A BANNER IS UNFURLED

BE STILL MY SOUL

VOLUME 2

OTHER BOOKS AND AUDIO BOOKS
BY MARCIE GALLACHER AND
KERRI ROBINSON:

A Banner Is Unfurled: Volume 1

A BANNER IS UNFURLED

BE STILL MY SOUL

VOLUME 2

MARCIE GALLACHER
KERRI ROBINSON

Covenant Communications, Inc.

Covenant

Cover images: background painting *Zion's Camp* © Judith Mehr;
couple illustration by Dave Malan, reference photo by Brett Thelin.

Cover design copyrighted 2006 by Covenant Communications, Inc.

Published by Covenant Communications, Inc.
American Fork, Utah

Printed in Canada
First Printing: October 2006

11 10 09 08 07 06   10 9 8 7 6 5 4 3 2 1

ISBN 978-1-59811-177-4

This volume is dedicated to David Johnson, our third great uncle.

Dear Readers,

It has been said that *all history is fiction.* Historians help us comprehend a fraction of the past, a section of the truth. Yet, in reality, so much has been left unrecorded. We can never fully understand the depth and breadth of those human souls who lived before us, thus we bring our own perception into past events—our own unique experiences, thoughts and feelings applied to the past but influencing our lives today.

As writers, this has been both the challenge and the joy of recreating the Johnson family story. We delved into mountains of historical renditions and primary documents. As we studied journal accounts, newspaper articles, and minutes from meetings, we were deeply moved by the voices we heard. We held on to rich stories from family histories recognizing their personal perspectives and possible fallibility. We weeded out some events and hilighted others. We noted but minimized minor discrepancies and adapted our own impressions into the storyline. As we filled in the missing pieces, we saw with new eyes those who really lived, who were as human as ourselves.

In *Be Still My Soul,* the Johnson family moves to Kirtland. They become even more closely intertwined with the miracle of the restoration as they witness the growing development of the fledgling Church of Jesus Christ. They live among and interact with other real families from Church history including the Joseph Smith Sr. family, the Frederick G. Williams family, the Murdock family, and the Hancocks. These firsthand observations provide a fascinating window into life in the early Church and the joys and struggles of those who embraced it. The heritage of these families touched our lives, so much like these individuals, in reality, enriched the lives of the Johnsons.

Seth, Almon, and Lyman travel with Zion's Camp. In researching and writing of this experience, we came to see the Prophet, Joseph Smith, with a clarity never before imagined. We discovered how he struggled to teach rough-hewn frontiersmen what it means to be men of God. We envisioned Zion's Camp in a personal light as we imagined our characters' faith tried, tested, and purified in that refiner's fire.

Amidst the historical detail shines the reality of the Johnson family who lived through these experiences and left a record for us to ponder on. In this volume, the Johnsons, like so many families both past and present, experience devastating sorrow and indescribable triumph. We share our own version of their story with you—as honestly and truthfully as we can, hoping that their lives change and illuminate yours as they have ours.

Marcie Gallacher
Kerri Robinson

EZEKIEL AND JULIA JOHNSON FAMILY
1832

Joel Hills [b. 1802] [m. Annie Pixley Johnson, 1826]
  Julianne [b. 1827–d. 1829]
  Sixtus [b. 1829]
  Sariah [b. 1832]
Nancy Maria [b. 1803]
Seth Guernsey [b. 1805]
Delcena Diadamia [b. 1806] [m. Lyman Sherman, 1829]
  Alvira [b. 1830]
  Baby son [b. 1830–d. before 1831]
  Mary [b. 1831]
  Albey [b. 1832]
Julia Ann (Julianne) [b. 1808]
David [b. 1810]
Almera Woodward [b. 1812]
Susan Ellen [b. 1814]
Joseph Ellis [b. 1817]
Benjamin Franklin [b. 1818]
Mary Ellen [b. 1820]
Elmer Wood [b. 1822–d. 1823]
George Washington [b. 1823]
William Derby [b. 1824]
Esther Melita [b. 1827]
Amos Partridge [b. 1829]

For a timeline of *A Banner Is Unfurled*, vol. 1, please see the additional material at the end of the book.

ACKNOWLEDGMENTS

As the Johnson saga continues, we have heard from many readers whose kind words have encouraged and sustained us—thank you so much. Our deepest gratitude goes to our husbands—to Gray Gallacher, whose personal sacrifices and contributions to this project are too numerous to list, and to Brent Robinson, whose commitment, wisdom, and editing skills are essential. We are indebted to our parents, Tal and LaRae Huber, and to our children, whose loving support never slackens. A special thank you to Denise Brasher, without whose friendship and help, deadlines could not have been met. Thank you to Jamie Gallacher and Kelby Hutchings, both descendants of Ezekiel and Julia Johnson, for their modeling for the cover. We are grateful to the journal keepers and letter writers of the past, and the professional and family historians of today, who preserve and explain our Latter-day heritage. Without them, there would be no story to tell. Once again, the Covenant staff has done an amazing job bringing this project to fruition. Thank you.

Oh Lord, in thee I take delight,
I on thy care depend,
Thou art my guide, by day and night
My great, eternal friend.

When all my earthly helps have failed,
Thy goodness was the same,
O'er all my foes I have prevailed,
Through faith in thy great name.

No good upon the earth is found
But what proceeds from thee;
I shall with every need be crowned,
While thou are friend to me.

Joel Hills Johnson
(*Hymns of Praise for the Young,* Hymn 328, 305)

November 1832—Pomfret, New York

Twenty-nine-year-old Nancy, the eldest daughter of Julia and Ezekiel Johnson, awakened to the pungent smell of warm lye. She lay on a bed in the sitting room next to the kitchen. Closing her eyes, she pictured what was happening—her mother, with her long black-gray hair and regal bearing, ladled the warm soap mixture from the blackened kettle into the wooden molds lined with cool, damp rags.

Nancy's father's voice—as direct and penetrating as an arrow—startled her. "Julia, I've sold the farm! Come early spring, I'll sail to Fort Dearborn. The land's been platted and the new town will be called Chicago. When I've bought a place, I'll send for you and the children."

Nancy took a deep breath. Her gray eyes were moist. It was now decided. She would have to go with her parents and the little ones rather than move with her adult siblings and their families to Kirtland, Ohio. She would always be dependent, one of the children. Her disability confined her, like the bars on a prison cell.

Nancy hoisted herself into a sitting position. Her light brown hair tumbled down her back. She heard her mother's response. "Zeke, if the farm is sold, please let us move to Kirtland. Joel and Annie are already there. Delcena and Lyman will be moving soon."

"No!"

"Zeke, I beg you." Nancy heard the tears in her mother's voice.

Nancy reached for the wooden crutches that leaned against the wall. She knew that pain would shoot through her hip when she stood. Pain had been her companion for the past three years, ever since a young horse had thrown her. The fall broke her hip bone near the socket. That had been a dark day. She remembered her brother, David, begging her to live. But was life really a choice? Her heart kept beating. Doing the best with what life handed you—*that* was the choice.

"Do you think I *want* to move?" She could tell from his voice that her father was not drunk. Yet his voice rose nonetheless. "Start over again at my age? Don't forget that this obsession with Mormonism nearly destroyed Seth! I won't have the young ones sucked into such . . . such darkness!"

Nancy thought of how she had been "sucked in,"—into a light so brilliant that even the shadows fled. She now knew that the gospel of Jesus Christ had been restored to the earth, along with the authority to baptize. Signs and miracles followed the believer just like in Christ's ancient Church.

"God's power healed Seth, Zeke. He is well now."

Nancy knew the bitterness of her father's response. "It sure didn't heal Nancy. Like the paper said, 'It wasn't for lack of faith.'"

Her mother rebutted. "Our Nancy understood. She accepted God's will."

"It's Nancy's sweetness that saved her from despair, not God. Do you think I'm blind, Julia? I know how it nearly broke David—realizing his God wouldn't heal his sister! The delusions are over, Julia! Over!"

There was a moment of silence, then a cry bordering on despair. "I beg you, Zeke. Don't move us against our will!"

There were footfalls, then her father's voice, softer this time, lined with hurt. Nancy imagined him walking toward her mother, reaching out his hand. "Julia, they're my children. A man can't stop what must be done."

Nothing. Then quick footsteps. Her father's voice was sharp again, like his blue-gray eyes. "I'll be in Fredonia the rest of the week—under friendlier skies." The front door opened and slammed shut. A single sob escaped her mother.

Nancy winced as she gripped her crutches and began to stand. Her mother needed her. Nancy heard the front door open and close again. Then the house was silent. With the aid of her crutches, Nancy stood and limped into the kitchen. Her injured hip ached. She looked out the window and saw her mother walking toward the woodland. Her father rode a horse in the opposite direction, down the road that led first to the tavern, and then to Fredonia.

Nancy made her way to the table, her injured hip dragging behind her. Was there no way to be of use? To relieve some of the burdens on her mother, some of the bitterness within her father? She saw the forgotten kettle sitting on the table, next to the soap molds. She began clumsily ladling the lye mixture into the molds before it hardened and became useless.

* * *

David had been in the woods since daybreak. He had seen the light spread through the eastern sky, transforming the shadowy trees into quivering color. Though it was cold, he was warm from hard labor. He shucked his coat and rolled up his shirtsleeves. To David, work was sport and he the victor. The twenty-two-year-old had just felled a stately tree. It was time now to turn it into kindling.

David paused for a moment at a sound—a crackling of branches in the woods. He turned to see his mother walking down the path toward him. She wore her navy cloak and her long, dark hair billowed behind her in the wind. From the look in her eyes he knew that something was wrong. David buried the ax head in a tree stump and hurried to her.

"Your father sold the farm," Julia exclaimed. Her breath was quick, her cheeks stained with tears. "David, he will move us away from here to Fort Dearborn where there are no members of the Church. What will become of your younger brothers and sisters? What am I to do?"

David embraced his mother. Her voice broke as she continued. "We must give up occupancy in June. Seven months from now. We will be separated from the body of the Church." Julia shook despite the warmth of David's arms around her.

David's brown-gold eyes flashed. "Pa's heart is hard against the Church, Mother, and drink is making him mean. God does not require you to live this way anymore. Seth and I will take you and the children to Kirtland."

"Hard hearts shatter, David. How can I leave the one who has supported and loved us these many years?" Julia's chest convulsed with pain. "But if we don't gather with the Saints, my children will lose the blessings of the gospel! What am I to do when there is unbearable sorrow behind both doors?"

David held his weeping mother tenderly in his arms. He spoke gently. "Seth will get back from Ohio soon and counsel us. Together we'll decide what to do."

Julia closed her eyes as she struggled to stop crying. David's strength steadied her, yet she knew that on one account he was mistaken. Her children could not help her with this decision—not her beloved grown sons, Joel, Seth, and David, nor her good son-in-law, Lyman Sherman, nor her precious elder daughters, Nancy, Delcena, and Julianne. Julia alone had covenanted to be Ezekiel Johnson's wife. Only God, the Eternal Father of them all, could show her the way.

* * *

A stiff, cold wind blew through Amherst, Ohio on the afternoon Seth Johnson arrived. He would soon be at his brother Joel's. Seth's task was to bring home his younger brother, fourteen-year-old Benjamin, who had been living with and helping Joel for the past eight months. Seth breathed in the cold air and put his hands in his pockets to warm them against the November chill. He gazed at the trees lining the road, their leaves losing color and drying fast. He thought about the last time he had been there—three months ago when the leaves were green and moist with humidity.

Last August, Seth, his father, and his seventeen-year-old sister, Susan, had traveled to Kirtland to meet the Prophet, Joseph Smith. Afterwards, they had gone on to Amherst, Ohio, to visit Joel's family and Benjamin.

At the time, Seth had been obsessed with the desire that his father would be converted to Mormonism and overcome his drunkenness, that there would be redemption for his father and peace for his mother and siblings. Seth's mind had been like a fiddle string, stretched so tight that it was at the point of breaking—all his energy quivering on that one note. But in Amherst, Ezekiel's drinking had continued, along with his rampage against God and Mormonism.

Seth had not been able to cope when his hope snapped. One sweltering night, he had run the fifty miles from Amherst to Kirtland. His reason had collapsed as he visualized the flames of

Satan destroying all he held dear. Mentally fragile, he had returned to New York with his father and Susan. There he had grasped the single thread of hope—his knowledge of Christ's healing power bought through the Redeemer's atoning sacrifice. He had worked the harvest during the days and had prayed fervently at night. Like the slow mending of a broken limb, healing had come. Now he was back in Ohio in the chill fall weather. He would tell Joel and Annie that all was well with him now. He would bring Bennie home.

* * *

The cow licked Benjamin Johnson's dark hair with her rough tongue. "Get away, Frannie," Ben ordered as he tilted his head out of the cow's reach and continued to milk her.

"She thinks you're her calf!" Almon Babbitt laughed from the barn door. Almon was nineteen and a close family friend of the Johnsons.

Ben scowled. In many families, milking was a woman's work. It annoyed fourteen-year-old Benjamin that milking had been his chore ever since he could remember—both at home in New York and now in Ohio. "A man shouldn't have to squat by a cow's udder," Benjamin muttered darkly.

Almon chuckled. "Unless he ain't a man yet. Move over, and I'll finish." Benjamin eyed Almon, who looked as dapper as ever, with his brown hair combed back and his green eyes keen with life. He was a great fellow to talk to and fish with, but he was also the type to play a practical joke rather than offer to finish someone's work.

"Why?" Benjamin asked suspiciously.

"Don't be daft," Almon said. "There's a surprise waiting for you outside the barn."

"Maybe I don't want it," Benjamin said.

"I know you do," Almon retorted. "Now go!"

Benjamin slowly stood up, his dark eyes fixed on Almon. "If this is a joke, I swear . . ."

His words were interrupted by a voice at the entrance to the barn. "Bennie."

Benjamin turned. He knew that voice. It was the voice of his older brother—the man who had taught him in school, who had encouraged him at home, who had answered his questions about God. It was the voice of the one who had watched over his childhood, of the one he idealized and loved more than any other in the wide world. But it was also the voice of the brother whose mind had broken this summer. And with Seth's breakdown, the earth had trembled under Benjamin's feet.

"Seth?" There was a question in Ben's voice as he looked into his brother's eyes.

Seth smiled, and Benjamin saw the peace there. Seth spoke, "Ben, I'm here to take you home." Ben ran to his brother, and Seth clasped him to his heart. "Through the grace of our Lord, Bennie, all is well with me now."

With their arms around each other's shoulders, the brothers walked toward Joel's log house. They stopped a moment when they heard Almon's shout from the barn. "Blast it, you beast! I just combed my hair! Ben, git back here!"

* * *

Later that evening Joel and Seth sat together at the kitchen table. "So, Father has really sold the place," Joel commented. Seth heard the sound of Joel's wife, Annie, singing to the children as she put them to bed. Ben was off with Almon Babbitt.

Seth nodded. "He told me in Jamestown the morning I left. Mother didn't know at the time. It will be a blow to her. When I visited the Prophet last week, he advised us to have hope. He believes a way will open for Mother and the children to come to Kirtland. But I don't believe she will come if it means leaving Father."

Joel sat silently for a moment. "I've sold the sawmill for a good price," he commented.

"I've put some earnings away as well," Seth said as his eyes met his brother's. "The prophet showed me a piece of property on the flats near the schoolhouse and Whitney store. It will be for sale this spring. A large frame house is already built there. An orchard extends to the hill behind the house and bears fruit. It would suit Mother and the children."

Joel looked into the fire. He was tall and lanky, with serious brown eyes and receding hair. He had a persistent cough and sloping shoulders. He looked back at Seth. "But what of Father? We are bound as sons to honor him."

Seth sighed deeply. He stood and added a log to the hearth fire. He was nearly as tall as Joel, but slim and straight. His eyes were brown and deep as he sat back down and sought the words to explain his feelings to Joel. "Through prayer I have come to realize that I must leave Father to God. The greatest honor we can bestow on Father is to guide his children to eternal life. That is my duty— to Father as much as to Mother."

Joel nodded as his brow relaxed. "I'll go to Kirtland as soon as I can and take a look at that property."

Oh! Take my yoke, and learn to be
Of meek and lowly mind!
And all who will thus come to me,
Pure joy and peace shall find.

For light and easy is my yoke,
The burden I impose
Shall heal the heart by sorrow broke,
And drive away its woes.

Joel Hills Johnson
(*Hymns of Praise for the Young,* Hymn 130, 131)

Three days later—Pomfret, New York

Joseph Ellis Johnson, Ezekiel and Julia's fifteen-year-old son, sat cross-legged in the hut of his old friend, Injun Goldfinger. He liked the strange smells, the low ceiling, and the black fire pit in the center of the tiny room. It took his mind off of all that was going on at home.

"Mr. Goldfinger, I'm a newspaper man now! *The Westfield Eagle's* been printing letters I wrote." Joe said with a grin and chuckle. "The thing is, nobody knows it's me! Except Rachel Risley." The youth was brown eyed and long legged with an angular face. His knees stuck out at odd angles in the cramped hovel. The old man's skin looked like a piece of wadded tow cloth, dipped in a rusty dye, dried in the sun, then stretched over bone in wrinkled dignity.

Joe grinned and kept talking. "I sign my name *Amicus,* which means 'friend' in Latin. I write about politics and stuff like that. The readers in Westfield think I'm an old, learned gentleman."

The Indian listened without commenting. "My sister Sue suspects me." Joe chuckled again. "She cut out one of the articles and put it on my bed."

"But she didn't say anything to you?' The Indian raised an eyebrow.

"Not a word!"

"Your sister is like an Indian woman. She knows the wisdom of silence. Something my young friend *Amicus* has not learned."

Joe laughed out loud. But the Indian did not smile. Joe quieted quickly, feeling awkwardly defensive.

"I know the wisdom of silence!" Joe insisted. The old man raised both eyebrows.

Joseph snapped his mouth closed. He would prove to his old friend that he knew the value of quiet, even though he itched for talk. He felt a sudden surge of longing for moody Ben, his brother and best friend.

Without a word, the old Indian began working on a pair of decorated moccasins. It was the old fellow's ornate crafts that had earned him the nickname, "Goldfinger." Joe sat still, mesmerized by the Indian's nimble, wrinkled fingers as he wove deer sinew in and out of soft leather. After a time, the Indian spoke. Joe smiled to himself. Injun Goldfinger wouldn't admit it, but he liked to talk as much as Joe.

"The white man calls this county after the Indian Lake, Chautauqua. Long ago, Seneca warriors crossed the lake and caught a strange fish, a type they had never seen before. They threw the fish into their canoe. They descended to the creek and came to the great lake you call Erie. The braves were astonished to find that the fish still lived. Because of its great strength, they threw this fish back into the water. From that time forth, the fish multiplied abundantly. The people named this lake Ga-ja-dah-gwah from the words Ga-jah, meaning fish, and the word ga-da-gwah, *taken out.*"

Joe smiled. "Ga-jah-dah-gwah. Chautauqua. That's a fine story."

"There is another," the Indian continued. "It is said that a Seneca maiden ate of a root growing on the banks of the lake. This root caused unquenchable thirst. The maiden stooped to drink of the lake's clear waters. As she drank, she disappeared into the waters forever. Hence, the name of this place changed to Ja-Da-Qua, the land of easy death, where one is seen no more."

The hut was silent for a time. Joe's smile vanished. He couldn't help thinking about home—about his father's anger and his mother's sorrow, about being hated by people because of their religion, about moving soon, away from his friends, his religion—away from everything. Joe's eyes became sober and moist. His voice was quiet when he spoke, "Our family multiplied here—like the fish. We're going to leave this place come June, and never be seen more in these parts. Pa's sold the farm and plans to settle in Fort Dearborn. Away from the Mormons. Mama is sad. She wants to join our people and our Prophet in Kirtland."

"So I have heard at the tavern. And what is your wish, Amicus, friend to all?"

Joe shrugged. "Mr. Goldfinger, my mother's never led me wrong. I figure that if Ma believes in Mormonism, then it must be true. But religion riles my pa. He thinks preachers are hypocrites and that the Prophet Joseph Smith is crazy. Sometimes I think Pa has a point. Remember Elder Brackenbury, the Mormon missionary who died last winter? I've never met a nicer fellow. Our prayers didn't save him. That doesn't seem reasonable to me. Does God really care about us? Is He really there? But I can't tell my ma and my brothers and sisters how I feel, because it might hurt them or disappoint them. I can't tell Pa either, because he thinks it's all hogwash."

The old Indian studied the boy for a moment, and then spoke. "To the red man, God is the sacred mystery. The life of Father Sun. The nourishment of Mother Earth. We stand erect as sons and daughters of Him, the sacred mystery. Then the white man came. His diseases killed us. His lies betrayed us. His liquid fire stole our souls. My people no longer stand erect as children of God. My young friend, liquid fire steals your father's soul. Your mother stands erect. Does this prophet, Joseph Smith? Does he know the sacred mystery? Will you?"

Joseph shrugged. "I don't know."

"The sacred mystery is here," the old Indian pointed to his chest. "In the silent drumbeat of a man's heart."

* * *

That evening, in Jamestown, New York, thirty miles south of Pomfret, Lyman Sherman walked the wooden floor of his cousin's house with his infant son in his arms. Albey had been born in that house just three weeks ago, a month following their move from Pomfret. They had come to Jamestown in order to gather with a group of Saints who were preparing to move to Kirtland, Ohio. Lyman was the presiding elder. At the moment, his wife Delcena was in the other room with their little girls, three-year-old Alvira and one-year-old Mary.

With one hand, Lyman pushed up his spectacles. He was near-sighted, and his glasses caused his eyes to appear almost common. But Lyman's brown eyes were anything but common. Large, expressive, energetic, and compelling, his eyes held others captive when he spoke. Had he been a gambler, Lyman Sherman could have fooled the world with those eyes. But Lyman Sherman was not a gambler. He was an honest man, a man who loved God to the very core, who embraced Mormonism as the gospel of Jesus Christ, who gave his heart and hands to the Lord. Lyman strode back and forth, singing softly to the babe about the restoration of Christ's gospel.

A few moments later, Lyman's cousin, Doctor Philastus Hurlbut, burst into the house. Hurlbut, a strong, powerfully built man in his mid-twenties, ran his fingers through his shock of thick, black hair. Doctor was his given name, not his title. "Another case of the disease has been reported—the Reynolds child. It appears to be smallpox. How fortunate that no one has died yet. Some say it is a milder strain of the disease."

"I'll go tonight and administer to the child," Lyman commented.

Hurlbut gaped at his cousin. "What! Do you want to bring the disease to this house? To your own little ones?"

"Philastus, I'm the presiding elder."

"Other elders have blessed the child, Lyman," Philastus lied. He figured Abraham had done as much when he said Sarah was his sister in order to protect himself. He added, "The priesthood is the same regardless of who wields it."

Lyman did not respond. The baby in his arms began to cry from hunger. Lyman shifted Albey to his shoulder and patted his tiny back. "What noise you make for such a little thing."

Philastus warmed his hands by the fire. "I still can not find my wallet! Are you certain Alvira didn't take it?"

The baby cried more loudly. Lyman answered, his voice louder than the cry, "I don't think so. Delcena has searched the house and yard."

"Where is Delcena?"

"Putting the girls to bed."

"How do you bear the crying and prattle of three children?" Hurlbut exclaimed.

Delcena stepped quickly into the room. She was a tall, young mother, with bright, light brown eyes and smooth dark hair that framed her face and was piled into a low bun. She glanced sharply at Philastus, then quickly took the baby from Lyman's arms. She locked eyes with Lyman, and then left the room without another word.

When all was quiet, Lyman gazed steadily at his cousin and spoke, "After our little Lyman died, my children's noise ceased to bother me. Only their silence is threatening. Philastus, we won't intrude on your hospitality much longer."

Philastus Hurlbut turned to his cousin and changed his tone, speaking lightly as he thumped him on the back. "Come, Lyman, don't be offended. You know you are always welcome here. Delcena is a good cook and I adore your offspring. I shall repent of my impatience."

Lyman sighed and spoke thoughtfully. "With the smallpox threat and Albey so young, Delcena wishes we were spending the winter in Pomfret. But I have sold the house and land. How I hope to be in Kirtland soon!"

"Hmm," Philastus replied, raising his eyebrows. "You might be able to go someday, if you don't spend all of your money helping the rest of the Saints purchase wagons and teams. Everyone has needs, Cousin. You have a wife and children. You must protect your own."

Lyman looked seriously at his cousin. "And what do you need, D. P.?"

Philastus met Lyman's eyes. "A cousin who is like a brother to me. Baptism in Christ's Church." Then Philastus laughed handsomely. "But those I already have. I also need my lost wallet and a pretty wife. Now, I'm off in search of the first. Don't wait up for me. I may find a quieter place in which to spend the night."

Lyman watched as Philastus stood and doffed his hat. After bidding Philastus good-bye, Lyman thought a moment about his cousin. He remembered months back when he had taught Philastus the gospel. There had been moments when Philastus's handsome mouth had softened, and his eyes had lost their self-aware look, and he had just listened. Yet, Lyman also knew Philastus's inborn drive—that boldness that was often proud. His cousin was charismatic and generous, but he could be calculating as well. As a young child, Philastus had not gotten on well with his own father, and had spent a good deal of time with Lyman's family. Lyman loved Philastus like a brother, but sometimes felt concern for his soul.

Lyman walked into the bedroom. Delcena had just finished nursing the baby. She laid him in the cradle at the foot of the bed. The little girls were asleep on the trundle. "How quickly the house became quiet," Lyman commented.

"The babies are asleep, and Philastus is gone," Delcena smiled wryly. "Heavenly Father does answer prayers."

Lyman looked tenderly at his wife. She was heavier than she had been as a maiden, but she carried herself handsomely. Her nose was straight and narrow. Her eyes were as soft and lovely as ever.

"Oh, Lyman," she exclaimed as they sat down on the bed together, "did I hear Philastus say that another child has come down with the pox?"

Lyman nodded as he put his arm around her waist. "The Reynolds babe."

Lyman pulled her close. Delcena leaned into him as he kissed the base of her neck. Her eyes were troubled. "Lyman, Philastus doesn't want us here. And the pox, how it frightens me!"

A sharp knock at the front door interrupted the couple. Delcena's head jerked toward the entry of the room. The babe in the cradle startled.

Lyman moved his hand to her shoulder as he stood. "Wait here. I'll answer it."

"Take the gun," Delcena whispered.

Lyman reached for the firearm against the wall. Then he smiled reassuringly at his wife. "Don't worry. It's likely a friend."

Lyman walked out of the room and to the front door, fully aware of the deep prejudice against their religion. Just last spring in Ohio, their leaders, Joseph Smith and Sidney Rigdon, had been brutally beaten and tarred and feathered. Lyman was a leader in Chautauqua County. He was not afraid, but his eyes were wide and alert, and his shotgun was ready as he opened the door.

Three strangers stood in the gathering darkness outside. "We are looking for Lyman Sherman, an elder in the Mormon Church," the foremost said. He was of average height, broad shouldered, and blue-eyed.

"I'm he," Lyman answered, his voice level and his eyes steady.

The leading man's face broke into a smile. He held out his hand. "Elder Sherman, I'm Brigham Young. This is my brother, Joseph, and my friend, Heber Kimball. Do you have room for weary travelers who are on their way to Kirtland to meet God's Prophet?"

Lyman's eyes transformed with gladness. "Always," he exclaimed as he grasped the man's hand and welcomed the group into the house.

* * *

An hour later, Delcena sat slightly apart from the men as she mended Lyman's shirts. The night was cold, and a fire roared in the hearth. The men were enjoying themselves. Lyman and Heber Kimball had just finished telling about themselves and their conversions. Now it was the Young brothers' turn. Delcena listened attentively as Brigham Young spoke of his childhood.

"We were dirt poor, and Father raised us on fear of God's punishments."

Joseph Young added, "We weren't allowed to even listen to a violin. Not that we could afford any such luxury."

Brigham chuckled. "If we had a pair of pants that would cover us, we were lucky."

Heber Kimball cut in. "And now, Brother Lyman, my friend, Brigham here, has a valuable trade. Brigham is an excellent carpenter with his own shop. He is also a talented glazier."

"Yes, but I'll leave all I have built to follow God's Prophet," Brigham commented, turning thoughtful. "I searched long for a church such as that described in the New Testament, with prophets, apostles, baptism by immersion, and the gift of tongues. It seemed to me that most preachers fell into two categories—those who enchained followers with the fear of hellfire, and those who were hypocrites, professing religion on Sundays and cheating their neighbors come Monday morning. I sought Christ's ancient Church full of the joy of the gospel and the gifts of the Spirit."

"And now you have found it," Lyman commented. "Christ's ancient Church restored with signs following the believers."

Joseph Young spoke. "We have experienced these signs recently. Brigham has spoken in unknown tongues."

Lyman's dark eyes turned to Brigham. "I have been in meetings of other sects where I've seen men and women seized with strange spirits, their bodies gyrating wildly as they speak strange words. Is this the gift you speak of? It did not seem of God to me, but of the adversary."

Brigham met Lyman's gaze. "For me, this gift came not with strange gyrations, but with dignity, light, and joy. It seems to be from God. But I'll ask the Prophet. He'll know for certain."

Lyman nodded, and his eyes softened. "Tell me more of your conversion, Brother Brigham."

Brigham gazed into the fire, then back at his host. "I wasn't as fervent as you from the start, Brother Lyman. I was given a Book of Mormon in 1830. I studied it for two years until I knew it was true—as well as I know that I can see with my eyes and feel with my fingertips. I was baptized on April fourteenth of this year."

Delcena was interested in the men's stories, but felt slightly bothered that their wives were absent from their conversation. "Brother Young, does your wife share your testimony?" she suddenly questioned. The men all turned to look at her as if they had forgotten that she was in the room.

Brigham's eyes met Delcena's. He spoke painfully. "Sister Sherman, my wife, Miriam, believed the gospel and was baptized in May. She died a short time ago, leaving me with two little girls to raise."

"I'm so sorry," Delcena said. Tears sprang to her eyes as her former annoyance slid away. She thought of the loss of her own son. Death seemed to visit every family. Did joy and sorrow always come hand in hand when one accepted Christ's gospel? She remembered how the joy of her conversion was followed on its heels by terrible sorrow when their friend and mentor, Elder Brackenbury, died.

Brigham looked into the fire. His blue eyes shone with both grief and joy. "Though I sorrow in the separation from my beloved, I rejoice in the restored gospel of Jesus Christ, in the knowledge that my wife dwells in the Savior's arms. My daughters shall have a childhood far different from mine. They shall be filled with a knowledge of Christ's true gospel." Brigham paused for an instant. He turned back to Delcena and added, "And they shall dance, study music, and do anything else that will improve their minds and make them feel free and untrammeled."

Delcena nodded at Brother Brigham as she wiped away her tears. "I'm sure they will grow into fine, talented women."

Heber Kimball shook his head, both doubtfully and playfully. "If Brigham does not spoil them first."

Delcena's thoughts turned to Brigham's wife and her own little ones. She would not want to leave them, even for heaven. Yet when the body completely succumbed to illness and pain, release into the Savior's arms was the only comfort. Delcena shuddered, thinking about how death awaited them all. She heard Albey fuss in the other room. Earlier, he had fallen asleep before eating his fill. Delcena stood up and gracefully excused herself, bidding her guests good night. She would leave the warmth of this discussion about heaven for the warmth of her babe tugging at her breast. For both blessings she thanked her Heavenly Father.

As the men continued to discuss the gospel in the sitting room, the dying embers glowed in the hearth. By candlelight, they opened their scriptures and read the prophecy of Enoch that Elder Brackenbury had copied and brought with him last winter. Then they read of the Brother of Jared's faith and his vision of the Lord in the Book of Mormon.

As they discussed the scriptures, Lyman and Brigham spoke of their love for the Lord and their gratitude to Him for condescending to earth and giving hope and salvation to man. They did not notice the fire dying in the hearth due to the warmth within their own souls. They finished reading the scriptures, and each man bore his testimony once more. When Brigham spoke, it was as if his grief for his wife was swallowed up by his joy in the Savior, both emotions fused together into a bright light radiating from the depths of his soul.

Suddenly, Brigham was speaking in an unknown tongue, yet Lyman Sherman understood each word. After Brigham finished, Lyman's voice was soft with emotion as he spoke. Tears coursed down his cheeks. He interpreted the words of eternal life uttered by Brigham Young. Then Lyman bore his own testimony. It too came forth in the gift of tongues. Brother Brigham interpreted.

As the fire died and the men sat in silence, Heber Kimball whispered the question that came from deep within their souls. "Is this gift of tongues truly from God? Only the Prophet will know for sure."

"Now, I believe it to be God's witness to His Saints during their trials, a testimony to His new, fledgling Church," Lyman answered quietly. Brigham nodded.

In the bedroom, separated from the men by a thin wooden door, Delcena had heard the testimonies. She felt certain that her husband was correct. When she had heard Brother Brigham and her husband speak in tongues, an assurance had filled her soul, a testimony of the unspeakable reality of God's love, of the existence of His restored Church, and of the joy that comes to the faithful after the trial of their faith. She gave this memory place in her heart and prayed that it would help carry her through whatever might come, whether it be smallpox or persecution, or the life or death of those she treasured. She lay in bed and slept with her babe in her arms and peace in her soul.

3

In Autumn, when the mellow fruit was red,
To "paring-bees" with lightened step we tread;
We peeled the fruit, told yarns, and joked and laughed
We kissed the girls—new cider then we quaffed
Then homeward we with blushing fair ones go
And little else but happiness did know.

Joseph Ellis Johnson
("The Old Schoolhouse," *Jottings by the Way,* xix)

Amherst, Ohio

It was nearly dusk and raining steadily when Almon Babbitt arrived at the log house. He slid off the mule, tied the drenched animal to the post, and rapped on the door. Annie Johnson answered it. Her unruly auburn hair lay tamed beneath a white knitted hair net. She held her eight-month-old baby girl, Sariah, in her arms. A petite, roundish woman with a freckled nose and rosy cheeks, Annie smiled as she greeted Almon. "Hello, Almon! You're shivering. Come in and get warm." Annie herded Almon into the kitchen. Almon set down his soaked hat, peeled off his coat, and hung it over a chair. Then Annie handed him the baby while she stirred the pork and potato stew bubbling in a kettle over the fire.

"I hear Seth and Ben are leaving at dawn," Almon commented as he breathed in the lovely aroma of the stew.

Annie nodded. She ladled a bit of stew and tasted it. Then she added a bit of thyme and a pinch of salt. "Yes. Unless this downpour gets worse."

"I wanted to come and say good-bye."

Annie set the spoon on the board and looked at Almon curiously. "I thought you'd be at the meeting with Seth and Joel. Did you know that Jared Carter is leaving for his mission to Michigan tomorrow morning? Don't you want to bid *him* farewell too?"

Baby Sariah whined and reached for her mother. Almon handed the baby back to Annie. His green eyes twinkled as he grinned. "I cut out of the meeting today. I'll repent tomorrow. I feared I would fall asleep at more talk of becoming of one mind and one heart. Now if it were a good debate, that would be different."

Annie laughed. "Save your debating for when you're a lawyer. You are a funny fellow, Almon. Thank you for befriending Benjamin. If it weren't for you, I don't think he would have smiled since Seth's breakdown this summer."

Almon laughed out loud. "That's my specialty—making people smile." He made a fish face at the baby. Sariah's little face broke into a wide, gurgling grin.

Annie continued, "Ben and Sixtus are in the barn feeding the stock. Why don't you fetch them for supper? Joel and Seth can eat later tonight."

Almon donned his coat and doffed his soaking hat at Annie. She watched the young man as he obediently ducked out the door into the rain. She fondly thought of how he often showed up around dinnertime, as if he could smell her cooking from miles around.

A few minutes later, Almon opened the barn door to find five-year-old Sixtus jumping into a pile of straw, while Benjamin forked hay into the mangers. "Almy!" Sixtus exclaimed over the sound of the rain pounding on the roof.

"Ho Sixtus!" Almon called out. "Hello Ben!"

Benjamin nodded at Almon as he emptied the load of hay into a manger. Almon hefted the gangly Sixtus onto his shoulders and, holding the child's hands, helped him into a standing position. On cue, Sixtus jumped forward from Almon's shoulders, his skinny legs flailing in the air before he landed in the pile of hay, shrieking with laughter. "Another jump! Another!" The little boy danced around Almon.

After launching Sixtus three more times, Almon dramatically moaned and covered his face with his hands. "Oh, no! I'm in big trouble!"

"How come, Almy?" Sixtus questioned, his eyes wide with worry as he tugged on Almon's trouser leg.

"I forgot that your momma told me not to play with you! I was supposed to tell you to wash up for supper. Run inside before she thrashes me!"

"She don't thrash very hard," Sixtus comforted.

Almon moaned again. "Maybe not you. She has a soft spot for you. But me? Go tell her I didn't mean it. Otherwise she might send me away without supper."

Sixtus hurried from the barn. Once the child had left, Almon rubbed his hands together and walked over to Ben. After taking his seat on a cock of hay, he smiled up at his friend. "I hear you're heading for home tomorrow morning."

Benjamin set the pitchfork down. He nodded at Almon and said wistfully. "I hope the rain lets up. I can't wait to see everybody—Ma and Pa, Joe E., and the rest."

"I s'pose you'll forget about all of us here in Amherst?" Almon stated.

Ben sat down near Almon. "I'll miss fishing with you."

Almon raised his eyebrows. "You like being out-fished?"

Benjamin gave him a look but ignored the comment. "I guess I'll miss Joel and Annie, but at home there's more people to help with the work. Mary, George, and Will do the milking."

Almon stood up and took a sealed letter out of his pocket. "Here's a letter for you to give to your sister, Julianne."

"From who?" Benjamin asked honestly.

"Me," Almon said offhandedly.

"Why'd you write Julianne?" Benjamin asked with raised eyebrows.

"Why do you ask so many questions?" Almon snapped.

Benjamin took the letter and glanced sidewards at Almon. It was usually Almon who got the best of Ben. Now the tables had turned. Benjamin held the letter near the lantern like he was trying to make out the words inside.

Almon grabbed for it, but Ben held it high. Although more than four years younger than Almon, Ben was two inches taller. Almon's green eyes narrowed. He was not in the mood to be toyed with. "Knock it off Ben, and give me the letter! I'll have Seth take it to her. I forgot that you're as daft as an ornery mule."

Benjamin chuckled and tucked the letter into his coat pocket. "Don't get riled, Almon. I'll give the letter to Juli. I'll take good care of it."

Almon glared at Benjamin. "This is an important letter. Promise me that you won't talk to anybody about it, that you will just deliver it to Julianne."

Benjamin stuck out his hand and shook Almon's. "I promise."

Forcing himself to relax, Almon thumped Benjamin on the back. "I know you always keep your word, just like your daddy. Let's go eat some of Annie's stew."

Ben swung the barn door open. Ignoring the gray drizzle outside, he turned to Almon. "There's one thing perplexing me."

"What's that, Bennie Boy?"

"Why are you sweet on my sister when she's old enough to be your aunt?" Ben dodged Almon's fist and dashed through the rain, laughing.

* * *

Pomfret, New York

Despite the threatening sky in the west, Joe whistled as he strode quickly to the place where a sweep of land enclosed a bit of Lake

Erie—the old lonely gulf, as Rachel Risley called it. Shortly, he would meet her there amidst the tall, bending grasses where the timeless lake extended out on one side and the forest rose on the other. It was a private place. Although Joe hadn't seen Rachel for over two weeks, he was confident she'd come. She was his best friend.

When Joe arrived, Rachel was nowhere in sight. Joe stopped whistling. Maybe she had trouble getting away. He thought of the day eight months ago when she had suggested they must meet on the sly. Her cheeks had been bright red with emotion, and her blue eyes had flashed. She had flipped her head in exasperation, her long, light brown hair splashing down her back. "Mother and Daddy are worried about me learning too much about the Mormons—especially from somebody I admire as much as you, Joseph E. Johnson."

The memory of those words echoed in Joe's mind. *She admired him!* And how he admired her! When they were little, he had stolen kisses from her each fall at the paring bees. He pictured those long-ago days, with her long braids bouncing as she laughed and pushed him away. Now he dreamed too much of kissing her to actually try it.

"Joseph E.," Rachel called out as she emerged from the woods. He ran toward her. She looked furtively behind her.

"Did anyone follow you?" Joe asked.

"I thought I heard something. Blanchard was watching me when I left school. I hope he doesn't tell my father."

"Why would he tell?" Joe questioned. "He's my friend."

Coloring slightly, Rachel shook her head briskly as if to dismiss some thought. "Never you mind." She opened her knapsack. "Joe, I've brought you copies of *Scientific American*. Morris sent them. We all miss you at school. Now that harvest is over, won't you come back?"

Joe shrugged as he put the books in his sack. "It's no fun anymore, Rache. Not with your cousins watching my every move and making sure we don't talk to each other. Besides, I've read more books than the master, Mr. Cheney. I've been helping my sister Juli teach a little winter school full of Mormons. I've some rising scholars."

Rachel humphed. "I don't see why you should abandon all of your plans just because you are a Mormon. You should attend the new academy at Fredonia. You could become a great, famous doctor, very kind, good, and wise."

Joe shrugged. "I'm not officially a Mormon yet. Pa won't give his permission. Anyway, I don't want to be a doctor anymore. Injun Goldfinger taught me how to heal people without bleeding and purging them."

"But Joe, it was your dream," Rachel countered as she put her hand on his arm.

"Sometimes dreams change. The success of our friend Amicus has changed mine. I think that I'll be a newspaper man instead of a doctor."

Rachel laughed delightedly and clapped her hands. "That reminds me! Daddy read the latest editorial by Amicus. The one where you wrote about Indian rights. Daddy said that Mr. Amicus is rather clever and fair-minded. I had to go outside to stop from laughing. If he knew it was you, Daddy would sing a different song! And now Joe, I'll tell you what I heard the ladies at church discussing. Amicus might be interested. There is a Jewish man named Mr. Levi who lives in Westfield. At least he *did* live there. He recently died. His friends want his funeral sermon delivered by a rabbi at the big Presbyterian meetinghouse. The trustees of the Presbyterian Church denied them its use unless they have a Christian minister speak. The interesting fact is that the meeting-house is not just owned by the Presbyterians; others donated funds when it was built, including Mr. Levi."

Joe's eyes lighted. "That is a story that Friend Amicus is very interested in!"

"I thought so!" Rachel smiled. The two walked and talked together, creating their own sunshine, until the wind picked up and clouds darkened overhead. It began to sprinkle, and the rain-drops were cold. Rachel grabbed Joe's hand. She pulled him in the direction from which she had come. "I saw some wintergreen on my way here! On one of the plants there is a lonesome, little bell-shaped flower left over from summer. Let's go pick it before it is soaked by the rain."

They ran hand in hand through the forest looking for the wintergreen. Joseph was eight inches taller than Rachel and rail thin. He had to duck under branches. She was quick on her feet. Suddenly Rachel hesitated, not remembering exactly where she had seen the blossom. Joe's heart pounded in his chest. Then she spotted it and ran over. They squatted side by side, picking the aromatic leaves, and admiring the dainty bell flower. Joe put the leaves in his sack. Then, he carefully detached the flower. Rachel thought of how his fingers were slender and careful—a scholar's fingers, much like his brother Seth's, their old schoolmaster. She would never forget how Seth Johnson had been dismissed from his position because of his religion. She knew that Joseph E. was determined to fight such injustice. That was what Amicus was all about.

It began to rain harder. Rachel looked up into Joe's dark, happy eyes. She still hadn't told him that Blanchard Darby was courting her. Blanchard was curly haired and manly. He had invited her to Fredonia next week to watch the militia march in the town square.

"Here, my lady." Joe bowed gallantly as he handed her the flower. "You've gained the prize. You've rescued the blossom. It shall be your talisman forevermore. Make sure it is not eaten by small animals nor injured by clumsy persons!"

"Thank you, my lord," she said with a curtsey, the rain in her eyelashes. She wouldn't tell Joseph about Blanchard. She knew it would erase his smile, quiet his soft laugh. He was her friend, her dear, kind, happy Joe. She kissed him on the cheek and hurried away, the wintergreen blossom cupped protectively in her hand.

As he watched her go, Joseph realized that he had forgotten to tell her that his father had sold the farm, that they would be moving come spring. He turned and loped home through the wind and rain, glad that spring was still a long way off.

* * *

Seth and Benjamin plodded through the steady rain, the mud sucking at their boots with each step. "How are you doing, Bennie?" Seth questioned. "Does your foot still pain you?"

"Not anymore. But it did last March when I traveled with Joel," Ben said. "We're not pushing as hard to get home as Joel did to get to Amherst. My foot hurt real bad then."

"I'm glad it's better now," Seth commented. "I remember how Joel wanted to get back and make sure that Annie and the baby had pulled through. There's no stopping a man when he's worried about his family."

Benjamin shrugged. "He sure didn't take much notice of how bad my foot hurt."

Seth smiled at his younger brother. "Or of how much you hate to milk cows. When I saw you milking away without a complaint, I figured old brother Joel knew how to work miracles."

Ben shrugged. "There wasn't anybody else to do it. I can't wait to get home. What's changed?"

Seth hesitated for a moment. "Lyman and Delcena moved to Jamestown. They have a new baby boy named Albey. They hope to gather with the Saints in Kirtland as soon as they can."

"That's good." Benjamin took a piece of jerky out of his coat pocket and bit into it. As he chewed on it, he thought about how the rain didn't bother him. He felt warm walking and talking with Seth. "Anything else?"

"Remember that steer Joseph E. named Hercules?"

Ben nodded. "Did Pa slaughter him?"

"No. Mary's trained him. He's handy now, a real good ox."

"Good for Mary! I didn't think anybody could save that one." Ben thought about his sister, Mary. She was two years his junior. Though she was demure looking with long, blonde hair and large brown eyes, Mary's looks were deceptive. She was very talkative and easily held her own if anyone crossed her. Mary loved animals—dogs, cats, lambs, pigs, cows, and horses. Pa made sure she was far away during slaughter time.

Seth spoke. "Mary was determined to save Hercules from becoming roast beef. Mary's skilled with creatures. Nancy was like that too."

"Until she was thrown by the colt."

"Yes, Bennie. Now Nancy gives all her kindness to her family."

Ben grinned. "I wish Mary would give more of her kindness to us too." Then he thought about how good it would be to see Nancy. Throughout his childhood, Nancy and Seth had been like second parents to him. They had taught him his first lessons, both academically and religiously. They had always taken time to counsel and comfort him and had become part of the structure and stability of his world. Benjamin asked Seth the question that plagued him. "Seth, are you sure your mind is strong now?"

"I'm sure, Bennie."

"You don't think it will happen again?"

"The Prophet gave me a blessing. He promised that I would be well. I've prayed a great deal, Ben, and I've tried to understand what happened. It took some time, but the Lord healed me. He heals all of us, Ben, if we believe on His name and keep His commandments. But we must be patient. Always remember that."

Benjamin nodded. "I won't forget. I'm glad we can talk again. I hated it when you were sick."

Seth put his arm around his brother. "That's why I came to get you. So that we could talk all the way back to New York."

Benjamin nodded. "It's going to be dark in a few hours. Are we going to find a grove to sleep in? If the evergreen branches are thick enough, they'll block the rain, and we could build a fire." Ben knew he could sleep the night in the cold and wet, under the tree branches, unafraid because his brother was with him.

Seth shook his head. The temperature was dropping, and the raindrops were beginning to spread into flakes of snow. "We should be getting close to Lyman's mother's place. We better pick up the pace and get there before nightfall."

"Just one more question, Seth." Benjamin took Seth's arm and stopped a moment. Seth turned to him. The boy's eyes were dark and imploring. "Are Ma and Pa still fighting?"

Seth shifted his weight. He wasn't sure exactly how to answer this question. At Seth's silence, Benjamin shoved his hands into his coat pockets.

Seth spoke, his voice gentle. "Pa's sold the farm. He plans on moving the family to Fort Dearborn come spring. I'm sure it's hard on Ma. You know how much she wants to go to Kirtland. But Pa's feelings haven't changed about the Church, and he's still drinking."

Benjamin thought about how cold it was getting. "Where will you go, Seth?"

"To Kirtland, Ben. With Joel's help, I'll buy a home and make a place for everyone who wants to come."

"I hope I can go with you, Seth!" Tears gathered in the boy's eyes.

Seth pulled him close. This time he had no words of wisdom or counsel. "We have to wait to see what happens, Bennie," he whispered. "And have faith."

A few moments later the brothers began walking side by side, quickly moving toward their goal. The rain changed into the first snow of the season. Seth struck up a conversation. "I hear you still haven't met the Prophet."

Ben nodded and commented. "All this time I've been helping Joel in Ohio, I never once went to Kirtland to meet Brother Joseph."

"Then imagine him," Seth said. "He's a big man, Ben, with strong arms and broad shoulders. He looks like he'd be as handy with an ax as our brother David. He's tall as a Johnson. His hair is fair, his nose is straight, and his forehead is high and wide. He speaks with a slight whistle because his front tooth was chipped off by a mob. But he speaks with authority mixed with kindness and wisdom. His eyes are blue, and they see straight into your heart."

"Sounds like you, Seth, except for his coloring and chipped tooth."

Seth chuckled. "There's a wagon load of differences. I'd never challenge him to a wrestling match. He's much stronger than I. Though not a scholar, his natural intellect is apparent. The Prophet's knowledge comes straight from God rather than from books. His nature is more flamboyant and cheerful than mine. If our Mary had met the Prophet, she would describe him as strong like an ox, merry like a colt, wise as an owl, and gentle as a lamb. He is God's anointed."

* * *

Five days later, Seth and Benjamin neared home. The sun was lowering over Lake Erie, and it looked as if the expansive body of water glowed with light. The sky was clear and the air cold and fresh. A light snow dusted the ground, and walking was difficult; the deep mud had hardened like clay, making the road jagged and uneven.

The brothers turned northeast toward Pomfret. Footsore, they trudged past the cemetery where Elder Brackenbury's body lay in an unmarked grave. Seth would never forget his love for the missionary who had baptized him, nor his deep sorrow at this friend's death. Almost worse had been Seth's horror when medical students secretly attempted to dig up the body in order to dissect it. Although David had apprehended one of the perpetrators, the man had been immediately released. Seth thought sadly of how the protection of a Mormon elder's body was beneath the notice of courts in the land of the free and the home of the brave.

"Seth," Ben commented. "The mill is so quiet."

Seth turned toward the gristmill across the street. "They must have closed down and headed toward home."

"Or the tavern," Ben said.

Seth nodded. The tavern windows were already ablaze with candlelight. Seth could faintly smell the tavern's hearth fire in the chill air. It was no wonder that the warmth of drink and fellowship tempted weary travelers. He sighed deeply, remembering the many hours he had spent at a lone table in the back of the tavern, trying to study amid the stench of tobacco, beer, and men's sweat, while he waited to escort his drunken father home.

"Think Pa's in there?" Ben questioned.

"I don't think so. He's probably working in Fredonia. You could ride to the shop tomorrow and tell him you're home."

Seth noticed Benjamin's silence following this suggestion. They passed the tavern and set out on the final mile of their journey. As they neared the farm, Benjamin's pace increased. Seth laughed, "You're like a barn-sour horse who's forgotten his sore feet in a rush to get home."

Seth matched Ben's energetic gait as they strode quickly toward their goal. It was almost dark when the house came into view. It was a simple, brown-colored house, more square than rectangular, with smoke curling up from the chimney. As they neared it, Seth noticed a figure behind the glass of one of the windows that was sealed for the winter. Whoever it was quickly disappeared. Seth smiled, "Bennie, brace yourself for the stampede."

A moment later, the family poured from the house. After greeting his brothers and sisters, Seth broke through the crowd and gained the porch where his mother and Nancy waited. Despite the lines of worry on her forehead, Julia smiled warmly at Seth as she embraced him. "Son, I'm glad you're home safely. How's Ben?"

"Fine." Seth watched as his mother strained her eyes to see Benjamin through the crowd of surrounding siblings. Seth chuckled. "Sure would be nice if your offspring would give you a chance to greet your son." Seth put his fingers in his mouth and whistled loudly. His brothers and sisters were startled into silence. "Ben needs to greet his mother."

Julia thanked Seth before directing her other children. "Come inside out of the cold. Supper's ready." Then she held her arms out to Benjamin. "Dear Ben, how I've missed you." Benjamin leapt up the porch steps to his mother.

After their embrace, Julia and Benjamin followed the children inside. Seth and Nancy lingered on the porch. Seth noticed that Nancy shivered from cold as she leaned on her crutches. He took off his coat and put it around her shoulders.

"Seth," Nancy said quietly, "Papa's sold the farm."

"I know," Seth answered. "He told me in Jamestown before I left. How's Mother taking it?'

"She's sad and worried. But you know Mama; she marches on."

"Is Father here?"

Nancy shook her head. "He's working in Fredonia."

"Nance, Joel and I have found a place to buy in Kirtland—a house big enough for whoever wants to come."

"We are under Papa's authority. Even if Mama refused to move to Fort Dearborn, he wouldn't let her take the little ones. The law would back him."

"You are of age, and David, and Juli. Almera and Susan will soon be, also. I don't think Father would or could stop any of you from coming with me."

Nancy looked at her crutches. "Being of age makes no difference for me, Seth."

Seth breathed deeply. "Nancy, isn't it time to live your own life—outside the perimeter of Father's influence? It doesn't mean that you are shirking your duty to the little ones. Mother will teach them the gospel until they can join us."

"I can't walk, Seth," Nancy implored.

The door creaked open, and David joined them on the porch. Nancy addressed him. "David, Seth and Joel have found a house in Kirtland. You can go there like the Prophet directed, like you have dreamed of!" Then she looked from David to Seth. "Perhaps this is why God did not heal me. Perhaps He wanted me to stay with Mama—as both a comfort and burden." Nancy swallowed. "But I don't know how I will bear saying good-bye to the two of you."

"It won't be for long. I'll convince you to join us one day," David exclaimed warmly. He lifted Nancy in his arms as her crutches dropped and clattered. "I will carry you wherever you want to go—whether it's Kirtland or the North Pole. But at the moment, it's to the kitchen table. Everyone's waiting."

With Nancy's smile as a reward, David carried his older sister into the house. Seth picked up Nancy's crutches and followed them.

* * *

After supper, twenty-four-year-old Julianne watched in amusement as twelve-year-old Mary ran up and linked elbows with Benjamin. "Come to the barn with me, Ben! I want to show you how I can drive Hercules!"

"Wait your turn, Mare," Joe countered as he stretched his arm around Ben's other shoulder. "Ben, we've got to talk. I've loads to tell you!"

"Not without me!" Mary countered.

Julianne laughed. "You two stop bombarding poor Benja! He's just gotten home from a long and exhausting journey."

"I'm not tired right now," Benjamin responded. Then he remembered the letter in his pocket. "Juli, I have something for you."

"What about me?" Mary demanded with hands on her hips.

Benjamin shook his head. "It's not a present. Just a letter."

"From who?" Joe asked.

Benjamin shook his head briefly as he remembered his promise to Almon. "Nobody important." He handed his sister the envelope.

"From nobody?" Joe raised his eyebrows as he directed Ben toward the sitting room. "Come tell me who nobody is!"

"Me too!" Mary shouted as she leapt after them.

Julianne quickly tucked the letter into her apron pocket. After she finished scouring the trenchers, she slipped upstairs to the girls' room. She heard the sounds of the others gathering around the hearth to talk. Julianne lit a candle, then sat down on the bed and took the letter out. She recognized the handwriting on the envelope.

As she carefully unfolded the paper, she remembered the darling young man she had met last winter. *Wait for me to grow up,* he had said in January with a glint in his green eyes. She had treated him as a tease, had let him know that he was five years her junior and still a child. But today she could not take her eyes from Almon's neat hand. His words thrilled her, even though a part of her felt obligated to a different man.

Dearest Miss Julianne Johnson,

When your sister Susan was here in August she gave me hope that you had not yet given your heart to another. I pray that is still the case.

*   Miss Julianne, surely you are aware of how much I admire your beauty and vivacity, your charm, your wit, and your*

kindness. Last winter all of my jokes were in earnest, and my jests were the only way I knew to confess my feelings.

I know I seem a boy to you and probably always will be so. Can you find any comfort in the fact that when an old man, my heart will be youthful, and we will sing and dance with each other to the grave? (That is, if you will have me. If not, I will quickly become a worn, crotchety creature and, thus, die young.)

Juli, in all seriousness, I am cuttingly aware that I am not, nor ever can be your equal in goodness or worth to God and man. Perhaps my youthful nature makes me reckless and gives me courage to selfishly ask what I do not deserve. Will you consider me? For I adore you. Your merriness rises before me like a bubbling brook, and your goodness is as bright as the full moon. I imagine your lips and your form and such things as I cannot pen and should not imagine. Forgive my boldness, but dear Juli, I love you forever.

Think of the laughter and talk at our hearth! Can you hear the sweet voices of our children? (when they are not mischief making, for they would be mine as well as yours. Thus, sometimes they will be tyrants, and you will understand that it is their daddy's fault and not their own).

All jests aside, I have turned nineteen. My family circumstances have caused me to live my own life for as many years as I can remember. I will be an attorney one day and am currently gathering information about a new law school in Cincinnati. As soon as I can, I will obtain the education I need to make myself of use to the Church and to society and acceptable to you.

My plans are to move to Kirtland in early spring. I will become an elder and fulfill whatever missions Brother Joseph sends me on. Though my mind spins in many directions, my soul is with the kingdom of God. You alone own my heart.

I hope earnestly that you will come and live in Kirtland, where your brothers, Joel and Seth (and I hope David), plan to settle. I don't know exactly how long it will take me to get my affairs in order so that I am worthy to marry. When that day comes, I will sail to Chicago to ask your father for your hand. Until then, would you wait for me and send all other suitors packing (with a swift kick to hurry them on their way)?

I will not sleep until you pen an answer to me. I won't eat either, but will stare into the sky—a forlorn good-for-nothing! If you already love another, or if you cannot love me, then I will try to go on living by admiring you from afar.

Dearest one, please consider my suit. Do not give yourself to another whose nature could not rejoice with yours as I know that ours can together. Write to me for I am in agony. Farewell.

From the boy who would be yours,
Almon Whiting Babbitt

After finishing the letter, Julianne lay back on the bed, holding the paper tightly in her hands. Her cheerful nature trembled. She closed her eyes to blink back her tears. Circumstances confused everything! At one time, her sister Susan had cared for Almon, so Juli had kept her distance. And now a man named Jeffrey Howell sought her hand. He had joined the Church six months ago. He was fifteen years Juli's senior and a widower with six children. He was a good farmer and a blacksmith with money enough for a start in Kirtland. He was in great need of a woman to help him. He was also very kind. Though Juli had postponed giving him an answer, she had also at times encouraged him.

"Juli, are you all right?"

Julianne looked over to see her eighteen-year-old sister, Susan, at the door of the room watching her. Juli sat up. "I have just received a letter from Almon Babbitt."

Susan studied her sister and blurted out, "You should marry Almon, Juli, not Brother Howell."

"Oh Sue, are you always right? When you came back from Amherst this summer, you told me that Almon is a man now, that he loves me, and that I should consider him as a suitor. I saw the tears in your eyes, Susie. How good you are and how sorry I am that his caring for me might have hurt you—you who are my dearest younger sister, and so much wiser than myself."

"Juli, now I only love Almon like a brother. Promise me you will marry him."

"He is so young, merry, and smart. He has every hope before him. How selfish it is of me to love Almon when Brother Howell is in such great need! Dear Susie, I am not unselfish like you."

"Juli, you must marry Almon."

"Susie, is it cruel of me to ask you to sit by me and tell me why I must marry him? Oh, give me a thousand reasons, for I need them to wash away my guilt!"

Susan sat down on the bed next to her sister. She was taller than Julianne, and her features were not as pert, nor her form as graceful. But Julianne knew that shyness covered her sister's intelligence and wit like a layer of clouds covers the blue sky above. She waited patiently until Susan spoke.

"Because you are young and merry too. Because you and Almon suit each other. Because you would be happy together. Because you love each other." Susan blinked the tears from her eyes and smiled wryly. "Not that love has anything to do with marriage."

Julianne took a trembling breath. "I wonder if Mother will be disappointed if I choose a reckless boy rather than a steady man. Will Nancy advise me differently? Almera will understand me wanting to marry for love rather than reason. But she won't be able to imagine why I would love Almon who so annoys her. But you, Susie, you understand my heart. But is a heart's choice reason enough for marriage? Will you help me write the letter to Brother Howell denying my hand?"

"Of course I'll help you write the letter," Susan replied. "I'll go get the pen and ink now."

* * *

Susan swallowed as she retrieved the writing materials from her brothers' room. She had not answered Julianne's other question. *Is a heart's choice reason enough for marriage?*

Her soul cried out the words she could not say. *My heart's choice wasn't enough. But that was because it was one heart choosing, not two. Juli, if you don't marry him, my sacrifice will be for naught, my pain worth nothing.*

Susan could not speak these words aloud, for she had not told Julianne the details of last summer. When Susan had visited Amherst with her father and Seth, Almon had been certain that Julianne would never return his affection. In response, he had tried to court Susan. But quiet Susan had known that Almon loved her sister and had explained to him that Julianne secretly cared about him as well. Almon had rejoiced at the hope, though it broke Susan's heart.

Susan walked back into the girls' room and set the paper, quill, and ink on the night table. Julianne stood up and hugged her. Scarcely able to return the embrace, Susan closed her eyes and prayed inwardly that she would be forgiven for telling her sister that simple lie, which seemed such a necessity. *Dear Father in Heaven,* Susan's voiceless prayer echoed, *help my falsehood become a reality. Help me only to love Almon as a brother.*

* * *

Ezekiel left the carpenter shop in the late afternoon. He mounted Old Katy and rode to the tavern for a drink and bite to eat before setting off on the five-mile journey home. He had finished eating a bowl of corn chowder and was sipping a brandy when a local farmer named Aaron Whittingham walked up to him. Holding a newspaper in his hand, Aaron asked, "Zeke, did you know that your oldest boy's name's in today's paper?"

Ezekiel's brow furrowed. "No, Aaron, I did not know that."

The man folded the paper and handed it to Ezekiel. He sat down and pointed to an article. "Shows the Mormonites in their true light. Makes a man's blood boil. Those Mormonite preachers are taking folks' money and sending them to some promised land in Missouri. Some of their converts are defenseless, single females.

To make matters worse, one's a gal with consumption. They baptized her because she had eight hundred dollars to give them. She's bound to die on the journey."

Ezekiel squinted at the article as he slowly read the words. His glower deepened with each passing moment. At the end of the article there was a footnote by the editor of *The Fredonia Censor*. It read: *One of these Mormon preachers, we believe, is Joel H. Johnson of this town.*

Ezekiel's features darkened with anger. "What proof do they have that one of those preachers is my son? My son's been working the harvest to provide food for his family!" Ezekiel slammed his fist down on the table.

The man named Aaron spoke carefully. "It's an honest mistake, Zeke. Joel *was* here preaching Mormonism last winter. You're doin' right getting your wife and kids away."

"You're darn right I'm doin' right," Ezekiel muttered. His stomach knotted. He gulped down the last swallow of brandy. Then he pushed his chair back and moodily stalked out of the tavern.

4

How kindly they watched o'er my once tender years,
Such kindness one ne'er can forget;
How oft in my dreams I embrace them, with tears,
Their images dwell with me yet.

Joseph Ellis Johnson
("The Graves of My Kindred," *Jottings by the Way,* xv)

Ezekiel's mood softened as he rode home. There was a brisk, cold wind at his back, an honest horse beneath him, and the road stretching before him. It was dusk when he approached his farm. From a distance he saw his daughter, Mary. Her lithe form silhouetted against the glowing western sky. She teetered on the brink of womanhood, but was a child still. Unaware that her father watched, Mary raced awkwardly from the barn toward the house with both arms wrapped around a large pail of milk. Nine-year-old George was just behind her, struggling to pull ahead and keep his milk from spilling at the same time.

"Mary! George!" Ezekiel called out. There wasn't so much as a hesitation in either child's stride. Disappointed, Ezekiel snorted. His voice had been lost in the wind.

"Papa, welcome home."

Ezekiel turned to see twenty-year-old Almera emerge from the woods and stroll up to him. In her arms lay a bundle of slender, twisted branches. Even after two decades of raising this daughter, her beauty still struck Ezekiel. Almera's features were soft and lovely, her skin fair and flawless, her eyes dark and long-lashed, as if a master sculptor had a hand in the shaping of her. The ever-changing nuance of color in her cheeks betrayed each shadow of emotion that crossed her soul. Slightly taller than average, she carried herself with grace and passion. Ezekiel feared for this daughter. A woman should not be so beautiful.

"Almera, what are you doing out here alone?"

"Just collecting branches. I'll put them in the vase with some evergreens. That will have to do until we have flowers this spring."

Ezekiel swung down from the horse, his legs slightly wobbly, betraying his visit to the tavern. He led the horse as he walked with Almera toward the house. "Anything of import happen here this week?"

"Nothing. Just Seth and Ben coming home."

Ezekiel's brow furrowed. "When did your brothers get here?"

"Yesterday." Almera glanced at her father. "Didn't you see Joseph and Benjamin today? They went to Fredonia to look for you and watch the militia march tonight."

Ezekiel shook his head. "I had a few stops to make on the way home and must have missed them. Did they say anything about Joel's whereabouts?"

Almera looked at his father, mystified. "Joel's home in Ohio with Annie, and they are all in good health."

Ezekiel nodded and exhaled quickly.

"Papa, why do you ask?" Almera questioned.

Ezekiel looked directly into her eyes. "Some Mormon elders from Ohio are back in New York. The paper mentioned that Joel might be one of them. It also says that these missionaries converted young, single, defenseless women. They took all their money and convinced them to walk to that Zion place in Missouri. The poor women were left destitute. One of them is a consumptive. It's a crime."

"The paper lies all the time!" Almera exclaimed.

Ezekiel snorted. "Don't be so certain! Sometimes you have to look past the lies to find the truth!"

Almera's face reddened. Didn't her father remember the hurtful half-truths the paper printed after Elder Brackenbury's death? "Papa, if you want to know the truth about the Mormon missionaries, why don't you ask Seth and Lyman, rather than believe the *Censor?*" she snapped.

"Do you think your brother and brother-in-law know more about the truth than your own father?" Ezekiel's voice rose a notch.

Almera glanced furtively at her father. "It's just that they're Mormon elders, Papa. They know firsthand."

Ezekiel put his hands on Almera's shoulders and spoke sternly. "I know a good deal more about the ways of men in the world than your elder brothers or Lyman Sherman. Be careful, Almera. There are wolves in the forest, men who prey on young, lovely women. Don't let anyone convince you to do something you'd be sorry about for the rest of your life, even if he is Mormon."

"Don't worry, Papa. I'm not a child," Almera said. "I won't easily trust any man—Mormon or not."

Ezekiel noticed the fire in her eyes. It would serve her well. He snorted and let go of Almera's arm. "The fact that you're not a child is what worries me! Now go on home. Tell your mother I'll be in for supper." He turned from his daughter and led the horse toward the corral.

* * *

For a moment Almera watched after him. Her father's shoulders were stooped from age and hard work, but there were still power and pride in his torso and in his arms. Almera longed to shout to him, to tell him so many things. She knew more about the ways of men than he realized. She had never told him that Philastus Hurlbut had made frightening advances toward her a few years ago. Philastus was now a devout Mormon, but Almera would never trust him. And last winter, Elijah Handy had professed his unconditional love. But Elijah's promises were false. He had shunned her because of her belief in Mormonism. Then there was Almera's own father.

He drank too much and was going to move the family against their will. Almera knew the peril of trusting men.

Almera turned away from the pain of watching Ezekiel's retreating form. He was a man and her father. These facts gave him so much more position and power than she would ever possess. Sometimes the hardest thing of all was that she knew beyond doubt how much he loved her. If you couldn't completely trust a father who would die or kill to protect you, then who could you trust?

Almera walked toward the house. Loneliness filled her. Her mind wandered back to earlier that day when Ben and Joe had invited her to go to Fredonia with them. The Fredonia town square would be full of life tonight, with the militia marching, the bands playing, and natural gas lighting up a hundred crystal lamps. How she used to love it there! She loved it so much that she could no longer bear to go.

Her eyes clouded with tears. This time last year Elijah had taken her to the Fredonia Inn and bought her a meal cooked on a gas stove. "This is the best place on earth," Elijah had said. "The only place in America with gas lights. My father helped dig that well in 1820. God willing, I will build you a home fit for a queen with a light in every room."

But God had not been willing. The joy of their relationship had turned to darkness when Elijah, the Baptist minister's son, found out that Almera believed in Mormonism. Elijah's anger had broken her heart. Would her father's anger now break all of their hearts? What would Papa do when he found out that Seth and Joel were buying a place in Kirtland and had invited any of them who wanted to join them there? Papa would not give in. He would rage at them all. And if he had enough drink in him, he would weep as well.

Almera felt tears on her cheeks, but she couldn't wipe them away because of the branches in her arms. Her face was chapped from the cold, and her tears stung her skin. Someday she would be away from all of this, and the world would be bright and clear once more. She would have a man who would hold her in his arms, who would believe in the gospel as she did, who would build a life with her, who would warm her and protect her every single day. Together they would sing the songs of Zion. They would have the light of Christ's gospel in their home. Almera wiped her eyes with her sleeve while still holding the branches in her hands.

As Almera lowered her arms, Nancy happened to look out of the window from her cot in the sitting room. She saw the twisted branches dividing her sister Almera's lovely features into sections.

* * *

The Fredonia town square teemed with lights and life. Joe stretched up so that he could see over the crowd. The militia had just finished marching. He glimpsed Injun Goldfinger who had set up a table to peddle his crafts. Joe put both hands over his head and waved to him. The old man nodded and smiled.

Benjamin pulled his hat down to cover his eyes. "We ought to go, Joe. I don't see any other Mormons. And we never found Pa. The way home is gonna be dark and cold."

"Ben, do you remember when we were little boys and Pa brought us here to see the French General Lafayette? He was as impressed with our gas lights as we were with him!"

"I remember," Benjamin grumbled.

"That was a good day, Ben. Pa hoisted us up on his shoulders."

"That was a long time ago."

"Not when you compare it with eternity. There's Morris and Willard."

Joe called out to his friends, who pushed their way through the crowd to join him. Laughing, Morris thumped Joseph playfully on the back. Morris's cheeks were red, and his eyes gleamed. His blond hair glistened under the lights. "I just beat Willard at *Hunker Down and Hassle for the Hauser.* I took that rope and pulled him clean off the box!"

"You lie like the devil, Morris! Joe, I beat him two out of three. Morris, let's take Joe over to the phrenologist and have his head examined! We had ours done an hour ago. It's a laugh."

Grinning, Willard and Morris each took one of Joe's arms and escorted him to a peddler's booth. Benjamin followed.

Scratching his head, Joe studied the drawing nailed to the phrenologist's booth. It was of the side of a man's head. The skull was mapped and divided into squares, each with a word and picture describing a personality trait.

A heavyset gentleman with a red silk vest, gold-chained pocket watch, long gray sideburns, and tattered boots greeted Joe. "Professor C. J. Harness, Certified Phrenologist, at your service."

"Professor," Joe said with an engaging smile, "my friends tell me I'm in need of your skills."

"Splendid." The professor smiled back. His teeth looked like blackened stumps. The man took off his gloves and blew on his hands to warm them. His blunt fingernails were caked with dirt. "Sit down, young friend." Joe obediently lowered himself into a wicker chair in the center of the booth. "Twenty-five cents, please."

Joseph dug in his pocket and pulled out the needed change. A group of people gathered around. Professor Harness began probing Joe's scalp with his fingers. Whenever he felt a depression or lump he called out a personality component. "Young man, you have the gift of friendship."

"Hear, hear," Morris and Willard chimed.

"Ah, you are benevolent. Tut, tut, but calculating. You are amative, disposed to love, but unfortunately, you lack continuity and firmness."

"It's true. Joe E. has kissed many a girl," Willard declared.

"He'll never stay with one woman," Morris added. "No continuity." Willard doubled over laughing. Joe grinned at Ben and rolled his eyes.

"Silence, young men!" the professor ordered. Morris and Willard tried to stop laughing, but it was like putting a lid on a pot that was already boiling over. The phrenologist's face reddened.

"Listen to me, you upstarts!" the man exploded. People turned in their direction like a changing wind. The man raged. "The doctrine of phrenology is a science and not to be meddled with! Last spring I studied the head of a man—destructive with no compassion. The next week he gunned down his brother! His own brother! A month ago, a woman came to me! She was idealistic and vulnerable. Not very intelligent. She has now been stolen away by Mormonites!"

Joe's grin evaporated. Willard and Morris were instantly silent. The crowd stirred. The professor continued. Now that he had a congregation, he worked them like a preacher. "Yes, she is the one you read about in your local paper! She was a pretty slip of a thing who suffered from consumption. The Mormonites took her, leaving her family without hope for her soul!" the man roared. "My skill can protect you from yourselves! Safeguard your children! If you don't hearken, it is at your own peril!"

A woman named Mrs. Cornwall pointed at Joe. Her eyes were angry and accusatory. "I read the paper. That boy's eldest brother is one of the Mormonites who converted the poor girl."

Joe sat frozen in the chair. What was she talking about? Desperately, his eyes scanned the crowd for friendly faces. He had grown up around these people. Surely, they loved him. He glimpsed Rachel Risley, recognizing the color of her hair deep in the crowd. Blanchard Darby was next to her. She stretched on tiptoes trying to see what was going on. Joe tried to get up out of the chair, but the man's hands on his head were like iron.

"Aha!" the professor exclaimed as he rubbed an area behind Joseph's ear. "There is a lack of honesty in you, boy! You need to be taught a lesson."

Benjamin scrambled to Joseph. His face was flushed, and his voice trembled. "Joe, let's get out of here!"

"Cursed Mormons," a drunken voice called out. "It'll be a glorious day when you Johnsons leave town!"

"Your sister Nancy is still a cripple! Why do you boys believe that hogwash?" another shouted. Joseph felt Benjamin pull him from the booth and nearly drag him past Morris and Willard.

"Yes, go!" someone screamed.

The professor grinned and shouted amicably to the crowd. "Would any of you good people like your head examined? Or perhaps your wife's? Your daughter's intended?"

"Joe, I'm sorry," Morris called out. Joe realized they were heading toward Rachel. Joe's eyes fastened on her face. She looked as if she were about to cry. Blanchard's arm wrapped around her possessively. Benjamin pulled Joe forward. A passerby hit Joe hard in the chest with his fist. Joe lurched, nearly falling.

Rachel screamed. Shaking, with his fists doubled, Ben spun around, but the perpetrator had disappeared into the crowd. An instant later, Injun Goldfinger stood beside Joseph. He stretched one arm around the boy and held a tomahawk in the other. The crowd backed away. The dignified timbre of the Indian's voice silenced those close by. "Stand tall, Joseph Johnson, friend to all. Come with me. Your brother too."

Injun Goldfinger escorted Joe and Ben out of the town square. Then he stopped abruptly. For a moment, the old man stood statue still, gazing back at the crowd and the lights. When the Indian was confident that no one had followed, he spoke, "Friend Joseph, can you walk home?"

Joseph nodded, not telling the Indian that each breath hurt like a knife in his side.

"I will stay here and make sure no one follows," the Indian said. He watched in silence as the boys began the five-mile journey home.

* * *

Ten minutes later, the dirt road loomed ahead of them. Black trees towered on both sides casting ghostly shadows. The full moon was a sphere of light. It was slow going. "Joe, are you going to make it?" Benjamin questioned worriedly.

"I don't know," Joseph mumbled painfully. A bat winged by.

"Just keep going." Benjamin put his arm around Joseph to support him.

The boys trudged forward. They had been walking for nearly an hour when two men approached them on horseback—dark, towering shadows in the moonlight. Joseph shuddered and leaned into Benjamin, pressing his sore ribs with his hand. For the first time in his life Joseph Johnson was fearful of other human beings.

"David! Seth!" Benjamin called out.

"How do you know?" Joe whispered brokenly as the horsemen galloped toward them.

"I can tell it's Katy and Leo. Look at their shapes."

No longer in danger, Joseph crumbled. He sobbed uncontrollably, his long, youthful body doubled over in pain and grief. Ben put his hand on his brother's shoulder. In a moment, David and Seth were with them.

"Joe's hurt," Ben explained as the men swung down from their mounts. Benjamin took the horses' reins. Seth and David ran to Joe.

"Joe, we're here. Everything is all right now," David exclaimed as he wrapped his arms around his younger brother's shoulders. Gaining control, Joe forced himself to stop crying.

"Where are you hurt?" Seth questioned worriedly.

"My ribs," Joe gasped as he tried to straighten.

David gently felt Joe's injured ribs with his fingers. "Nothing is out of place. Can you breathe all right?"

Joe nodded. "It just hurts."

"What happened?" Seth queried.

Benjamin explained, "The crowd turned mean, and someone hit Joe. I think it happened because the paper printed another lie about the Mormons. Injun Goldfinger helped us get away."

Seth affectionately ruffled Joseph's hair. "Pa told us about the article and said that the *Censor* mentioned Joel. We decided to come find you two. *Johnson* isn't a very popular name right now."

David shed his coat and shirt. Bare-chested, with his coat crumpled on the ground, David tied his shirt around Joseph's chest to give support to his ribs.

"Put your coat back on. David. You won't be any help to Joe frozen," Seth said as he picked up the coat and handed it to David.

David grinned as he stretched the coat back on. "Joe, do you feel any better now? Do you think you can ride Katy?"

Joe shrugged and took a tremulous breath. "I don't know."

"We'll lift you on," David offered.

Seth looked at Joseph thoughtfully. "Joe, would you like me to give you a blessing first?"

Joseph nodded. As Joe leaned into David, Seth reached up and laid his hands on Joseph's head. With tender gentleness, Seth prayed, blessing Joe with comfort and strength, promising him that power from on high would guide him throughout his life, assuring him that his Father in Heaven knew him and would bless and protect him always.

Then a moment later, with Seth on one side and David on the other, Joe felt himself lifted into the saddle. Benjamin mounted Leo and patted the gelding's neck.

Under the glow of the full moon, in the black and white world of nighttime, Joe and Ben rode the horses home, while David and Seth walked beside them. They talked of the restored gospel, the Prophet Joseph Smith, the unrest in the world, the Savior's Second Coming, and the uncertain future of their family. By the time they arrived at the house, much of Joseph's pain had gone like night flees from the light of dawn.

Joe went into the house while his brothers unsaddled the horses. Everyone was asleep. He lit a candle in the kitchen hearth and used it to light his way. Still sore, he carefully climbed the stairs, holding onto the smooth oaken rail that his father had crafted. He went into the boys' room where George and Will snored peacefully, their childhood features innocent and lovely in sleep. Joe noticed that there was a piece of paper on the bed he shared with Benjamin. He walked over and picked it up. He held the candle close enough that the light fell on the paper. It was a note from Sue attached to a clipping cut out from *The American Eagle*, Westfield's newspaper. Sue's note read:

I like Amicus a great deal and look forward to more of his letters to the editor. The public thinks he is a wise, old

*gentleman. But I beg to differ. I believe he is a very smart
young man, probably 15 years old. What is your opinion, Joe?
From your dedicated sister, Sue.*

Joseph held the newspaper article in his fingers. He had
planned to buy a copy of the *Eagle* while he was in Fredonia. But
so much had happened. He thought of Rachel with Blanchard's
arm around her. Tears clouded his eyes, for he knew that Rachel
would never meet him again in the lonely old gulf to pick wintergreen. Would he be as outcast in Chicago as he was here? Should
he move to Kirtland with Seth? Would his father allow it? Joseph
walked slowly to the desk, set the candle in the candlestick, and sat
down to read the printed article that he had penned.

Mr. Editor,

*I wish to state to the public a simple unvarnished fact without
any comments. On Monday of last week, a certain man in this
town died and went the way of all the earth. Being in his lifetime a believer in the faith of Abraham, he requested that his
funeral sermon might be delivered by a man of his own faith.
His request was complied with, and his friends applied to the
trustees of the Presbyterian Church, in this village, for the use of
their meetinghouse to conduct the exercises in—but they were
denied this humble privilege—nor is this all. I am informed
that the house is partly owned by men of liberal principles and
does not belong exclusively to the Presbyterians. AMICUS*

Joe closed his eyes. He felt so tired. His chest ached. He heard
the door open downstairs and the sound of his brothers' voices. He
picked up a quill and wrote a note on the back of the piece of paper.

Dear Sister Sue,

*Amicus is not nearly as smart as you think. Until this night,
Amicus has been so foolish as to not fully appreciate his good*

fortune. He has the kindest, most affectionate, elder brothers and sisters. One sister, in particular, who I believe is 18 years old, is especially wise. Her unsolicited advice will always be heeded by Mr. Amicus.

Your devoted brother,
Joseph Ellis Johnson

* * *

At dawn, Joe awakened from an uncomfortable sleep to see David leaping from his bed. The room was frigid. David pulled his trousers and coat on as quickly as possible. Once dressed, he shook Benjamin's shoulder. "Up and at 'em," he announced cheerfully.

"I'm awake," Ben muttered as he rubbed his eyes. It was Ben's duty to chop wood with David before breakfast.

"Good!" David exclaimed. "Now for George and Will. Get up, you scamps! Mary is already downstairs waiting for you with the milk buckets."

"Where's Seth?" Benjamin asked, shivering as he dressed.

"In the sitting room writing letters to Lyman and Joel," David answered as he threw clothes to George and Will and told them to get dressed under the covers.

"How are you feeling, Joe?" David questioned.

Joseph tried to sit up, but laid back down groaning. "It hurts more than last night when I went to bed."

David grinned and tousled Joseph's shock of dark hair. "Bruised ribs always hurt more the morning after. Sleep in and take it slow today."

Benjamin eyed Joseph and muttered, "Lucky dog, Joe. Next time I want to be the one hurt." Joe chuckled, but was quieted immediately by a lancing pain in his side.

Thirty minutes later, Joe carefully sat up in bed, wincing. He was alone in the room, but could hear his mother and sisters preparing breakfast downstairs. He wasn't sure if he was hungry enough to make it worth the pain of getting up. There was a knock at the bedroom door. "Come in," Joe called out.

Sue walked into the room carrying a tray that included a plate brimming with pork, fried potatoes, cornbread with apple butter, and a glass of cider. "Don't get up, Josie. Seth told me what happened. You shouldn't have written me that note last night when you were hurting."

Joe grinned. "I didn't hurt so much last night. So you found me out, Sue."

Susan propped the tray up for Joseph and sat down on the side of the bed. "I've suspected you were Amicus for some time. But I wasn't sure."

"What gave me away?"

"The way you write—sassy and wise with a bit of Latin thrown in now and then."

Joe grinned. "You know writing styles, and Ben knows horses' shapes. I'm an ignorant fellow."

Susan raised her eyebrows. "You know you are the smartest of all of us."

Joe smiled. "I'm too intelligent to suppose that I'm smarter than you, Sue."

Susan smiled wryly. "Joe, you are smart *and* charming. Everyone's favorite."

Joseph's eyes clouded, and his voice was tinged with uncharacteristic melancholy. "Not everyone's favorite. Last night I saw Rachel with Blanchard. It hurt worse than getting hit. I wondered if it was because I'm Mormon. Probably not. Charming and smart aren't everything. Blanchard is handsome. I'm not."

Susan looked down at her hands. Then she looked up and spoke frankly. "I know how you feel, Joe. I'm not pretty like Almera and Julianne. The trouble is that women are dependent on men. If I were a man, I could at least make my own way in the world."

"I'm glad I'm not a woman," Joe said thoughtfully.

Susan raised her eyebrows. "Then again, we don't have to plow or chop wood. I suppose I should count my blessings and beware of jealousy."

Their conversation reminded Joe of a poem he had once heard. He closed his eyes to get the words right. "'And like a cinder that has life and feeling seemed his face with inward pining to be what he could not be.' If you could be anything at all, Sue, man or woman, what would it be?"

"A member of Christ's Church. A Mormonite," Susan said honestly. "Do you want that too, Joe?"

Joseph was quiet for a moment. Then he nodded. "Yes. Isn't it ironic that we want that very thing that separates us from our friends?"

"I suppose it's time to make new friends," Susan commented. "But that might be hard to do in Fort Dearborn."

* * *

Ezekiel and Julia sat down at the breakfast table and waited for their children. Benjamin and David walked into the kitchen after chopping wood. In an instant, Ezekiel left his chair at the table's head to embrace Ben. "It's good to have you back, son! Have you heard the news? The farm is sold, and we'll be moving to Fort Dearborn come spring."

"I heard, Pa," Benjamin answered with a quick glance at David.

"Would you like to go with me in early spring as soon as the waterways open?" Ezekiel questioned. "You can help me pick out some land and put seed in. We'll send word for your mother and the others."

"I don't know," Benjamin muttered as he looked down. He stepped back from the embrace and made his way to his seat on one of the long benches that flanked the table. His father stared after him. Benjamin's face turned crimson, and the boy glanced at his mother. Ezekiel saw the look of compassion and under-standing in Julia's eyes. He glowered. Their attitudes made him the villain!

One by one, Ezekiel's children sat down at the breakfast table. The fire blazed in the hearth. Julianne cheerfully poured coffee.

When she poured Ezekiel's she kissed his cheek. "It's good to have you home from Fredonia, Papa," she said.

Her warmth thawed the edge of his mood. "Thank you." Ezekiel patted Julianne's hand.

"It looks like it will snow today," David commented. Ezekiel nodded in agreement.

"Where's Joseph?" Ezekiel questioned as he took count of his children.

Susan lifted her head and looked at her father. "I gave him breakfast in bed. His side hurts."

Ezekiel's eyes filled with concern. He had known men with stabbing pain in their side, who were dead within a week. He pushed his chair back.

"Where are you going, Ezekiel?" Julia questioned.

"To check on my boy. I want to know exactly where his pain is located."

"He's all right, Pa," David said. "He was hit in the ribs last night. He's sore, but he'll be fine."

"How'd he get hit in the ribs?" Ezekiel demanded. "Joe's never been a fighter."

"It was in Fredonia. Someone in the crowd just hit him," Benjamin blurted. "I couldn't tell who it was. It happened so fast."

"Why, Ben?" Ezekiel's countenance darkened. "Why do you think someone would come up and just hit Joe?"

Benjamin looked down at his pork and cornbread.

"Answer me Benjamin!"

"Because we are Mormon," Ben said quietly.

Ezekiel slammed his fist onto the table. "Benjamin Franklin Johnson, you are not Mormon, and neither is your brother! You both are under age and subject to my authority!"

With tears in his eyes, Benjamin burst out, "Pa, I want to move to Kirtland with Seth and David. Please don't make me go to Chicago!"

Ezekiel's eyes darted to his wife at the other end of the table. "This is your doing Julia!" he thundered. Julia's hands shook.

There was a time, not many years ago, when she could not have imagined being afraid of her husband.

Seth's voice broke the instant of strained silence. "This is not Mother's doing. This is mine. I plan to purchase land in Kirtland. I've told Ben and the rest that there will be a place for them there, if they want to come."

Ezekiel stared at Seth in disbelief. "You, my own son, will take my children from me?"

"Pa, it should be their choice," Seth said gently. "Not mine, nor yours. Consider Benjamin's pain, Father, and your daughters' tears. I too love them. I will not close my heart nor home to them."

Ezekiel stood up from the table and stepped toward Seth. Seth arose, meeting his father's gaze. David left the bench and stood next to Seth. Ezekiel shouted, "It is not their choice! They are not of age! It is not your mother's choice! She is my wife! Seth, though you are of age, you have a duty to honor your father! I deserve better than this at your hands!"

Seth's level, dark eyes did not waver. It was as if Seth had known this storm would come, and he was prepared to meet it head on. "Father, I honor you. But I have a duty to God and to my brothers and sisters who would follow Him. I pray that you will forgive me and understand one day."

Ezekiel spun toward David. "What do you say to all of this? Will you leave me to clear the land on my own?"

David's sentences were short. "I'll help you clear the land. And build a house for Mother. But I will live in Kirtland."

With fists knotted at his sides, Ezekiel's voice vibrated with rage. "Your brothers will live with me until they are of age! By then, their eyes will open, and they will see Mormonism for what it is! Your sisters are subject to me until they have husbands of their own! I warn you not to divide this family!"

When Seth and David did not answer, Ezekiel pounded both fists on the table. Dishes clattered, and coffee spilled as he roared again, "I warn you!"

Little Esther and Amos began sobbing loudly. Almera and Benjamin stood up with tears in their eyes, wanting to escape. "Sit back down and eat your breakfast!" Ezekiel shouted. Seth and David stoically complied.

"I can't, Papa," Almera cried as she ran from the table. Benjamin followed her. Susan bowed her head and cried silently. Nancy was weeping. Young Mary took her eldest sister's hand and held it tightly. Julianne pulled Esther and Amos into her arms to quiet and comfort them.

Ezekiel's knees bent as he sat down in his chair, breathing raggedly. His wife's hands were folded in her lap, and her head was bowed as she desperately prayed for the strength to endure another day.

5

And many a time did I list to his voice,
When the words he did utter, caused me to rejoice;
He taught to us lessons of light, and of truth,
I have treasured them up since the days of my youth.

George Washington Johnson
(*Jottings by the Way*, 13)

February 5, 1833

Delcena rocked Albey in the sitting room. The relaxing baby calmed her tension as the child lost his battle to keep his eyes open. The room was bright with a fire in the hearth. The flames of a few lighted candles blazed in sconces on the wall. Philastus Hurlbut came into the room from his bedroom, sat close by the fire, and nervously tapped his foot. Delcena did not look over at him. His arrogance had been difficult for her to cope with for the past six months, and tonight she had other worries on her mind as well.

A few minutes later, Lyman entered the cabin and immediately shut and latched the door behind him, leaving the wind and darkness outside. Delcena glanced over at him and saw a look of both sorrow and peace in his eyes. He shook his head as he shed his coat and gloves. Delcena closed her eyes as sorrow welled inside her. Lyman embraced his wife and baby, but did not speak. His hands were cold.

Hurlbut's head jerked up. He ran his fingers through his wavy dark hair, pushing it out of his eyes. "So, cousin, what has happened?"

Lyman moved closer to the fire for warmth. "We did all we could for Sister Clark," he said quietly. "We gave her a priesthood blessing, but she passed on."

"How is Brother Clark holding up?" Delcena questioned. Now fear crept through her, colder than Lyman's hands.

"God will comfort him," her husband answered.

"What comfort is there when his wife died of smallpox?" Hurlbut snapped as he sprang to his feet. "Shouldn't God support His Saints better than this? Lyman, you or I could be the next! Or Delcena and the children! I won't wait here for it to happen. Tomorrow, I'm leaving for Kirtland. Judge me as you will."

Lyman's eyes met his cousin's. "D. P., I'm not your judge. The stars are out tonight. I don't think it will snow tomorrow. Go if you must."

"Lyman, come with me! Leave Delcena with her parents for the winter. The pox is here in Jamestown, not in Pomfret. We'll come back and get your family in the spring." Lyman shook his head resolutely but said nothing.

Hurlbut went on, "What's keeping you here? Smallpox is threatening your family! Joseph Smith is in Kirtland!"

"Duty," Lyman answered simply. "There are families interested in the Church. I might be an instrument in God's hands in their conversions."

"Leave them in God's hands," Philastus rebutted. "Your first responsibility is to your family. Get them out of here."

Delcena glanced at Philastus, feeling a rare gratitude for him. His genuine concern for their welfare touched her. Delcena spoke, "Lyman, I agree with Philastus. We shouldn't stay here any longer. Not with smallpox among the Saints. We have three children."

Lyman turned to his wife. "Delcena, we have consecrated all to the Lord. I believe that he will protect us. Did you read the newspaper? Dr. Proudfit doesn't think the disease is smallpox, but a less dangerous disease called varioloid."

Delcena responded with tears in her voice. "Smallpox or vari-oloid, I won't stay here, Lyman."

Philastus let out a short laugh. Lyman's eyes darted to his cousin. "I see no humor here."

Philastus's voice was conciliatory. "It's just that I'm surprised that Delcena is on my side—a rare reversal in my fortune. Lyman, it is two votes to one. Be a good loser, and I'll help you pack. The house can remain vacant until the new renters come in the spring."

Lyman stared back into the fire, the reflection of the flames dancing in the lenses of his glasses. He turned to his wife, "Delcena, there isn't room in your parents' home for all of us. Your father's drunkenness would not be good for our children. How I wish I could take you to Kirtland now! But my mission here isn't finished, and we would have to depend on charity until we could build a cabin of our own. Can't you be patient until spring and trust in God's will?"

Delcena looked over at her husband, her dark eyes moist. She cradled her baby boy protectively in her arms, remembering her first little son's illness and death. It was like a scar in her soul that was opening once more. She slowly shook her head, and her voice, though slightly shaking, was resolute. "I have faith, Lyman, but I can't stay here. We've already lost one baby. I won't lose Albey or the girls to smallpox. Not if there is a choice. We could live in Joel's old cabin on Annie's father's land."

Hurlbut looked from Delcena to Lyman. "Cousin, listen to your beautiful wife. With your family safe in Pomfret, you would be free to travel to and from Kirtland this winter. If duty requires you to be here in Jamestown much of the time, so be it."

"Lyman, please," Delcena begged.

* * *

The room was silent save for the crackling fire, the wind outside, and the baby's soft snores. Delcena and Philastus said nothing as Lyman looked into the fire and listened to the voices in his own soul. How he would love to see Brother Joseph again, to be invited to study with the School of the Prophets. Words from a recent revelation, which Elder Rigdon brought to Jamestown, ran through his mind. *He that ascended up on high, as also he descended below all things, in that he comprehendeth all things, that he might be in all and through all things, the light of truth; which truth shineth . . . This is the light of Christ.*

Lyman pictured Sister Clark with sores on her skin as she hovered between life and death. She had not lived when he had laid his hands on her head and, by the power of the priesthood, blessed her. Instead her breath stopped, her body stilled, and her spirit fled. That too had been an answer to his prayer. Lyman took his glasses off and rubbed his eyes. He looked in the direction of his wife and baby. Without his spectacles, they blurred together, blending in with the shadows and earth tones in the cabin. More words from the revelation reverberated in his heart. *And if your eye be single to my glory, your whole bodies shall be filled with light, and there shall be no darkness in you; and that body which is filled with light comprehendeth all things. Therefore, sanctify yourselves that your minds become single to God, and the days will come that you shall see him; for he will unveil his face unto you, and it shall be in his own time, and in his own way, and according to his own will.*

Hurlbut stomped his foot in frustration. "Lyman! Come out of your trance and make a decision."

Lyman jerked his shoulders almost as if he had awakened. He put his glasses back on and said briskly, "Delcena, tomorrow we go to Pomfret and see if Joel's old cabin is available. Philastus, go to Kirtland. I will continue missionary work here in Chautauqua County, but will visit you in March if I can. Delcena, in the spring, it's Kirtland ho!"

A relieved smile lit Delcena's features as a tear escaped her eyes. "Yes, Lyman, it's Kirtland ho! I can scarcely wait until that day!"

Hurlbut raised his eyebrows. "And if I know Lyman, it will be *Zion ho!* Or *mission ho!* after a month in Kirtland. You have a great deal to look forward to, Delcena."

Delcena raised her eyebrows slightly. "It may be *mission ho*, for you too, Philastus."

Philastus grinned. "I suppose. I would like to be ordained an elder. If a mission is in store, I hope it is to an agreeable place, not one infested with disease and poverty."

Lyman's forehead creased as he focused on his cousin. "The gospel is for all people, in all places."

Hurlbut laughed and spoke lightly. "Well put, Lyman. But I cannot be in all places, nor amongst all people. Let us hope that the Prophet Joseph sends me to that place where I can be of the most use. For it has been revealed to me that pleasant places and pleasant people need the gospel."

Lyman's brow furrowed, "D. P., you should not make light of sacred things. Elder Brackenbury went where the Lord called him. He gave his life serving a mission."

"But his life was cut short by years," Hurlbut rebutted as his pleasant look flickered and his eyes became troubled and combative. "He would have been more use to the Lord had he lived longer. You know that, Lyman."

"I do not know that! That good man's life was in God's hands. We do not comprehend what God comprehends. *That* is what I know."

Philastus closed his eyes briefly. When he opened them again, they were unreadable. "Come Lyman, let's not argue now and upset Delcena. We can debate later."

"I don't want to debate with you." Lyman swallowed and did not take his gaze from his cousin. He felt as if he were searching to know who Philastus really was. Lyman swallowed and spoke. "I want us both to be men of integrity, testimony, and faith. You are as a brother to me. I know of your generous heart. I want us to be undivided, one in purpose."

Philastus Hurlbut let out a quick breath. When he spoke, his voice was entreating, almost begging. "Lyman, you are the only man I trust. But I fear that the real world is far different from what you see and that someday you will be sorely disappointed.

We are very different men. But promise me, Lyman, that we will always be friends."

"Of course, Philastus," Lyman said quickly as he stood and embraced his cousin.

* * *

Delcena stroked her baby's hand as she watched the two men. A shadow passed over her heart. They were cousins, both men of passion and action. Philastus was the more striking to look at— with broad shoulders and a fine physique. His chiseled features and wavy hair could break a woman's heart. But he was proud, and sometimes his integrity seemed to waver. Would he always be a friend to Lyman? Delcena shuddered. She did not like the thought of Philastus as an enemy. Yet, why did she fear? These two men shared a deep bond. Baby Albey's eyelids fluttered in his sleep. Distracted from her concerns, Delcena kissed her child's cheek. She stood and carried him into the bedroom where his sisters slept, and where his cradle awaited him.

* * *

A week later, Philastus Hurlbut knocked on the door of an unfa-miliar, weather-worn farmhouse in Erie County, Pennsylvania. Snow swirled around him, catching in his dark hair and speckling it gray. He was in the Pennsylvania borderlands on his way to his uncle's home in Elk Creek Township. Philastus had planned to spend the night at the home of a fellow Mormon named Erastus Rudd. But with the storm brewing and night approaching, he knew that he could be frozen before finding the place. He cursed himself for attempting this journey alone. Perhaps he would have been better off risking smallpox in Jamestown with Lyman.

He waited a few moments for someone to answer the door. He reasoned that if he had to wait much longer, he would break the hinges off. Then the door creaked open, and a wizened old man with a sallow face and dim, bloodshot eyes, stood before him.

"Hello sir." Philastus stuck out his gloved hand. "I'm a stranger in these parts and lost in the storm."

"You alone?" the man questioned suspiciously, not taking Philastus's hand. Philastus nodded.

"Name's John Miller," the man said as he studied Philastus. "You look hardy enough to weather this storm. But you're welcome to my fire and ale as long as you ain't one of those cursed Mormon elders."

"I'm not," Philastus answered. He had not been ordained an elder and was technically telling the truth. Philastus followed the man into a damp parlor and found a seat in front of the fire. Hurlbut took off his gloves and rubbed his hands together. The heat from the blaze seemed to go up and out the chimney, rather than warm the room. Miller retrieved two cups of ale. After handing one to Philastus, he slowly lowered himself into a dusty chair.

The two sat quietly for a time sipping their ale, listening to the wind whistle and the fire crackle. As warmth spread through his powerful frame, Philastus asked his host a question. "So what do you have against the Mormons?"

The old man eyed his young guest. "Their lies are spreading all over these parts. Even my neighbor, Erastus Rudd, has joined them."

Hurlbut raised his eyebrows.

The old man's dry, thin lips twisted, and he continued. "That young deceiver, Jo Smith, got hold of Solomon Spaulding's manuscript. He used it to write his cursed Book of Mormon. The thing that galls me is that Solomon wrote most of his book in the Rudd home. Now the Rudds harbor Mormon missionaries and hold meetings in the very same room."

"Are you certain?" Philastus asked.

"Of course I'm certain," the old man grumbled. "Spaulding was my friend. In the old days, I visited with Solomon in that room a hundred times."

Hurlbut smiled slightly. "I don't question your memory, sir. Are you certain that the Book of Mormon was taken from your friend's romance novel?"

The old man narrowed his eyes at Hurlbut. "I never told you it was a romance novel."

"Word travels. I've done some investigating of the Mormon religion."

"And what have you learned?" the old man spit out.

Hurlbut measured his words carefully, speaking somewhat truthfully. "That this religion is compelling but rather difficult to believe. Yet one wants to believe that God again speaks to man, that the confusion of the ages is knit into a new hope. But that hope grows more elusive to me with each passing day. But there are good people who believe it. My cousin and aunt, for example."

Miller wagged his head back and forth. "I'm an old man, and no one listens much to me. That's what happens when you're old or dead. People throw you away and use whatever's left for their own purposes. Just like Jo Smith did to Solomon's story."

"Do you have a copy of your friend's manuscript?"

"No, but I could get it. His wife's got it locked away in a trunk back east."

"Have you read the Book of Mormon?"

"I've thumbed through it."

"And you are certain that they are one in the same?"

"Not the same. Smith changed things." John Miller folded his arms and let out a sharp breath. "Jo Smith isn't stupid. But where else would he have gotten his book from?"

Philastus Hurlbut mirrored John Miller by folding his arms. He raised his eyebrows. "That seems to be the question of the day."

John Miller shuffled to his feet and laid a bony hand on Philastus's shoulder. "Tomorrow, I'll take you to see Nehemiah King and Henry Lake. They'll convince you."

Philastus shook his head. "I have business. Tomorrow I visit my aunts and uncles in Elk Creek."

"Who are your people?" Miller questioned.

"The Hurlbuts, Shermans, and Winchesters."

Miller nodded slowly. "I know your people. Asenath Sherman is Mormonite. She and her girls moved to Thompson for the winter. The Winchesters just joined the Mormons. With a family like that, you are swimming in dangerous waters, boy."

Philastus laughed. "You don't know the half of it. But don't worry about me, Mr. Miller. I'm a darn good swimmer."

John Miller shrugged his shoulders. "You look like it. What's your name anyway?"

"Doctor Philastus Hurlbut."

"Doctor? Where's your physician's bag?"

Philastus grinned. "You're an observant old man. I'm not a physician. Doctor is a given name. My mother gave me the name because I am her seventh son."

"Be wise as a serpent, Seventh Son."

"And harmless as a dove?" Philastus asked with an ironic chuckle.

"Unless you're dealing with Mormonites," Miller remarked, the corner of his mouth lifting in a smile. Philastus noticed that most of his teeth were missing.

* * *

Four days later, the morning was cold and clear as Philastus Hurlbut and Joel Johnson walked toward the Kirtland flats where Joel would take part in a meeting of the School of the Prophets. As they neared the Whitney store, Joel gestured toward a house about two hundred yards away. "D. P., that is the home and property I will own come spring. Right now, the downstairs is for rent. Consider it. Then you could stay after I buy the place." Joel gestured toward a two-story brown house and the surrounding land.

"A fine idea," Hurlbut said as he rubbed his hands together. When Hurlbut had arrived at the Kirtland Tavern that previous evening, he had been pleased to find that Joel Johnson was already a guest. Hurlbut continued, "The more of your family who come to Kirtland, the merrier it will be for me."

Joel grinned and coughed. "I've already spoken to the owner about a price. He wants three hundred and fifty dollars for the plot with the house and orchard on it. As soon as I talk him down, the deal will be clinched. Seth will buy the two and one half acres of wild land adjoining. It will go for about forty dollars an acre."

Philastus smiled. "Wonderful."

Joel clapped Philastus on the back "I'm off to the meeting. I'd be obliged if you will take a good look at the house and orchard and tell me what you think."

"Certainly," Hurlbut answered. He watched Joel as the tall, lanky man walked toward the Whitney store. Then Hurlbut turned and strolled toward the house that Joel planned to buy. As he walked through the snowy orchard, Philastus paid little attention to the winter skeletons of the fruit trees, but instead thought about his conversation four days ago with John Miller. He liked the idea of living with the Johnsons. He could keep a close watch on Joseph Smith, who was living in an apartment in the nearby Whitney store. Hurlbut wondered where the truth lay. Was it possible that Smith was divinely inspired as he once thought? If he discovered that Joseph Smith was a fraud, would he tell Lyman? He didn't like the idea of Lyman spending his life taken in by Smith's delusions. Or should Philastus keep this knowledge to himself and enjoy the Mormon society while he gained position and standing in the Church?

The sound of voices interrupted Philastus's thoughts. He pivoted and glimpsed a group of young ladies whispering and giggling as they rounded the back of the Whitney store and made their way toward a nearby millpond. They pulled a long, slim wooden plank and laid it across the icy water. Once done, they gathered to one side of the pond, and a girl stepped out onto the plank. The wooden beam teetered under her weight. She took a deep breath and continued precariously forward. When she reached the other side, the other girls laughed and cheered. Hurlbut moved closer so that he could see the girls more clearly and hear distinctly what they were saying. A tree concealed him from their view.

"Eleanor, it's your turn!" a pretty, spirited girl exclaimed.

A thick-framed young lady responded, "Lovina, the pond isn't frozen clear through. If I fall, I could drown."

"Oh, Eleanor, it's safe enough, unless you're an ox. This is good exercise. It will increase your balance and grace."

Hurlbut whistled softly under his breath. This Lovina was tall and shapely, with shiny brown ringlets and flashing eyes. She wore slender black gloves and a fur-trimmed cape. The girl was fascinating.

Eleanor navigated the plank carefully, putting one foot forward and then sliding the next foot up to meet it. A young boy ran out of the Whitney store, momentarily distracting the girls. Eleanor tottered and regained her balance. The boy tugged on Lovina's cape. "Ina, Mama will be out soon. Pa will give you a licking if you cross the pond."

Lovina turned to her little brother, "I'm too big for lickings, but you better not tell him, Ezra, or I'll give you the licking of your life."

"Shut your mouth, Lovina," Ezra snapped.

Lovina rolled her eyes at her brother, then cupped her hands over her pretty mouth and shouted, "Hurry Eleanor, before my mother comes out! I want a turn!"

"I can't do it!" Eleanor called back, her voice shaking.

"You have to! You're halfway across. Hurry!" Lovina yelled.

Nearly in tears, Eleanor summoned the courage to move forward, but as she shifted her weight, her foot slid off the plank. With a scream she tumbled through the layer of ice and into the frigid water. "Eleanor, grab the plank!" Lovina shrieked. Eleanor reached out and grasped the board. Lovina tugged desperately on the wooden plank, trying to pull Eleanor out of the pond. But the struggling, sopping girl was too heavy. In an instant Philastus was to them. He took the plank and easily pulled Eleanor to the side. He squatted down, put his arms around the freezing, drenched girl and dragged her out. Lovina gaped at him with tears in her eyes and her hand covering her mouth. Gratefully she gasped, "Sir, thank goodness you were near."

Philastus lifted the shaking, half-conscious girl in his arms. "We need to get her warm."

"Take her to the store; my father will know what to do," Lovina said quickly. Then she cried out in dismay, "Oh, I am going to be in such trouble!"

"I hope not," Philastus answered. "Who is your father?"

Lovina looked at him strangely. "Dr. Frederick G. Williams, scribe of the Prophet."

* * *

"What happened?" Mrs. Rebecca Williams cried out as the group entered the store.

"Eleanor fell in the millpond, Mama," Lovina sobbed. "This gentleman saved her life."

"Follow me!" Rebecca addressed Hurlbut. An energetic, confident woman, she turned to her daughter. "Lovina, get Emma and Sister Whitney. Tell them to bring blankets and dry clothes to the kitchen."

A few moments later Emma Smith held Eleanor, while Elizabeth Whitney and Rebecca Williams began peeling off her frigid clothing. Rebecca Williams spoke to Philastus. "Sir, please get my husband. Tell him to bring his medicine bag. He's upstairs with the brethren."

"I'll show you the way," Lovina added quickly.

As Lovina led Philastus to the stairs, she began crying again. "It's all my fault," she whimpered. "You must think me a brute."

Philastus took her hand and kissed her gloved fingers. "I think you're beautiful and spirited," he said with feeling. "I saw the whole thing. Trust me, you have done nothing wrong."

When they reached the staircase, Lovina gave Hurlbut directions. Philastus bounded upstairs. He knocked on the schoolroom door. A voice called out, inviting him in. Philastus stepped inside. About twenty men were crowded in a small room. The Prophet stood in front of them. He smiled at Philastus "Can I help you, Brother Hurlbut?" Philastus was surprised that Joseph Smith remembered his name.

Philastus nodded. "Sir, Dr. Williams is needed downstairs. Mrs. Williams asks that he bring his medical bag." A tall, middle-aged man with kind eyes and pleasant features sat at the desk with a quill in his hand. He stood up and retrieved a large canvas bag from under the desk.

Joseph spoke. "Brother Sidney, please continue instructing the brethren while I go with Brother Frederick."

Once out of the room, Joseph turned to Philastus. "What happened?"

"A young woman fell in the millpond. The sisters are attending her in the kitchen."

"Do you know her name?" Dr. Williams questioned quickly.

"I heard her called Eleanor."

Dr. Williams hurried down the steps. When he found his daughter, Lovina, waiting at the bottom of the stairs with her hair disheveled and her cheeks tearstained, he immediately addressed her. "Ina, are you all right?"

Lovina nodded, but her lovely, green eyes swam with additional tears. "Papa," she gasped, "I didn't mean for it to happen."

Dr. Williams' brow furrowed, and he spoke authoritatively. "Lovina, we'll talk about what happened later. Take me to Eleanor."

When they reached the kitchen, Dr. Williams and Lovina went in, leaving Hurlbut and Joseph Smith waiting outside the door. Joseph turned to Hurlbut. "Brother Philastus, did you see what happened?"

Philastus nodded. "Yes, I was taking a stroll across the property that my friend, Joel Johnson, plans to purchase. I heard screams. Miss Eleanor had fallen in the pond after attempting to cross over on a wooden plank. Miss Lovina was trying desperately to rescue the girl, but she hadn't the strength. I aided them. Eleanor wasn't in the water long."

Joseph put his hand on Hurlbut's shoulder. "Thanks to you, Brother Philastus. When did you arrive in Kirtland?"

"Yesterday evening."

"Tomorrow, the brethren are meeting in the schoolroom. Please join us."

A few minutes later, the door to the kitchen opened, and warmth spread into the chill hallway. Dr. Williams walked out, followed by Lovina. He closed the door behind them. "How is Sister Eleanor?" Joseph queried. "Would she like a blessing?"

Dr. Williams nodded. "I believe she will recover. I told her I would bring you back in with me." Then he turned to his daughter. "Lovina, what did you have to do with this?"

Hurlbut spoke before Lovina could answer. "Dr. Williams, I saw the whole thing. Miss Lovina only tried to help Miss Eleanor. Your daughter's feelings of guilt lie in the fact that she was not strong enough to pull her friend to safety. Fortunately, I was in the vicinity."

Dr. Williams looked carefully at Philastus. He gazed briefly at Lovina and added to no one in particular. "Eleanor is one of Lovina's closest companions and usually does whatever Lovina bids her to do." Lovina's face reddened.

Philastus smiled boldly at her and then turned to her father. "I would think that all young ladies would want to follow your lovely daughter's advice. Dr. Williams, these events have strained Miss Lovina. Please allow me to escort her home."

"Lovina?" Williams questioned. The young lady nodded. Her eyes were dry now, and there was a daring lilt to her chin.

Dr. Williams added, "Take Ezra with you. Your mother is staying with Eleanor until her father arrives. Lovina, some things occurred in the Council this morning that I need to discuss with you later. Do not leave the house or allow anyone in until your mother or I get home." Lovina nodded dutifully, but Philastus noticed the hidden glint in her eye. This filly was not easy to control. How he would love the challenge!

* * *

Five minutes later Philastus, Lovina, and Ezra had rounded the bend beyond the Whitney store when a man galloped up to them on horseback. "Lovina!" he exclaimed. "I've found you!"

"I can't go with you, Burr. Father has told Brother Hurlbut to escort me home," Lovina retorted with a defiant shake of her head.

The man spun his horse in front of them and reined in, forcing the group to stop. Hurlbut eyed him. The man was in his twenties and wore a palm-leaf hat that shaded his eyes. He swung down from the horse. He focused on Lovina, completely ignoring Philastus. Hurlbut studied him coolly, rubbing his hands together. The man spoke. "Lovina, do you know what happened in the Council this morning?"

"No Burr," Lovina flashed. "I've had a busy morning. Lo and behold, the world doesn't revolve around you." Hurlbut smiled to himself, enjoying this beautiful girl's spunk. Young Ezra shuffled his feet nervously. Philastus patted the boy's shoulder.

"They excommunicated me. Your father did not defend me," Burr spit out, his voice dripping anger. "I told them I didn't care how soon I was cut off."

"You shouldn't have treated the Council with contempt," Lovina said hotly. "What were you thinking?"

"They wanted to send me on a mission to get me away from you!"

"Stop making excuses, Burr," Lovina exclaimed. "Everyone is going on missions. Now father will never let you marry me."

"As if he could stop you," Burr responded.

Lovina glared back. "I won't marry anyone who isn't an elder in the Church!" Then she turned her back to him, took Ezra's hand, and marched away. Hurlbut doffed his hat to the young man and followed them.

With a curse, the man mounted his horse. "This isn't finished, Lovina!" Burr called out.

"It is until you repent!" Lovina retorted without looking back.

Philastus had to step quickly to keep up with Lovina as she marched forward, dragging her little brother along. When she finally tired and slowed down, he began a conversation. "Who is the poor fellow you were talking to?"

She glanced at Philastus. "Burr Riggs. He used to be the handsomest bachelor in Kirtland."

"Until I arrived." Hurlbut raised his eyebrows and chuckled.

Lovina looked sideways at Philastus and added, "If Burr wasn't so stupid I would marry him."

"Perhaps his loss will be my gain."

Lovina stopped and looked boldly at Philastus Hurlbut. Ezra skipped on ahead, clearly bored with his sister's exploits. Her exquisite, spirited beauty enthralled Philastus. Folding her arms, Lovina asked, "Are you asking for my hand in marriage, Brother Hurlbut?"

Philastus grinned at her and winked. "I had a revelation when you and your father were in with Eleanor. We are to marry. It is God's will."

Lovina smiled engagingly, "I'll give you my answer as soon as I receive a similar revelation."

"Fair enough." Hurlbut laughed out loud. They walked in silence for a few moments, and Lovina allowed Philastus to take her hand.

She did not speak again until she announced that they were at their destination. "Thank you for your kindness," she said prettily. "I do hope Eleanor is going to be all right."

Hurlbut's mouth twisted upward. "I'm sure Miss Ox will survive."

Lovina giggled. Hurlbut noticed two beautiful horses in the corral attached to a small barn. They were stately, powerful creatures. Their black coats complemented the dark, bare trees and white snow. "What beautiful animals," he commented.

"Father bred them," Lovina said.

Philastus looked significantly at her. "Your father breeds beautiful creatures."

Lovina laughed. "I suppose Papa loves his horses as much as his children. He says they are far more obedient." With that, she tossed her head and ordered her little brother into the house. She pulled off her gloves and held them in her left hand.

Hurlbut took her slender fingers in his gloved hand and brought them to his lips. "Good day, Sister Lovina," he said softy, after kissing her hand.

"You may call on me, Brother Hurlbut," she said as she withdrew her fingers.

"Shouldn't I ask your father's permission first?"

Lovina raised her eyebrows and smiled. "Of course. You are a gentleman, aren't you?"

* * *

"Welcome Brother Joel, Brother Philastus." Joseph Smith shook the men's hands as they entered the Whitney store the following morning. Joseph directed them toward the stairs. "The brethren are gathering in the schoolroom. Brother Frederick and I have some business to attend to and will join all of you shortly."

Frederick G. Williams and Joseph Smith walked together into a small office, unaware that Philastus Hurlbut's eyes followed them. Dr. Williams was older, a soft-spoken, poised man with polished manners, but he did not have Smith's self-confidence, charisma, or magnetism. The men's friendship and familiarity were obvious. The two conversed as they walked with their heads inclined toward each other, completely at ease, the Prophet Joseph's hand resting affectionately on Dr. Williams' shoulder.

A few moments later Joel and Philastus entered a small upstairs schoolroom. An older, distinguished-looking man greeted them. "Good morning, Brother Joel."

"Brother Sidney, have you met my friend, Brother Philastus Hurlbut?"

Rigdon vigorously shook Philastus's hand and smiled warmly. "Yes, we briefly met when I was in Jamestown. It's wonderful seeing you again, Brother Philastus. I trust that you will find great joy during your stay here in Kirtland with your brethren."

"Thank you, Elder Rigdon," Philastus said with a friendly smile. "I have so much to learn."

"And so much to offer as well," Rigdon said.

As Philastus and Joel took their seats on a bench, Philastus watched Sidney Rigdon greet the incoming men. Hurlbut knew that

Rigdon had been a famous Campbellite minister who converted to
Mormonism, bringing a good deal of his congregation with him. The
local Campbellite preachers were incensed at Rigdon's defection, and
this fueled the prejudice against the Mormons.

Philastus stretched his legs out, and Joel took out his pipe and
began smoking. Other men in the room made themselves comfortable as well, smoking and chewing tobacco, discussing the
kingdom of God as they waited for their prophet. Twenty minutes
later, Joseph Smith entered the room followed by Dr. Williams.
Philastus could not take his eyes off Joseph Smith's face.

Sidney Rigdon walked over to Philastus and put his arm
around his shoulder. "I can tell you are in awe," Sidney whispered.
"You see the light in the Prophet's eyes, the near transparency to
his features. This happens when he has just received a revelation
from God."

The room was instantly silent. Joseph held a piece of paper in
his hand. "Beloved brothers, our Father in Heaven in His mercy
has opened the heavens once more, and I have received this." With
his voice firm and full of feeling, Joseph began reading the words
of the revelation:

> *"Behold, verily thus saith the Lord unto you: In consequence of
> evils and designs which do and will exist in the hearts of
> conspiring men in the last days, I have warned you, and fore-
> warn you, by giving unto you this word of wisdom by
> revelation—*
>
> *"That inasmuch as any man drinketh wine or strong drink
> among you, behold it is not good, neither meet in the sight of
> your Father . . .*
>
> *"And again, tobacco is not for the body, neither for the
> belly, and is not good for man, but is an herb for bruises and
> all sick cattle, to be used with judgment and skill.*
>
> *"And again, hot drinks are not for the body or belly . . ."*

Hurlbut glanced around the room as Joseph continued reading.
Joel Johnson was among the first to put down his pipe. One by

one every other man did so as well. As the smoke cleared from the room, Philastus Hurlbut looked back at Joseph Smith. He was naturally fair, and the light streaming in from the window could have given him that look of heavenly brightness. Was he an actor or a prophet-saint? Were these words from Joseph Smith, God, or Frederick G. Williams? Philastus could not tell. But he knew one truth—Joseph Smith held incredible power over other men's lives! Hurlbut listened as Joseph continued:

> *"And all the saints who remember to keep and do these sayings, walking in obedience to the commandments, shall receive health in their navel and marrow to their bones;*
>
> *"And shall find wisdom and great treasures of knowledge, even hidden treasures;*
>
> *"And shall run and not be weary, and shall walk and not faint.*
>
> *"And I, the Lord, give unto them a promise, that the destroying angel shall pass by them, as the children of Israel, and not slay them. Amen."*

After the meeting, Sidney Rigdon brought Joseph Smith over to Philastus. "Brother Joseph, Brother Philastus had never seen you receive a revelation before. He was deeply moved and will make a fine elder someday soon."

Joseph once again shook Hurlbut's hand warmly. "It's good to have you here, Brother Philastus."

6

Methought I viewed the garden round,
Our mutual handiwork had crowned
With trees and shrubs, and flowers so sweet,
Which lingered still when my lone feet
Turned far from thee.

Benjamin F. Johnson
(*Jottings by the Way*, xxvi)

Early March, 1833

Julia packed Ezekiel's things with a heavy heart. The salt pork, biscuits, dried fruit, and honey seemed a sorry compensation when her soul was severed from her husband's. She folded a change of clothes and placed them in Ezekiel's trunk. She and her daughters had made everything he wore with their own hands. His anger and intemperance had worn the weave of matrimony that bound them, leaving it threadbare. She sighed, relieved that the thaw had come, that the waterways were open, and that Ezekiel was going. There would be some peace now, at least for a time. She would rest for a little while—pushing back the painful thought that she would be required to join him, that she would be separated from her religion, her elder children, and her grandchildren, that her heart would be torn in pieces.

Julia lugged the trunk outside, where Ezekiel and David were harnessing the horse in preparation for the drive to Dunkirk. From there, Zeke would travel by water to Fort Dearborn. The morning was dim with low, thick, gray clouds. Ezekiel finished fastening the harness before looking up at his wife. His eyes were bloodshot. Julia didn't know if it was from drink or emotion. It was so hard to tell these days. Without speaking, David reached out and took the trunk from his mother, hefting it to the back of the wagon.

Ezekiel spoke to his wife. "I'll send you instructions when I have a place."

"I know."

"Take good care of the children. Keep them safe."

"I will," Julia answered. She remembered how Ezekiel had kissed each one good-bye before they left for school earlier that morning. She had been grateful that he had not pressed Benjamin to go with him.

The door opened, and Nancy stood in the door frame, leaning on one crutch. Ezekiel walked quickly up the steps to her. "Good-bye, dear Papa," Nancy whispered.

"Good-bye Darlin'. Paint a picture to hang over the new hearth," Ezekiel said as he kissed her cheek.

"I love you, Papa," Nancy whispered. Her gray eyes held more melancholy than joy.

"And I love you," Ezekiel returned.

Julia felt David put his arm around her shoulders. Ezekiel turned from Nancy and took out his pocket watch. After checking the time, he looked over at Julia and David. His brow furrowed, and he spoke gruffly. "David, let's go."

David nodded curtly and addressed Julia. "Mother, I'll be back by nightfall." Without a word to his father, he leapt into the wagon seat.

Conflicting emotions bound Julia as Ezekiel turned to her. Her husband's eyes became moist as they looked into hers. It was as if he wanted to explain something, but could not. Did he struggle to put into words a lifetime of memories, of joy and terrible pain? And she had nothing more to say. He quickly kissed her chill cheek. His voice cracked. "Julia, good-bye."

For a brief instant, she laid her hand against his grizzled face. "Farewell, Zeke." He somberly climbed into the wagon next to David.

David tapped the whip on the horse's rump. Julia turned around and began walking toward the house. Her legs felt very heavy. When she reached the porch steps she heard Ezekiel's voice. "Julia, come when I send word!" he shouted.

Julia looked over her shoulder and saw her husband looking back at the house as David drove the horse onward. "Good-bye, Zeke," she called back. As Julia joined Nancy on the doorstep, her breathing was labored. Profound sorrow pressed heavily upon her. The presence of her gentle, crippled daughter supported the weight of her pain.

* * *

It was a hazy, dull, gray afternoon as Almon Babbitt and Frank Hills walked down a muddy road in Newport, Kentucky. Almon's mood was as bleak as the weather. He gazed back in the direction of the pier they had just come from, where people and supplies were ferried across the river to and from Cincinnati. Almon's boots sucked in the mud. He glanced at the man next to him who had a pleasant look and seemed to be enjoying this miserable outing. He was Frank Hills, son of Joel and Rhoda Hills, relatives of the Johnsons. Joel and Annie had suggested Almon stay with the Hills family on his venture. Other than Frank's acquaintance, Almon's trip had been filled with one disappointment after another.

Almon pondered the details of the morning's failure. Frank had accompanied him to the newly established College of Law in Cincinnati. A gray-haired professor with pointed teeth and sparse sideburns had questioned Almon extensively about his past schooling, his religion, and his financial circumstances. Not daring to stretch the truth with Frank standing there next to him, Almon had answered the questions honestly. The scholarly gentleman then told him sternly that there was no room for a poor, Mormon boy in their institution.

It made Almon mad—the way he was caught between a rock and a hard place. Had he lied, he might have been accepted into the school where he could prepare himself to practice a vocation necessary to sustain a family. But if Julianne had heard from her cousin, Frank, that Almon was false, she would never consent to marry him. "You're making a mistake," Almon had told the professor before leaving. He had walked away with his head held high, even though he smarted from the rejection.

Now as they walked toward the Hills' home, Frank remarked pleasantly, almost as if he read Almon's thoughts. "You're a fool to have told the truth about your religion. But an honest fool is worth a good deal more than a wise old liar."

Almon spun toward him. "I'm one of the smartest fellows to ever come your way. I'll be back here someday! You wait and see."

A mule-drawn cart passed the young men. Almon jumped to the other side of Frank, causing his new friend to take the full splatter. But the mud on Frank's trousers did not dampen his spirits. Frank flipped his reddish-brown hair out of his eyes and laughed. "I wouldn't want to come up against you in a court-room. I believe, old chap, that no one can stop your boat from coming in."

"My boat may be too late for Julianne Johnson to get on board," Almon muttered dismally.

"Love isn't a footrace, but a field to be planted and nour-ished—or so my mother says. I think it's more of a gamble." Frank laughed as he rolled his shoulders, loosening the muscles of his large frame. He grinned, wrinkling his freckled nose. "If you're serious about marrying my cousin, buy a farm."

"I hate farming," Almon retorted, but Frank's jovial mood was slowly rubbing off on him. "I spent every penny on passage here. Gambling it is."

Frank whistled. "You'll sink in that family as a gambler. Win a fortune, but lose your love."

"That's the truth." Almon smiled slightly. "There never was a more religious bunch than Mrs. Julia Johnson and her brood."

Frank laughed. "I know Joel, Seth, and David. But the girls and youngsters are a mystery. I hear one boy is named after me—Benjamin Franklin."

Almon suddenly grinned, remembering the jokes he'd played on Benjamin. "Unlike you, he goes by Ben. The boy is tall and thin, boorish and sweet, a fine, fun fellow to tease and fish with. Then there is Joe, the smart one who laughs and loves a game. Nancy is crippled but has the patience of Job. Delcena is married to Lyman Sherman. Almera is a beauty, young Mary a feisty cat. George and William are pups still—hardly distinguishable. There are the babies, Esther and Amos. Susan is one of my favorites. She's a sweet thing, thoughtful as an owl, and Julianne—Julianne is indescribable."

Frank slapped Almon on the back. "She's that pretty?"

"Pretty! That's only the start of it. She's witty, sweet, and wise. Her form is . . ." Almon whistled, then shook his head briskly and snorted. "But what does she have to do with me? It will be a long while before I'm fit to take a wife."

"Come," Frank said. "Don't be discouraged. How do you know them all so well? I thought you lived in Amherst, near Cousin Joel."

"I stayed with them in New York last winter. I was one of the missionaries who taught them."

Frank raised his eyebrows. "My father was baffled when he found out that Aunt Julia had joined the Mormons."

"If you think your father was baffled, you should have seen your Uncle Zeke," Almon whistled. "What a row! Still is, I'd wager." Then he added warmly. "But know this, Frank Hills; I am determined to become part of that family. I will marry your cousin, Julianne or die trying."

* * *

Ezekiel ate his supper at a tavern in Detroit, Michigan. The captain of the steamer had decided to lay over until the weather improved. Ezekiel drank a good deal, and his mood became increasingly dark as he listened to a group of people talk at a table near him.

"I tell you it's true," a large woman with a mass of brown hair piled high on top of her head chattered excitedly. "I knew Mr. Wilkinson before he became associated with the Mormons. His arm was painful and numb and his knee frozen with arthritis. He heard about the Mormons and opposed them—like all of us. Then, he was alone in the woods one day when he heard a voice from the sky saying he should not fight against the Book of Mormon."

"I'd wager that voice wasn't from heaven!" a gentlemen commented with a sardonic smile. "Probably some Mormon missionary hiding in the woods! I hear some of them have as much New England ingenuity as any of us." Laughter broke out in the group.

"Who knows?" the lady continued mysteriously. "All I know is that a short time later a Mormon elder named Jared Carter came to Michigan to preach. He laid his hands on Mr. Wilkinson's arm and leg and now they are as whole as whole can be. I've seen it myself!"

Ezekiel stood up and stalked over to the group. They quieted as he approached.

"Are you offended by our conversation?" the woman asked boldly.

Ezekiel shook his head, but his face was a mask of anger. "Just thought I'd shed some light on the matter. I know Jared Carter, the Mormon," Ezekiel spat out. "He came and preached to my family last spring. My oldest daughter's been lame for years, ever since she fell off a wild colt. She's as lame after meeting Mr. Jared Carter as she was before. That's the Mormon God for you. Healing an old man and leaving a young lady crippled."

No one responded. Ezekiel turned and walked to his room, gripping his bottle of brandy so tightly that the glass nearly cracked.

* * *

March 13, 1833

Philastus Hurlbut knocked on the door of Joseph Smith's upstairs apartment off the Whitney Store. A middle-aged man, whom

Hurlbut did not recognize, answered. He held a dark-haired little girl in his arms. She was laughing and pulling on his ears. In an instant, Hurlbut sized him up. The man was average—thin brown hair, rather short, neither handsome nor plain, neither old nor young—of no account.

"Hello." The man balanced the child on his hip and held out his hand to Philastus. "I don't believe we've met. Name's John Murdock."

"Hello, Brother John," Hurlbut pumped his hand. "D. P. Hurlbut. And who is this enchantress?" Hurlbut stretched out one of the child's curls, let go, and watched it bounce back onto her head.

Murdock's eyes softened, and he held the little girl close. "This is Julia Smith, Joseph and Emma's darling."

"Well, little Julia," Hurlbut said affably to the baby, "Where's your papa? He's expecting me."

Julia pointed a chubby forefinger to a nearby door. "Papa in there."

Murdock kissed the baby's hair, and his eyes misted. Hurlbut thought that this must be a weak and sentimental man to be so taken in by a little child.

The door to the office opened, and Joseph filled the door frame. "Good morning, Brother Philastus," he said affably as he shook Hurlbut's hand. Julia stretched out her arms to Joseph, whining and crying, "Papa, Papa!"

John handed the child to Joseph who hugged and kissed her. The Prophet put his free arm around Murdock's shoulder. "She reminds me of her mother."

"Aye. A good deal so," Murdock commented quietly.

Joseph turned his head and spoke to the child. "Now Julia, Papa has business, and you shall go with Uncle John. He has a treat for you."

"Yes, I do, Miss Julia, downstairs in the store." John Murdock quickly took the little girl and swung her up onto his shoulders, ignoring her loud protests. Her tears turned to giggles as he tickled her bare foot.

"Thank you, John," Joseph said warmly as the man and child left the apartment.

"Can't think of a nicer way to spend the morning," Murdock called back.

Joseph put his hand on Hurlbut's shoulder and led him into the office. The two men were equal in size and weight, both broad shouldered and strong. They would have been well balanced in a wrestling match.

"You are fortunate to have a friend who is willing to tend your child," Philastus commented.

"John Murdock's friendship is a pearl beyond price," Joseph said with feeling. He pointed to a chair for Hurlbut to sit in and then settled behind his desk. "Now, Brother Hurlbut, what can I do for you?"

Philastus looked squarely in Joseph's eyes. "Tell me about the coming forth of the Book of Mormon. I have heard rumors and whispers and want to know exactly what happened."

Joseph studied Philastus Hurlbut for a moment. "It is a long story," he began, his blue eyes moist with memory and his voice resonant. "Thousands of years old. My part in it began ten years ago. It was the twenty-first of September, eighteen hundred twenty-three. At nightfall, I was praying beside my bed when a light filled the room and a personage stood by my bedside. He told me that he was a messenger sent from the presence of God and that his name was Moroni. He explained that God had a work for me to do and that my name would be known for both good and evil among all people. He told me there was a book buried in the earth. It was written upon golden plates and contained an account of the former inhabitants of this continent and the everlasting gospel as delivered by the Savior. With these plates were two stones in silver bows with an attached breastplate called the Urim and Thummim, which God had prepared for the purpose of translating this book."

Joseph paused for a moment. Hurlbut stared at his hands, his brows knit together. The whole story was so fantastical. It couldn't possibly be true. On the other hand, Joseph Smith seemed so genuine. Yet Philastus knew how genuine a man could pretend to be. He had pretended himself on a few occasions. He scratched his head and looked up at Smith, "An angel from the presence of God. What was the date again?"

"September twenty-one, eighteen hundred twenty-three."

"Are you certain?"

Joseph exhaled and nodded. "Yes. Some dates you do not forget."

"For me this will be one of those days." Philastus smiled, his voice friendly. "March thirteenth, eighteen hundred and thirty-three."

Joseph smiled back warmly. "Perhaps we will both remember it as the day we talked together of the Book of Mormon."

Hurlbut rubbed his chin, and his brow furrowed slightly in concentration. "Tell me about the translation and publication of the record, of how a simple farm boy accomplished such a momentous task."

"Through the gift and power of God," Joseph said quickly. "In His wisdom, God chose one young and unlearned who could not have done this work on his own."

"Tell me," Hurlbut pressed. The morning passed as Joseph continued talking. He told Philastus Hurlbut of the years of preparation before he obtained the plates. He described the process of translation and spoke of the lost manuscript and subsequent darkness. He described the vision of the three witnesses and spoke of his own joy when others heard the words of the angel and saw and felt the record. He mentioned Martin Harris's unselfishness in mortgaging his farm.

Hurlbut listened intently to every word, asking questions occasionally. He filed Joseph's answers away in his mind. Finally, when Joseph was finished, Hurlbut looked into his eyes and queried, "It is nearly unbelievable. Did it really happen as you have described it to me?"

Joseph nodded and exclaimed, "Yes, Brother Philastus!" Then Joseph took a deep breath that was almost a sigh. "Yet I would not have believed the story myself had it not happened to me. But I witness to you that it was so."

Hurlbut exhaled sharply. "You're an extraordinary man." Then Hurlbut looked intently at the Prophet. "Brother Joseph, I am staking my life, everything I am and have on your honesty. If I ever find out you are lying, I will kill you."

Joseph did not flinch. "Others have said the same, dear brother. Pray earnestly and exercise faith. Then the Lord will bless you."

There was a knock at the door. Joseph stood up and opened it. Sidney Rigdon entered the room and strode over to Philastus and shook his hand. "Brother Hurlbut, did Joseph tell you our plans? Five days from now the high priests will be meeting in the schoolroom. Join us and we will ordain you to the office of an elder in the Melchizedek Priesthood."

Philastus's color deepened, and a shudder passed through him. He felt Joseph Smith's eyes on him, perhaps gauging his reaction as he had gauged Smith's reaction to each of his earlier questions. The possibility that Smith might be telling the truth struck him. But how could he know for sure? Should he become an elder when he had so many doubts and suspicions?

Hurlbut pictured the bewitching Lovina and remembered her declaration that she would only marry an elder in the Church of Christ. He wanted her, come what may. He looked from Sidney to Joseph and said with warmth, "You cannot comprehend how eagerly I look forward to that day."

Joseph nodded and shook his hand, looking once more into Philastus's dark eyes. "We meet in the schoolhouse at sunrise, each man fasting and dressed in clean clothing. Come, dear Brother Philastus, and join with the School of the Prophets."

* * *

March 18, 1833

The gray sky glowed pink along the edge of the eastern horizon, and the air was absolutely still, as if waiting for something. Clad in a dark broadcloth suit and top hat, Philastus Hurlbut cut a smart figure striding across the Kirtland Flats to the Whitney Store. Only one other man was out that morning. Hurlbut had met him before. His name was Zebedee Coltrin. Hatless, Coltrin trotted up to Philastus. At twenty-nine years old, Zebedee was slender and bald, with an unusual clarity to his wide-set eyes. After introductions, Coltrin asked, "Are you headed to the School of the Prophets?"

"Yes," Philastus answered. "To be ordained an elder."

"Marvelous," Coltrin exclaimed with warmth.

"I must confess some apprehension at the thought of mingling with such illustrious brethren," Hurlbut commented.

"'Tis a wondrous experience," Zebedee said. He described how they would be welcomed into the schoolroom with a specific salutation from the Prophet, after which he would perform the ordinance of the washing of feet like the Savior did in olden times.

A few minutes later, Coltrin opened the door of the Whitney store and motioned for Hurlbut to cross the threshold. Philastus stepped inside and smelled the warm aroma of fresh-baked bread.

"For the sacrament," Coltrin explained. Philastus Hurlbut raised his eyebrows and took a deep breath. He concluded that at least this morning he would imagine that Joseph Smith was a prophet of God.

Zebedee Coltrin and Philastus Hurlbut were the final two to enter the schoolroom. A fire blazed in the hearth. Hurlbut recognized a number of the eleven men sitting in chairs in a semicircle. There was Joseph Smith and his brothers—Hyrum, William, and Samuel. Sidney Rigdon and Frederick G. Williams were there of course. He also knew Newel K. Whitney, the owner of the store, and John Murdock, the man who tended the Prophet's child.

Joseph stood and greeted the two men with outstretched arms. "I salute you in the name of the Lord Jesus Christ, in token or remembrance of the everlasting covenant, in which covenant I receive you to fellowship, in a determination that is fixed, immovable, and unchangeable, to be your friend and brother through the grace of God in the bonds of love, to walk in all the commandments of God blameless, in thanksgiving, forever and ever. Amen."

Philastus sat down in a empty chair near William Smith. He followed the other men's lead as they took off their boots and stockings. The Prophet girded a towel around his waist and lifted a basin of water warmed by the fire. He knelt down by each brother and silently washed his feet. Philastus felt uncomfortable when it was his turn. Here was Joseph Smith kneeling before him like a lowly servant. Could this man's motives be as pure as they seemed? He thought about what it would mean to Lyman if he were here. Then his mind wandered along a different path. He imagined himself married to Lovina Williams. He would immensely enjoy the girl washing his feet like this.

Joseph silently dried Hurlbut's feet with the towel. Philastus watched the other men's reactions as Joseph moved around the room. Most were very reverent and visibly touched. John Murdock wept openly when Joseph's hands touched his callused feet. Philastus Hurlbut closed his eyes. He could not comprehend such emotions.

* * *

In the soul of John Murdock the past surfaced before his eyes. The day was April thirtieth, two years ago. His wife, the best part of his life, lay ill. She called John to her bedside. He was glad, for she looked better; there was color in her cheeks and a look of peace in her eyes. She held out her hand to John, and he quickly took it. *I am going, John,* she had said gently. *Farewell.* Then she let go of his hand and laid her own across her chest. She went to sleep, her breath stopping without a struggle.

John was left to groan in anguish, for his precious wife was gone, leaving him with five children. The eldest two were little boys, Orrice and John, the middle child was four-year-old Phebe, his precocious girl, the youngest two were twins, a boy and a girl, just six hours old. John had no family to turn to for help; his own mother was dead, and his in-laws were among the most virulent anti-Mormons in the Kirtland area.

The Prophet, grieving over the deaths of his own infant twins, had come to see John. After the men had talked and wept together, John carried the babies to Joseph's home and laid them in the arms of Emma, who was gray and haggard from enduring the deaths of her children. John had watched Emma's cold sorrow turned to warm tears as she held his little ones. Though his heart was breaking, John had promised that they would be Emma and Joseph's children completely. John knew that in losing them, he had given the babes and Sister Emma life. But eleven months later, John had received terrible news. The infant boy, Joseph Murdock Smith, had died as a result of the mob violence in Hiram, Ohio.

Now, in the School of the Prophets, John wept as his beloved Prophet, the father of his sweet baby girl, knelt before him and washed his feet. Trembling, John laid a hand on Joseph's shoulder. Joseph looked up at his friend, and John saw the Prophet's tears as well.

After this ordinance, the room was silent as Joseph announced that Sidney Rigdon would say an opening prayer. Then Doctor Philastus Hurlbut was ordained an elder. Following Hurlbut's ordination, the Prophet laid his hands on the heads of Sidney Rigdon and Frederick G. Williams. He ordained them to the office of Presidents of the High Priesthood to take part with Joseph in holding the keys of the last kingdom and to assist in the presidency as his counselors. After the ordination, the Prophet first embraced Sidney, then Frederick.

"I will be with you," Frederick said clearly. "Whether in suffering or journeying, whether in life or in death, I will stand continually on your right hand."

"Thank you, Brother Frederick," Joseph exclaimed. "I accept you in the name of our God."

And I too, John Murdock thought, *I will stand with you, the Prophet of God, forevermore.*

Brother Joseph looked at all the brethren in the room. The Prophet instructed them to pray silently while he broke the bread, poured the wine, and blessed the sacrament. Then the Prophet's eyes rested briefly on John. He turned to the rest of the men. "I promise you," Joseph Smith said, "that the Spirit of God will be poured out upon us and that the pure in heart will behold a heavenly vision this day."

As John Murdock partook of the sacrament, this promise became a reality. The visions of his mind opened. He beheld a man, most lovely; the visage of his face was sound and fair as the sun. He was covered from his neck to his feet with a loose robe, pure white, whiter than any cloth John had ever seen before. His hair, a bright, silver gray, curled in the most majestic form. His eyes were keen and penetrating. As John endeavored to comprehend the whole personage, the vision closed, leaving John comforted and filled with love and joy. All would be well. The King of heaven and earth reigned supreme.

* * *

As the sacrament was passed and the brethren prayed and meditated, Philastus Hurlbut looked around the room. He ate the chunk of warm bread and drank the cup of wine. He saw the look of rapture on John Murdock's face, as if the man saw or felt something that Philastus could not comprehend. Philastus felt exasperated, for Murdock's look reminded him of Lyman. Though he regarded Lyman more highly than any other man, Philastus felt shut out from a part of Lyman's life, that part that communed with God. Hurlbut suddenly felt pointedly alone, a stranger in the School of the Prophets.

But regardless of his separateness, Philastus knew that he had discovered something of what he was searching for. He now knew a great deal more about the strange depth of power wielded by Joseph Smith Jr.

* * *

April 12, 1833—Jamestown, New York

Lyman Sherman walked through the evening drizzle with Zebedee Coltrin and John Murdock. The two elders had arrived in Jamestown early that morning. Lyman took a deep breath. These missionaries had come at a difficult time. More Saints had come down with the pox. One man had died earlier in the week. Lyman, who had always been so full of faith, felt cords of fear knotting within. Delcena had written, begging him to come to Pomfret and stop risking exposure. But Lyman had stayed in Jamestown. He felt both guilty and grateful that his family was tucked safely away. Yet, he could not leave the people of Jamestown to face this malady or the increasingly brazen hatred of the Jamestown residents without him.

As Lyman and the missionaries returned home from the Barker farm in West Jamestown where they had spent the day blessing the sick, Lyman thought of how Saints had gathered there through the fall and winter, many hastily building cabins on the Barker property. New members were still arriving. Last month, Brother Barker had rented a row of homes on West Third Street to accommodate them. Two weeks ago, when Philastus's property sold, Lyman had moved into one of the cabins. Now that the pox had broken out among the Mormons, the enraged, frightened people of Jamestown had erected a fence at the intersection of Third Street and Lafayette to isolate the Mormons and prevent them from entering town. A brute named Big Simmons acted as watchman and beat anyone trying to leave the "Mormon Quarter."

The members of the Church were discouraged, threatened by their neighbors and by this disease. Lyman knew that it was providence that brought these faithful elders to them. The elders had healed four people that day. Lyman feared that his own faith would not have been strong enough. When he had dressed that morning, he had noticed a small pimple beginning to form in the soft skin on the inside of his elbow joint. Fearing that it was smallpox, he had agonized, wondering if he would see Delcena and his children again. Even more terrible was the fact that there was a fissure in the armor of his faith.

"Brother Sherman, what troubles you?" Zebedee Coltrin suddenly asked.

Lyman looked over at the man walking next to him. The rain clearly did not dampen Coltrin's spirits. He was hatless, and his bald head seemed waterproof. "Is it so obvious that my faith lags?" Lyman questioned.

"Only to those of us who have felt their own faith falter," John Murdock said gently. "You have not been blessed to attend the School of the Prophets in Kirtland. To see your faith transformed to knowledge."

"My cousin is in Kirtland. Philastus Hurlbut," Lyman commented. "Have you met him? He left in February when the pox broke out."

"We know him," Zebedee said. "A fine-looking fellow. He was ordained an elder in a meeting of the School of the Prophets, the same day Frederick G. Williams and Sidney Rigdon were ordained to the First Presidency, to serve as counselors to Joseph. What a day that was!"

"Tell me about it," Lyman said quickly. The knowledge that Philastus was well, both spiritually and physically, lifted his spirits.

John Murdock stopped walking. He buried his hands deep within his pockets. Rain dripped from his hat as he spoke. "That day, the Prophet told us that if we should be humble before God and exercise strong faith, the visions of heaven would open to the pure in heart. Brother Lyman, I am not usually a visionary man like Brother Zebedee," John Murdock continued. Then he described his vision of the Savior to Lyman. "The love from this vision still tarries with me," he concluded.

"I saw the God of Heaven surrounded by a flame of fire," Zebedee Coltrin added, his voice full of awe. "His appearance was so grand and overwhelming that I thought I should melt down in

His presence, and the sensation was so powerful that it thrilled through my whole system, and I felt it in the marrow of my bones."

Through the dim twilight, the visions of these men penetrated Lyman's heart. "I am so glad that Philastus was there that day!" Lyman said.

"We saw your cousin again a week ago in a missionary meeting in Elk Creek," Zebedee Coltrin added.

"Philastus, a missionary!" Lyman smiled.

John Murdock nodded. "Yes. At the time, his companion was a timid young man named Daniel Copley. But Brother Daniel had difficulty preaching and often left your cousin to go forth on his own. In Elk Creek, Brother Hyrum Smith reassigned companionships. Brother Orson Hyde, a man of mighty faith and knowledge, is now preaching the gospel with your cousin."

"Then Philastus is in good hands," Lyman exclaimed. "God bless you both for coming!"

A moment later, the group rounded a corner. Candlelight gleamed in the windows of the house Lyman rented. "No one should be at my place tonight," he said warily.

"If it's a foe, there are three of us to reckon with," Murdock commented.

"It would take more than three of us to tackle Simmons and his hickory stick." Lyman exhaled, deeply concerned, then rapped on the door. "Who's in there?" he yelled loudly.

The door swung open, and a powerful man grabbed Lyman around the waist. The missionaries instinctively pulled him off and tackled him to the floor, pinning him. They wouldn't have been able to hold the man had he not gone limp from laughter.

Lyman rocked back on his heals and grinned. Another man was there as well. A tall gentleman stood by the fire and lifted his hand in a friendly wave. "Lyman," he said with a chuckle. "It's good to see you!"

Lyman hurried over and embraced him. "Hello, Seth! Looks like David has finally met his match."

David shrugged off the confused elders and jumped to his feet. "Only because there were two of them," he declared. "I already took care of that big fellow by the fence."

"How?" Lyman questioned.

Seth chuckled. "By bribing him with Father's leftover brandy."

David reached a hand down and pulled each elder up, introducing himself and Seth at the same time. He laughed when he noticed Lyman looking in the direction of the pot of stew steaming over the fire.

"It smells so good. I've eaten nothing but cornbread and salt pork for a month," Lyman admitted as he looked from David to Seth. "Which one of you trespassers is the cook?"

"Delcena," Seth smiled. "We are here at your wife's command."

"God bless her!" Lyman exclaimed.

David continued, "Delcie told us to feed you before we hogtied you and brought you home. Come with us. At least for a few days!"

Lyman was quiet for moment. His worry that he might be coming down with smallpox resurfaced. He shook his head.

"Go, Brother Sherman," John Murdock cut in. "Brother Zebedee and I will minister to the Saints here for a few days, and then we will join you in Pomfret. You can return to Jamestown at that time."

"I can't," Lyman said.

John Murdock studied him. "Brother Lyman, my wife died two years ago. My little girl, Phebe, is in Missouri in Sister Gilbert's care. My boys are living with other families while I serve my mission. Our time together as a family was so short. Spend time with your wife and little ones when you can. It is the Lord's will."

Lyman folded his arms and felt for the bump he had noticed on his arm that morning. It was gone. He sighed deeply "I'll go gladly," he said. "Brethren, I am unworthy of the Lord's blessings this day."

Seth nodded with satisfaction. "Delcena will be overjoyed," he commented.

David threw his arm around Lyman's shoulder. "Now that your wife will have her way, let's eat, man!"

* * *

As the last morsel of stew was devoured, Zebedee Coltrin spoke up. "Tonight I'm visiting Hiram Winters, the fellow who runs the Jamestown sawmill. A few years ago, I worked for Hiram. Boarded there. I wager that he and his wife, Rebecca, will accept the gospel. Rebecca's people, the Burdicks, live close by. They're good folks. You fellows ought to come with me."

"I know the family," Seth commented. "Years ago, I sold them one of Joel's shingle cutters. They're honest men."

Lyman raised his eyebrows. "We can't get there without crossing the barricade. Simmons knocks Mormons out with one stroke of his hickory stick. David, you bribed him to get in, but I don't think we can bribe him to get out."

David grinned broadly. "I'm not too worried about getting around Big Simmons tonight. His reflexes will be slow from the brandy."

The men prayed together before leaving. Seth, Lyman, and the missionaries lit a lantern and walked down the dark road toward the barricade. The drizzle had stopped but the air felt dense, the moon and stars obscured by clouds. The lantern lighted their path and drew Simmon's attention.

Crouching in darkness, David ran quickly to a point farther down along the barricade. His footsteps were soundless in the soft, rain-soaked ground.

"Mr. Simmons," Seth called out as they approached. "It's Seth Johnson. We met earlier this evening. I'm back with my friends and need to pass by."

"Over my dead body," Simmons called back, brandishing his stick. "Cursed Mormons! It's my job to protect the good people of Jamestown from smallpox."

"Don't fear, sir," Seth went on. "We are hearty—free from any disease."

"Then *you* should fear," Simmons sneered.

During this interchange, David soundlessly climbed the fence and moved into the pool of dark behind Simmons.

"We will pass by," Seth said authoritatively. Then he, Lyman, and the elders began climbing over the fence. Simmons lifted his stick high into the air and was about to bring it down heavily on Seth when he was tackled from behind. Simmons dropped the hickory stick. He fell to the ground with David on top of him. The four men leapt over the fence. David sprang away from Simmons before he could get a hold. Then the five Mormons sprinted down the street. Simmons picked up the stick and waved it at the men, shouting furiously, "I'll teach you boys a lesson when you come back this way later tonight!"

* * *

Twenty minutes later, Hiram and Rebecca Winters greeted an exhausted Zebedee Coltrin and his four winded friends. Coltrin quickly told Winters about Simmons. Hiram took the men inside and bolted the door behind them.

"Mr. Johnson." Hiram greeted Seth with a warm handshake. "That shingle cutter is worth its weight in gold."

Seth smiled warmly. "The message we bring you tonight is worth far more than earthly gold. We'd like to share it with you and your kin."

Hiram looked thoughtfully at the men. "Then you shall."

Rebecca Winters fed her guests cake and cider while Hiram went to the neighboring homes to invite his father-in-law, Gideon Burdick, and his brothers-in-law, Alden and Thomas Burdick, to hear the message of the Mormon missionaries. After they arrived, the men talked around the blazing hearth until late into the night. The Mormons declined Rebecca's offers of tea and Hiram's of chewing tobacco. Zebedee explained the new law of health that had come to Joseph Smith, the Prophet. Together, the group read in the Bible and the Book of Mormon. Each of the guests bore personal witness of the restored gospel of Jesus Christ. Seth was the last, and he spoke with eloquence and conviction.

As the conversation drew to a close, Hiram Winters looked into Seth's eyes and commented, "Your faith is intriguing."

"Gentlemen, come back and teach us more," old Gideon Burdick, a revolutionary war veteran, commented. "There must be something to your religion or people wouldn't be up in arms about it."

Lyman smiled. "It might be hard getting through that barricade when Brother David goes back to Pomfret. Old Simmons carries a big stick."

David raised his eyebrows and laughed.

Alden Burdick chuckled. He was a tall, sturdy man and had enjoyed the story of David tackling Big Simmons. "Tonight, we'll take you the back way to the Barker's place. Row you across Chautauqua Lake. You can walk home from there. Unless young David wants a second try for the hickory stick."

David laughed. "Not tonight. I'll let Simmons keep his toy."

It was past midnight when Hiram Winters and Alden Burdick rowed the men across the lake. Lantern light reflected on the dark ripples as they cut through the water in the canoe. When they were on the other side and had climbed out of the boat, Winters embraced Zebedee Coltrin. "When will I see you again, my friend?" he questioned.

"Tomorrow night at eight o'clock? Brother Murdock and I will meet you here."

"Zebedee, you never were one for mincing words," Hiram commented. "I'll be here." He showed the men a path that led to the Barker property. Then he climbed back into the boat with Alden, and the two rowed away in silence.

The group of men talked for the hour it took to skirt the Barker's property and walk the road back to Lyman's place. Only Seth was quiet, lost in his own train of thought. The night's missionary experience brought memories of Joseph Brackenbury into his soul. He would never forget that kind and intelligent man who taught him the gospel of Jesus Christ. Joseph Brackenbury had died on his mission, giving his life in serving God. Seth wondered what sacrifices lay in store for himself and his family.

Seth sighed deeply and glanced at David, who was talking animatedly to Lyman and the missionaries. He hoped he would soon hear from Joel about the purchase of the Kirtland property. David, Julianne, and Almera had decided to move to Kirtland with him. Benjamin was confused. He wanted desperately to go with Seth, but was torn with guilt because of his father. Susan and Joe had decided to go to Chicago with their mother. Seth sighed and prayed that the Lord would consecrate his actions that they might be according to God's holy will.

7

Dear Lord while I upon thee call
Make known thy will to me
That I may justify do I with all
And humbly walk with thee.

Be merciful, true, just, and kind
More loving, meek, and mild
More to thy heavenly will resigned
And like a faithful child.

Give me more wisdom, faith, and grace
To know and love thee still
And faithful labor in each place
That I am called to fill.

Joel Hills Johnson
(*Diary,* 63)

April 1833

Ezekiel paced the length of the room while a stout, hairy young
man named Jacob Underwood made himself comfortable at the
narrow desk. For ten dollars Ezekiel had hired Mr. Underwood to
perform two services. First, Underwood was to write the letter that
Ezekiel dictated. Second, he would drop the letter off at the

Dunkirk port on his journey. Mr. Underwood licked his thumb and forefinger, picked up the quill, dipped it in the ink well, and nodded for Ezekiel to begin.

"Dear wife," Ezekiel said, hesitating between each phrase. "I have bought a quarter section of land with a log house already built upon it. Title to the land will be ours when you come bringing the final payment from the Pomfret farm. A portion of the land has already been cleared. Today I bought a mule team and will begin sowing corn and wheat on the morrow. Sell what goods and animals you can and send the rest by water. Obtain passage so that you and the children will arrive here the first week of June. I will go to the port those days and look for you. If I am not there to meet your boat, I'll leave word at the tavern. If you are delayed due to accident or sickness, send me word, and I will come for you." Ezekiel paused.

Following a long moment, Underwood lifted his head and looked over at him. "Are you finished, sir?"

Ezekiel hesitated. *Was he finished?* What else was there to say? That he felt older and more tired each day? That the world was dark without his family? That even drink could not deaden his emptiness? *Was he finished?*

"Is that all, sir?" Mr. Underwood raised his bushy eyebrows.

"No," Ezekiel snapped. He went on. "Give the children my affection. And keep a generous portion for yourself. From your husband."

Underwood handed Ezekiel the letter. With work-worn hands, Ezekiel clumsily signed his name. Then he folded the paper, slipped it into the envelope, and sealed the flap with wax from the near-extinguished candle on the table. On the outside, Ezekiel printed: *To Mrs. Julia Hills Johnson. Pomfret Township, New York.*

Without glancing at the name on the envelope, Underwood took the letter and tucked it away in the pocket of his coat. Ezekiel handed the man ten dollars. The two men shook hands. Ezekiel spoke gravely. "You've given me your word that you will take this letter to the Dunkirk tavern. The innkeeper knows me. He will see it gets to my wife."

"My word is my bond," Underwood promised.

Ezekiel watched the man leave the room.

* * *

Jacob Underwood felt somewhat ill the first four days of his journey as the Steamer chugged north on Lake Michigan. The fifth day dawned bright. After lunch, he ventured out onto the deck. With the noon sun beating down on him, he began to sweat. Underwood took off his coat and tucked it beneath a bench. Twenty minutes later, he felt increasingly light-headed and nauseated. He leaned over the rail and retched. A fellow passenger helped him to his berth and covered him with a wool blanket. That night, Mr. Underwood was stricken with fever and chills. Twenty-four hours later, when Mr. Underwood arose from his bed to look for his coat, it was gone. After questioning the captain, Mr. Underwood learned that the fellow who had helped him to bed had disembarked at the last port. Mr. Underwood searched the ship, but to no avail. "'Tis stolen," the captain said and shrugged.

Underwood shook his head and went back to bed, relieved that his money and valuables were packed in his trunk. Days later, when they stopped at Dunkirk, he remembered the letter inside the coat pocket. But he felt no obligation to contact Mrs. Johnson, as the ten dollars were lost with the coat. Underwood sighed. It was the thief's business now. If he were an honest thief, he would send the letter on its way.

* * *

May 1833

Coals flickered in the hearth as Julia walked into the dark kitchen. Her long, gray-streaked tresses tumbled over her shoulders. She could not sleep. In two weeks she had to give up occupancy, but she still had not heard from Ezekiel.

After lighting a candle, she slumped into a chair at the kitchen table. She stared into the deep shadows in the corners. It had been a strange spring, spent packing rather than planting. The dark night's uncertainty haunted her.

She thought about the peace in her home during the past two months. When Ezekiel left in March, they had all breathed a great cumulative sigh of relief. In April, they had enjoyed a wonderful visit with Elder Murdock and Elder Coltrin. Julia had cooked her best meals for the missionaries. Seth and David had talked with them until late each night. Each day, her family read, prayed, and sang together. The children laughed and played without restraint or worry. Their eyes were calmer and brighter as they escaped the daily reminder of the chasm separating their parents and tearing at their loyalties.

Julia's shoulders sagged. What was she to do? The current peace in her home felt like Zion. Must she return her children to that life of division and strife? If no word came from Zeke, they would all go to Kirtland with Seth and David. Was Ezekiel's silence an answer to her countless prayers?

Julia shuddered as the opposite side of the coin numbed her. She did not know where Zeke was or what had happened to him! But she knew that he would never abandon his family if it were in his power to do otherwise. Was he ill or injured? The thought of him dying alone was more terrible than the thought of moving with him.

The night closed in around an exhausted and worried Julia, as the embers in the hearth died away. Was it possible that her own prayers to move to Kirtland had caused her husband's death? That did not seem the way of a loving God. But Julia remembered how Nephi was told by an angel to kill Laban so that a whole nation would not dwindle and perish in unbelief. Had God taken her husband's life so that her children could have eternal life?

Julia's hands began to shake. Memories of their years together seized her. Despite all the pain, that part of her that was once young treasured a portion of his soul. She prayed that such a sacrifice was not God's will. She would have her husband alive, regardless of the cost. Julia put her head into her arms and wept.

There was a tug at Julia's nightdress. "Mama." Julia wiped her eyes and looked down at Esther. The little girl had been sleeping in bed with her since the day Zeke left.

Julia pulled her six-year-old daughter into her lap and kissed her hair. "Why are you sad, Mama?" Esther questioned.

"I was thinking about Papa," Julia explained. "And missing him."

"Chin up, Mama," Esther advised as she lifted her mother's chin with her soft, small hand. Julia smiled. Only her eyes reflected her sorrow. Then, she took her daughter's hand, and together they walked into the bedroom.

* * *

The next afternoon, Julianne, Almera, and Susan were hanging out the white clothes, their arms sore from a morning spent washing. A stiff breeze pulled at Almera's white knitted cap, liberating more than a few strands of her dark, silky hair. With an exasperated humph, she threw the shirt over the line in a heap and shoved her hair back under the cap. She looked restlessly out at the blue, wind-washed sky. Her eyes swept past the house and up the lane. She saw Seth and David returning from their trip to town.

"Seth's back," Almera commented.

Julianne looked up. She glimpsed a flash of white paper in his hand. She dropped a wet towel in the basket and called back to her sisters as she ran to meet her brothers. "A letter, Seth has a letter!"

David chuckled as he watched Julianne tear toward them, holding her skirt up with her hands. "Is it from Father?" she gasped as she reached them.

Seth shook his head. "No."

Julianne's forehead creased with disappointment. "Almon?"

"Ah, now we know why you ran so fast," David teased. "It's not from your sweetheart either."

Julianne eyed David, but did not condescend to reply. Almera and Susan joined the group. Seth's shake of the head communicated that the expected letter had not come.

"If it isn't from Papa, then who *is* it from?" Almera asked edgily.

"Joel and Annie," Seth said. "Let's go find Mother and Nancy and I'll read it to all of you."

Five minutes later, the group gathered around the kitchen table.

"There are two letters," Seth explained. "One is addressed to me from Joel, and the other is to Nancy." He handed one piece of paper to Nancy. Then he unfolded the other letter and read aloud.

Brother Seth,

I hope that this letter finds all of you well. Annie and the children enjoy good health. My cough continues. Much has happened in Kirtland this spring. In April the School of the Prophets concluded, and many have gone on missions.

I am purchasing the house on the flats that we spoke of last fall. Surrounding land may become available soon for you to buy. We will discuss the possibilities when you arrive. I am also considering buying a piece of wild land on the outskirts of town.

You may have already heard that God has commanded us to build a temple. It will be a daunting task. So many are poor, having left all to gather with the Saints. Don Carlos Smith asked me to send David his best and to tell him that strong backs are needed to work on the House of the Lord. They will wield axes and hammers together.

Annie and I move to Kirtland at the end of May. My skills in the brickyard or at the sawmill will be used in the building of God's house. There is so much work to be done, but the miracles of God continue, and He upholds His Saints.

I am hopeful that Mother is well. Is all in order for her departure? Does Father have a house and land secured? There is room in my house for you and David and any of the others who desire to come to Kirtland. Mother and all are welcome if

the need arises. Come to Kirtland quickly so that you can
choose what rooms you want. The others I will rent out. D. P.
Hurlbut has requested we hold a room for him to lease when
he returns from his mission. Annie has written Nancy. May
God be with you.

Joel H. Johnson

Seth lifted his head and looked around the room at his family. A question hung in each of their minds. How long should they wait before they make a decision?

"David," Seth suggested, "perhaps you should go to Kirtland alone and meet Joel. Tell him we are waiting to hear from Father."

"But we have to give up occupancy in less than two weeks," David said. "We haven't even started looking for a place for Mother to lease. I think we should take Mother and the family to Kirtland. Then I'll go find Father."

"Then Mother would have to move again when Papa comes back," Julianne voiced her thoughts aloud. "Unless Papa changes his mind once he finds all of us in Kirtland."

"Can't we leave someone here to wait for Father?" Nancy questioned.

"But he might not ever come," Susan whispered.

Almera kneaded her hands in her lap. She blurted out, "Someone needs to get to Joel and tell him not to rent any rooms out. Or we won't have any place to live in Kirtland. Or worse, we'll have scoundrels living in the house with us!"

"Joel wouldn't rent rooms to scoundrels," Seth assured her.

As her children weighed the alternatives, a strange weightlessness began to fill Julia. Gone was the terror of last night. She knew that God was with them all. She knew what had to be done. Julia straightened her shoulders. "If we don't hear from your father, we will leave him in God's hands and travel to Kirtland a week from today. All of us together. After we are settled, Seth or David will go and find Father.

"But first, things must be put in order. The house will be scrubbed inside and out. Since we'll be traveling by land, new wagons and teams need to be purchased. We will use the payment on the farm to do so. We no longer have the luxury to wait and wonder."

"But what of Papa?" Susan begged.

"Our Father in Heaven loves your father. We will pray for him continually," Julia said gently. "If we hear from him, we will change our course. But until then, we must go forward trusting in God."

"But what if he comes back and finds us gone?" Nancy questioned.

Julia was quiet for a moment. "We'll leave word with the neighbors."

"After everyone is settled in Kirtland, I'll find him," Seth promised.

Julia was grateful for Seth's comforting presence and nodded her approval. Then she looked at the girls and added, "All is well, except for the baskets of wet clothes left in the yard."

As the girls went outside to finish the wash, Almera muttered. "When the Lord comes again, we'll be outside hanging laundry."

"Then we'll be the first to see Him step out of the sky," Julianne responded.

* * *

While the rest of the Johnson family busied themselves with their chores, Nancy lingered at the table. She opened the letter that Annie had sent her. As she read, tears filled her eyes. She pictured her sister-in-law, with her bushy auburn hair and freckled hands, sitting at the table balancing one child on her lap while another tugged at her skirts as she wrote.

Dearest Nancy,

Sariah is teething. I've tied up little bags of caraway seeds and dipped them in sweet milk. Chewing on them relieves

her somewhat as long as I'm holding her. Sixtus begs me to
play with him. He is so tall now you won't recognize him.
How did your mother manage all of you? Joel must have
whined like Sixtus. I'm sure you and Seth were solid little
troopers who never gave her a moment's trouble. But Julianne
and David?

    Anyway, dear Nancy, as I tend to my little ones, I think of
you. Do you want to come to Kirtland with Seth and David?
Do you hesitate because of your infirmity? My darling friend, if
it is in your heart to come, then come. If you desire to dwell
with the Lord's people, then come dwell with me. Your face
will always be a joy in my house, and I will never tire of your
company. Joel wants you here as well. Sariah is trying to tip
over the inkwell. Come, dear Nancy, if it is in your heart.

With warmest affection,
Annie

* * *

Outside, Joe and the younger children sat on the fence watching as Benjamin worked the ox, Hercules. Benjamin whacked Hercules on the shoulder with a short whip. Instead of switching directions like he was supposed to, the ox butted Benjamin and knocked him down. Esther and Amos screamed. Benjamin scrambled to his feet and stared angrily at the ox. Hercules snorted. George and Will snickered.

Exasperated, Mary called out to her brother, "You can't do it that way, Ben. Stand up straighter like you're the boss. Talk soft like you're his friend. Don't look straight into his eyes like you want a fight, but don't look away either. Watch his ears all the time so you know what he's thinking. Tap him, don't smack him."

Red-faced, Benjamin tried again, more gently. The huge animal walked away from him and chomped on a tuft of grass. Ben threw the whip down and whirled around facing Mary. "Hercules isn't any handier than he used to be!" Benjamin said in an accusatory tone. "You said you trained him."

"I did." Mary humphed and slid from the fence. Her braids flipped behind her as she picked up the whip. In a moment, she had Hercules walking placidly next to her and turning whichever way she desired at the slightest tap.

Benjamin glared at her. "That ox won't let anyone else drive him. If you aren't around, he'll end up in the stew!"

"You're the fellow in a stew!" Mary retorted. "Come on, Ben. Aren't you proud of me?"

"I guess," Benjamin said with a grudging smile.

A moment later, Seth came out of the house and called Joe and Benjamin over to him. "I heard that John Smith, the Prophet's uncle, is in Westfield today on his way to Kirtland. He's going to preach there tonight. Want to come with David and me and meet him?"

Joe shook his head. "I promised the girls I'd read to them while they mend. If you get a chance, get me a copy of Tuesday's *Eagle*."

Seth nodded and looked over at Benjamin. "Bennie?"

"I'll go," Ben said quickly.

Seth put his hand on Benjamin's shoulder. "Go get something to eat, and change your shirt. It looks like you've been rolling in the dirt."

* * *

Thirty minutes later, the three brothers headed toward Westfield. The early evening was warm and humid. Gold and crimson clouds stretched along the horizon. Seth handled the reins as their horse, Katy, pulled the wagon. Ben sat on the wagon seat next to him. David stretched out in the back of the wagon and napped. When they arrived in Westfield, Seth stopped briefly at the tavern and bought a copy of the *Westfield Eagle*, the local newspaper. They continued north to a farm owned by a member of the Church. When they arrived at their destination, Seth reined in Katie. David sat up and stretched. Ben climbed down from the wagon.

Gathering darkness dimmed the orange sky. A group of men were setting out benches for the meeting. David jumped out of the wagon. Seth descended, and the two went to introduce themselves. After unhitching Katie and getting her settled, Benjamin spotted his brothers and hurried to join them.

"Hello. My name's John Smith." A tall gentleman in his fifties shook Seth's hand.

"It's a pleasure," Seth responded. "I've met your nephew, the Prophet Joseph. I see a family resemblance."

John Smith smiled. "Then you have one on me. I've never met Joseph Junior. But I'm looking forward to the day."

David stuck out his hand and heartily shook the older gentleman's. "Glad to meet you, sir. Another nephew of yours, Don Carlos, is a great friend of mine."

"Now Don Carlos I've met." John Smith grinned. "Three years ago, my brother, Joseph Senior, brought Carlos with him when he gave me a Book of Mormon. That visit caused quite a stir among the men in the family. At that tender age, Don Carlos bore a strong witness to the truth of this work. It made his Uncle Jesse hopping mad."

David grinned, remembering his own experiences with Don Carlos. "Carlos caused quite a stir with me when he bore his testimony. Up to that time, I was determined not to believe. Old Don Carlos is a troublemaker for sure. I can't wait to see him again."

John Smith chuckled. Together the men continued setting out the benches. They were nearly finished when a young man about Ben's age ran toward them from the direction of the barn. "My son, George Albert," John Smith explained gravely. "Brother Brown, our companion on the trip, has a horse sick with colic."

"He's down, Pa! We can't get him up! If we don't do something, he's going to roll!" George Albert gasped, breathing heavily, his round face and thick features contorted in frustration.

"We'll help." David said. The men ran to the barn. The horse was on his back, his powerful body writhing, his legs churning the air. The two men in the stall with the horse had dropped the ropes tied around the horse's neck and hindquarters. "It's too late," young Norman Brown cried. "He's already rolled over. His gut's twisted."

Ignoring the man's words, David went into the stall. "Seth, Ben, help me," he ordered. David picked up one of the ropes, and Seth and Ben the other. The brothers pulled with all their strength. The horse did not rise, but bellowed in pain as the rope broke. The horse stilled for an instant. Then he writhed weakly, his dark eyes rolling back in his head.

"Get my gun, Norman," Brother Brown spoke in a voice close to tears. "I won't have him suffer anymore."

David squatted down and stroked the horse's head, calming the suffering creature. He looked up gravely. "Seth, I think it best if you take Ben out of here."

"Come on, Ben," Seth said as he touched Benjamin's elbow.

Ben looked at George Albert who stood stoically next to his father. Benjamin shook his head as tears gathered in his eyes. "I'm stayin', Seth."

Norman Brown handed his father the gun. The men tightened the ropes around the suffering animal so that only one shot would be required.

"If this is the work of the Lord," Brother Brown muttered angrily as he shouldered his gun, "He would not suffer our horse to die when we are on the way to Zion."

* * *

Before the meeting started, the men lit lanterns and worked in the darkness, helping Brother Brown bury his horse. Then they washed their hands and faces in a nearby stream. The moon was full, and a chorus of crickets filled the warm night air. John Smith's wife, Clarissa, a round, gray-haired woman with a cheerful voice, unpacked a clean shirt from the wagon and brought it to George Albert.

"Clean up, son," she said with a smile. George Albert ducked into one of his family's five wagons to change his clothes and comb his hair.

A few moments later, the Smiths and Johnsons joined the thirty other people gathering for the meeting. John Smith walked up to the stand. Moonlight and lantern light illuminated his finely chiseled features. There was dignity in his presence. He spoke of the promise of Jesus in the New Testament—that He would go to other sheep of a different fold. He spoke of the need for a restoration of the ancient Church and explained the passages in the Book of Mormon and the Bible about the gathering of Israel. He continued the discourse with power, describing the new latter-day work, the signs following the believers, and the prophetic call of his nephew, Joseph Smith Junior.

As John Smith spoke, Benjamin looked over at George Albert, whose head lolled from exhaustion.

"Go George," Clarissa Smith whispered to her son. "Your bed is made up in the wagon."

George quietly stood and left the meeting, his broad shoulders sagging. Ben gazed after George Albert, who trudged toward the darkness of the camp.

"He needs to rest," his mother whispered softly to the girl sitting next to her. "Father will understand."

Benjamin turned around and looked back at John Smith as the man testified of God's reality and of the mission of the Lord, Jesus Christ. Ben thought of his own father, Ezekiel Johnson, and of the countless times he came home from the tavern drunk. Ben wondered if George Albert Smith knew how lucky he was.

* * *

Four days later, back at home, in mid-afternoon, Ben and Joe loaded barrels of grain into one of the wagons. Joe whistled as he worked, but Benjamin was quiet and brooding. After finishing, the boys sat together on the bumper of the wagon. Ben moodily chewed on a kernel of dried corn.

"Ben, what's the matter?" Joe asked.

"I've changed my mind. If Pa's still alive, I'm going to Chicago, not Kirtland," Benjamin muttered as he spit out the corn.

Joseph raised his eyebrows and squinted at the sun. "Good. Chicago wouldn't be any fun without you. Why'd you change your mind?"

"If I see Pa again, I won't ever let him down."

"Don't worry about Pa. It takes weeks for letters to get from one place to another. Pa's tough. He can take care of himself. We might hear from him tomorrow."

Joe was quiet for a moment, then added. "When we are both of age, I'll go with you to Kirtland, or to Independence, Missouri. We'll be baptized. We'll buy a farm, and I'll start a newspaper. Things will work out."

"Pa's probably dead, Joe," Benjamin said bitterly.

Joe's eyes flashed. "You think like Will's jumping beans, *wrong end up*! Pa's fine. We'll get a letter from him soon. Or he'll meet up with us in Kirtland."

Benjamin's voice rose with emotion. "Pa would have written us by now, and you know it!"

Joe stared at Benjamin. "You talk like you don't even want to believe Pa's alive!"

Benjamin shouted at his brother as tears gathered in his eyes. "You think I don't want Pa to be alive, Joe? Is that what you think? Because I'll tell you something—part of me doesn't want to hear from Pa! That part of me wants so bad for all of us to live in Kirtland together. But another part of me hates me for thinking that and loves Pa so much that it wants to die if anything has happened to him. Pa wanted me to go with him. It'll be my fault if he's hurt or dead. And those two parts of me are knocking heads together all the time. Knocking heads inside of me!"

Benjamin stood up and ran toward the woods.

"I'm sorry, Ben! I didn't mean it," Joseph yelled after him.

* * *

After his brother disappeared into the trees, Joe stood up and dejectedly walked toward the house.

When he entered the kitchen, Susan looked up from the table where she was packing the silverware. "What's the matter?" she asked.

"Ben's riled. He ran off."

"He's worried about Pa. Like all of us," Sue commented. Joe nodded dismally. Susan continued, "Seth and David are back from Westfield. They brought a team of oxen and today's *Eagle*."

"Where's the newspaper?" Joe questioned.

"On the mantle in the sitting room. I looked at it. There's a letter from a fellow called 'Mr. Anti-Mormon' accusing Amicus of being a Mormon."

Astounded, Joe dropped into a chair next to Susan. "You're joking! I've never written anything about the Church. I've purposely stayed away from it!"

"Go read it, Joe," Susan said with a small smile. "We're leaving soon. I think the Westfield readers deserve one more letter from the witty Amicus."

Joe stood up and went into the sitting room. He thought about his response last month to the writer who called himself "Equal Rights." Under the guise of Amicus, Joe had accused him of *non compus mentis*. The man had no common sense in stating that Indians would never have the right to vote. He took the newspaper to the desk and read the letter to the editor from Mr. Anti-Mormon.

Mr. Editor.—I observed in the communication of your very learned correspondent "Amicus" this Italicized sentence, "non compus mentis," *in endeavoring to come at the meaning of which I spent much labor to no purpose. Neither the Latin or Greek Lexicon, though searched with great care, could furnish the word* "compus." *And at last in despair I came to the conclusion that Mr.* "Amicus" *must be a Mormon. And being very anxious to learn the definition of this strange word* "compus," *& understanding that those Mormons who speak or write in unknown tongues are able to translate them into our language, I would most earnestly request our Mormon friend* "Amicus" *to interpret without delay. ANTI-MORMON*

Joe shook his head at the absurdity of it all. First, a man who denied people rights called himself "Equal Rights." Another fellow called himself "Anti-Mormon" and figured he would offend Amicus by sarcastically calling him a "Mormon." Wouldn't they laugh if they knew that Amicus was a youth who wanted very much to be baptized into that despised sect, but his father would not allow it? Joe shook his head. There were so many contradictions. He didn't want to be separated from his family, yet he loved his father. He wanted to go to Kirtland, but hated the fact that he would never see his friends again.

Joe sighed. An optimist at heart, he clung to the belief that everything really would work out for the best. A thought struck him. Was this hope the greatest absurdity of all? Blood rushed to Joe's face. He was more like Ben than he realized—parts of himself at odds within. He ached one moment, joked the next. The life surrounding him was unstable—fluid and moving. Only one thing was certain—this place would be behind him soon. The old hawthorn tree, the glade full of wildflowers, the fields and hives, the lonely gulf, the whitecaps on Lake Erie, the schoolhouse gleaming on the hill, the harvest parties and sleigh rides, Rachel and Morris, the friends who had loved him.

Though Mormonism separated him from so much of what he loved, in his heart he believed it was true. Joe picked up the pen and dipped it in the ink. He wrote the verse for Susie, Benjamin, and that part of himself that longed to be Mormon. He wrote the letter from that other part—that side of himself that feared absurdity would tarnish all of his dreams.

For the Eagle:
And like
A cinder that had life and feeling, seem'd
His face, with inward pining, to be what
He could not be—

Mr. Editor,

A correspondent of yours comes out over the signature "Anti-Mormon" *wishing to know* something *about* something, *but*

it would puzzle Jo Smith himself with all his profundity in the
mysteries of Mormonism, to perpetrate the deep obscurity which
clouds his communication and ascertain the desires of this
gentleman. I am afraid that like the boy's beans his thoughts
came "wrong end up" when he penned his witticism. Now I am
willing to accommodate this candid solicitor with any thing
that I know if only I find out what he wants, but my opportu-
nities to improve my mind have been so few that I can not delve
into the meaning of hieroglyphical sentences. I would that he
had been more explicit . . . To conclude, I advise him never
again to attempt to criticize the orthography of words borrowed
from a dead language, till he shall have made such proficiency
in his own native tongue as to write COMMON SENSE.

AMICUS

* * *

Near the end of May, Seth and David purchased two more wagons, three oxen, and a team of mules. That made a total of six wagons for Julia Johnson, her children, and their belongings. Saturday was spent making the final preparations and packing the food they would take on their journey.

On Sunday, after church services, Harriet Bull came to say good-bye. She embraced Julia and told her once more that they all would have believed if only dear Nancy had been healed. Julia held the corpulent lady's hands and begged her to watch for Ezekiel, to tell him of their love, and to send him to Kirtland if he came looking.

On Monday morning Lyman brought Delcena over with their wagon packed and ready. Now the entourage contained seven covered wagons, eighteen people, and fifteen animals. With tears in her eyes, Delcena tenderly kissed Lyman good-bye. Three days ago Sylvester Smith had come to Chautauqua County and asked Lyman to stay and continue preaching there as his missionary companion.

As they pulled away from Pomfret, New York, forever, Julia, Joe, Nancy, and Susan looked back as tears burned their eyes.

Julia's heart lingered on the memories of births and deaths, joy and pain, the gospel found, and her husband lost. Joe reflected on the friends that he would never see again, the highlights of Rachel Risley's hair, the wisdom of Injun Goldfinger, and the clasp of Morris Cook's hand in his. Nancy and Susan wept for the pain their father would feel when he came back and found them gone.

My sisters loved, and brothers kind . . .
I kissed them each, and warmly pressed their hands—
And clasped them to my breast.

Joseph Ellis Johnson,
("The Dreamer," *Jottings by the Way,* xviii)

Saturday, June 1, 1833

The sun had edged beyond the horizon, and the long shadows of twilight dimmed the colors of the countryside as the Johnson entourage approached the Kirtland flats. Julia sat next to Seth on the seat of the lead wagon. She was grateful that the weather had been dry and mild, that the journey had been unusually smooth and unhampered. Benjamin was close by, riding Leo. Some of the children walked. The youngest ones slept.

As they passed the Whitney store a group of curious onlookers stared at them. Seth halted the wagon train and introduced himself. A man ducked inside the store, and a moment later, Joseph Smith stepped out.

Benjamin gaped and moved the horse close to Julia. "Mother," he whispered. "The prophet looks like any other man."

Julia nodded reassuringly at Benjamin, then turned to see Joseph Smith walk up and heartily shake Seth's hand.

"Hello, Seth. Your brother Joel arrived a week ago. I didn't expect you so soon or with such a large company. Did you have a safe journey? I couldn't be more pleased had I prayed you here myself."

"Brother Joseph," Seth returned with a smile, "I'm sure glad to be back in Kirtland. I would like you to meet my mother, Mrs. Julia Johnson."

Joseph leaned across Seth and shook Julia's hand. "Sister Johnson, it's a pleasure meeting you."

Julia nodded, and her eyes filled with tears. A part of her agreed with Benjamin. This friendly young man with blue eyes and a seamless forehead felt more like a son of hers than a prophet of God. Even with this sweet sense of familiarity, she marveled at his calling. "Thank you, Brother Joseph."

"I remember your husband well, Sister Johnson. He is a rough, honest-speaking man. The kind of man I like best."

Julia's dark eyes suddenly clouded as she said, "He left for Chicago months ago, and we haven't heard from him since."

"I'll pray for his safe return to you," Joseph responded, and then gently counseled, "The Lord knows your needs, Sister Johnson. You must trust in Him now and in all trials that may come. Your choice to come to Kirtland and join the Saints was not easy, and you will be blessed."

Julia's heart filled with warmth as hope rushed in through the darkness of her worries about Ezekiel. She knew that this young man was the mouthpiece of the Lord. Not only for Christ's Church, but for her.

Other members of the family gathered around, anxious to get a closer look at the Prophet. Julia looked at their travel-worn clothing, dirty fingernails, and dust-covered faces. They were hardly fit to meet this man of God. She watched as the Prophet graciously, and with sincere interest, began greeting each child, communicating his delight that they would now be his neighbors.

Joseph gripped David's hand. "Brother David, welcome! We've been commanded to build a house of God, but the laborers are few and nearly penniless. Don Carlos will be overjoyed to have you working next to him."

David grinned. "Not more than I!"

Upon seeing Susan, the Prophet spoke and smiled, "Miss Susan, I remember meeting you in Kirtland last summer. Welcome." Susan's color deepened as she smiled and thanked the Prophet.

Then a noise coming from the direction of the schoolhouse caught Julia's attention. Annie appeared from around the corner. She was running toward them with her skirts held high, her auburn hair in disarray, her face effervescent. Joel followed close behind with Sariah in his arms. Julia's heart leapt.

"Good new travels fast." Joseph laughed as he turned back to Julia and grinned. He shook Seth's hand once more. "God bless you all for gathering with the Saints."

* * *

That night Julia couldn't sleep despite the long journey. Her mind retraced the past hours. She shivered and hugged herself. Could it be that she was really here in Kirtland, that such a wonder had occurred! What a joy it was to see Joel, Annie, and her grandchildren. How tall Sixtus had grown! What a beauty Sariah was! And she had met the Prophet and joined the Saints—a dream she had thought well beyond her reach. Julia wrapped a light cloak around her nightdress and walked out to the porch where Joel, Seth, and David were sitting and talking.

"Mother, it's past ten," Joel commented. "Aren't you weary from the journey?"

Seth stood up and offered his mother the chair. Julia smiled and sat down. "I can't sleep for the wonder of this place." Julia gazed upward, her eyes reflecting the starlight. She continued. "Now that I'm here, I can't bear the thought of leaving. I pray for your father constantly, yet after today, I know that it is right that we have come. Joel, I have wagons and teams that I no longer need. And we can't live off your charity. Should I sell them or give them to you as payment for us living here?"

Joel replied thoughtfully. "I think I'll keep them. Then you can have a percentage of ownership in the house. I've bought some wild land on the outskirts of town. As soon as I can, I want to build a house there for Annie and me. I could use the wagons and teams. The boys can help me clear the land." He paused and turned to his brothers, "Seth, when do you and David plan on leaving to look for Father?"

"As soon as possible," Seth replied.

"I hope he is safe and that no illness or accident has befallen him," Joel commented, his brown eyes serious.

Julia spoke softly as she looked down at her hands. "Little else could have kept your father from contacting us."

"The letter could have been lost en route," Joel said to his mother. "If that's the case and you don't arrive in Fort Dearborn as instructed, he'll look for you in Pomfret, and folks there will send him here."

David took a deep breath. "If he finds Mother here, he'll be brimful of rage and hurt. And we won't be here, Seth. Mother would have to deal with him without us."

Seth's eyes looked very tired. "What do you suggest, Joel?"

"Stay here for awhile and wait," Joel stated. "Give him a few weeks so you don't miss him if he comes here looking for you. There is something else to consider. Today, Brother Joseph received a revelation. God chastised his people because they have not started building His house. There is now a real urgency to begin. Hyrum Smith brought me a copy of the revelation. He also said that Brothers Thomas and Joseph Hancock will supervise the brickyard. I have been asked to help them, to burn the bricks for the House of the Lord. But I haven't the strength to fell the vast number of trees needed to fire so many bricks. Now the Lord has sent David here with his strong arms. It seems like providence."

Julia breathed out slowly. "But what of your father?" Her sons were silent for a moment as if unanswered questions lay before them like missing pieces to a puzzle.

"Joel, read the revelation to us," Seth requested.

Joel went inside and retrieved the lantern and piece of paper. He hung the lantern on the porch hook. Insects swarmed the light. Joel read aloud.

"Verily, thus saith the Lord unto you whom I love, and whom I love I also chasten that their sins may be forgiven, for with the chastisement I prepare a way for their deliverance in all things out of temptation, and I have loved you—

"Wherefore, ye must needs be chastened and stand rebuked before my face;

"For ye have sinned against me a very grievous sin, in that ye have not considered the great commandment in all things, that I have given unto you concerning the building of mine house;

"For the preparation wherewith I design to prepare mine apostles to prune my vineyard for the last time, that I may bring to pass my strange act, that I may pour out my Spirit upon all flesh . . .

"Yea, verily I say unto you, I gave unto you a commandment that you should build a house, in the which house I design to endow those whom I have chosen with power from on high . . .

"Verily I say unto you, it is my will that you should build a house. If you keep my commandments you shall have power to build it.

"If you keep not my commandments, the love of the Father shall not continue with you, therefore you shall walk in darkness."

Julia saw David tremble and turn to his brother. "Seth, we must have the love of our Father in Heaven. I have walked in darkness before and will not do so again. A strange urgency spreads through me. I must give my all in building this house. It is God's will!"

Julia looked at Seth. Seth put a hand on David's shoulder and looked into his mother's eyes. Julia knew he was remembering his own time of darkness. Seth took a deep breath. "Mother, I suggest we stay here three weeks. If Father hasn't come by then, David and I will not rest until we find him."

Julia stood and put her arms around Seth, laying her head for a moment on his shoulder. Then she stepped back and looked at his dear, intelligent face, the sorrow and gentleness of his features. His eyes contained an eternity of feeling. She looked over at her darling David, a man of such goodness, joy, and passion. A part of her would forever love the man who gave her these sons. Julia said softly, "Sons, if you think that is best, then I am certain it is God's will."

* * *

Two days later, Seth strode through a steady drizzle to the Whitney Store. He wiped the mud off his boots before entering. As he stepped through the doorway, his attention riveted to the conversation of two men standing near the entrance. One of them was Jared Carter, who had once stayed with the Johnsons in Pomfret and had rebaptized David. Seth knew that Jared had recently returned from an extremely successful mission to Michigan.

"We should not have excommunicated Hurlbut without giving the man a chance to defend himself!" The comment came from the other man, a tall muscular fellow with classic facial features and the burly, jaunty toughness of a sailor.

"William, you heard the testimonies against him. What else could we have done when Brother Philastus seems to have disappeared from the face of the earth?" Carter defended.

Uncomfortable and concerned, Seth immediately turned to them. "Good morning."

Jared Carter's face broke into a smile. "Brother Seth Johnson! I heard you had come to Kirtland!" He shook Seth's hand.

The stranger stepped forward. "I'm William Smith. It's good to have you here. You related to Joel Johnson?"

"My brother," Seth remarked.

"Does every man live in the shadow of his brother?" William asked. Without waiting for an answer, he doffed his hat to Seth and ducked out the door.

"William is the Prophet's brother," Brother Carter explained as Seth watched William leave. "A man of varying passions."

Seth turned back to Jared. "Speaking of men of varying passions, I overheard you speak of Philastus Hurlbut. He's an acquaintance of mine and kinsman to my brother-in-law, Lyman Sherman. What's happened?"

Jared spoke thoughtfully. "I remember Brother Sherman. Brother Joseph is still upstairs in the schoolroom. I think it would be best if you spoke with him about it."

After Seth gained the stairs, he found Joseph in the schoolroom talking with two gentlemen. The Prophet warmly welcomed Seth and introduced him to Frederick G. Williams and Sidney Rigdon. "Now how can we help you, Brother Seth?" Joseph queried.

"I overheard two of the brethren talking about D. P. Hurlbut. Has he truly been cut off from the Church?"

The joy left Joseph's eyes. He nodded. "This morning he was excommunicated by a council of high priests. I'm sorry."

Seth exhaled slowly, then spoke, "This will be a blow to my friend and brother-in-law, Lyman Sherman. D. P. is his cousin and dear to him. What happened?"

The Prophet was silent for a moment as if considering. Then he spoke. "Brother Hurlbut was found guilty of unvirtuous conduct toward a woman while on his mission. Orson Hyde and Hyrum, my brother, testified against him. Brother Hurlbut wasn't present at the trial. It seems he abruptly left the mission field. We don't know where he is, for he hasn't returned to Kirtland."

"And the lady he offended? Is she with him?"

Joseph shook his head. "She is left to sorrow alone."

Seth closed his eyes for an instant. He spoke with concern, "Lyman will be ashamed. I will write him today so he doesn't hear it from another."

"Brother Hurlbut's sins don't shame Brother Sherman or his family," Joseph said quickly. "Tell Brother Lyman we pray that his cousin repents and comes back into the fold of God."

* * *

The first light of morning lay shrouded in dark mist. David opened the door, sending his younger brothers and sisters outside to do their chores.

"David!" A duet of voices startled him. David peered through the mist and saw Don Carlos Smith and Almon Babbitt leaning against the trunk of a ghostly oak tree in the foggy semidarkness. Don Carlos stood tall and straight. Almon was dwarfed standing next to him. The two friends each embraced David.

Carlos exclaimed, "Joseph and the First Presidency are meeting right now. Then the temple committee will come to discuss the location for the House of the Lord. Come with us, and we'll see if they'll let us join them."

Almon moved his feet anxiously. "Wait. Before we go, I need to welcome Julianne to Kirtland."

David's face lit up. "Let's go now! Almon, my sisters aren't ready for visitors. They would have my head if I let you in! I'll go tell them that you and Carlos will be here for lunch. You can greet Juli then."

Carlos chuckled at Almon's look of sheer disappointment. "Patience, Almon my boy, patience."

David ducked inside to tell his family to expect guests for the noon meal.

A few minutes later, as the three young men walked the short distance to the Whitney Store, David asked Don Carlos to tell every detail about plans for the temple. Before Carlos could speak, Almon thudded David between the shoulder blades and changed the subject.

"Patience, David, my boy, patience. We'll hear all about the House of the Lord soon. Ask Carlos about the wagon full of Bostonian females that rolled into Kirtland late Saturday night!"

David raised his eyebrows. "Well?" Don Carlos broke into a grin.

"Unmarried Bostonian ladies," Almon expounded. "Currently staying with Don Carlos's family. Very attractive sisters in the gospel."

David eyed his friend, awaiting an explanation.

Don Carlos answered sheepishly, his blue eyes bright and his finely chiseled features gaining light as the sun rose. "My brother

Samuel is already courting one of them. Her name's Mary Bailey."

"And another's name is Agnes Coolbrith," Almon cut in. "Carlos can't keep his eyes off of her."

David nudged Don Carlos with his elbow. "And. . . ?"

Carlos shrugged. "She's an angel, David. Light brown hair, white skin, eyes nearly the same color as yours. She's intelligent and sweet. But she's considerably older than I am. I don't want to make the same mistake as Almon and fall in love with a girl before I can take care of her as my wife."

Almon snorted. "Julianne Johnson is not a mistake. I won't let her slip through my fingers." Then he added in a low voice as they entered the Whitney store, "Carlos, I think you're just scared of being henpecked by an older woman like Emma henpecks Joseph."

Don Carlos laughed out loud. "Almon, if Joseph hears you talk that way, he'll throw you out by your ear. He loves Emma and thinks that she is the best thing that ever happened to him."

David chuckled. It was so good to be with his friends again. "I think we should eat lunch with the Smiths, not the Johnsons," he mused. "I should like very much to meet Miss Agnes."

Don Carlos looked over at David, noting his handsome, masculine features and broad shoulders. "On second thought," Carlos mused, "I'd like to get to know Miss Agnes before *you* have the chance."

Almon grinned. "Then it's two votes to one, David. The voice of the majority is the will of God! It's lunch at the Johnsons'."

The young men hurried up the steps only to find the door to the schoolroom shut. They heard low voices within. Instinctively they knew to wait rather than knock on the door. As moments passed, a handful of other men joined them. The only one whom David recognized was Jared Carter.

Carter was friendly enough, but looked at David and Almon as if he weren't sure what they were doing there. Don Carlos quickly introduced David to his father, his brother Hyrum, the storekeeper, Newel Whitney, and Elder Reynolds Cahoon, a member of the temple committee. David felt uncomfortable, wondering if they were being too bold.

A moment later, Joseph Smith opened the door. Frederick G. Williams and Sidney Rigdon were sitting in the room, so intent on their own thoughts that they hardly seemed to notice the brethren filing in. David lingered outside the door with Don Carlos and Almon. After Joseph greeted and welcomed the older brethren, he stepped into the hallway, placing his hand on his brother's shoulder. "Carlos, come in with your companions. You young brethren sit on the back bench and listen. We have just beheld a vision from our God." David's apprehension turned quickly to joy as he followed Don Carlos and Almon into the room.

After the prayer, Joseph asked the brethren to give their suggestions about constructing the House of the Lord. Newel Whitney spoke with concern in his voice. "Is it possible to build the house of logs?" he asked. "The Church is so poor right now, and the people are buying so much on credit. Procuring enough wood to burn bricks would be a formidable task, and we haven't enough brethren for such labor. It would take less time and expense to build a log structure."

"It would have to be a frame house, rather than a log house, if it is to be a house of God," Joseph Smith Sr. commented.

Joseph looked at his counselors, then turned to the other men. "Shall we brethren build a house for our God of logs?" he questioned with a smile. "We now have a plan from the Lord, given by Himself; and you will soon see, the difference between our calculations and His idea. Before you arrived this morning, we knelt in prayer, and the building appeared before us in vision." Joseph then described a beautiful building of either brick or stone, with an inner court, a lower court, and a higher court, with tiers of pulpits on each end, and table leafs in the shape of yokes attached to the lower tiers for the administration of the sacrament.

Tears filled David's eyes as he listened to the Prophet of God. After he finished describing the building, Joseph suggested that the brethren walk together to the property that the Church had purchased. Together they would decide on a location suitable for the house of God.

As the men headed for the door, Joseph pulled David aside for a moment. The Prophet's face was alight with excitement. "Brother David," he whispered, "a scythe is leaning against the back door. Bring it with you."

Thirty minutes later, the men stood together on a piece of property that was officially part of the French farm, though it bordered Frederick G. Williams's land. Not far away was the log house where Mother and Father Smith lived. The plot was situated in the north-west corner of a field of wheat, which the Smith brothers had sown the previous fall. In minutes the men pulled down the fence. With the scythe, David leveled the standing grain to prepare a place for the building.

"Joseph, I will be the first to work on the Lord's house." Hyrum grinned. Dropping to his knees, without a tool in his hands, Hyrum began digging a trench for the wall. Reynolds Cahoon joined him, also digging with his bare hands.

Joseph Smith Sr. and his household joined the group. Samuel Smith watched while holding Mary Bailey's hand. Agnes Coolbrith stood next to them, her soft brown eyes happy. David knew who she was instantly, for she was as lovely as Don Carlos had described. The Prophet walked up to David, Don Carlos, and Almon. "Will you brethren chop the trees needed to burn the brick for the Lord's house?" he asked.

"With every particle of my strength," David promised.

"I'll do all in my power," Don Carlos added.

"And you, Brother Almon?" Joseph questioned.

"I'll work by my friends' sides." Almon grinned.

"Your Father in Heaven will accept your sacrifice, my dear young brothers," Joseph said as he embraced each of them.

* * *

Two hours later, at one o'clock, the sun shone brightly through the window of the Johnson home. Nancy sat by this window folding napkins as her sisters set food on the table. She saw David and his companions returning. "They're nearly here," she commented. Julianne walked over to the window and broke into a bright smile.

Susan did not look up. "Is Almon with them?" she questioned as she set out the silverware.

Julianne nodded. "Yes. I don't know how to act after the letters between us."

Susan glanced over at her sister. "You'll know when you see him," she assured her.

Nancy turned to Julianne who looked so fresh with her pink cheeks, upturned nose, expressive eyes, and narrow jawline. Nancy thought of her sister's lively, affectionate, unselfish ways and wondered if Almon was noble enough for her. "Be careful, Juli," Nancy advised. "I don't know if Mr. Babbitt suits you."

Julianne hugged her sister's shoulders. "Oh, Nancy, I'm most anxious to find out. I can't go forward until then."

"Dearest Juli, don't close your eyes to other prospects," Nancy begged.

The sisters watched the young men approach. Julianne commented, "The other must be Don Carlos Smith. He is as tall and well built as David. Yet he has something of the look of the Prophet."

Almera put the pitcher of milk on the table and walked over to stand by them. She peered out the window with a wrinkle in her brow. "Don Carlos is handsome," she admitted, "but he has such a boyish look about him."

"They all three do," Julianne added with a wistful smile. "They look like pups from the same litter. And poor Almon is the runt."

"There are more to those three than appears," Nancy said quietly as Susan walked over. "After the Lord's house is built, they will attend the School of the Prophets."

"And they need it," Almera said wryly as she watched David and Don Carlos mischievously push Almon toward the house.

Susan turned and went back to setting the table. Nancy watched after her and wondered if she was all right. She knew that Susan had once had feelings for Almon. Was it painful for her now? Nancy remembered how it had long ago been difficult for her to watch Delcena and Lyman's joy.

* * *

Thirty minutes later, the noon meal was a noisy affair with Julia's younger children competing with their smaller nieces and nephews for her attention. Julia felt some trepidation as she looked around at all of the mouths to feed. Ezekiel's absence burdened her, yet she squared her shoulders, reminding herself that she had money from the Pomfret sale that would last her at least until the end of the year. She had hardworking sons and daughters as well. With the Lord's aid, they would make it. She glanced over at Almon Babbitt; he was the reason Julianne had rejected Brother Howell's proposal. Julia had mixed feelings about Julianne's choice. She liked Almon, but he was young and restless. Ezekiel had once been young and restless too. She had hoped to see her daughter happily settled.

Julianne flashed Almon a smile as she poured the children glasses of milk. Then she squeezed onto the bench between Will and George, across the table from Almon.

"Brother Almon," Julia said above the hubbub of noise. "Annie tells me you went to Cincinnati and stayed with my elder brother. How is he?"

Almon swallowed the bite of cornbread. "Mr. Hills is very well, Sister Johnson. He spoke of you with the warmest sentiments. Mrs. Hills also said that she would dearly love to see you again."

"When we were young, Rhoda and I were the best of friends," Julia remarked. "Did you talk with them about the gospel?"

Almon shook his head. "Mr. Hills refused to converse on the topic of religion, though he wanted to know every other detail of your family."

Julia sighed. "How are their children?"

"In good health. I enjoyed the company of your nephew, Frank. He is a giant of a fellow, jolly and freckled, full of fun." Almon smiled, remembering.

There was a hint of longing in Julia's voice. "How I should like to see them again."

Julia took a deep breath. Ezekiel was not here to question this boy who had come to call on their daughter. Julia's tone changed and became matter-of-fact. "Brother Babbitt, did you visit the law school in Cincinnati? Will you be attending after harvest?"

A brief shadow crossed Almon's eyes. "Not this year. I'll stay here and work on the Lord's house." Almon's eyes strayed to Julianne and caught her encouraging smile.

Almon grinned ruefully. "I couldn't convince the old professor that I'm well-read and an excellent debater. He wouldn't consider a poor, unpolished Mormon boy. I'll keep knocking on his door. I'm hoping that he'll change his tune someday and come to appreciate my virtues."

"One of which is humility," Almera commented, raising a pretty eyebrow. Almon reddened. David choked on a bite of pork. Don Carlos covered his mouth with a napkin as he suppressed a chuckle.

Julia noticed that Annie came quickly to Almon's rescue. Her redheaded daughter-in-law spoke with warmth. "Almon's confidence becomes him. He was the most wonderful friend to us in Amherst. Isn't that right, Benjamin?"

"Almon is the best fellow," Ben answered with a grin. "When he isn't bragging about catching a fish."

"I'm sure it was rejoicing, not bragging," Annie corrected.

"Rejoicing!" David guffawed. Benjamin broke up with such force that a piece of food flew out of his mouth. The younger children howled.

Annie cleared her throat. "I should be surprised if Brothers Almon and Don Carlos ever visit us again."

David took a drink of cider to douse his mirth. "You misread me, Annie," he said. "I'm very glad to have Almon here with us."

"Me too," Ben added. "Bragging and all."

"I . . . " Julianne began. The table was suddenly silent as all eyes turned to her. She smiled quickly, "I—I hope Brother Babbitt rejoices in our home often."

"I will," Almon said, his eyes only on Julianne's face. "Every day of the week if I'm allowed."

"You're allowed," Julianne whispered.

"Except, Juli, you aren't the head of this household," Seth said quietly and directly.

Julianne's color rose in surprise as she turned to her brother. "Nor are you, Seth."

"I am," Julia said quickly. "And Brother Almon is always welcome here." Then she turned to David and changed the direction of the conversation. "Son, could you and your friends tell us all about the meeting this morning? We are all anxious to know the details about the House of the Lord."

David looked at his mother, and his eyes lit with great joy as he began describing all that he had experienced.

* * *

Later that week Almera attended a quilting bee with her mother and Susan. During the course of conversation, one of the women asked about Philastus Hurlbut. Another told the sordid story of Brother Hurlbut's affair in the mission field and of his subsequent disappearance and excommunication. Almera's face grew hot. She dared not look at Susan, the only person she had told of Hurlbut's inappropriate advances. *Why hadn't Brother Joseph known that Hurlbut was not an honest man, unworthy to hold the priesthood of God? Shouldn't the Lord whisper those impressions to a prophet of God?* Almera glanced at her mother. Julia concentrated on her sewing, her face unreadable.

That evening when the younger children had gone to bed, Almera was present when Julia brought up the subject with the older members of the family. Julia told Seth and Joel about the gossip and asked if they had any knowledge of whether or not it was true.

Seth nodded. "I've spoken to the Prophet Joseph. Philastus was excommunicated, but he was not here to defend himself. No one knows where he is. The testimonies against him were clear and irrefutable."

Almera glanced over at Delcena who was in the rocking chair with baby Albey. The chair stopped moving. "Seth, why didn't you tell me of this?" Delcena questioned.

Seth looked at her. "I didn't want to burden you. And I didn't know if it would be fair to Philastus. I had hoped that this would not be fodder for quilting bees."

"Not burden me, Lyman's wife?" Delcena questioned, clearly upset. "Did you think I would bring this up as idle gossip?"

"No, Delce. I didn't mean that," Seth said quickly. "I've written to Lyman."

Delcena suddenly turned to Joel. "When Philastus returns, will you still rent a room to him?"

Joel spoke honestly. "I don't know. I've given him my word. And he has paid in advance. But if he has been cast out from the Church?"

Almera's voice shook slightly, "There are people coming to Kirtland every day who need places to live. Find someone else, Joel. We can't rent a room to a man like that!"

Joel took a deep breath. "We need the money, and most people cannot pay."

"No amount of money is worth harboring a wicked man!" Almera snapped. "He shouldn't have been given the priesthood in the first place!"

"Almera, the Prophet believes in the good in people and in what they can become," Seth countered.

"Is it possible that he is repentant?" Delcena cried out. "He gave me and my family a home. He tried to protect my children from smallpox."

Julia spoke. "When you lived with him, was his conduct in any way uncomfortable for you, Delcena, as a woman?"

Delcena shook her head. "No."

Almera's pretty features reddened, and she twisted her hands in her lap. She would not be able to rest if Philastus Hurlbut lived under the same roof. She looked over at Susan as if begging for help.

Susan cut into the conversation. "Doctor Hurlbut was expelled from his congregation in Jamestown on similar charges."

There were tears in Delcena's eyes. "I know. Lyman must feel so badly. Sometimes when we lived with Philastus, his pride annoyed us. Yet Philastus has always been generous, and Lyman loves him and believes in the good in him. The thought of Philastus cut off from the Church is terrible."

"Maybe he will come back and answer the charges. Don't give up on him yet, Delce. Repentance is a gift from the Lord," Seth said.

"But he had been ordained to the high priesthood. That makes his sin so much darker," David commented.

"Delcena, what do you think Lyman would have us do?" Joel asked.

"Lyman wouldn't turn him out," Delcena said. "He would have us continue to be his friends and pray for him."

Joel sighed. "Then that is the course we'll take. For now."

Almera stood up. "Father wouldn't stand for this!" she cried hotly. Her cheeks were bright, and sweat beaded on her forehead. She left the room.

* * *

Susan watched after Almera, wondering if she should follow.

"Susan." Nancy's gray eyes filled with concern. "Do you know why Almera feels so strongly about this?"

For a moment Susan considered telling them about Hurlbut's advances toward Almera years ago. But a confidence was like a gift for one person alone, not something to be given to others. "She doesn't trust him," Sue replied. "Nor do I. And she misses Father's protection. As do I."

Nancy spoke gently, "Sue, you know that if Hurlbut made advances toward any of you, our brothers would turn him out faster than lightning strikes."

"After we thrashed him within an inch of his life," David added, his brown-gold eyes flashing. "You are all protected with your brothers here."

Susan stood and looked from David to Seth. "Thank you," she said softly. "I'll go tell Almera."

* * *

Ezekiel popped the slug of tobacco into his mouth, his jaw clenching with each chew. It was late afternoon as he waited for the steamboat to arrive, which he hoped carried his wife and children. He squinted and gazed up at the sky. It was overcast, with only a few patches of blue showing through the gray clouds.

He chewed and waited while the boat docked. He had come to the dock each day for the past two weeks. He spit out the tobacco as he watched the group of travelers disembark. Julia and his children were not among them. Ezekiel ground his teeth. If tragedy had befallen them, wouldn't someone have sent word?

A drunkard who frequented the dock each day walked up to him. "Bad news again, heh? Everybody's waitin' for somethin'. You waitin' for a woman?"

Ezekiel nodded, looking at the man levelly. "My wife and children."

The man raised his eyebrows and grinned. "My wife ran off fifteen years back. Warn't much of a loss."

Ezekiel spun away from the drunk as his temper rose. He stalked to a nearby building and bought passage on the steamboat heading east in the morning. It was possible that his letter had never made it to Pomfret. Julia could be there renting a place and waiting for him to come for her. He walked back to the tavern and bought a drink. He sat down at a table alone. Another thought tortured him. Had she abandoned him? He shook his head and swallowed the burning liquor. He remembered the lovely depth of his wife's eyes. Could it be possible that she was capable of such betrayal? He stood up and bought another drink.

* * *

On horseback, Philastus Hurlbut made his way to Kirtland. He had left his mission rather abruptly five days ago before Orson Hyde could confront him about his relationship with Miss Huldah Barnes.

Miss Barnes was a rather corpulent young lady, a member of the family that the elders had been staying with. She had nimble feet and a quick wit—often poking fun at her own unattractiveness. One evening Philastus had found himself alone with her in the sitting room. He had told her of her womanly charms and beauty. She had giggled and had claimed she didn't believe him. To prove it, he had kissed her warmly. It had seemed a little thing to Philastus. But the girl had told her sister, who asked him his intentions and warned him that she would speak of it to Orson Hyde. Philastus had decided to leave quickly, without a word, before Hyde accused him and a scandal erupted.

On the way back to Kirtland, he had stopped in Thompson to spend a few days with Lyman's mother and sisters, hoping that the Barnes affair would blow over. He had found his cousin Electa as lovely as ever. He had spent a good deal of time with her, winning her devotion, but knowing all the while that he preferred Lovina's colorful beauty to Electa's charming prettiness. He also knew that Electa basked in his gentlemanly affection, never imagining that another woman's image was part of every breath he took, nor that his one regret was that he would never fully enjoy his darling cousin. He had charmed his Aunt Asenath and his cousin Cornelia as well by helping them get their affairs in order so that they would be ready to leave as soon as Lyman came for them.

All had gone well in Thompson. But now Philastus felt a driving need to get back to Kirtland. Leaving thoughts of Electa behind, he spurred his horse forward, desire for Lovina surging through him. He did not rest until eight hours later when he stood at the door of Frederick G. Williams' home.

Philastus knocked. The door opened a crack, and Lovina peeked out.

"Lovina, is anyone else home?" Philastus asked. Lovina shook her head coolly.

Philastus pushed the door wide open, grabbed her hand and pulled her out onto the porch. She did not protest. He kissed her. Though she allowed it, she remained unresponsive.

"This is like kissing a wall!" Hurlbut exclaimed. "Is this any way to treat your love who has just returned from a mission?"

Lovina glared at him, incredulous. "You don't know, do you?"

"Don't know what?" Philastus asked. "I came here as soon as I arrived in Kirtland."

"You've been cut off from the Church. I'm not allowed to see you again."

"What?"

"Why do you act so innocent?" Lovina stomped her foot. "Father said that if I knew the details I would not want to see you again! The Prophet agrees that you are not worthy to court me!"

"I can't believe this! Am I not allowed to defend myself?"

"No one knew where you were!" Lovina cried. "You disappeared from your mission. And not to come back for me."

Hurlbut stepped away from her and pulled his hat down to shade his eyes. He spoke. "I was with my Aunt Asenath and cousins in Thompson. They are three women living alone and they needed help getting their affairs in order before they move to Kirtland. My cousin Lyman, their son and brother, is too busy preaching the gospel in New York to come to their aid."

"I don't believe you!" Lovina cried. "Brother Joseph said that you aren't an honest man."

"Brother Joseph is a hypocrite!" Philastus shouted raggedly. "Yet you believe his every word! Ask my aunt and cousins where I was!"

"Brother Joseph is the Prophet!" Lovina shouted back with her chin lifted high. She broke into tears. "I loved you! But I won't marry anyone who has been cut off from Christ's Church!"

Philastus Hurlbut folded Lovina Williams in his arms.

"Let go of me, D. P. Mother and Father will be home any moment." She wept as she tried to push him away.

He held her more tightly, anger, frustration, and desire pounding through his veins. "I'll fix everything," he hissed in her ear. "We'll be together yet."

"They're coming!" Lovina gasped, glimpsing the family's buggy and team rounding the bend in the road. Philastus stepped back from her. Lovina bit down on her lip. Her father's team was fast approaching.

Philastus looked into her eyes. "I'll be back," he promised.

Lovina swallowed and nodded. "Good-bye, dear D. P.," she whispered. For a moment she watched him ride away, the handsomest man in Kirtland. Then she turned and went into the house and up to her room before her father could ask her who had called.

9

When trembling sinners wish to know
How they may shun the road to woe,
And have pure joy within,
We tell them, though by men despis'd
They must repent and be baptized,
And wash away their sin.

Joel Hills Johnson
(*Hymns of Praise for the Young,* Hymn 125, 127)

June 21, 1833

Philastus bowed his head before the council of high priests. During the prayer, he thought about the part he had played for the past two weeks—that of the repentant sinner. He had never imagined that a man as proud as himself could play it so well. Yet he did not want to lose Lovina, nor the brotherhood he felt with Lyman. Whether or not he believed in Mormonism, his future depended on which way the scale tipped today.

Sweat beaded beneath Hurlbut's shock of dark, wavy hair. After the prayer, Joseph Smith stood up and focused on him. The Prophet's high forehead shone in the cramped, humid room. He spoke. "Brother Hurlbut, you were charged with unchristian-like conduct toward the opposite sex and duly cut off from the Church of Christ. You are now invited to speak before the council."

Philastus stood, his heart pounding. He was outnumbered. How strange that these weak men could frighten him so! Only Smith held any real power. Thoughts of Lovina's beauty shot through him. He had not seen her for these long two weeks, but her image burned in his mind night and day.

"I do not protest my own weakness and sin," Philastus began. "Only that I was absent at the time of the council—thus strict justice was not done in removing me from the Church."

Frederick G. Williams looked intently at Hurlbut, his quill momentarily still. Philastus felt the sting. If he lost in this council, his one priceless treasure was gone forever. Tears of frustration filled his eyes. He would prostrate himself before God and the devil to claim Lovina Williams as his own. As Hurlbut spoke, he cried openly, begging the council's forgiveness and promising to live a virtuous life from that moment forward.

"Are you willing to fulfill your mission, to continue preaching the gospel? To confess before the Church and before the woman you have injured?" Joseph questioned.

"Yes. With heaven's speed," Philastus said. He swallowed and rubbed his hands together, feeling the sweat on his palms and the damp tears on his face. He hated this helplessness with every fiber of his being.

Sidney Rigdon spoke. "I move that because of his liberal confession and the intents of his heart, that Brother Philastus Hurlbut be rebaptized, and all of his priesthood blessings restored—this very day. This would allow him to continue his mission on the morrow. All in favor show by the sign."

Philastus watched as man after man raised his hand. The final two people to give the sign were Frederick G. Williams and Joseph Smith Jr. Philastus took out a handkerchief and wiped his eyes as his tears disappeared. His visage remained appropriately humble and thankful.

"Brother Hurlbut," Joseph said without a smile, "I welcome you back into the fold of Christ. Please leave us for an hour. We have other business to attend to. Then return, and we will proceed with your baptism."

Philastus nodded and shook Joseph's hand. After Hurlbut left the room, Joseph was quiet a moment, focusing on the door closing behind Philastus.

"What is it, Joseph?" Hyrum questioned.

The brethren in the room waited silently as Joseph turned around. They were used to the Prophet's revelations, the change that came over his features, the brightness that infused him when flashes of insight poured forth the words of God. But today Joseph's eyes were sorrowful, veiled beneath their long, light lashes. "I fear for Brother Hurlbut. Will he be able to fulfill the promises he has made? Did his confession truly reveal the intents of his heart?"

"Time will answer your questions," Frederick commented.

Joseph nodded. "But if he is honest, he deserves our trust and a restoration of his blessings."

Sidney Rigdon stood and put his arm around the young prophet. "Should he choose, young Brother Hurlbut has the energy and passion to do the Church great good."

Joseph nodded slowly. "Should he choose." Frederick G. Williams did not speak further, but added another note to the minutes of the meeting.

* * *

It was mid afternoon. Almera sat on the porch bench knitting. She dropped another stitch and swatted at a fly landing on her wrist. She couldn't concentrate on the work before her. Her mind was troubled. At the noon meal, Joel had told them that Philastus Hurlbut had been rebaptized and had his blessings restored. He was going back out on his mission to the same area he had left. Almera could hardly believe it.

She thought about her reaction when Hurlbut had come back to Kirtland two weeks ago. Initially, she had felt extremely distraught. However, she had soon realized that his mind was elsewhere, probably on the woman he had offended on his mission.

Nancy hobbled out of the front door and sat down next to Almera. "A penny for your thoughts, Mera."

"I'm knitting about as well as David today," Almera sniffed. "It's no use."

"Let me help," Nancy offered. Almera handed her the half-finished cap, knitting needles, and yarn. Nancy deftly began fixing the flawed stitches.

"What do you think about Brother Philastus being rebaptized?" Nancy asked.

"I don't think he is truly repentant!" Almera said. "Nor do I think he should be sent back out on a mission."

"I understand how you feel," Nancy commented.

"Why can't the Prophet see through him?" Almera questioned.

"I think the Prophet knows that everyone deserves a second chance. Brother Joseph is quick to forgive. He trusts that God will deal justice in the end."

"How do you know that, Nancy?"

Nancy smiled. "When he preaches, I listen to each word. He is a prophet of God, but he is also human. Mera, I trust in our Heavenly Father and our Prophet."

Almera nodded slowly and allowed the burden of concern to ease from her shoulders. "I do too," she said as she took a deep breath. "And Hurlbut won't be living here for a time. That's good news."

"Indeed it is," Nancy agreed.

* * *

That evening an elated Philastus Hurlbut galloped his horse to the Williams' residence while Frederick and Rebecca Williams dined with the Smiths. His hope was to happen upon their daughter without a chaperone.

After tying his horse, he knocked on the Williams' door, but no one opened it. Then he heard Lovina's laughter floating to him from behind the barn. He grinned and walked toward the sound. When he rounded the corner of the house, his smile faded. A young man was pulling sticks with Lovina's little brother, Ezra. Hurlbut recognized the man. It was Burr Riggs, the fellow Lovina had shunned months ago. Riggs animatedly fell forward, allowing the boy to win.

"Bravo, Ezra! Bravo!" Lovina squealed and clapped her hands while perched on a stack of hay. Her dress was green and matched her eyes, her hair curled in ringlets down her back. "Oh, poor, handsome Burr, you've lost again," she commiserated coyly.

Hurlbut cleared his throat to make the threesome aware of his presence. *Yes, poor Burr, you've lost again,* he thought maliciously as Lovina started and turned toward him. She jumped down from the hay and nervously dusted off her dress. Her forehead scrunched. "D. P., why are you here?"

He glanced challengingly at Riggs, then back to Lovina. "To speak to you. Alone."

"Stay here with Ezra, Burr. I'll be back in a minute," Lovina said. She flounced away before Riggs could protest. Hurlbut followed her around the barn, toward the side of the house, out of earshot.

When she turned around to face him, her green eyes held fire. Philastus took her hands. She pulled them away. He took them again and held them tightly. "Lovina, all is well. I've been rebaptized. There is nothing to separate us now." Then he chuckled. "Except the mission I must fulfill to convince them that I'm fully repentant."

Lovina forcefully pulled her hands away and tucked them behind her back. She stepped back from him. "Mr. Hurlbut, things have changed. Two weeks ago, Father gave Burr permission to court me again. He, too, is now in full fellowship in the Church. We have fallen back in love."

Hurlbut stared at her in disbelief, "What do you mean? Is this some game?"

Lovina stomped her foot. "I love Burr, not you! That's what I mean."

"Surely you're joking. Riggs is a sniveling pup!"

Lovina glared at him hotly, "Burr has never sniveled in another woman's arms! I overheard Father and the Prophet talking. I know about Miss Barnes. I've made up my mind. I will never marry you. I'm engaged to Burr."

Philastus Hurlbut stared at her. "I'm dedicated to you. I will have you."

"No, you will *not* have me!" Lovina's eyes narrowed. Then she lifted her chin courageously. "I thought you suited me. But I was wrong. I love Burr with all my soul. I will have Burr. I will never change my mind again."

He took her shoulders between his hands. Had he prostrated himself and still lost this game? "To think of what I did for you!" he raged.

Lovina paled, suddenly afraid. "Let go of me," she whispered, "or I'll shout for Burr."

"Think twice, Lovina—I could kill Burr with my hands tied behind my back!"

Lovina screamed. Hurlbut pushed her away. "You aren't worth the trouble. There is another woman waiting for me."

* * *

The next morning Philastus left before dawn under the pretense of continuing his mission in the east. He galloped his horse toward Thompson, Ohio. It was mid-afternoon when he arrived at the house that Asenath Sherman rented for herself and two daughters. Hurlbut swung down from the horse, took a long drink from his flask of water, and combed his black hair back with his fingers. He would marry Electa, his pretty, blonde cousin, to combat the rage and hurt churning within. He would have a wife as sweet and fresh as morning.

Philastus rapped on the door. His diffident cousin Cornelia answered. "Hello, Philastus," she said distinctly. Intent on his errand, he didn't notice the way Cornelia studied him as he entered the house. Philastus helped himself to a chair in the sitting room. His complexion was ruddy from the heat of the day. "How are you, Cornelia?"

"Well," she answered. "And you?"

Philastus grinned. There was a reckless, nervous edge to his usually confident demeanor. "As right as rain. Who else is home?"

Cornelia eyed him. "Mother is gone. Electa is spinning."

"Please get Electa. I've come to speak with her."

"Electa!" Cornelia called out as she turned her head toward the open door. Then she turned back to Hurlbut. "Yesterday, we received a letter from Lyman."

"Is he well?"

"Yes, considering the circumstances."

Before Philastus could ask about the circumstances, Electa walked into the room. Her flaxen hair was braided and tied back in a low bun. "Hello, Philastus," she said. Her cheeks were pink from the humidity and her eyes bright and moist with conflicting emotions as she looked at her dark, handsome cousin.

Hurlbut stood. "Electa, I've come back for you. Nelia, will you leave so I can speak to your sister alone?"

Cornelia looked significantly toward her sister. Electa nodded. Cornelia exhaled sharply as she stood up. "I'll be in the kitchen."

Electa sat down. Her skirt was lavender and her blouse white. Hurlbut noticed her chest rise and fall as she breathed. His heart pounded. How fortunate he was that this flower was close by, ready to be plucked. If Lovina was storm and beating sun, fierce heat and lightning, here was morning dew and soft spring sunlight. She would be better for him. Electa's coolness would douse his burning.

He went down on his knees before her and took her small white hand in his. He looked into her blue eyes. Her cheeks were fever red, but her hand was cool as he brought it to his lips. "Electa, are you well?" he queried. She trembled, and tears gathered in her eyes.

Hurlbut stood and drew her into his arms. He continued, "I love you, darling Electa. I've come for you, to marry you. Our love will know no bounds. You will never weep again."

Electa gently withdrew. She took her handkerchief out of her apron pocket and wept. "Electa, what is it?" Hurlbut questioned. "Are these tears of sorrow or joy?"

She wiped her eyes and swallowed. "We received a letter from Lyman."

"What is it, my darling? Bad news?"

"Oh, Philastus, you act as if you don't know!" Distraught, Electa paced the room. Finally she stopped and gathered her composure enough to speak. "The bad news is about you. Lyman will never consent to our marrying. Nor will I choose a man who is not honorable. Yet I love you as my cousin. But Philastus, who are you?"

Hurlbut spun toward her and took hold of her arm, "Who told Lyman these lies?"

"Seth Johnson wrote him," Electa cried. "Mr. Johnson heard the sad news from the Prophet himself."

Hurlbut shook his head and exhaled. He spoke more to himself than to Electa. "He will pay dearly!"

"Who will pay? Seth Johnson?" Electa's voice was suddenly quiet and piercing. "He wrote out of love for Lyman and concern for you."

Rage seeped through every fiber of Philastus Hurlbut's being. He stepped back from Electa, his hands hardening into fists. "Joseph Smith has spread these evil tales about me. The man is a fraud, and I will prove it!" he hissed. "He has taken from me all that is dear! The women I love! The brother I had in Lyman! I will be avenged!"

"Philastus, I beg you not to fight against God!" Electa cried.

"Smith knows nothing of God!"

Hurlbut stared at his weeping cousin for a moment, wrapped in too much anger to speak. Then there was a knock at the door. From the sitting room he heard Cornelia answer it. Electa turned and ran from the room.

A moment later, Brother Amos Hodges entered the sitting room followed by Cornelia. Hodges greeted Philastus with a handshake. "Brother Hurlbut, the Prophet asked me to accompany you on your mission. When I went to find you this morning, you were already gone. Sister Johnson directed me here. Are you ready to preach tonight?"

Philastus Hurlbut's color was high. He scoffed. Pulling his hand away, he looked briefly at the astounded Cornelia, then turned back to Hodges, his voice dripping sarcasm. "Yes, I'm ready to preach!" He turned to his cousin. "Cornelia, I've been re-baptized. Should I tell the good people of the Thompson Branch how I deceived Joseph Smith's God? How I proved that his council has no wisdom? Yes, I told them I was sorry! They believed it to be an honest confession! I deceived the whole of them and made them restore me to the Church!"

Amos Hodges's mouth turned into a grim line. He spoke between clenched teeth. "If that's the case, I have no business here. Sister Cornelia, would you like me to turn him out for you?"

"He is our kinsman," Cornelia said stoically, "and will not be turned out. You can go, Brother Hodges, and may the Lord accompany you." Hodges respectfully nodded and left the house.

"Philastus, you can have supper with us as long as you do not speak against the Lord's anointed."

Philastus looked bitterly at Cornelia. "Don't put yourself out, Nellie. I know the details of Joe Smith's fraud. The Solomon Spaulding tale is true! I'll prove it with such force that even Lyman will be free of Mormonism!"

"Lyman already knows the truth." Cornelia stared at him. "Leave, Philastus Hurlbut. You are no longer welcome here."

Hurlbut glared back at Cornelia. "Joseph Smith will fall. He won't destroy another man's prospects like he has destroyed mine, or defraud another honest fool like Lyman! Mark my words, Cornelia. I will discredit Smith or wash my hands in his blood!"

* * *

The cerulean sky lay calm amid puffs of sun-dipped clouds. Lyman Sherman stood on the banks of Lake Chautauqua near Hiram Winters's mill and sang to the group before him:

> *"Down in old Jordan's rolling stream;*
> *The prophet led the holy Lamb,*
> *And there did him baptize:*
> *Jehovah saw his darling Son,*
> *And was well pleas'd in what he'd done,*
> *And own'd him from the skies.*

"Believing children gather round,
And let your joyful songs abound,
With cheerful hearts arise;
See, here is water, here is room,
A loving Savior calling, come,
O children, be baptiz'd.

"Behold, his servant waiting stands,
With willing heart and ready hands
To wait upon the Bride;
Ye candidates your hearts prepare,
And let us join in solemn prayer,
Down by the water side."

The small congregation followed Lyman to the water's edge. He stepped into the cool lake and, one by one, baptized a family—a good family, with hearts as honest as the soil. First came Gideon Burdick, a revolutionary war veteran, next his wife Jane, then Gideon's sons and their spouses, Thomas and Anna, Alden and Jerusha, and then finally, Gideon's beloved daughter, Rebecca, with her husband, Hiram Winters. They were warm-hearted, hard-working, God-fearing folk—the substance that made the nation great. Lyman watched as the family embraced each other, laughed, cried, and explained to the little children about God.

A joy beyond expression filled Lyman as water streamed from his clothes. The remembrance of the frigid night when Elder Brackenbury baptized Lyman beat like fire in his veins. Today, Lyman Sherman beheld a family whose goodness and faith extended beyond time and into the glory of eternal worlds. Had Elder Brackenbury beheld the same vision when he baptized the Johnson family? How it must have comforted him when he died so far away from his wife and children. Like missionaries before and after Joseph Brackenbury and Lyman Sherman, their sacrifice had yielded gold—the priceless mettle of souls brought to God, sanctified from sin with power to rise in the resurrection like shining stars, the sons and daughters of Christ. Lyman knew that this joy for others was what Philastus had never really understood, one of the reasons he had lost his way. Had Lyman taught him too much of doctrine and too little of love? The thought brought tears to Lyman's eyes.

Lyman took his glasses off. He tried drying them by taking a handkerchief out of his pocket. The handkerchief was soaked from the baptism. Rebecca Winters noticed. She smiled at her husband, Hiram, and handed him the baby. She unpinned a dry handkerchief from the line and gave it to their beloved missionary. Lyman thanked her. He dried his glasses and wiped his eyes. Then he put his spectacles back on.

Gideon brought a chair outside and set it on the porch in preparation for the confirmations. He mentioned how their wet clothes felt refreshing on a hot day. There was no reason to wait. Lyman and Sylvester Smith confirmed the new converts. Afterwards, Jane, Rebecca, Anna, and Jerusha fed them a dinner of roasted chicken.

At sunset, Lyman left the Burdicks and started home alone. He planned to pack and leave for Kirtland in the morning. As he neared the house he rented, a lone figure stood by the porch. Lyman could not make out his features because of the brightness of the setting sun. He wondered if it was a scout sent by the good citizens of Jamestown, lying in wait to punish the Mormon elder. Was Big Simmons nearby with his hickory stick? Strangely, Lyman didn't feel the least shadow of fear.

The figure began walking forward. Lyman squinted, knowing that there was something familiar about the outline of this man. Then a rifle went to the man's shoulder, pointed straight at Lyman's chest. Lyman's stomach knotted, for he didn't have a weapon with him. How he had hoped to be with his wife and children again!

"Who goes there?" the man called out.

Lyman gasped as relief flooded through him. He recognized the voice. "Father Johnson! It's me, Lyman!" he exclaimed and broke into a trot.

As Lyman approached, Ezekiel did not lower the gun. Lyman's welcoming smile dimmed.

"Where's my family?" Ezekiel shouted.

"In Kirtland," Lyman said steadily. He stepped closer and reached out his hand touching the warm barrel of the gun. "Are you going to shoot me?"

"I haven't decided whether to protect you or shoot you!"

Lyman saw the pain and rage in the man's eyes. "I went to Pomfret, and they weren't there," Ezekiel growled as he lowered the gun. "Disappeared. Like they never were."

Lyman took a deep breath. "You've got it wrong. They've been worried—didn't know what happened to you. I'll explain."

Ezekiel exhaled sharply. "I sent my wife instructions."

Lyman shook his head. "The letter never came. Mother Johnson looked for it each day. Time ran out. Then they went to Kirtland. Seth and David are probably in Chicago now, searching for you."

Ezekiel's eyes narrowed. "You expect me to believe that! Julia wanted to go to Kirtland more than she ever wanted anything."

"Believe what you will," Lyman returned. "But I'm telling you the truth."

The two men stared at each other. Ezekiel was the first to lower his eyes. He spoke. "Are they all well?"

"Yes," Lyman said gently.

Ezekiel took a deep, trembling breath. "Then I leave for Kirtland tomorrow," he said gruffly.

"My work here is complete," Lyman said. "Can I travel with you as far as Thompson, Ohio?"

Ezekiel snorted. "If you don't preach Mormonism the whole way."

* * *

Five days later, Ezekiel and Lyman arrived at Asenath Sherman's home. The day was cloudy and humid, the air thick with moisture. Both men dismounted, Lyman from his horse and Ezekiel from a large mule he had purchased before leaving Jamestown. Lyman knocked on the door. Ezekiel stood back for a moment, his hand resting on the mule's neck. He watched as Lyman warmly embraced his mother and sisters. He wondered what kind of reception he would get when he arrived in Kirtland. Asenath turned to Ezekiel. "Come in and rest, Mr. Johnson. Electa will get you a cool drink of water and something to eat."

Ezekiel took off his hat. "Thank you, Mrs. Sherman."

Ezekiel felt restless and isolated while he sat in the muggy room and listened to the Shermans talk about their plans and their family. He broke off a piece of bread and dipped it in milk. He ate his portion quickly, then took the small bottle of liquor out of his pocket and swallowed a mouthful. He wouldn't rest until he saw his family again and had them safely on their way to Fort Dearborn. If he left within the hour, he'd get to Kirtland by eleven o'clock that night. The days were long this time of year, and he'd only have a couple of hours of darkness to travel through. He looked up and heard a bit of the conversation floating around him.

"Son, there was news of Philastus today," Asenath Sherman said to Lyman as she pushed a damp, errant strand of gray hair back from her face.

Electa looked up from her knitting. "Must we speak of it, Mother?" she asked, her voice pained.

Cornelia eyed her sister. "Of course, Electa. Lyman ought to know."

Electa looked down, her youthful jaw set. Asenath glanced at both of her daughters, then continued, "Philastus has sworn revenge on the Saints. He's gathered information about Solomon Spaulding's manuscript and is taking donations from an anti-Mormon group in Mentor. He plans to travel east where he swears he will get proof that will discredit Joseph."

Lyman took a deep breath. "Is he still living with Delcena and her mother?" Asenath nodded.

Ezekiel's attention riveted toward the group. They were talking about his wife and children as if he weren't there! He broke into the conversation. "Do you mean that D. P. Hurlbut has left the Mormon Church and is living in the same house as my family?"

Asenath Sherman glanced sharply at her guest. She nodded. "Yes. My nephew has a contract with your son Joel to rent a room."

"That will change when I get there," Ezekiel muttered.

Asenath replied tartly, "I don't see why Philastus's religious aspirations bother you, Mr. Johnson, as you claim Joseph Smith is deluded."

"Deluded, but not dishonest," Ezekiel growled.

"Sir, don't forget that Philastus shared his home with Lyman and Delcena and our grandchildren!" Asenath returned hotly. "Our hearts are breaking over his sins and his fall from the Church of Christ. His faults are not for you to judge! We pray for him and leave him to a just God who knows his generous heart."

Ezekiel clamped his mouth shut. It seemed that all women were as strong willed as Julia. Had it always been this way? The room was silent for a few moments. Finally, Lyman spoke. "Father Johnson, are you going to stay the night?"

Ezekiel shook his head and stood up. "No. I'll be going on to Kirtland now." He picked up his hat and gripped the brim. "Thank you, Mrs. Sherman, for your hospitality."

Asenath looked at him squarely, "Mr. Johnson, I hope you aren't shortening your stay over our difference of opinion."

"No, Ma'am. I planned all along to get to Kirtland tonight," Ezekiel said quickly.

Lyman took a letter out of his pocket and handed it to his father-in-law. "For Delcena. Tell her that I'll be in Kirtland with my mother and sisters within a week."

Ezekiel took the letter and put his hand on Lyman's shoulder. "I'll see this gets to your wife." He turned to go.

"Farewell, Mr. Johnson," Asenath said as she stood and walked Ezekiel to the door. "Tell Mrs. Johnson that I look forward to seeing her next week."

Ezekiel donned his hat. "I'll give my wife your regards, Mrs. Sherman. But we'll be on our way to Fort Dearborn before you arrive in Kirtland."

* * *

It was past eleven when Ezekiel found the home on the flats where his family lived. He held a lantern in one hand and was leading the mule with the other. Candlelight shone in one of the downstairs windows. The rest of the house was dark. Someone was awake.

With a pounding heart, Ezekiel turned away from the house and made his way toward the barn. His old dog, Chief, jumped out of the shadows and barked out an enthusiastic greeting. Ezekiel leaned down and affectionately scratched the animal's ears. At least someone was glad to see him. A moment later, the man, dog, and mule entered the barn together. Leo whinnied loudly. The mule brayed back an answer that was both a greeting and a warning. Ezekiel noticed that the barn smelled more of fresh-cut hay than manure. He had taught his boys well. He untacked the mule, then led him to a straw-softened stall. Ezekiel was lifting a forkful of hay into the stall when he heard a voice outside the barn door.

"Hey, Pa. Welcome home!"

Ezekiel turned as Joe entered the barn. In the shadowy lantern light, the angles of Joe's face broke into a wide grin. The two hugged long and warmly.

After the embrace, Joe brushed his tears away with a soft laugh. "I told Ben you were all right," he said.

"I'm all right, and you are even taller," Ezekiel answered. "Are the rest asleep?"

Joe nodded. "I was up late reading some books that this root doctor named Williams lent me."

"Is everybody here?"

"Yes, more than everybody. Joel and his family. Delcena and her kids, and D. P. Hurlbut. But David and Seth are packed up. They booked passage on a boat for the day after tomorrow. They were going to Chicago to find you."

Ezekiel snorted. "They waited long enough."

Joe put his arm around his pa's shoulders. "That's just because they wanted to give you a chance to find us first. Let's go in and wake everybody up."

Ezekiel shook his head. "Not tonight. Just point the way to Mother's room."

Once inside the house, Joe showed Ezekiel the downstairs room where Julia slept. Before going upstairs, he embraced his father once more. "I'm glad you're home, Pa," Joe whispered.

Ezekiel nodded. He decided to wait until tomorrow to remind Joe that this place was not home.

Ezekiel dimmed the lantern before opening the door to Julia's room. After stepping quietly in, he placed the lantern on the floor. The shallow light cast high ghostly shadows on the walls. He turned and looked at Julia. She slept on her back, the coverlet clumped at her ankles. Her white linen gown twisted around her legs and her long, loose hair framed her face. To him, she was not a middle-aged mother, but a maiden still. Amos was curled up next to her.

Julia stirred. Her consciousness lingered in that dimly lit place between sleep and wakefulness. She blinked, confused and vulnerable. Ezekiel saw that she looked frightened. He moved quickly to the edge of the bed. He cleared his throat. "Julia, it's me, Zeke."

"Zeke?" she questioned as her look transformed from fear to radiance. In her dream-like state she was young again, and the man she loved had come for her, like one rising from the mists of the dead, to lift her in his strong arms. Ezekiel saw the rapture in her look. One hoarse, gasping sob clutched him as he clasped his wife in his arms. His silent tears wet her hair and cheek.

In a moment, Julia was fully awake. "Oh, my husband, my husband! You are alive!" she cried as she wrapped her arms around him so tightly that she could feel their hearts beat as one.

* * *

"Ben!" Joe held the candle in one hand and shook his brother's shoulder with the other. Benjamin jerked awake. Joe chuckled at his confusion.

"What is it?" Benjamin growled.

"Pa's home," Joseph whispered. "I thought you would want to know. He's fine."

Benjamin shot up into a sitting position. Joe put a hand on his shoulder and pushed him back down.

"I want to see Pa."

Joe grinned and blew out the candle. "Ben, my boy, Pa's so glad to be with Mother again that he doesn't want to see anyone else until morning."

"Are you sure?" Ben questioned, dumbfounded.

"Positive," Joe answered as he crawled into bed. "Go back to sleep, Ben. I just thought you would want to know. Tomorrow's going to be a great day."

"If you're funnin' with me, Joe, I will kill you," Benjamin said.

Joe suppressed a chuckle and whispered back. "Ben, you know that I would never tease about something like this. But if you wake up George and Will, Pa will murder us both."

Benjamin lay back down on his pillow. His heart beat quickly, and he felt an inner glow, like the sun beaming out from inside of him. He couldn't remember feeling this happy in a long, long time.

10

I want my children living near, their faces I must see,
For life would give but little joy, if they were far from me.

George Washington Johnson
(from "The Home I'd Love," *Jottings by the Way,* 34)

The next morning, an hour before daybreak, a congregation of children gathered outside Julia and Ezekiel's closed bedroom door. Mary put the candle in a sconce. Their youthful shadows were long and distorted on the surrounding walls.

"Papa looks dead," four-year-old Amos whispered, enjoying his rare moment as the center of attention. "'Cept for snoring. I sneaked out."

"I bet you're lying." George elbowed his little brother as he stared at the closed door.

"Am not!" The little boy's whisper was nearly a shout.

"Hush, Amos," Esther warned as she put her arm around him. Then her look became doubtful. "But you aren't telling stories, are you?" Amos virulently shook his head.

"Come on!" William exploded. "Let's look and see for ourselves. We only have a minute before David's at us for chores."

"We can't just barge in there like a herd of buffalo!" Mary insisted, her voice of reason rising over her brothers' and sisters'. "We have to knock!"

"If we knock, we'll wake him up," George argued. "Make Pa mad as a bear."

"No. If we interrupt him and Mama without knocking, he'll be mad as a bear," Mary explained.

"Is Grandpa mean?" Sixtus questioned.

William shook his head, "No. But he ain't always nice either."

"He's *always* nice to little grandkids," Esther assured Sixtus.

"Quiet everybody!" William hissed. "I'm peekin' in."

But William didn't have a chance to open the door. As he reached for it, the handle moved. The door creaked open on its own accord. William jumped back. Wide-eyed, the children watched as Ezekiel sprang out, roaring like a bear. He grabbed William and George, his gray hair awry as he picked them up off their feet and hugged them tight. Afterwards, he lifted Esther and Amos and kissed them. They felt his scratchy chin against their soft, young faces and wrapped their arms around his neck. He set them down gently, then picked up his grandson, Sixtus, and swung him high into the air. Before releasing the gangly little boy, Ezekiel chuckled. "Esther spoke the truth! I'm always nice to little grand-kids, though my own kids best beware of Papa Bear!" Ezekiel roared again.

Mary threw her head back and laughed. Ezekiel turned to her, his blonde, brown-eyed girl standing back from the rest, as if teetering on the far brink of childhood. She ran into her father's waiting arms. After hugging Mary, Ezekiel saw Benjamin waiting half-way up the stairs, fighting tears. David and Seth stood behind him.

Joe, Julianne, Almera, and Susan were farther back, leaning on the banister rail. The girls stared in near disbelief. Joe winked at his father and chuckled.

Ezekiel cleared his throat. "The bunch of you are a sight for sore eyes. Come here." Ezekiel opened his arms to his children.

"I won't let you down again, Pa," Benjamin promised as they embraced.

"You never let me down, son," Ezekiel whispered. After he released Benjamin, his eyes met David's and Seth's, the sons he had lost to Mormonism, the two who strove to lead his younger children away from him. There was tension in the air as he locked eyes with them. Finally, Ezekiel let out a breath. "Hello, Seth, David. I hope you've been takin' good care of the family whilst I've been away."

David grinned and stepped forward. He put one arm around his father and the other around Ben. He nodded his head. "You bet, Pa. You had us worried."

Seth put his arm around his father's other shoulder. "Looks like you've saved us a trip. Welcome to Kirtland, Pa."

"Can't say I'm glad to be in Kirtland," Ezekiel snorted. "But I'm glad to see my family in good health."

Then Julianne, Almera, and Susan hurried down the staircase to embrace their father. Julianne led the way. Her feet were light and her smile joyous. Almera rubbed sleep and tears out of her lovely, dark eyes before she kissed her father's ruddy cheek. Then Ezekiel greeted Susie, whose black, tear-filled eyes held such tenderness that it nearly broke his heart.

Delcena came with a baby in her arms and two little girls pulling on her skirts. Ezekiel was to them in an instant. He kissed the little girls and wrapped his arms around his daughter and grandson. "Princess, I've a letter for you from Lyman."

Before Delcena responded, Ezekiel suddenly stopped and turned. He had heard the sound of Nancy's crutches. Her gait was broken and painful, her gray eyes so much like his mother's.

"Papa, dearest Papa," Nancy cried out.

"Beloved child," he said as he held her close, unable to stop his tears. "My precious Nancy."

After the embrace, Ezekiel brushed the tears from his eyes and turned back to the rest. He said, "Looks like we're all here, but one. Where's Joel?"

"Up here, Pa!" Joel called from the top of the stairs. Sariah fussed in his arms. "Annie will be out in a moment. She's not feeling too chipper this morning. You are going to be a grandfather again."

Ezekiel shouted a congratulatory "Hurrah!" Then he looked once more at the eager, beautiful, apprehensive faces of those around him, and for a fleeting moment he believed in the possibility of heaven.

* * *

In the early afternoon, Julia took a break from the laundry to walk through the orchard. She stopped for a moment and leaned against a tree in the cool shade. Last night had brought into the forefront of her mind the depth of the bond she shared with her husband. It had been like traveling back in time, and the spark of their relationship had flamed brightly for a moment. But it was daylight now, and accounts would soon be due. Little between them had really changed. She would have to tell him that she would not move to Chicago.

Ezekiel stepped out onto the porch and called her name. "I'm here, Zeke," she called back.

He walked over through the stark sunlight. Julia thought again of the tenderness of his homecoming. Was there a way to convince him that they could build a life here?

Julia smiled at her husband and spoke. "Look how the peaches are coming, and the apple trees look healthy. The maples will yield ample syrup next year. We'll have surplus to sell or trade."

Ezekiel looked out at the orchard. His words were blunt. "Julia, I've a quarter section of land with a cabin on it in Fort Dearborn. Begin packing. We leave in two days."

Julia's eyes burned, but her spine straightened, and her muscles tensed. She had to be strong right now, as strong as the prophetess Deborah. Her voice was crystal clear. "God brought us here. This is our home now."

Ezekiel's head jerked back to her. "Your home is with me."

"I traded Joel the teams and oxen for ownership in this house. I'm staying, Ezekiel."

His chill, gray eyes bored into her. "You've been planning this all along. You never meant to join me."

"That's not true! I feared for you and prayed for you," Julia cried out, wishing there were a way to make him understand. "Had I received your letter, I would have gone to Fort Dearborn. But it was Providence that kept your letter from us. It was God who brought us here and you safely back to us. I will not take my children from this place! Not after all our Heavenly Father has done."

"*Our* children!" Ezekiel roared as he broke. "They are not *your* children alone!"

"I know that," Julia whispered. His children were his saving grace, the purpose of his life. "I will not leave. Can't you stay here with us?"

"Julia! What evil choices you hand me!" Ezekiel cried out. His pain shot through Julia. "Must I live without the love of my wife and children, or break like a dumb animal under your yoke? How can you do this to the husband who loves you?"

"Forgive me, Ezekiel," Julia said with tears in her voice. "But when my Heavenly Father speaks, I cannot disobey. I beg you to stay here with us! The children love you. I love you."

"The law will support me." Ezekiel's voice was cutting as a knife. "Is that what you want? It will cut Ben in two! Like the child brought before King Solomon."

"It will cut us all in two," Julia whispered brokenly.

Ezekiel breathed raggedly, his face reddening as he shook with frustration and rage. Julia's dark eyes filled with tears of compassion and sorrow, mingled with the slightest shadow of fear. Yet her shoulders were straight, and she would not bend.

When Ezekiel spoke, his words were bitter, and his fists were knotted at his sides. "I'll stay, but against my will. I'll not cut my children in two!" He spun around and walked quickly away.

Julia could not stop her tears. Last night her husband had enfolded her in loving arms. Would that moment ever come again? "Zeke," she cried out before he was out of earshot. "My heart breaks!"

His head pivoted, and he looked at her standing there, her shoulders straight, with tears shining on her face. "And mine is shattered."

* * *

Nancy had been watching her parents out the window. She rose to her crutches and limped out of the door and carefully down the porch steps. As she hobbled over to Julia, she called out, "Mother, are you all right?"

Julia leaned against the tree for support. Sorrow and relief flooded her soul. Sorrow for the wedge between them, and relief that the family would not be torn asunder. "Oh Nancy, your father is staying," she cried, with tears streaming down her face. "But I fear—I fear it has cost me his love!"

Nancy joined Julia under the tree. "Papa's love for you runs deep, Mama. As deep as the ocean."

* * *

A day later, at dusk, Ezekiel rode his mule across the bridge that spanned the Chagrin River and led into the town of Mentor. His mood was dark. He made his way to the tavern.

After buying a drink, Ezekiel sat down at a corner table. He downed his brandy, then went to the counter to purchase another. The liquor would soon warm him and bring temporary solace.

Three men, dressed in broadcloth suits, entered the tavern. Ezekiel watched them stride in with an air of superiority and purpose. He let out a mirthless laugh when he noticed that one of them was D. P. Hurlbut, Julia's house guest. Ezekiel turned to the bartender and spoke in a low voice. "I know the young one; who are the other two?"

"Sir, you are a unique customer. That young fellow is the only person in here I don't know, other than you," the bartender said, obviously curious. When Ezekiel did not offer any more information, he added, "The old fellow is Orris Clapp, a rich Campbellite. The other's Grandison Newell, a farmer and business man, one of the most well-to-do fellows in these parts."

Ezekiel nodded, wondering what Hurlbut was up to. The three approached a group of men toward the front of the tavern. Hurlbut and Orris Clapp sat down. Grandison Newell spoke like an orator. "My friends, I want you to meet Doctor Philastus Hurlbut. This gentleman has just returned to us from a Mormon mission."

A man called out, "Grandison, what are you doin' bringing a Mormon missionary here? Do we get to tar and feather 'im?"

Newel raised his hand to quiet the fellow. "Isaiah, I said that Doctor Hurlbut has returned to *us*. He is no longer a Mormon."

A spontaneous cheer went up. Newel continued. "Doctor Hurlbut has discovered an interesting fact. The notorious Book of Mormon is a work of fiction and imagination and was written more than twenty years ago. If his hunch proves true, this will completely divest Joseph Smith of all claims to the character of an honest man, and place him an immeasurable distance from the high station he pretends to occupy as prophet of God." Cheers erupted around the room, and Hurlbut rose to shake hands like a politician.

"Where's the proof?" Ezekiel called out from the counter.

All eyes reverted to him. Newel addressed Ezekiel. "You're a newcomer, sir. Are you Mormon?"

Ezekiel glanced from Newel to Hurlbut. Philastus gazed at him with a calculating smile, but did not offer any obvious public recognition. Ezekiel snorted. The drink had gone to his head, but it was not bringing comfort. "Good day, Philastus," he said sarcastically. Then he looked back at Newel. "No, I ain't Mormon. That church took my wife from me."

The elderly man named Orris Clapp stood up, walked over to Ezekiel, and shook his hand. "Welcome, sir. 'Tis no shame to have kin who are Mormonites. Mormonism ensnared my daughter and her husband, John Murdock. When she sickened, the fool tried to bless her rather than call a doctor. She's dead now and my grandchildren are farmed out to other Mormons while their no account father walks the country preaching false doctrine."

Ezekiel nodded slightly to the man, then looked back at Hurlbut. "Philastus, where's your proof?"

Hurlbut stood and smiled at the group. "As you can see, Mr. Johnson and I are old friends from Chautauqua County, New York."

Ezekiel snorted again.

Hurlbut went on, "We both know firsthand the way Joseph Smith destroys families, coercing money from his innocent followers, demanding obedience like a cursed king. He wields ungodly power. And there are the countless poor who are flooding into Kirtland under his command. This will wreck the county economically and politically."

Hurlbut waited briefly for his listeners to absorb what he had said, then continued. "Let us put this evil to rest. I am acquainted with individuals who told me that the Book of Mormon was copied from the writings of a man who is deceased. It was originally intended to be a fictional romance. I am willing to travel and obtain written statements. This charade will end."

"Good luck to you!" someone called out. The men at the tables applauded. At that point, Grandison Newel stood up and put his arm around Hurlbut. "Sadly, this young gentleman has lost his fortune and friends to Mormonism. It is up to us to organize as a committee and help him in his quest."

Orris Clapp took off his hat and put twenty dollars in it. "Let me be the first to contribute. Gentlemen, this endeavor is worth our time and our money."

As Clapp passed around the hat, Ezekiel dug into his pocket. When the hat came his way, he put in a dollar. Looking levelly into Orris Clapp's eyes, he commented bitterly. "Today's my lucky day. I'd pay a pretty penny to get Philastus Hurlbut out of town."

* * *

The slanted rays of the sun bent and hazed over the brickyard. Steam rose from three out of the ten kilns where low fires removed the water from the bricks. This water-smoke blurred the blue of the sky as it rose to meet the black smoke billowing out of four other kilns to the east. In these kilns, the bricks were being fired at a high temperature, twenty-four hours a day for seven days. If it was not done correctly, the bricks would either explode or become clinkers—too cracked or warped to be usable. In the remaining three kilns the fire hole had been bricked over, allowing the heat to slowly dissipate from the previously fired bricks inside. This cooling process took an additional week.

Under Joel's supervision, the men worked in the yard. Seth, Benjamin, and Joe E. labored as off-bearers, moving the bricks from the molding table to the drying table, then to the kilns. They stoked the fires during the day and dissembled the kilns when a load was finished. Joel constantly watched the color and density of the smoke, making sure the temperature was gauged correctly.

To David, Don Carlos, and Almon fell the task of procuring the necessary wood to burn the bricks. During daylight hours, they felled trees and chopped logs, hauling load after load to the brickyard. They stayed at the brickyard each night so that Joel could go home to his wife and children. When darkness fell, they slept under the stars or beneath a wagon when it rained. They labored like sentries, taking turns stoking the fires, constantly protecting the bricks they burned for the House of the Lord.

* * *

One evening Julianne and Susan drove the wagon to the yard to bring food to the men. Julianne noticed that while David and Don Carlos stoked one of the kilns, Almon stood close by—chatting, not working.

When Almon noticed the women, he left his friends and ran over. "Allow me," he said gallantly as he gave his hand to Susan and helped her down first. As Susan stepped out of the wagon, Juli observed that Almon's hair was combed and his clothes relatively clean. Almon grinned up at Julianne and offered his hand. She took it. Even his fingernails were clean.

After helping Juli out of the wagon, he continued holding her hand. "Almon, did you know we were coming?" Julianne questioned with a bright smile.

Almon's green eyes sparkled. "David told me earlier." He kissed her hand. "Hence a bath in the Chagrin."

David looked over at his sisters. "I'll never tell him again when ladies are coming. We haven't gotten any work out of him for the past hour."

"Two hours," Don Carlos corrected.

Almon laughed. "They are making me pay by taking the first watch tonight. Ladies, when Miss Agnes brought breakfast this morning, Carlos ran to the river to wash the soot off his face. David is the only one of us immune to the charms of the female sex. He must have too many sisters."

Julianne nudged Almon with her elbow. "No one can have too many sisters."

Susan smiled slightly, "No Juli, I think it depends on who the sisters are."

A moment later, Carlos and David finished stoking the fire and joined the group. Joel, Seth, Joe, and Ben approached from the far section of the yard where they had just dissembled a kiln.

Almon helped Julianne spread out an old quilt. The group sat down. Susan and Julianne served them fried chicken, thick slices of bread, and fresh vegetables. After Joel blessed the food, Susan sat down near Ben and Joe. "How are the bricks coming?" she queried.

Joel's brow furrowed. He shook his head, "Not good."

Seth explained, "Susie, we're still getting a good deal of clinkers. We can't use them to build the House of God."

"What causes that?" Susan asked.

Seth shrugged. "Sometimes it's the judgment of the brick makers. But not in this case. Joel is meticulous, and the fires are roaring all night. It has to be the quality of the clay. At the rate we're going, it will take years to burn enough bricks for the Lord's house."

"Joseph and Hyrum are considering hauling stone from a nearby quarry," Don Carlos remarked.

"But for now, we burn bricks," David added. "We work harder and faster. We make up for the clinkers by increasing our own efforts. We dig more clay, build more kilns, and chop more wood."

Almon raised his eyebrows. "How can we do that, David? We're already working twenty-six out of every twenty-four hours."

Joe E., whose usually lively brown eyes were dimmed and red from exhaustion and smoke, leaned back on his elbow. "I'm with Almon. I don't see how we can do more."

"Me neither," Ben added.

Julianne looked around at their worn faces. Seth was stoic, but tired. Benjamin and Joe looked utterly exhausted. Last night, Joel had mentioned that he didn't see how David and Don Carlos could keep up the pace they had set for themselves. Only Almon looked chipper, and Juli smiled inside, knowing why.

She turned her gaze from the men and watched thoughtfully as the black smoke from the kilns seeped into the crimson sky. Then she turned back and addressed her eldest brother. "Joel, can't the bricks burn by themselves for an hour or so while we play some games? I think what we all need is some fun!"

"Hear! Hear!" Almon agreed.

Joel surveyed the brickyard, then nodded. "The bricks should be all right for a couple of hours. I'll check the kilns and head home. Julianne, if you can get this bunch interested in a game, more power to you." Joel stood up and added, "Seth, you coming with me? Ben and Joe can escort the girls home."

Susan glanced sharply at her oldest brother. "Girls?" Sue questioned. "Juli and I are women and could escort our little brothers home."

The setting sun lit the gold in David's eyes. "Susie, you are certainly a grown lady. But Julianne?" he teased. Julianne humphed at her brother.

"I'll look out for the ladies," Almon offered quickly. "Seth, you can go or stay, whatever you please."

Seth eyed Almon, who was sitting extremely close to Julianne. "I'll stay."

Carlos looked over at David, and the two chuckled. "Almon, my friend," David declared, "you are as predictable as the seasons."

After the meal, Juli and Almon conferred in whispers. They built eight low stool-like seats from the brick clinkers and set them in a circle. Almon kindled a campfire in the center. Darkness descended, the smoke giving the sky a grayish, purple hue. A quarter moon rose. Julianne asked them all to move from the blanket and take a seat around the fire.

After a nod from Julianne, Almon picked up a stick, about an inch in diameter and two feet long. He stuck the end of it into the fire until it flamed. Taking the stick out of the fire and holding it up, the flames lighted his features. He raised his eyebrows twice. "The bunch of you look half dead. So Juli and I have decided that its time to play JACK'S ALIVE!"

Almon immediately handed the stick to Juli, who held it for a handful of seconds and passed it off to Seth. Seth gave it to Sue, who gave it to Joe. Joe held it for a full moment before handing it to Ben. Ben quickly handed it to Don Carlos. Carlos forced it into David's hand just as the spark died. "David, you lose!" Carlos laughed. "Susan, would you do the honors? I'm sure you're a better artist than I."

Don Carlos handed Susan the stick. With a self-conscious half smile, Sue carefully drew a mustache under David's nose with the charred end of the stick. Then she stood back to look at him.

"You better be done, Sue." David grinned evilly. "Or watch out!" Quietly and fearlessly, Susan added curly-cues on the ends of the mustache.

The game continued until most of the men in the group had ash-drawn mustaches, whiskers, pointed beards, and exaggerated eyebrows. Somehow, only Susan and Juli managed to escape without "Jack" dying in their hands. But on the final round, Almon held the stick until the spark appeared dead. Then Almon handed the stick to Julianne and blew fiercely on the hot end. The ember reddened for a split second and died out. Juli was left with the dead "Jack" in her hands.

"That's cheating," Juli exclaimed. "You can't revive Jack by blowing on him!"

"Let's take a vote," Almon suggested. Only Susan and Seth voted in their sister's behalf. The rest agreed with Almon. Julianne lost.

Almon took the stick from her. "All right, lovely one," he said. "Would you like a mustache, beard, or sideburns? Your eyebrows are too perfect to tamper with."

"None of them," Juli smiled. "I choose the penalty."

"If you choose *the* penalty, you realize that I get to choose *what* penalty," Almon said playfully.

"Of course. What do you want?" Juli questioned with a coy twinkle in her eye. "My hairpin, my brooch, or a stocking?"

Almon scratched his chin. His eyes glinted mischievously. "Hmm. Something more personal." Joe and Ben eyed each other.

"Give him a strand of your hair," Don Carlos suggested.

"Or a bit of toenail," David said, laughing.

Almon shook his head. "There's only one thing I'll take in payment."

"Just ask for a kiss and get it over with," Ben blurted out.

"Tell Juli to strike hands with the wittiest, nod at the prettiest, and kiss the one she loves best," Joe suggested with a grin.

Almon glanced at Joe. "A good idea, but not what I had in mind." He turned to Juli. "Miss Julianne Johnson, I will only be satisfied with one gift in payment. Your hand."

Julianne was momentarily speechless.

Seth cut in quickly. "Julianne's hand is attached to her wrist and therefore unavailable."

Almon turned to Julianne, his eyes searching hers in the firelight. "Is Seth right, dearest Juli?"

"My hand is unavailable as payment in a game," Julianne said clearly. "But if a walk would do as payment, I would love to take one with you."

Almon nodded and stood up. He and Julianne left the group. Almon kept his distance from her as the two strolled to the far side of the glowing kilns.

When they were out of sight, Julianne stopped. "Almon, what's wrong?"

"How can you ask me that after telling me that your hand is unavailable?"

Julianne took both his hands in hers. Should she tell Almon how he filled her soul, stirring great tenderness there? "I can't give something away in a game that is already gone. My hand and heart have long belonged to you."

"Then why didn't you say so, Juli? In front of your brothers. Seth looks at me like I'm trespassing whenever I touch you. David and Carlos make a joke of how much I love you."

"You aren't a joke, Almon, though you make others laugh. That is part of what I love about you."

Almon pulled Julianne close to him. She felt his heart pounding. Juli shivered though the night was warm.

"I'm frightened, Almon," she whispered as she rested her head on his shoulder.

"Of what?"

Juli smelled the smoke from the kilns. She remembered Seth's explanation about the bricks. If the quality of the clay wasn't strong enough, they exploded or warped in the heat. "Almon, are we made of stuff strong enough to hold together through the fires of life? Will God walk with us down our path of matrimony, keeping us safe like Shadrach, Meshach, and Abednego?"

Almon enfolded her in his arms. "We're not clinkers, Juli. We'll hold together through whatever God or the devil sends our way. You can be sure of that. I'll shield you from any fire that surrounds us. You are my sunrise, the answer to my every prayer!"

Julianne looked into his eyes. "My hand is here, darling Almon, awaiting the moment when you are ready to claim it in matrimony." Almon Babbitt confidently and tenderly kissed the woman he loved.

* * *

On the other side of the brickyard, the rest of the group stood and bid David and Don Carlos farewell. Susan explained to Seth that she wanted to walk home tonight. She had spent the day working in the house. The warm, night air felt soothing. Ben and Joe agreed to drive the wagon home.

As they headed through the darkness, Seth carried the lantern, and Sue's arms swung gently at her sides.

"Does Julianne really love Almon?" Seth asked.

Sue nodded. "With all of her heart."

"Do you think he would make her a good husband?"

Susan was quiet for a moment, thinking of the time when she had loved Almon. Yet tonight she felt peace. Julianne and Almon were made for each other. She answered softly. "Yes, Seth. I think that they will be very happy together. They fit together somehow."

"But I worry that he isn't steady enough. That she might be unhappy someday."

"Annie, Joel, and David know him the best and esteem him highly. And he has always been steady in his kindness toward our family, his commitment to the gospel, and in his love for Julianne. It won't do anyone any good to fight against the force that pulls those two together."

Seth sighed. "Then I suppose I should start treating Almon like a brother rather than like a cockroach."

Sue giggled. "If you've treated him as a cockroach, I don't suppose anyone has noticed. Thank goodness you are a gentleman, or poor Almon would be squashed."

Susan and Seth walked on companionably. Though Seth was nine years older and a man, there were ways in which they were much alike.

"Is there anything you don't know, little sister?"

Susan's smile dimmed. "I don't know how we will ever get the temple finished with so many clinkers."

"I don't know either," Seth answered. "Yet with God's help, we will build it. The cornerstones are to be laid three days from now."

In the lantern light, Susan's smile lit her eyes. "How I am looking forward to sewing the curtains and cloths for the House of the Lord."

* * *

Back at the brickyard, David and Don Carlos spread out their bedrolls and climbed between the quilts. There was a spot in the sky where the stars were bright, too far away for the smoke from the kilns to touch their glory. Both young men focused on that portion of the sky.

"David," Carlos said, "three days from now, on the morning that the cornerstones are laid for the temple, I'm to be given the Melchizedek Priesthood, to be ordained an elder."

David was silent, still staring at the sky. Don Carlos continued. "That way I can be one of the twenty-four elders who lay the cornerstones. Joseph says it's right, but I'm so much younger than the others. And no one has worked harder for the Lord's house than you, David."

David turned to look in the direction of his friend. But it was too dark to see Carlos's features. Yet David felt the warmth of their companionship. It touched David that Carlos was concerned that he might be saddened that he had not been chosen. David looked back up at the sky.

"Of course it's right," David said quietly. "Carlos, no one is more worthy to bear the high priesthood than you."

"But there are so many older than me, David. With so much more experience. Will they hate me for this honor?"

David smiled slightly. "The people admire you, Carlos. This will bring them joy, and you will bless the lives of the Saints."

"And you, David, will it bring you joy?"

"Yes, Carlos, oh yes!" David exclaimed. "And someday, when I have done all that God has asked me to do, when my sacrifice is acceptable to my Savior, I too will be an elder in Israel."

"God has already accepted your sacrifice, David. He knows your great heart. If you speak to Joseph, I think you will receive the priesthood now."

"Not yet, Carlos. I must know, from God, that I'm fully ready for that blessing, that I am pure and clean before Him."

"Then will you come to our home in the morning on the day the cornerstones are laid, and see me ordained? It's a journey I would share with you."

"Of course I'll be there. One of many journeys together."

After a few moments of quiet, Carlos spoke again. "Twenty-four elders will participate in the ceremony, each six laying one of the stones. Joseph showed me a list of the elders. He wants Joel, Seth, and Lyman Sherman to participate."

David grinned. "Let's hope that Lyman is back by then."

Carlos chuckled. "I suppose Joseph's faith will get him here in time."

David lay awake for a time, sleep eluding him. "Carlos," he ventured quietly, unsure if his friend was still awake.

"Yes."

"Have you ever experienced the gift of tongues?"

Carlos spoke quietly. "No. Have you?"

"No."

Carlos went on. "But I've seen others sing and speak in tongues. Joseph has talked to me about this gift. He told me that it is sometimes the ability to understand and speak other languages when preaching the gospel. It is also manifest when righteous men, like Brigham Young, speak in the pure tongue of Father Adam, and someone else interprets by the power of the Holy Ghost. Joseph explained that this is a gift that we need to be very careful with as a church. When it is from God, there are no wild gyrations, only dignity and sacredness. This gift can easily be misinterpreted by men, or twisted by the adversary."

David did not speak again. Don Carlos's breathing became heavy and regular with sleep. But David lay awake, thinking about his friend's words, knowing that if he ever experienced such a gift from God, then he would know with a surety that he was worthy to hold that high and holy priesthood. He did not sleep until he heard Almon return and check the fires.

11

On Zion's sacred hill,
And by the Lord's command,
The Saints, his temple build,
In Joseph's promised land . . .

. . . With heart and hand,
His Saints obey
His just command,
Without delay.

Joel Hills Johnson
(*Hymns of Praise for the Young*, Hymn 141, 139–140)

June 23, 1833

In the morning, David knocked on the door of the Smith home. He wore a stock tie, a pressed linen shirt, a vest, and clean trousers. Hyrum answered the door, his eyes characteristically calm, his smile welcoming. "Hello Brother David. Come wait in the sitting room while I go and get the rest of the family."

David walked in. He was greeted by Mother Smith, Carlos's younger sister, Lucy, Mary Bailey, and Agnes Coolbrith. The ladies were sitting in chairs around the perimeter of the room. Mother Smith explained that they had just finished putting the house in order and were now waiting for the men to join them. Agnes sat very still with her white hands folded in her lap. She looked up at

David. Her loveliness did not escape him. Agnes caught his eye and smiled a "hello."

A few moments later, Father Smith, Joseph, Samuel, and Don Carlos entered the room together. Samuel took a seat next to Mary Bailey. Don Carlos beamed as he shook David's hand. After the greetings, Mother Smith directed David to a seat near the hearth. "You and my Carlos do clean up well," she whispered with a twinkle in her eye.

Joseph lifted a chair and moved it to the center of the small room. He invited Don Carlos to sit down. Father Smith, Joseph, and Hyrum stood around his chair and placed their hands on Carlos's head. Father Smith spoke, "By the power of the Holy Melchizedek Priesthood, we lay our hands upon your head and confer upon you the Melchizedek Priesthood and ordain you to the office of elder therein."

Father Smith continued blessing his seventeen-year-old son, his darling boy. "Don Carlos, you shall be great in the sight of the Lord, for He sees and knows the integrity of your heart, and you shall be blessed; all that know you shall bless you. You shall live to fulfill all that the Lord has sent you to do. Even so. Amen."

A burning filled David as he listened to Don Carlos's blessing, a pulsating desire to hold this priesthood that was the power of God given to man to act in His name. Yet he remembered his weaknesses—his frustration with this very power when Nancy was not healed, his inability to stop the anger he sometimes felt toward his father, and the way he had deeply hurt Kathryn Clay and Hope Randall. The muscles in David's arms and shoulders tensed. He thought about how Philastus Hurlbut had been ordained an elder and fallen. Before David received this gift, he must know that he would not fall again, that he had gained power over his passions, his temper, and his own will. *Trust in the Lord with all thy heart.* These words entered David's mind as if spoken by a voice. David breathed out slowly, his shoulders relaxing.

After the ordination, he embraced Don Carlos. "A new journey has begun, my friend," David said warmly.

"A path we journey down together," Carlos commented.

David then turned as the Prophet said, "Now to lay those cornerstones."

"Yes!" David exclaimed jubilantly.

Joseph smiled at David. "This is a great day, Brother David, one of those days when we shall witness an outpouring of the Spirit of God."

David grinned. "One of those days that makes the others worth living."

Father Smith put his arm around David's shoulder. "Yes. It's good to have you here, David. Your friendship with my Carlos is a great blessing."

* * *

At noon, when the sun was its highest point in the sky, a congregation gathered at the temple lot to attend the ceremony. Julia stood with her own crowd of children. David, who had walked over with the Smiths, came up to her and kissed her cheek. He stood on her right hand, swinging Amos up on his shoulders so that the little boy could see. Ben and Joe did the same with Joel's Sixtus and Delcena's Alvira.

Nearby, William and George caused a mild ruckus by stepping on each other's toes. Julianne and Almon stepped between them. Almon threatened to torture the younger boys if they made another sound.

Mary bounced her namesake, little Mary Sherman, in her arms. She pointed at Lyman, who stood with the elders. "Lookie! There's your daddy. Aren't you happy he came home yesterday?"

Next to Mary, Nancy sat in a chair. She had her arm around Esther, who leaned into her. Esther squinted in the bright sunlight. In front of them, also in chairs, Delcena cradled her baby boy, and Annie softly crooned into Sariah's ear.

Slightly in front of the rest of the family, Almera and Susan stood together whispering. The sun beat down brightly on their white bonnets. Julia wondered what men would be lucky enough to marry them one day. Then a feeling of warmth encircled her.

She felt the hope and joy of the moment, glad about the House of God and glad to be with the Saints.

A few minutes later, Julia watched in awe as the First Presidency laid the first stone. As the ceremony continued, she saw the dignity of her sons, Joel and Seth, as they worked with the other elders, laying another granite stone as gently as if it had living breath.

When the next stone was laid, Julia looked over and saw the joy in Lucy Mack Smith's eyes. Sister Smith's husband and four of her sons were participating. Julia's breath caught in her throat for an instant as she felt the old, familiar heartache, that wedge between herself and Ezekiel.

A few moments later, the final group of elders laid the last stone. Among them was Edmund Durfee, one of the missionaries who had taught Julia the gospel. Her son-in-law, Lyman Sherman, was next to him. Julia thought of another who had been so close to these two—Joseph Brackenbury who was no longer with them in this world. Her family was indebted to him.

Julia noticed that Delcena was crying. Was she moved by the ceremony or was it more than that? Her husband was with her again but would almost certainly leave soon on another mission. After laying the stone, Lyman stood and looked over at Delcena. She smiled at him through her tears. Julia was moved by her daughter's courage.

Then, the ceremony was complete. Julia's voice joined Emma Smith's clear, strong soprano.

May peace attend thy gate,
And joy within thee wait,
To bless the soul of every guest:
The man that seeks thy peace,
And wishes thine increase,
A thousand blessings on him rest!

My tongue repeats her vows,
"Peace to this sacred house!

For here my friends and kindred dwell:"
And since my glorious God
Makes thee his blest abode,
My soul shall ever love thee well.

* * *

Two hundred yards away, unnoticed by those who gathered, Ezekiel stood beneath a tree with a bottle of brandy in his hand. He turned his head away from the Mormon meeting and noticed two men approaching the Methodist meetinghouse, the only other public building in sight of the temple lot. They did not notice him, but looked at the singing congregation.

Ezekiel heard the first gentleman snort derisively. "Do those people really believe in their own doctrines? In Joe Smith's idle, foolish whims?"

The other scratched his chin and shook his head, mystified. "Some of them sacrifice much; they leave their homes, family, and sometimes wealth." Shaking his head, he continued, "These things denote sincerity, almost plead in their behalf."

The first man looked keenly at the second. "You sound as if you want the Mormonites here in Kirtland!"

The man shook his head and smiled sadly. "No. But perhaps we judge them too harshly. I suppose man has ever been, and perhaps ever will be, the sport of some delusion."

A sense of foreboding and powerlessness coursed through Ezekiel. *My family is the sport of this delusion. And there is nothing I can do about it.*

* * *

The next afternoon, Ezekiel rode to Mentor looking for a carpentry shop where he could practice his trade. He stopped to buy a drink at the tavern and to inquire about work. The bartender gave Ezekiel directions to an old carpentry shop near the river. He explained that the owner of the shop was on his deathbed. A young man named Samuel Prescott now rented it. There might be room for another man.

Ezekiel downed his brandy and left the tavern. He rode directly to Prescott's shop. As he tied his mule to a post, he glimpsed an empty carpenter's bench through a small side window. When Ezekiel walked through the front door, a man looked up from working, and his hammer stilled.

"Samuel Prescott?" Ezekiel queried.

The man nodded and walked over to Ezekiel and put out his hand. "Sounds as though you know me, but I don't believe I've met you, sir."

Ezekiel briskly shook the man's hand. "The name's Ezekiel Johnson. I'm new in town and looking for a carpenter's bench to rent. Did some work in Fredonia, New York, previously."

Prescott was of average height, and broadly built, with hair as flaxen as a child's. He had full cheeks and a full mouth. His wide-set blue eyes were heavily lidded and his hands overly large. He considered a moment, then spoke, "You can work the bench for twenty dollars a month."

Ezekiel whistled and shook his head. "I can't afford it. I've a family of fifteen children to feed."

Prescott raised his light eyebrows. "Any good-looking daughters?"

"Just seven of them."

Prescott chuckled. "Fifteen dollars a month, one for each of your children. On the condition that I get to meet your girls."

Ezekiel snorted and nodded. He reached into his pocket and took fifteen dollars out. He handed the money to Samuel Prescott. "As for my girls, we'll see about that after I get to know you better."

"Done," Samuel Prescott said as he emphatically shook Ezekiel's hand.

* * *

That evening, as the moon rose in the summer sky, Ezekiel walked out onto the porch where Seth, Lyman, and Delcena were talking.

His son-in-law was the first to speak to him. "Father Johnson, I've rented some land." Lyman glanced over at Delcena, who was sitting on the porch bench, covered with a linen blanket as she nursed Albey. "As soon as I can I'll get a cabin built, then we'll be moving out."

"When do you plan to start building?" Ezekiel questioned.

"Tomorrow."

Seth spoke up. "I'll talk to David and Joel. We'll rotate men at the brickyard so that you have someone working each day."

"That's still not much manpower," Ezekiel commented gruffly. "The Shermans need their own place as soon as possible. I'll be there tomorrow morning."

Delcena glanced at her father. "Are you that anxious to have us out of your house, Papa?" she asked, half teasing.

"It's not my house, Princess," Ezekiel answered. His words contained a bitter edge. He turned to Lyman and continued. "I heard Philastus Hurlbut talk in the tavern before he left town. When he gets back, he aims to destroy Mormonism, and he thinks he'll have the tools to do it. He'll be working from this house trying to ruin the very thing that you and my boys are dedicated to." Ezekiel snorted softly, but without mirth. "All of you know how I feel about Philastus Hurlbut and about Mormonism. It seems like God Himself would find this situation laughable."

A tense silence filled the porch. In the distance, laughter floated to them from the back of the house. It was the sound of the children, watching for fireflies.

Ezekiel noted the frustrated tension in Lyman's jaw at the mention of Hurlbut. Ezekiel shook his head and added, "Lyman, you need to get your house done before Philastus gets back. You and your cousin can't live under the same roof—not with things the way they are."

Ezekiel then looked at his daughter nursing the baby, her eyes troubled. He affectionately touched her shoulder. "Princess, I'm gong to the tavern for a spell. Tell your mother not to wait up."

* * *

The next morning, Ezekiel and Lyman hauled wooden planks from the flats to Lyman's lot. When they arrived, a man was walking around the land as if he were studying out the best place for the foundation. Lyman grinned and greeted him with an enthusiastic shout. "Brother Brigham, I thought you were leaving this week."

Brigham Young's temples crinkled when he smiled. "Father Bosley and I leave in a few days. In the meantime, word is that you could use a hand."

Lyman grinned. "I wish I could pay you what you're worth."

"Let's trade a day for a day. I'll be back in a month to settle here in Kirtland. I'll come calling."

Lyman nodded. "And I'll have my tools ready."

While Lyman continued to talk with Young, Ezekiel slowly lifted a plank from the wagon. He remembered meeting Young nearly a year ago when the man came through Chautauqua County. He knew that Young had left his motherless children to serve a mission for the Mormons. The man had come to Kirtland after his mission to see Joseph Smith before returning home. Ezekiel couldn't understand how a man could put religion before his little ones. Ezekiel stopped momentarily and watched the two men talking like brothers. Young spoke simply and directly, while Lyman talked with his hands and his eyes.

The morning lengthened as the men worked together. A stiff breeze arose, the clouds moving overhead, the world switching every few minutes from shadow to bright sunlight. As he worked the boards, Ezekiel thought about Joseph Smith's God. He was illusive, like a blinking star, a magnetic weight drawing men and women with such force that they couldn't break loose. He wondered what information Philastus Hurlbut would bring back. Like the vacillating sunshine and shadow, he couldn't decide whether he wished Hurlbut success or failure.

As the hours passed, Ezekiel noted that Young was a hard worker, unspoiled by wealth or greed. The man didn't talk too much or too little, but when he spoke, his words had purpose. Young was clearly a skilled carpenter, though his boots had holes in them, and his trousers were threadbare. Missionary work didn't pay very well. At the end of the day, Ezekiel shook Young's hand. "I've rented a carpenter's bench in Mentor," he offered. "When you come back, I'm willing to share the bench with you."

Brigham smiled broadly. "Thank you, Father Johnson."

A moment later, as Ezekiel watched Brigham shake Lyman's hand in farewell, Ezekiel wondered how many more times he'd be fool enough to help some young Mormon.

* * *

August 10, 1833

The morning sun bathed the fields of Kirtland in light as Don Carlos spurred the chestnut mare and galloped to the brickyard. He had gone home last night while David and Almon tended the kilns. But it had not been a restful evening. After dinner, a message had come for the Smith men to make haste to the Whitney store.

There they had found Oliver Cowdery, who had just arrived from Missouri. Oliver's sensitive features had looked haggard, and his eyes were dull from sorrow and exhaustion. Carlos had listened as Oliver described the scenes of terror in Jackson County. Then Oliver had read aloud the mocking and threatening manifesto signed by the mob. Carlos's vision had blurred with tears, in part for the agony in Joseph's eyes. Now it was Carlos's task to take the dire news to his friends.

"Carlos, what is it?" David asked as Carlos reined in the mare. David held the horse while his friend dismounted.

"Terrible news from Zion."

Almon, who was rubbing the sleep out of his eyes, hurried over. Seth, Joe, and Benjamin had arrived a half hour previous and were checking the kilns. Following a shout from David, they quickly joined the others.

Carlos swallowed and began. "Oliver Cowdery came last night from Missouri. On July twentieth, a mob of old citizens gathered in Jackson County, pledging their lives and sacred honor to remove the Saints. They wrote down their demands and threats and took them to Bishop Partridge and Elder Gilbert. When Bishop Partridge asked for time to consult with the First Presidency here in Ohio, the mob threw down Brother Phelps's home, turning his family out, destroying the press and his furnishings. They threatened others and drove women and children into cornfields and thickets. Bishop Partridge was taken from his house and marched to the Independence town square where he and Brother Charles Allen were abused and tarred and feathered. Acid was added to the tar to burn their flesh. Bishop Partridge took it all with such humility and Christlike resignation that the crowd finally dispersed."

Almon's green eyes flashed. "I wouldn't have stood still for that kind of abuse."

Joe E. glanced at Almon, a shudder running through him. "Then you might have ended up dead."

Don Carlos went on. "On July twenty-third, the mob gathered again, bearing bayonets, guns, and a red battle flag. The brethren signed an agreement that half the Saints will leave by January first, and the other half by April first."

"How can they give up Zion?" Ben exclaimed. "Won't the Lord fight our battles?"

"The law is on our side," Seth remarked. "The Saints can't be legally thrown off of the property they lawfully purchased. The courts will rule in their favor."

"They're buying time and avoiding bloodshed," Don Carlos explained. "Oliver asked Joseph what is to be done. Joseph was up all night praying. But he still doesn't have a definite answer."

Almon felt indignant. "How can the Lord be silent at a time like this?"

"That's what I'm wondering too," Ben admitted, his brown eyes confused. Joe nodded. David was silent.

Seth glanced at Almon, then spoke directly to his brothers. "Joe, Bennie, the Lord hasn't been silent. On August second, Joseph received a revelation stating that God has sworn to be Zion's salvation and high tower. In the same revelation, the Savior defines Zion as *the pure in heart.* And on July twenty-third, the very day the mob gathered, we laid the cornerstones for the House of God." Seth took a deep breath and glanced at Don Carlos. "And our beloved Brother Carlos, who has such a pure heart, was given the high priesthood. Aren't these things evidence, that even in the moment of peril, Zion flourishes?"

Benjamin looked into Seth's eyes and nodded briefly. Almon looked up at the fierce sun. He didn't look convinced.

Don Carlos spoke. "And Joseph received another revelation just four days ago." The tension in Carlos's frame began to relax as he spoke. "David and I lay awake two nights ago committing it to memory. *Ye shall live by every word which proceedeth forth out of the mouth of God. For he will give unto the faithful line upon line, precept upon precept; and I will try you and prove you herewith. And whoso layeth down his life in my cause, for my name's sake shall find it again, even life eternal.*"

Don Carlos paused and looked at David. David had been silent during the recital of the events, shock and horror etched in his features.

David drew a breath, then he spoke, his voice trembling with strong emotion. He continued quoting the revelation where Don Carlos left off. "*Therefore, be not afraid of your enemies, for I have decreed in my heart, saith the Lord, that I will prove you in all things, whether you will abide in my covenant, even unto death, that you may be found worthy. For if ye will not abide in my covenant ye are not worthy of me. Therefore, renounce war and proclaim peace, and seek diligently to turn the hearts of the children to their fathers, and the hearts of the fathers to the children.*"

Seth placed his hand on Ben's shoulder and smiled slightly, though there was sadness in his eyes. "The suffering and building of Zion is like this temple we've been commanded to build. We don't know how we shall do it, and the quality of the bricks isn't the best, but the House of God will be built, and we must each do our small part. So it is with Zion and the people, including each of us who is called to carry her forth to the world."

After Seth spoke, there was a pained stillness for a few moments. Don Carlos suggested that the group kneel down and pray together. Don Carlos offered the prayer, pleading for the cause of Zion and for the lives of the people in Jackson County. Then he asked God to purify their hearts that they might do their part and be worthy of eternal life.

When the prayer ended, David looked at the diminishing pile of wood which needed to be replenished in order to keep the bricks burning. He stood and stretched upward, the muscles in his tan arms rippling in the sunlight. "Now we chop wood and burn bricks. We build the temple. We fight today for Zion's cause!"

* * *

Philastus Hurlbut returned to Kirtland four days after Delcena and Lyman moved into their log home. Though he lived with the Johnsons, he had little to do with them. He slept late into the mornings, dining on a quick breakfast that Julia left out. He took supper in his room and seemed so preoccupied with his own thoughts that he hardly seemed to notice the existence of the Johnson family.

One night Philastus and Ezekiel happened to come home at the same time. As they stepped up onto the porch, Hurlbut touched Ezekiel's arm. "There's a meeting tomorrow morning at ten o'clock in the Methodist church. I'm lecturing to all opposed to Mormonism. I guarantee you'd be interested."

"I'll think about it," Ezekiel responded shortly before opening the door.

The next morning Ezekiel went to the brickyard. He walked past the shack where Joseph and Thomas Hancock were molding the bricks. He watched as Joel and Seth unloaded the raw bricks, while Lyman and Almon stacked them into a herringbone pattern to dry. He recalled working with his boys in their own brickyard on the Pomfret farm.

Joel and Seth walked up to their father. Seth held a raw brick in his hand. Joel started to speak, but was overtaken by a fit of coughing.

"You need to stay away from the fires," Ezekiel said shortly. "The smoke always makes your cough worse." He'd noticed a slight cough in David, too, and he wondered silently about the effects of the kiln smoke. Then he turned to Seth and took the brick from him. He studied it. "Are you getting a good deal of clinkers?"

Seth nodded. "Any suggestions?"

"Try drying the bricks longer before you fire them. This clay isn't the best. Are there any more deposits?"

"We keep looking," Seth said with a small smile. "Thanks for the instruction."

"I'm the one who taught you boys to make bricks. Just wanted to make sure you're doing it right."

"Are you headed to the shop?" Joel asked casually.

Lyman and Almon walked up. Ezekiel nodded a greeting before answering Joel's question. "Nope. I'm staying in Kirtland today. As a matter of fact, I'll be near your temple site."

Ezekiel glanced pointedly at Lyman. "Hurlbut's lecturing in the Methodist church at ten o'clock. Thought I'd go and hear what he has to say. I'll let you boys know if there's anything of import."

"If I were you, Pa, I wouldn't waste my time," Joel commented, struggling to keep his voice casual. It galled him that he was harboring in his house the man who was set on destroying the Prophet. He coughed once more. "Anyway, I've got bricks to burn. I'll see you at supper."

Ezekiel tipped his hat. "If I were you, son, I wouldn't waste my time on this quality of clay. Dig deeper for new deposits."

Joel walked away. Seth looked at his father. "We've got an extra spade, Pa, if you'd rather stay with us and dig deep."

Ezekiel cleared his throat. "If I felt like diggin' deep today, I wouldn't be goin' to hear Philastus."

* * *

After Ezekiel left, the men went back to work. As Lyman stacked the bricks with Almon and Seth, his movements were quick and jagged. He accidentally dropped a raw brick and it crumbled into a pile of dirt.

"Are you all right?" Seth asked.

Lyman's large, dark eyes simmered from behind his glasses. He dug his hands into his pockets. "I'm going to the Methodist church to see Philastus."

"I don't think that's a good idea," Seth said. "Lyman, leave Philastus to God. That's what I've had to do with Pa."

"Seth, I baptized him. I keep thinking about the times we stood by each other. I taught him the gospel, and we discussed the Book of Mormon. He asked honest questions, and we prayed together that he would find the answers. I can't put it to rest until I look him in the eye and see what's there."

Seth put his hand on Lyman's arm to detain him. "Not today Lyman. There will be fifty men there who hate the Mormons. How are you going to sit still and listen to Philastus's lies? If you speak up, they will make an example of you."

"I won't open my mouth unless I get a chance to talk to Philastus alone."

Almon spoke up. "Lyman, I'll go with you."

Lyman looked at Almon and nodded. "I'd like the company. I'm gonna go clean off my hands."

As Lyman walked toward the creek, Seth turned to Almon. His look was not friendly. "I can understand why Lyman is interested in what Hurlbut has to say. But why are you? Do you doubt the Book of Mormon?"

Almon's green eyes flashed, and he shot back. "No. But if Lyman and Philastus come to blows, I don't think Lyman will win.

He could use another Mormon boy close by. If need be, the two of us can take D. P."

Almon did not lower his gaze as Seth nodded slowly, changing course. "Pa will be at the meeting. You two should be all right. Whatever Pa's faults, he won't let anyone abuse his family."

Almon grinned, "Seth, are you calling *me* family?"

* * *

When Lyman and Almon arrived at the Methodist Church, the meeting hall was nearly packed. They saw the back of Ezekiel's head as he sat near the front of the room. Hurlbut stood to take the floor. As Lyman and Almon stood up in the back, Philastus's eyes met Lyman's before he began talking. Philastus nodded slightly to acknowledge his cousin. Lyman remained stoic. He did not nod, nor did he look away.

Hurlbut began speaking with great energy and emotion. He spoke of the evils of Mormonism, the sinister, charismatic power of Joe Smith, and the need to protect the believers from their own delusions. He claimed that he had uncovered a great secret—the Book of Mormon was not written by ancient inhabitants upon golden plates.

After a smattering of applause, Hurlbut continued. "I now know that it was originally written by a respected clergyman who is now deceased. It was written as a story, a romance, but he died before it was published. The text was changed by a modern hand, not a rough, unlearned hand like the scoundrel, Joe Smith, but another more delicate hand. It was done by a man desiring his own grandeur, one many of you once loved and respected—the notorious Sidney Rigdon."

The crowd rustled and some cheered. Hurlbut held up a piece of paper and spoke loudly above the din. "I have a written statement from the brother of the clergyman who wrote this romance! I know the location in the east where the original manuscript waits in an old trunk, a voice whispering from the dead to tell us truth!"

Hurlbut wiped the sweat from his brow. A man raised his hand. Hurlbut nodded toward him. "Pass around that paper so we can get a look," the man suggested.

Hurlbut shook his head. "I've shown it to a few select gentlemen, but I won't make the details public." Hurlbut paused significantly. "Not yet."

Philastus's eyes drifted briefly to Lyman and Almon. "If this information slipped into the wrong hands, Joe Smith's elders might try to intercede."

After taking a few more questions, Hurlbut added, "Some of the gentlemen here, namely Mr. Newell, Mr. Clapp, and Mr. Randall, have already agreed to help finance a trip to the east where I will obtain this manuscript and every other piece of information needed for Joe Smith's downfall. When I return, the results will be published, and the world will be free of Mormonism. Anyone who would like to help, please speak to Mr. Newell after the meeting. I will not let you down!" The audience rose to their feet, applauding.

"I can't stomach this," Lyman said briefly. He walked out the back door with Almon following.

Philastus saw them leave and shouted above the crowd. "Gentlemen, I must regrettably go, for I have pressing business to attend to. Thank you." Philastus put his hat on and strode through the crowd and out the door.

Ezekiel stood and walked out of the meetinghouse.

* * *

"Lyman, a word with you!" Philastus called out as he hurried toward Lyman and Almon.

Lyman turned around slowly. "Why Philastus? Why in heaven do you want to speak to me?"

Hurlbut's eyes bored into Lyman's. "You are my cousin, my brother."

"I was," Lyman said shortly. "I baptized you. I rejoiced when you made sacred covenants. Now I watch you turn to Satan, mocking everything we believe in."

Hurlbut's voice raised in frustration. "I know the truth. I listened to you once. Listen to me now!"

Lyman shook his head. "I've heard enough."

"Then you will live your life as a slave to Joseph Smith and his lies!"

Lyman's color rose in frustrated anger. "I am God's servant and a slave to no man. Stop, Philastus, before it is too late!"

"That's the way it is with you Mormons. If someone doesn't believe in your doctrine, they are in Satan's grip, ashes beneath your feet. There was a time when you promised to always be my friend."

Lyman gaped at Philastus. "Don't you have friends enough? You left a roomful."

Philastus exhaled sharply. "You, Lyman, are the only man on earth I trust. I do this for you most of all."

Lyman looked into his cousin's handsome face, the wavy dark hair, the chiseled features, the pride in his eyes. "No, Philastus. You are not doing this for me. I'm sorry." Lyman turned and walked away.

Philastus whirled toward Almon. "Babbitt, talk some sense into him!"

Almon raised an eyebrow. "Seems to me that Lyman has all the sense he needs. He sees through you."

Philastus's eyes narrowed. "Babbitt," he spit out, "someone should cut out your tongue. We both know that you are like me."

Almon shook his head. "I don't think so."

"I've seen you with Julianne Johnson," Hurlbut stated sharply. "I know what you'd do if Joe Smith destroyed your dreams!"

Almon looked momentarily shaken. He regained his confidence and shook his head. "There is a difference."

Philastus smirked. "When you put your finger on it, let me know what it is."

Almon cocked his head. "It has to do with other people, with loving other people. With knowing they are better than you, with wishing you were more like them. And with trying to change."

"Don't you think I've felt that way about Lyman? Don't you think I know the worth of kinship? I'm not some kind of monster."

"You're a proud and arrogant man," Almon said, his green eyes glittering in the sun, a light going off inside of him. "And I know pride and arrogance. I battle mine every day."

Almon turned and left. Ezekiel, watching and listening under the eaves of the Methodist meetinghouse, made a decision at that moment, a decision that had nothing to do with the Mormon Church or Hurlbut's claims. He decided that he would give permission when Almon Babbitt asked for Julianne's hand in marriage.

12

Our brother's work is done,
For which he now is blest;
His battle's fought, the victory won,
He's gone into his rest.
No more his voice we'll hear,
The Saints to faith inspire;
He'll in the dance no more appear
Nor chant the joyful lyre.
He labored with his might,
The work of God to aid;
In it he took supreme delight,
While on this earth he staid.
Triumphant in his death,
Eternal life he's won.
Peace reigned with his expiring breath,
To think his work was done.

Joel Hills Johnson
(*Hymns of Praise for the Young*, Hymn 221, 208–209)

October 4, 1833

Joseph Smith walked to the woodland where Don Carlos, David, and Almon were working. He suggested they lay down their axes and go hunting with him. The three had worked tirelessly and deserved some diversion. They buried their axes in a log to keep them out of the dirt and headed back to their houses for their guns.

An hour later, squatting low in the brush with their guns in their arms, they watched as small groups of two or three ducks began to cautiously approach the small pond looking for a safe place to bed down for the night. The sun was low in the sky and the wind brisk—perfect weather for duck hunting. A pair of green-headed mallards suddenly banked hard and flew straight into the concealed quartet. Joseph and David raised their guns to their shoulders and fired. One of the ducks flinched just enough to dodge the oncoming pellets. The other was not quite as agile.

"Bulls-eye! That's two for Joseph," Don Carlos said as the duck fell from the air.

"Brother Joseph, do you enjoy making jest of us?" Almon asked.

Joseph grinned. "Not really. But Emma will be glad for some meat for supper."

The men stood up. David set out to retrieve the bird—the penalty for having missed again. He had only taken a few steps when he doubled over, coughing. The Prophet looked at him with concern. "Are you all right, Brother David?"

David stopped coughing and wiped his mouth with his sleeve. He turned to his friends and smiled a bit sheepishly. "Been coughing a little lately—probably just a cold." His face was flushed.

"You've been coughing more than a little for the past two weeks, and it's getting worse," Don Carlos countered. His eyes looked worried.

"Carlos, Almon, why don't you two retrieve the duck for David," Joseph suggested.

When David began to argue, Almon cut in with a grin. "David, you've a good excuse for your poor shot today, so take advantage of it. But don't expect this treatment next time we go hunting." He and Carlos left before David could respond further.

Joseph turned to David and smiled. "I was hoping to have a word with you alone today, Brother David. I'm leaving for a mission tomorrow. Before I go, I want to ask you a question. Do you deem yourself worthy to become an elder in the Church of Christ?"

David looked down for a moment. Then he lifted his head and looked into Joseph's eyes. "I'm trying, Brother Joseph. I've repented and I seek each day to live my life according to the teachings in the Book of Mormon. But I don't know if God finds me worthy. Will I always have the self-mastery that becomes a man holding the priesthood? I've never experienced the spiritual gifts that follow so many of the believers. I've never spoken in tongues or experienced the gift of healing, or revelation, or visions." He smiled a bit ruefully. "When I catch a cold, it runs its natural course. I don't think that I have faith enough to be healed or to heal others."

Then David's eyes became serious, and his strong shoulders sagged. "There is a good deal of the natural man within me, Brother Joseph. I would give anything to know that God accepts me, that I can become a shaft in His hand."

Joseph smiled reassuringly at the young man. "David, there are many other spiritual gifts—the gifts of knowledge, of faith, of charity. A revelation from the Lord given to me a few years ago outlined the qualifications of those who would labor in the ministry.

> *"Therefore, if ye have desires to serve God ye are called to the work . . .*
>
> *"And faith, hope, charity and love, with an eye single to the glory of God, qualify him for the work.*
>
> *"Remember faith, virtue, knowledge, temperance, patience, brotherly kindness, godliness, charity, humility, diligence.*
>
> *"Ask, and ye shall receive; knock, and it shall be opened unto you."*

Joseph looked directly at David and spoke. "David Johnson, I see these qualities within you. You are worthy to serve the Master with your brethren in the priesthood. Prepare for that day which is at the doors. Obtain an assurance of your standing before God."

The gold in David's eyes shone with tears. "Brother Joseph," he began, hardly able to contain his emotion, "I will do anything. If need be, I will wrestle an angel, like Jacob did, to obtain that assurance."

The men were quiet for a moment. Then they heard footsteps in the woodland behind them, opposite the direction Almon and Don Carlos had gone. They turned around as a hunter stepped out of the dense trees. The man carried a gun and smiled broadly. "My place is about a mile from here. I was out looking for some deer when I got wind of you fellows. Which one of you shot that bird?"

Joseph stepped forward. "I did, sir."

"Excellent shot. I'm Hank Shelton. I don't believe I've met you."

Joseph put out his hand and shook Shelton's. "It good to meet you, Mr. Shelton. I'm Joseph Smith."

Shelton's eyes widened. "You're not Joe Smith, the Mormon prophet, are you?" David gripped his rifle a bit more tightly, but was caught off guard by another spasm of coughing.

After David quieted, Joseph smiled amicably at the stranger. "I'm one and the same."

Shelton dropped Joseph's hand and cocked his head. His eyes slanted quizzically. "So you foretell the future? Talk to angels? All that rubbish?"

The setting sun highlighted the reddish tint of Joseph's blond-brown hair. His clear blue eyes studied the man from beneath his long, light lashes. Joseph spoke. "When it is God's will."

Shelton laughed both derisively and uncomfortably. "Well, Mr. Joe Smith, do you have a revelation for me before I head back home?"

"No, Mr. Shelton," Joseph said. "*I* don't have a revelation for you. Revelations come from God." Joseph recognized the slightly friendly, slightly mocking expression in the man's eyes. He grinned and added, "Besides, you wouldn't believe my calling even if I told you the stars would fall from heaven within forty days and you saw it happen."

Hank Shelton smirked and shrugged his shoulders. "Don't take offense, Mr. Smith. It takes all kinds of folk to make up this wide world. I'll be a-watching the stars. Good evening."

Joseph spoke. "No offense taken. I would not believe my own story if it hadn't happened to me. Good-bye, Mr. Shelton."

Puzzled, Hank Shelton walked away. A few moments later, Don Carlos and Almon strolled up. The dead bird dangled from Almon's fingers.

Joseph put his arm around his brother's shoulders. "Carlos, I need to be getting back. Oliver left a few days ago for New York to purchase a press and type to replace the one destroyed by the mob in Missouri. We will move *The Star* here to Kirtland. When Oliver returns, would you like to learn the art of printing?"

"Yes!" Don Carlos's eyes lit up. He had always been interested in the press and had hoped for the opportunity to learn the trade.

"Good." Joseph chuckled. "And I'm leaving on a mission tomorrow with Elders Rigdon and Nickerson. We go northeast into Canada. I should be back sometime near the first of November. I'm worried about Emma and the children, but it is important for me to go. Would you watch out for them while I'm away?"

Don Carlos nodded. "Of course. But Joseph, is it a good time for you and Elder Rigdon to leave, what with the problems in Missouri, and with Oliver in New York?"

"I have the utmost confidence in Brother Williams. The Lord will guide him." Joseph glanced at all three young men. "You see, my friends, missionary work must go forth regardless of our personal circumstances. Jehovah is at the helm." Then Joseph smiled a bit ruefully. "And I must also admit that nothing comforts me like teaching the truth. A mission is the best kind of rest for me. Pray that God will seal my testimony to the people's hearts."

As the men voiced their agreement, David coughed again. Joseph went on, "There is one more thing I want to tell you boys. You can stop burning brick for a time. Even though we've decided to build the temple with stone, the brick you've already made will be used to build God's kingdom in many other ways. God bless you for your hard work. And you, David, stay home tomorrow and get well." He smiled again at David. "Be at peace in your soul. Your assurance from God will come like the dew from heaven."

Joseph's smile transformed into a lively grin. "You need not wrestle an angel, but I hope you will wrestle a prophet when I return."

* * *

During the middle of the night, Seth awakened to the sound of David choking. Seth quickly lit the lantern. Hardly able to catch his breath, David grasped the chamber pot and threw up. He continued coughing. Worried, Seth placed his hand on David's shoulder to steady him. He felt the heat from David's skin beneath the linen nightshirt.

Seth handed David a handkerchief, then he went to the dresser and drew a cup of water from the pitcher. Seth helped David take a few gulps. David grasped the handkerchief and coughed into it.

A few moments later the coughing subsided. "David, how long have you had this cough? Should I awaken Joel and give you a blessing?" Seth asked.

David shook his head and smiled weakly. "A couple weeks now, I guess. I'll be all right until morning. You make a good nurse."

"Then be a good patient and rest." Seth took the soiled handkerchief and set it down on the table near the lantern. He handed David a clean one. "I'll go empty this pot, or its smell will keep both of us awake tonight."

"Thank you. I'm sorry to be such a bother," David said.

Seth glanced kindly at David and teased. "What are younger brothers for anyway, but to be a bother?" Seth picked up the chamber pot, and then reached for the soiled handkerchief. It fell open. When he looked at it, Seth's heart sank, and a sickening fear crawled through him. There was a good deal of blood in on the cloth.

Seth looked over at David. His brother had turned the opposite way and was resting quietly on his side. Seth touched David's shoulder, but could not speak. David felt his brother's loving hand and closed his eyes. Almost blinded with tears, Seth took his hand off of David and folded up the ends of the putrid handkerchief. He carried the lantern and handkerchief in one hand, the chamber pot in the other. Once downstairs, Seth set the lantern on the kitchen table and went outside into the moonlight.

The moon was nearly full and the night cold and windy. He went to the stream on the property. He dumped out the contents of the chamber pot. Then he bent down and rinsed the handkerchief out over and over again until the dark stains slipped away into the frigid water and the handkerchief reflected the snowy whiteness of the moonlight. With the clean handkerchief in hand, hollow words echoed in Seth's mind, "David is going to get well. David is going to get well . . ."

Shivering with cold, Seth trudged back to the house. When he opened the door, he found Nancy sitting at the kitchen table where he had left the lantern. Her crutches stood balanced in the crook of her arm.

"Nance, why are you up?"

"The coughing awakened me. Is it David?"

Seth nodded heavily.

"Is he all right?" Nancy asked. Seth hesitated. "Seth, tell me," Nancy pressed.

"Nancy, he's coughing blood," Seth said quietly, coming to some kind of acceptance of what the symptoms meant. "It must be consumption."

Nancy felt if she had been shot. "But, Seth, he hasn't been languishing! It must be something else!"

Seth stood quiet. Nothing more needed to be said. He did not remind Nancy of quick consumption that took its victims in a matter of weeks. It was not only because he did not want to alarm her, but mostly to hang on to some hope that he was wrong.

Nancy's heart fluttered within. David was her precious, younger brother, her first responsibility and first burden. And during the years since her accident, he had become her strength and her joy. It was David who had found her broken on the ground after she fell from the horse. It was David who had made her promise to live. It was David who had spent countless hours at her side as she convalesced, telling her stories and making her laugh. He had carried her crippled body when she didn't have enough strength to walk.

She had comforted him when he was filled with anger at their father's drinking. She remembered his acceptance of the gospel, his urgent desire for her to be healed, and the depth of his disappointment when she was not. His searching and growing faith had burned brightly inside of her, and she lived in his light when discouraged.

Lately, after Sabbath meetings, she had watched David single out Agnes Coolbrith to speak with. Nancy saw their mutual attraction and imagined him marrying that sweet, lovely woman who lived with the Smith family. She saw her future self rocking David and Agnes's beautiful babies, and perhaps growing old in his home. But now her handsome, passionate, joyous David was gravely ill. How could it be that the tables had turned?

Seth saw that Nancy was shaken and spoke reassuringly. "Nancy, we must trust in our Heavenly Father and have faith."

Nancy's long hair tumbled around her face, and her gray eyes were luminous with worry. There was a sense of panic in her words. "But Seth, how can we? How can I go on if David is taken from us?"

Seth sighed deeply. "We will beseech the powers of heaven to keep him here."

* * *

Ezekiel awoke late the next morning. He went into the kitchen where Julianne, Almera, and Susan were finishing the breakfast dishes. They were unusually quiet as they worked. A plate of food awaited Ezekiel at the table. As he ate, he heard the sound of coughing coming from upstairs. "Is that David?" he questioned.

Julianne nodded. "He's worse, Papa."

Ezekiel took the stairs two at a time. Before entering the bedroom, he abruptly stopped. The door hung ajar. Joel and Seth had their hands on David's head and were giving him a blessing.

Julia sat at David's bedside with her head bowed. Seth prayed, "David, we bless you with comfort and strength. We promise that you will witness the hand of the Lord in your life at this time. We leave these blessings with you in the name of Jesus Christ. Amen."

As his loved ones raised their heads, Ezekiel walked into the room.

"Hello, Pa," David greeted. His breath was shallow.

Ezekiel thought of how he had seen little of David ever since he had been working in the brickyard. He walked over and stood by David's bedside next to Julia. "Son, when did the cough start?"

"Couple of weeks ago," David said. He struggled to sit up as a fit of coughing shook him. Ezekiel supported his son's back with his arm. Julia held a handkerchief to his mouth. Ezekiel saw the traces of blood in David's sputum.

When David's coughing was under control, Ezekiel gently lowered him back onto the feather pillow. Ezekiel looked at Julia. "Has anyone sent for Dr. Williams?" he questioned.

Julia shook her head.

"I think he's at the Whitney Store," Joel offered.

"I'll be back shortly," Ezekiel said. He turned from his wife and sons and strode out of the door.

The sky was overcast as Ezekiel ran to the Whitney store. Once inside, he found Elizabeth Whitney behind the counter. "I'm lookin' for Dr. Williams," he said abruptly.

"He's upstairs in a meeting with a group of the brethren," she explained. "Is this an emergency?"

"My son, David, is gravely ill."

"Come with me."

Ezekiel followed Elizabeth as she went up the stairs. She knocked on the school-room door. When it opened, she explained that young David Johnson needed immediate medical attention. Frederick asked Bishop Whitney to lead the meeting in his absence. The doctor hefted his bag. Don Carlos, who was in attendance, followed Frederick G. Williams out the door.

* * *

Julia and Seth met the men at the front door. "Brother Frederick. Don Carlos. Thank you for coming." They shook hands with Dr. Williams and embraced Don Carlos. Ezekiel stood apart. It was as if he wasn't there.

While Julia and Seth led the men upstairs to David's room, Ezekiel paused for a moment at the bottom of the steps. Looking toward the kitchen, he saw Julianne standing with a dishrag in her hands, watching him. Did she know how alone and out of place he felt in this house that was clearly not his own? He heard David's coughing. His son suffered. Turning, Ezekiel mounted the stairs. Julianne threw her dishrag down and caught up with him.

* * *

Ezekiel stood on the threshold of the bedroom, with Julianne next to him. Nancy, sitting at David's bedside, looked up. Outside, the clouds were dispersing, and patches of sunlight fell on Nancy's hair and the side of her face. Ezekiel imagined her braving the stairs this morning, slowly, slowly, using her crutches as she painfully gained one step at a time, her useless leg dragging behind her. Now she was beside her brother, their tenderness toward each other like the softness of summer twilight. Ezekiel's head began to throb. His heart ached.

Dr. Williams cleared his throat. "Good morning, Brother David."

Nancy slowly stood up on her crutches, then moved back next to Seth so that Dr. Williams could examine his patient. Julia went to the other side of David and sat down on the bed.

David sat up, triggering a coughing spasm. After he stopped, Dr. Williams examined the sputum, then listened carefully to the coarse breathing emanating from David's muscular chest.

"Brother David, I've some medicine to ease your cough. Take a pinch of it three times a day with a warm lemon tea." The doctor opened his bag and took out three powder-filled vials, a pocketknife, and a small cup. He pried the vials open. With the tip of his knife, he skillfully combined small amounts of the powders and emptied them into a cup. Then he turned to Julia. "Sister Johnson, do you know how to prepare a flax-seed poultice?" Julia nodded. The doctor continued. "Apply the poultice to David's chest morning and night."

Doctor Williams turned to the strapping young man who lay desperately ill. Shadows of exhaustion rimmed David's gold-brown eyes. The doctor spoke. "Brother David, you need bed rest. No chopping down trees or wrestling bulls for a season. If the weather is fair, open the windows or sit outside. The fresh air will do you good."

David looked up into the doctor's eyes. "Is it consumption, Brother Frederick?"

"It could be, though there is only a tinge of blood in the sputum this morning. So it could be pneumonia. You are young, strong, and haven't been languishing. With the Lord's help, we will pray for a full recovery."

Julia took her son's hand in hers. Ezekiel wondered if she were remembering that her father had died of consumption when she was a little girl.

Frederick went on, "Now, David, I must show your caretakers how to thump your chest to bring up the phlegm. This is very important if this is pneumonia. But if my thumping causes increased bleeding in your lungs, then we stop. In cases of consumption, thumping does not help."

Dr. Williams helped David sit up into a more forward position. Then, with one arm around David to support him, he thudded David's chest repeatedly with the heel of his hand. Wrenching coughs erupted from David, and blood spewed from his nose and mouth. The doctor immediately stopped.

Ezekiel could stand it no more. He turned and left the room. He heard light footsteps behind him and Julianne's voice. "Papa, wait."

Ezekiel stopped at the base of the steps and turned around. He stood absolutely still as pain coursed through him. It had to be quick consumption. David would die. Julianne ran to him. "Oh, Papa, Papa," she sobbed as she hugged her father. "What shall we do?"

A silent, wrenching sob shook Ezekiel's shoulders. He pulled it inward and held Julianne for a moment. Then he released her and took his coat off the hook. "I must be goin' now."

"Don't go, Papa," Julianne cried with tears streaming down her face.

"There's nothin' I can do here to help," Ezekiel muttered. He left the house and began the lonely walk to the tavern.

* * *

Upstairs in David's room, all were silent as Julia wiped the blood off of her son's mouth and nose. David saw the look of fear in Don Carlos's eyes and knew that it reflected his own.

Frederick G. Williams looked steadily at David. "Brother David, I've seen men and women healed by the power of God. And as a physician, I will do all within my power. Have faith, Brother David."

"I'll try, Brother Frederick," David said.

After Frederick and Don Carlos left, Julia kissed David, and with her fingertips she moved his brown, curly hair back from his eyes. Her hand trembled. "You were coughing so much last night," she said quietly. "Can you sleep now?"

David forced a smile. "I'll try, Mother."

"I need to go and pray. I'll come back soon. All will be well." Julia's voice trembled. She kissed David again.

David turned to Seth. "Go with Mother," he said softly. Seth nodded and put his hand on David's shoulder. Then he followed Julia out of the room.

As they descended the stairs, Julia felt Seth's arm around her shoulders. She was able to walk into the sitting room despite the crushing weight pushing on her chest. She crumbled onto the davenport. Seth sat down beside her and held her as she wept.

* * *

Nancy remained at David's bedside. "Nancy, I'm afraid," he whispered.

"Me too, David," Nancy responded.

"Dear Nancy, if I knew I was acceptable to God, I could bear dying."

"How could you not know that?" Nancy cried. "Your soul is precious, David, pure before him."

David fought tears, not wanting to bring on another fit of coughing. He whispered brokenly. "I'm afraid of falling into darkness—like in the nightmares. When we wake before we hit the ground. I'm afraid I will not wake in time."

Nancy swallowed and took her brother's hand. She would be his rock as he had been hers in her time of despair. When she spoke, her voice was composed. "Do you remember when you were a little boy and we watched the baby sparrow fall from its nest? It fell like a lead weight. But before it hit the ground, it opened its little wings and flew. And you chased it." Nancy smiled through her tears. "Thank goodness it flew faster than you could run."

Tears were on David's cheeks. He tried to smile. "It was fast."

Nancy wiped his tears with her handkerchief. She continued. "The Lord notices each sparrow's fall and flight. He will walk this road with you. You can lean on His omnipotent arm. David, you will not fall in the darkness; you will soar back into the arms of Jesus." Then Nancy's composure broke, and she wept. David held her slender hand. She could still feel the strength and gentleness in his grip. Nancy quieted and spoke again. "But I would be left behind without my darling brother. How I wish that you could promise me that you will not leave us."

"I promise," David whispered.

"Darling David," Nancy sobbed. "You were never very good at keeping your promises."

"I am now, Nancy," David said. "Whatever happens, wherever I am, I will always be with you, Seth, Mother, and the rest. Some bonds never break."

* * *

During the following weeks, David had many blessings and was the constant object of pleading prayers. Despite the prayers and blessings, David worsened. The Johnson family did all they could for David's comfort.

Julia and Ezekiel cared tenderly for their son. As David weakened, it felt as if the years disintegrated before them. He was their beautiful babe again, rather than the man he had become. Julia cooked David's favorite foods, even if he could only eat a few bites. She wept each day and sought solace through prayer.

Ezekiel struggled to remain stoic, to support his dying son. He greeted David each morning with a tender kiss before going to the shop. Yet after work, he often escaped to the tavern, weeping at a lonely table, remembering the infant whom his mother-in-law had suggested they name after a fallen king.

During the daylight hours, the house was quieter than usual as each family member strove to make David's final days joyful. Joe E. made David the medicinal teas suggested by Dr. Williams and saw that David drank them. Nancy spent each morning sitting by David's side, reading to him when he was awake. Julianne, Almera, and Susan washed his soiled bedclothes and bathed his forehead with wet cloths. Benjamin and Seth turned David from side to side to relieve his pain. After school each day, the younger children brought flowers, interesting rocks, leaves, bugs, and toads to David as gifts.

Don Carlos came over each evening after supper. If the weather was pleasant, Carlos helped David outside, and the two sat together, watching the sun lower and the sky redden to the color of the autumn leaves. They talked about the power of the Savior's Atonement. As time passed, David became more spirit than flesh, absorbing the abundant knowledge and faith that God granted him.

* * *

One morning, three weeks after David's diagnosis, Julianne wrapped her navy cloak around her shoulders and left the house.

She felt exhausted from watching over David the previous night, and knew she must get some fresh air before she broke into pieces.

The day was gray and cold, but not any bleaker than her soul. David had experienced a bad night, racked with pain. Seth had blessed him, and Julianne had prayed constantly as she labored to relieve him. Finally, in the early hours of the morning, David had slept.

But just as David rested, Joel had awakened with a fever. Annie, on edge from her pregnancy and saddened about David, was beside herself. She needed help. But Julianne didn't have any strength left to give. To make matters worse, Almon had not been around for over two weeks.

As Julianne walked, the wind kicked up, and the dark clouds thickened. Tears clouded Julianne's eyes. Sometimes it felt as if God had abandoned them. She had scarcely passed the Whitney store when she heard someone running toward her. Almon caught up to her, breathless. "Juli," he exclaimed as he took her hand. "How I have missed you!"

Julianne pulled her hand away as she turned around to face him, her brown eyes brimming with accusatory tears. "Why haven't you come to see David, Almon?"

"Carlos tells me how he is every day, and I send him my love."

"Almon, he's dying and you've left him alone. I thought Mormon boys stuck together. Have you forgotten that?"

Almon defended himself. "No! I love David. He saved me from a beating once. Maybe even saved my life. Don't you think I remember that? And now he is leaving. He was everything that I ever wanted in a friend. Everything! It hurts too much to see him like this when there's nothing I can do to stop it."

"Don't you think it's hard for me, Almon? For David? For all of us? Seth and I were up all night with David. I'm so tired! But I won't leave someone I love in their time of trial."

"Juli, David has all of you. He doesn't need me."

"He needs to know you care. I need to know," Julianne said in tears. "If I give myself to you, will you only be there during the good times? Papa drinks because he isn't strong enough to bear the weight of sorrow. Almon, I want a man strong enough to share whatever happens. I don't want someone who is only with me during the summer season."

Almon stared at Julianne, speechless. He saw her lovely form wrapped in the navy cloak, her upturned nose red from crying. He loved her, but he was not good enough for her. He felt as if she were receding from him and he were frozen—powerless to reach out and pull her back. Julianne turned and walked away.

* * *

Wednesday, October 30, 1833

The next evening, Don Carlos stayed at the Johnsons after nightfall. David's breathing was shallow, and he had been sleeping most of the day.

At nine o'clock that night there was a knock at the door. Julia answered it. Almon stood on the threshold. He took off his hat and kneaded the rim in his hands. "Sister Johnson, I was hoping to stay for awhile and sit with David—maybe let the rest of you get a good night's rest."

Julia's voice was welcoming. "Come in, Almon. Don Carlos is upstairs with David now."

Almon went up the stairs with Julia. Don Carlos, Seth, and Nancy were in David's room. Seth dipped a cloth into the basin of water and handed it to Nancy. She wet David's lips. Then Seth stepped back to the threshold of the room to make room for Julia and Almon. Julia walked over and kissed David's forehead.

"Hello, Almon." Carlos greeted his friend with a smile.

David's eyes opened. His cheeks were still rosy from fever, and to Almon, he did not look sick enough to die. David recognized Almon and looked at both of his friends. "Come closer to him," Carlos explained to Almon. "David wants to tell you something."

Almon bent down, his ear close to David. "You're here, Almon," David whispered. "I'm glad." It was hard for David to speak. He had so little air left in his lungs.

Almon forced a smile. "You bet, David. Us Mormon boys stick together."

David smiled. "Take care of Juli."

Almon blinked back tears as he patted David's shoulder. "I will."

"Carlos." David spoke to his other friend. "A little longer. I journey soon."

"I'll go with you as far as I can, my friend," Carlos promised.

David looked tenderly at Julia and Nancy. They moved closer, and he whispered to them. "Rest now. My brethren will wait with me. I love you, beloved Mother. I love you, dear Nancy."

"I love you, dearest son," Julia said as she kissed him again.

"Rest well, darling David," Nancy added as she smiled into her brother's eyes.

* * *

The night stretched out slowly before the men at David's bedside. Seth's eyes kept closing as he sat in a chair near David.

"Go to bed, Seth," Almon suggested, "before you fall off the chair."

Seth bid David a tender good night. "My beloved brother," Seth whispered. "Never doubt my affection."

"Go, Seth, and sleep," David whispered. "My dear brother. We will not be separated long."

"Only until morning," Seth whispered as he gently embraced his brother. David's eyes followed Seth as he left the room.

As the night passed, Almon did not flinch as he moistened David's lips and changed David's position so that he could continue to breathe. When David finally slept, Carlos and Almon talked about other things. Carlos told Almon that the Saints in Missouri had received a letter from Governor Dunklin advising them to seek redress from the appropriate authorities for their loss of property. Bishop Partridge and Sidney Gilbert were currently in the process of seeking help from lawyers in Clay County. But they didn't know if any lawyers would be willing to represent the Mormons.

"Someday that will change," Almon said quietly and determinedly. "I'll know the law inside and out. The Church won't have to go to others for legal counsel."

"I believe you'll do it, Almon," Carlos said. "You'll be a great man in the kingdom of God."

Suddenly David's body jerked, and his eyes opened. He looked past Almon and Carlos. His face shone with joy.

"Hurry, Almon, get the family," Carlos said.

Almon ran from the room. David struggled to sit up. Carlos sat on the bed next to David and held his friend in his arms. "David, I'm here," Carlos said. "The rest are coming. Can you wait?"

"They're already here, Carlos," David whispered. David spoke again, looking toward the window, his voice strong, clear, and joyous. Though the words were in another tongue, Don Carlos, holding his friend close, understood their meaning as clearly as if it were his native language.

Then David closed his eyes as his breath left his body. Carlos turned to see David's grieving parents in the doorway.

"My boy!" Ezekiel sobbed as he jerked forward and stared, almost in disbelief, at the two young men. David seemed to be sleeping in a friend's arms, but his chest was still. There was no more pained struggling for breath. Don Carlos Smith, his clear, handsome face beautiful in the candlelight, seemed to glow with an inner light.

"Loving spirits have escorted David home," Carlos said quietly. "To the mansion prepared for him."

Don Carlos moved aside. Ezekiel and Julia held the warm body of their son in their arms for the last time.

* * *

A few hours later, the sun rose. Almon and Don Carlos took word to the Whitney store of David's passing; then they returned to the Johnson home. They did the dishes and played with the little children. When Almon took his leave after lunch, Julianne walked outside with him. "David asked me to take care of you," Almon said quietly.

Julianne began to cry. "Never leave me, Almon. Please."

Almon put his arms around her and held her close while she wept. "I'll never leave you," he said quietly. "Never."

* * *

Late that afternoon, there was a knock at the door. Almera answered it, her eyes bloodshot from grief. A blond-haired young man stood before her. "Is this Zeke Johnson's home?" he asked.

"Yes," Almera said.

"I'm Sam Prescott," the man replied, thinking that this girl was absolutely lovely, even when her eyes were red and swollen from crying.

Lyman walked up and stood behind Almera. After introductions, Prescott addressed him. "I work with Zeke at the shop. When Brigham Young came in this morning he told me that Zeke's son died last night. We finished the coffin. We figure that no man should have to build his own son's casket. I brought it over."

Together, Lyman Sherman and Sam Prescott carried the coffin into the sitting room.

Upstairs, Seth and Don Carlos had dressed David's body in the white shroud that Susan had sewn earlier that week. The men carefully carried the body downstairs and laid it in the casket. Prescott watched as the family gathered together, holding each other and weeping.

Ezekiel walked over to Prescott. He shook his hand. "Sam, I'm in you're debt."

Prescott shook his head. "No. I'm sorry about your boy."

As he left the house, Prescott thought about how utterly haggard Zeke Johnson looked today, especially in comparison to flawless features of his son in the casket, and the beautiful face of his daughter.

* * *

The following morning, the small schoolhouse near the Johnson home overflowed with people who attended David's funeral.

Ezekiel sat on one side of Julia. Seth was on the other, holding her hand. Julia wept during the sermon, yet her shoulders remained erect as she found courage in the message of eternal life. But to Ezekiel, Jared Carter's words tasted bitter. His son was dead, yet Carter talked about David's good works following him to heaven. David had worked himself to death on the Mormon temple. To Ezekiel, it seemed that if there was a God, He was silent and cold as his son's body. His family lived in some strange world of faith, while Ezekiel was detached and alone, devastated by his loss. David had not been healed.

Following the service, Ezekiel watched in stony, pained silence while his precious son was buried in the loveliest section of the orchard on the hill behind the house that he had never wanted to live in.

* * *

Don Carlos went home exhausted. He lay down, but could not sleep. He went to the desk and took out a paper, quill, and an ink bottle. He thought about how he was still living while his best friend was gone. He would go on, learn the art of printing, probably marry and have children. Almon would be an attorney. But David was gone. They would never work together, or laugh together, again. Not on earth anyway. Carlos sat down and with tears in his eyes wrote the words that would memorialize his friend, David Johnson, the words that would be printed in the first Kirtland edition of the *Evening and Morning Star*.

> *But in the morning of his days he was called from a world of trouble and strife, to try the realities of eternity! In the flower of his age, in the vigor of his youth he was cut off from this life: God chose to take him to himself, though the affections of our hearts were closely allied to him.*
>
> *The afflictions of his body, during his last illness, he bore with that resignation and fortitude becoming a man. Not a*

*murmur escaped his lips against the providence of the Lord.
And when his body was wracked with pain, he stayed himself
upon the arm of Omnipotence, and rested his hope in the
promises of him who had given his life a ransom for his soul.
And in his last moments, while kindred spirits waited to escort
him away, he said,* "I am going home: there is a place in the
mansion of the Father that Christ has prepared for me, where I
shall rest: I am anxious to go: I am prepared to die! *And then,
without a struggle he fell asleep, and his spirit fled to the
paradise of God!*

*His funeral was attended with due solemnity, conducted by
the direction of brother J. Green; and discourse suited to the
occasion was delivered by brother J. S. Carter, from Rev. XIV.
13* "And I heard a voice from heaven saying unto me,
Write, Blessed are the dead which die in the Lord from
henceforth; Yea, saith the Spirit, that they may rest from
their labours; and their works do follow them." *And while
his numerous relatives and friends crowded round, eager to
drop the last tear over their kindred dust, we could not forbear
reflecting, that, though this body is now cold and inanimate,
soon it shall be reanimated again: yes, quickened and immor-
talized, no more to see corruption; for we could not forbear
saying in our hearts, Ah! He only sleeps! And while we mourn
his departure, may God enable us to appreciate our loss—while
he rests in peace!*

13

But when the truth arose,
With brilliant rays to shine,
The world sank back and darkness chose,
Instead of light divine.

The truth sends many a ray
To drive away the night,
And usher in the glorious day
Of the millennial light.

Joel Hills Johnson
(*Hymns of Praise for the Young*, Hymn 30, 35)

Monday, November 4, 1833

It was nearly ten o'clock in the morning. Emma Smith mended in her rocking chair while little Julia played on the floor with scraps of cloth. Emma already felt a little tired from awakening before dawn to feed her hungry baby. She had stayed up and begun her daily chores rather than go back to sleep. Baby Joseph now rested quietly after his second feeding of the morning. Emma watched as Julia lined up scraps of cloth into a colorful row. She was a particularly busy, observant child. Emma was jarred from her thoughts by the sound of the door opening. She turned her head and looked up, glimpsing her husband's light hair. "Joseph!"

Before she could set her work aside, Joseph dropped his knap-sack and swept Emma into his arms. After a long, warm embrace, he stepped back from Emma, bent over the cradle and touched the cheek of his sleeping son, then picked up his little girl, swung her around and kissed her. Julia squealed with glee. Joseph grinned at his wife. "You are all well, just as the Lord promised!" Joseph set Julia down, hung up his hat and coat, and pulled up a chair near Emma.

"Are you hungry?" Emma questioned.

"My family is safe and well! For the moment, that is meat enough."

Emma breathed deeply. Her husband was home! She cut a thick slice of bread and spread a generous portion of apple butter on it. Joseph poured himself a cup of milk and sat down to eat. "How have the children been?" Joseph asked between mouthfuls.

"Julia is learning the names of the colors, and little Joseph has taken his first step."

"And I have missed it all," Joseph said.

"Such is the life of a prophet," Emma remarked. She wondered how long she would have Joseph with her this time. "Tell me of your travels."

Joseph swallowed a mouthful, then began talking. "First we went to the borderlands and stayed with Brother Rudd in Springfield. We had a large congregation, Emma. I bore testimony of all the Lord has brought forth by His holy angels. I was saddened to learn that D. P. Hurlbut was there the week before lecturing against us, saying that Sidney stole the Book of Mormon from the writings of a deceased man named Spaulding—that we used that manuscript to fabricate the Book of Mormon. Hurlbut has a signed affidavit from Spaulding's brother."

"But Joseph, the Book of Mormon was translated before you knew Sidney! These lies will crumble without a foundation."

"Too often people don't take the time to learn the truth. How Philastus hates me, Emma! He, who used to be one of my brethren, wants to destroy me."

"He's not the first, Joseph."

"I know, but it still troubles me. And I am sure that he will not be the last."

Seeing the pain in her husband's eyes, Emma put her right hand over Joseph's left. His eyes and fair complexion always betrayed his emotion. It would appear rosy and joyous one moment, then a shadow would cross his heart, and Emma could see it in his face. She treasured his expressiveness. It was one of the things that drew her to him again and again.

Emma sighed as they sat in silent companionship. His life was so different from hers. Emma's days were consumed by everyday matters—caring for her toddlers, preparing food, sewing, washing, and running the household when he was so often away. She did not commune with angels. Sometimes it was difficult taking care of so many earthly things, while his world was full of heavenly visions.

Joseph spoke again, more cheerfully. "Many in Canada readily received the truth, for which we thank our Heavenly Father."

"I'm glad, Joseph," Emma said simply.

Joseph looked into Emma's dark eyes. "Tell me, Emma, how are things here and in Missouri? I haven't spoken to Frederick yet. I came straight home to you."

Emma looked away. Their moments together felt so fleeting, and she knew that her words would burden him. But he was the Prophet and it couldn't be helped. He needed to know. She looked back at him and began. "In Missouri, our brethren agreed to pay a group of lawyers from Clay County the outlandish fee of one thousand dollars to represent them. As soon as the Jackson County mob got wind of that, their threats of violence increased. We haven't heard any more since then. I fear for them, Joseph."

Joseph stood up, his eyes deeply troubled. He leaned into his hands that were pressed on the table. They were small hands for such a large frame. "We will pray for them with all the energy of our souls. May God protect our brothers and sisters in Zion!"

Emma went on slowly. "And here in Kirtland, Joseph, a tragedy. David Johnson died last week from quick consumption."

"Young David is dead?" Joseph repeated, his eyes widening in near disbelief. "Oh, Emma! His poor family! How do they bear up?"

Tears filled Emma's eyes. "They grieve, Joseph. We all grieve to lose one so young and full of promise. Poor Carlos has lost his friend."

Joseph quickly jumped up and put his hat and coat back on. "I must go to them."

Emma stood up. "Joseph, don't leave me yet! You just came home. You must be tired from traveling. Rest a bit first."

Joseph took her into his arms. "I remember what it was like for our family when Alvin died. I'll be back soon, Emma." Emma straightened and nodded. She turned back to her work as she listened to the door close behind her husband once again. Would she ever get used to it?

* * *

From the sitting-room window, Ezekiel saw Joseph Smith walk from the Whitney Store toward his house. Joseph's stride was long and purposeful despite a slight limp. Ezekiel stood up and walked over to the door. He opened it just as Joseph's hand was poised to knock.

"Welcome, Joseph," Ezekiel said, half sarcastically, as he motioned for Joseph to come in. Ezekiel's eyes were red, and his breath smelled of whiskey. "When did *you* get back?"

"An hour ago. Emma told me of David's passing."

Ezekiel spoke before Joseph could continue. His voice was bitter with pain. "No angel told you on your trip, eh? Didn't command you to come back and heal my boy?" Ezekiel snorted in disgust. "Or do you figure David's death was the just hand of Providence?"

Tears filled Joseph's eyes as he focused on Ezekiel Johnson. "I loved your son. Had I been able to help David, I would have come with Godspeed!"

Ezekiel ground his teeth together to keep his jaw from quivering. The man before him was so earnest. Ezekiel's fists clenched tight. "David worked himself to death for your temple! Worked himself to death in that cursed brickyard!"

Tears slid down Joseph's cheeks. "Father Johnson, David, your son, was a man of great worth. How we mourn his loss! We justly mourn his loss!"

Ezekiel's body began to shake with uncontrollable sobs. Joseph Smith took the elderly, half-drunken man into his arms and wept with him.

* * *

November thirteenth was clear and cold. In the late afternoon, Almon walked to the brickyard. He gazed woodenly at the silent kilns. He pulled off a tarp covering raw bricks. He stared at the unfired bricks lined up in a herringbone pattern, like strange, inanimate soldiers, waiting to be finished. He kicked one of them, and it knocked several more off the plank, like dominoes. The dry clay shattered.

Almon dug his hands into his coat pockets. David's soul was the fire that had kept the brickyard alive. Now it was doused. He thought about Juli. He still loved her, but she didn't laugh anymore, and the twinkle had vanished from her eyes. Life was too full of sorrow and toil. Almon dug the toe of his boot into the cold ground. How dare David leave them all like this! What good was priesthood power anyway, when it didn't save your best friend and left you alone and cold?

"Almon Babbitt!" Almon turned at the sound of the voice. Joseph Hancock was walking away from a log house located near the brickyard. Smoke curled up from the chimney and into the steel-blue sky. Hancock carried his gun. "I'm goin' deer hunting. Wanna come?" Joseph Hancock was in his early thirties. He and his brother, Thomas, had formed the bricks that the Johnson crew had burned.

Almon shrugged. "I left my gun at home."

"Come on. You can use Thomas's gun. He's sick in bed today."

"Let's go then," Almon said.

As the hours passed, the day did not improve. The two men followed a buck deep into the woodland. Almon felt frustrated. Hancock walked too loudly, his feet crackling in the leaves. They couldn't get close enough for a decent shot. As they watched the buck gallop off for the third time, Joseph Hancock shook his head. "It's getting late. We best give it up and get back home before dark."

"I suppose," Almon said. He looked around. Vast, endless trees towered in each direction. "I don't know where we are. You lead the way out."

Hancock raised his eyebrows. "I don't know which way to go either."

The two men wandered for two hours, searching for a way out of the forest. Darkness fell, swallowing up the light. Together they groped along a twisting path and followed it until they reached a brick house built deep within the woodland. Smoke rose from the chimney, and the windows glowed with candlelight.

Relieved, the men walked to the door together. Joseph Hancock knocked. A burly man with a friendly smile answered and invited the lost hunters inside to sit around his fire. He introduced himself as Hank Shelton.

Shelton ladled each man a generous portion of venison stew. They had each just taken a bite when he sat down next to them and asked, "Are you fellows Mormon?" Almon raised his eyebrows at Hancock and shoveled a heaping bite of stew into his mouth. The stew was good, and he wanted to have as much as possible before they were thrown out in the cold. Joseph Hancock swallowed and cleared his throat. Hank Shelton laughed out loud and slapped his thigh. "You two *are* Mormons!"

"Yes, sir."

Shelton licked his lips. "I don't believe I've ever been this lucky! Thirty-nine days ago, I met Joe Smith hunting duck in these very woods."

Almon's eyes riveted on Shelton. Could this be the hunter David had mentioned meeting? Could that really have been just thirty-nine days ago? Had this man been with David the day before his lungs started to bleed?

Shelton went on. "I asked Smith for a revelation, and he told me the stars would fall sometime in the next forty days. Well, this is day thirty-nine, and I haven't heard of one star falling! What do you fellows think of that?"

Joseph Hancock stared levelly at Shelton and remarked. "There is one night left. If Joseph said so, the stars will certainly fall tonight."

Shelton chuckled. "Well, I'm not waiting up tonight, though you fellows are welcome to. You'll need to sleep here. It's too late to get you back to Kirtland."

Almon set his bowl on the floor and spoke suddenly. "Were there any other men with Joseph Smith?"

Shelton eyed Almon. "Yes. Joe Smith and another man—a fine-looking young fellow. A couple of their companions were off fetching the duck Smith shot. Why do you ask?"

"I was there—fetching the duck," Almon stated, his eyes gleaming strangely. "The man with Joseph was my friend, David Johnson. If Joseph had made a prophecy about the stars falling, David would have told me."

"You calling me a liar, boy?"

Almon's green eyes flashed. "I'm stating facts."

Shelton bristled. "Tomorrow, you go ask your friend. He'll tell you the truth if he's honest."

Almon stared into the fire and clamped his mouth shut. Hank Shelton scoffed, "What do you have to say to that, boy? Are you afraid to ask your friend? Is he as dishonest as your Mormon prophet?"

Almon's green eyes darkened. He jumped to his feet. David had always said that Mormon boys stick together. Almon wanted to break something. Joseph Hancock stood quickly and put his hand on Almon's shoulder. "Babbitt, sit back down," he commanded.

Almon shot a look at Hancock, but complied. Joseph Hancock turned apologetically to their host. "Please excuse my companion.

He's upset because he can't ask his friend. David Johnson recently died of quick consumption. And, by the way, Joseph Smith is an honest man."

Hank Shelton looked at Almon who continued staring into the fire. Shelton's voice had softened when he spoke. "Son, I'm sorry about your friend, I truly am. But you need to think carefully about the man you're following. Your friend wasn't healed by Joe Smith's magic, and no stars have fallen from heaven. Think on that. Now, I'll go get you fellows some quilts. You can sleep here by the fire."

An hour later, Joseph Hancock and Almon lay by the fire, both wide awake. Finally, Hancock stood up. "I'm going outside to watch the stars. Want to wait with me?"

Almon shook his head. "Do you think Joseph really said that about the stars?"

"Mr. Shelton doesn't appear a liar," Hancock remarked as he stood up.

"People misunderstand. Get things wrong all the time," Almon muttered. "What's the truth anyway?" He rolled over and closed his eyes. He couldn't quit thinking about what their host had said. David was dead, and Almon wasn't about to watch for stars that wouldn't fall. It would be better to dream.

Two hours later, Almon awakened to Brother Hancock shaking his shoulder. "Almon, come outside quick!" Half asleep, Almon stumbled toward the open door while Joseph Hancock woke up Hank Shelton.

A few minutes later, the three men stood out in the yard, staring at the sky, dumbfounded. The heavens were afire with thousands of meteors streaking through the sky in every direction, some with twisting trains of light following them, some like large drops of rain falling through blazes of light.

Joseph Hancock watched in amazement. "Well, Mr. Shelton, would you look at that?"

Hank Shelton's voice was a whisper. "I'll send for Joe Smith on the morrow. You Mormon boys know something I don't."

Almon's heart pounded exuberantly. "You're right, Mr. Shelton! We Mormon boys do know something!" He flung his head back and grabbed at the sky as if he were catching the stars. Joseph, the Prophet, had sure gotten it right this time. Somewhere in heaven he pictured David laughing. Almon could almost hear him say, "Almon, my friend, Mormon boys stick together. Forever."

* * *

On the night of November thirteenth, in the Johnson home, Annie turned over in discomfort. It was the eighth month of her pregnancy, and the past three weeks had been terribly difficult. David had died, and his passing had broken all their hearts. Yet she had been so frightened by Joel's illness that David's last days seemed more of a blur than real. Her husband had been ill with bilious fever. She had feared for Joel's life, while the rest of the family was wrapped in David's struggle. The effort to keep her own children under control while attending to her sick husband had exhausted Annie.

Then David had died, and Annie had wept, sorry that she scarcely had a chance to say good-bye. To make matters worse, her Sixtus had grown increasingly temperamental. Annie knew that Ezekiel's drunkenness, Joel's illness, and David's death had confused the little boy. Annie also knew that she ought to feel thankful that Joel's fever had broken a few days ago. Yet she felt drained and discouraged.

Annie dismally thought of an incident earlier that evening. Sixtus had fought with Amos. Annie had taken him upstairs and spanked him. After she struck her boy, Sixtus had screamed that he hated Momma. Annie had broken down and cried. Joel, who was still weak from his illness, had come into the room to find his pregnant wife distraught. With swollen eyes, Annie had burst into sobs again, begging Joel to hurry and build a cabin on their wild land. Their baby was coming. They desperately needed a place of their own.

The baby squirmed inside Annie. Tears again gathered in her eyes. She wanted so much to have the birth over with, to be comfortable once more. She turned over so that she was facing the window and tried to think of her blessings. Joel's fever was gone. She would have loved ones around her for the delivery of this child. A prophet was again on the earth. Then, through her tears, Annie saw the night sky light up. She sat up and wiped her eyes. The lights of the meteors were blurred and diffused by the glass of the window. Annie reached over and shook Joel's shoulder

* * *

Fifteen minutes later, the Johnson clan stood outside on the porch. Only Ezekiel stayed inside, unable to awaken from his drunken sleep. Joel, Annie, and their children huddled under the same blanket. Julia and the others stood close by with their arms around each other as they watched the blazing storm in the night sky.

"The stars shall fall from heaven as a fig tree casteth her untimely figs," Seth whispered.

Healing tears coursed down Julia's face. She was not afraid, though it appeared as if heaven and earth were on fire. She was prepared for the Second Coming of Christ. It was then that she would see her son again. Her beautiful David was in the loving and powerful hands of the Creator, the Father of heaven and earth.

"David has not left us," Nancy whispered. "But waits beyond time for us to join him. What a beautiful sight to behold."

Benjamin stared at the sky. He whispered to Joe, "I'd sure be scared right now if I were a sinner. This is a sure sign of the last days."

Joe watched in awe, his hands in his pockets. He spoke. "How can it be that so many stars are hurled at once? Is there no law that confines the vast fields of heavenly ether?"

"Heavenly Father is throwing the stars," George stated, eyeing Joe as if he were an idiot.

"God can do whatever He wants," William added. "With Jesus' help."

"They took David," Mary whimpered.

Julianne put her arm around Mary. For the first time since David's death, Juli's smile was not forced. "David has a good throwing arm, a really good one. Remember how he used to skip rocks in Lake Chautauqua? Can't you imagine him in heaven throwing some of these stars?"

"I can," Almera said as her eyes filled with tears.

"Me too," Susie whispered.

* * *

In Missouri, hundreds of Saints had been driven from Jackson County. Their homes had been destroyed, their men beaten and whipped. Some had been shot. Women and children had crossed the frozen prairie alone, most without adequate shoes or clothing. Supplies were scarce. Ferrymen had taken them over the Missouri River out of Jackson County. Then rain had descended in torrents. The mud was soft and cold on their burning, bleeding feet.

They had camped near the cottonwoods on the Missouri River bottoms, cutting young trees and fashioning what shelter they could. It looked like a village of hundreds of hastily built wigwams. Men stared into the fires, women labored without joy, children cried in fright and hunger.

Then one night the sky was clear. At two o'clock in the morning, a shout went out in the camp. "Awaken! Awaken! A sign in heaven!" Men, women, and children stumbled outside. The fireballs hurling through the sky lighted their images, illuminating the dirt on their skirts and britches, and the flashes of pain, confusion, and triumph in their faces. They knew what this shower of meteors meant.

They had been driven from the garden of their every hope, their New Jerusalem, their Zion. They were bereft, and God knew it. Whatever their sins had been, for whatever reason they had lost Zion, the Lord of Heaven now comforted them with a night sky full of light. The spark of hope kindled in their hearts. They had faith that the Son of God would come to earth again, that Zion would be redeemed. For the moment they forgot about the gnawing in their stomachs, the fact that their children might weaken and die from cold and starvation. They simply watched the spectacular night sky, until daybreak hid the shower of falling stars.

* * *

Around the corner from the Johnsons, the Prophet Joseph stood at the front gate with Oliver Cowdery. He did not yet know of the Saints' plight in Missouri. Oliver spoke. "Joseph, the stars fall like a hailstorm. What does it mean?"

Illuminated by the heavenly light, the Prophet's face shone with joy. "It is a sure sign that Christ will come! Look at the marvelous works of the Lord, Oliver! How thankful I am for His mercy unto us, His servants! May each Saint in these latter days be saved in His kingdom through Jesus Christ, our Lord!"

14

Sinner, can you slight the Savior?
Can you scorn his dying love?
Can you shun the light, the favor,
Sent in mercy from above?

Joel Hills Johnson
(*Hymns of Praise for the Young,* Hymn 131, 131)

On a cold morning in late November, D. P. Hurlbut arrived at the home of Mr. Jerome Clark in Hartwick, New York. After introductions, Hurlbut gave the elderly Mr. Clark a letter from Solomon Spaulding's widow, Mrs. Matilda Spaulding Davison. Hurlbut shuffled his feet and ran his hand through his dark, wavy hair while Clark read the letter. He was here for one reason. Years ago, Spaulding's widow had left an old trunk in the keeping of Mr. Clark. The trunk contained Solomon Spaulding's handwritten novel entitled "Manuscript Found."

As Philastus waited, he thought about the past weeks. He had traveled extensively in his effort to find the manuscript. His journey had led him to Pittsburgh, New York, and, finally, to Massachusetts, where the widow lived with her daughter. When he had visited the widow, she had informed him that her late husband's papers were in the keeping of a Mr. Clark in Hardwick, New York. Philastus had spent an entire day convincing the elderly woman to write a letter giving him permission to take the manuscript. She had finally agreed when Hurlbut promised to have the manuscript published, give her half of the profits, and to return the original manuscript to her. Finally, Philastus was back in New York presenting the letter to Mr. Clark.

Mr. Clark raised his eyes and looked at Philastus. He carefully folded the letter up and put it in his vest pocket. "Follow me, Mr. Hurlbut." He led Philastus up a narrow staircase to a small, musty room. The door creaked as Clark opened it.

"There it is." Clark pointed a bony finger toward an old, dusty trunk in the corner of the room. "Solomon Spaulding's papers. Good luck finding what you're looking for." Mr. Clark shook Philastus's hand and left the cheerless room.

Philastus removed his gloves and rubbed his hands together to warm them. His quest was nearly complete. Dust spilled from the hair-covered trunk as Hurlbut pried it open. Engulfed in the musty smell of old papers and with his cold-stiffened fingers shaking from excitement, he shuffled through the trunk's contents until he found it—a collection of handwritten pages titled "Manuscript Found." He quickly glanced through each page, making sure the text was in order, and that no pages were missing. Then he gathered the papers up and carefully tucked them into his satchel. Relief swept over him. He finally possessed what he had promised to find. This would surely bring Smith down. Anxious to read the manuscript, he pulled his gloves back on and left the cold room.

That afternoon, seated in front of a roaring fire in a room in the tavern, Philastus studied the manuscript before him. He read until late in the night, only stopping to eat and stoke the fire. As time passed, he became increasingly agitated. Page after page passed before his eyes. When he had read the entire manuscript, he shoved it from him, stood up and paced the room. He cursed. The thing he read bore little resemblance to the Book of Mormon. It might not support his boasts nor justify the large sums of money that Grandison Newell and Orris Clapp had spent on his journey. He would have to adjust his plan. His jaw clenched tightly in determination. The second leg of his mission would succeed! He would travel to Palmyra, New York. He would find those who had known the Smiths and who despised their pride and blasphemy, those who would embellish every fault, every questionable story, those who would join him in tearing their credibility to shreds.

* * *

Monday, November 25

Benjamin ducked out the front door behind Joe E. and his younger brothers and sisters. He glanced briefly toward the schoolhouse where they were headed. Benjamin adjusted his hat to keep the rain out of his face and walked quickly in another direction—toward the Whitney store. He had decided not to go to school today, but to help Joel on his house instead. Before that, though, he needed to talk to Seth. He had a pressing concern on his mind.

Five minutes later, Ben was scraping the mud from his boots on the porch of the Whitney store. A hand fell on his shoulder. "Hello, young Benjamin!" Ben tilted his head up and saw the Prophet. He immediately straightened. They stood eye to eye; Benjamin was youthful, dark, and slender, in contrast to the Prophet's fair complexion and broad build.

"President Smith." Benjamin inclined his head, his face turning red with self-consciousness.

"Call me Brother Joseph." The Prophet smiled warmly as he shook Ben's hand. "I'm surprised you aren't in school today. What brings you to the store?"

"I'm looking for my brothers."

Joseph smiled, "Which ones? You have a gaggle of them."

Always sensitive to jesting, Ben felt his face grow hotter. "Seth and Joel."

The Prophet grinned reassuringly. "Seth and Joel are with Bishop Whitney near the creek, scouting out a spot for a sawmill. If we can get it built before the snows come, it will be ready to cut lumber for the Lord's house in the spring. I'm interested in knowing what they've decided. I'll go with you to find them."

As they started out together, Benjamin felt tongue-tied and nervous. It was difficult to believe that a prophet of God was interested in walking and talking with him.

Joseph continued the conversation. "Don Carlos moved in with me a few days ago in order to learn the art of printing. He speaks of your family with great affection. He tells me that you are an extraordinary young man who loves the Lord."

Benjamin nodded. "I do."

"Yet you have not had the opportunity to be baptized."

Benjamin felt the rain begin to saturate his hat. He turned to the Prophet, and a rush of words came out as his eyes filled with emotion. "I want to be baptized, but my father won't allow it until I'm of age."

"That day will come, Benjamin."

At the kind look in the Prophet's blue eyes, Ben went on. "But what if I take sick and die like David? My soul won't be saved. Yesterday I asked Seth if I ought to defy Pa."

"What was Seth's counsel?" the Prophet queried.

"He said he would pray earnestly about it," Ben answered, "and we would talk about it again today. That's why I'm lookin' for him."

Joseph nodded, his voice thoughtful. "Benjamin, your whole family mourns for David, but I think it is the worst for your father. He hasn't faith to comfort him." Then Joseph put his arm around the young man's shoulders. An inner light shone from Joseph's blue eyes. The Prophet spoke. "Ben, wait patiently upon the Lord. Be mindful of your father's wishes for a time."

Benjamin nodded, his heart pounding. The Prophet looked out toward the creek. He extended his hand. "There they are."

Seth and the other men were in the distance, standing on the bank of the creek. Their forms looked blurred in the drizzle. Benjamin and the Prophet walked quickly to join them.

Once they were with the men, Joel and Bishop Whitney showed the Prophet the location where a sawmill could most conveniently be constructed. Benjamin stood close to Seth, a short distance apart from the other men. The rain increased, and the Prophet, Bishop Whitney, and Joel turned and walked back toward the Whitney Store.

Benjamin and Seth followed a few paces behind. In a low voice, Benjamin told Seth of his conversation with Brother Joseph. Seth smiled at his younger brother. "Then put your mind at ease, Ben. Have faith that you will be baptized someday. For now, we have the comfort of knowing that our prayers have been answered by a prophet of God."

Once the group was back on the porch of the Whitney Store, Joel addressed Benjamin. "I could use some help on the house today. Annie's itching to move in before the baby comes."

Ben slowly smiled. "Sounds better than school."

The Prophet chuckled at Benjamin. "Next winter, my young friend, we will have a school which will suit you. You will be able to study the words of the prophets along with other subjects. I'll wager that you'll be itching to go to school then."

Seth put his arm on Benjamin's shoulder and raised his eyebrows. "That will be a welcome change." Then Seth added, "Bennie, I'll meet up with you and Joel after I pick up some supplies for Mother."

* * *

After Ben and Joel left, Seth walked into the store behind the Prophet and Bishop Whitney.

Lucy Mack Smith was waiting for Joseph just inside the doorway. Joseph kissed his mother's cheek. "Hello, Mother. Have you come to buy goods from Newel's store, or to see me?" When she didn't immediately respond, he teased. "Ah, I must not be the son you're looking for. You miss your darling, Carlos."

In response, Mother Smith took Joseph's hands in hers. Her eyes were grave and reddened. Joseph studied her features. "Mother, what is it?"

"Elders Hyde and Gould just arrived from Missouri. The Saints have been driven from Jackson County. The elders are in the translating room with Frederick and Sidney, waiting for you."

Joseph motioned to Bishop Whitney and Seth to follow. The Prophet's eyes were grim with worry. Lucy Mack Smith followed the men. When the Prophet walked in the room, he greeted and embraced his brethren. "What has happened? Have any been killed?"

"Joseph, sit down first," Mother Smith pleaded as she pulled up chairs for the men.

Seth sat down with the others and folded his hands in his lap. His knuckles whitened as Elder Hyde related the heart-wrenching details. "A mob collected on Monday, the fourth, in Independence—two or three hundred well-armed men. We tried to defend ourselves, and a battle was fought above the Blue River. Brother Barber and two members of the mob were killed. Others were wounded. I don't know how many. Philo Dibble severely. He may now be dead. Brother Gilbert's store has been broken open and Brothers Gilbert, Phelps, and one other brother taken as prisoners. The mob threatens that they will never let them escape alive. Some of the brethren have been beaten and whipped. Our homes and property are destroyed, our women and little ones driven like cattle. When we left, the people were fleeing from Jackson County with almost nothing but their lives. They are destitute and don't know what to do."

As Joseph heard this, grief overwhelmed him. For a moment he put his head in his hands, and his strong shoulders shook. Joseph cried aloud, as tears flowed down his face. "Oh my brethren! My brethren! Would that I had been with you, to have shared your fate! Oh my God, what shall I do in such a trial as this?"

* * *

December 12, 1833

Despite the early morning chill in her three-room frame house, sweat glistened on Annie's temples as she felt the pain of the contraction. Ten-month-old Sariah, who was sleeping cuddled up against Annie's side, felt her mother tense. The child startled awake, let out a cry, then fell back to sleep.

In the kitchen, stoking the fire, Julianne had heard Sariah cry out. She opened the bedroom door and saw that her sister-in-law was awake. "Annie?"

"It's time," Annie gasped.

"I'll go get Joel," Julianne said quickly. She threw her cloak on and ran out the door, through the crusty snow to the barn, her long braid bouncing on her back.

"Annie's in labor," she said breathlessly to her brother. "I'll awaken Sixtus so he can go with you. Bring Mother, Almera, and Susan back to help with the delivery."

"I'll get the wagon ready," Joel said. But instead of going straight to the wagon, he took a board and broke the ice in the trough so that the animals could drink.

"Can't you do that later, Joel?" Julianne exclaimed. "I've never midwifed all alone before. The baby could come fast. I need Mother here if Annie has any difficulty."

Julianne didn't wait for Joel's response but ran back to the house. Once inside, she opened the bedroom door and found Annie out of bed, lifting Sariah. "My water broke," Annie said almost apologetically as she hoisted the baby girl to her shoulder. Annie wore a white nightdress, and her hair was a wild, auburn mass of disarray. She glanced at her protruding abdomen. "This child is determined. He won't wait."

"He?" Juli asked with a slight raise of her slender eyebrows. She took Sariah from Annie and laid the little girl in the cradle. "Annie, get back under the covers. Aren't you frozen?"

Another contraction gripped Annie, and she sat down on the edge of the mattress. When it was over, she looked at Juli. "This must be a boy! Only a male would be so demanding!"

"I hope your husband is hurrying." Juli smiled and shook her head slightly as Annie lay down. "But Joel's never been a quick mover."

"Not like your Almon. He's quick as a cat. But I don't mind my Joel's lumbering ways."

"Annie, you're so relaxed. It's sure to be a smooth birth," Julianne commented as she forced a pert smile. She tucked Annie in under the quilts.

An instant later, Joel came in with Sixtus. He looked at Sariah sleeping in the cradle. He turned to Annie, a nervous look in his eyes. "The wagon's ready. Will the baby wait for Mother?"

"I'm not sure," Annie said with a small smile.

Joel swallowed. "Should I take Sariah with me?"

Annie shook her head. "No, she's sound asleep. Just take Sixtus. Juli's here with me to help." Then Annie cringed, wrapped in another contraction.

Julianne brought Sixtus into the room, dressed, but still droopy from sleep. Joel took his hand and explained that Sixtus was going to Grandma's to stay while Mama had the baby. Sixtus's eyes widened. He turned his head and stared at his mother, who was in obvious pain. He pulled away from his father and ran to the bed. "Mama!" Sixtus cried out, suddenly sobbing. "I'm feared you will die!"

Annie gritted her teeth and stroked her little boy's hair until the wave of pain passed. Then she took Sixtus's face between her hands and looked deep into his eyes. "Be brave, my Sixtus, and don't cry. It's just the baby coming. You go now and play with Amos. When you get back, you'll have a new brother."

"Named Nephi?" Sixtus sniffled.

"Yes," Annie responded. "Just like we talked about."

"What if Nephi's a girl?" Sixtus asked tearfully.

"I hope not. How people would torment her with a name like *Nephi!*" Annie teased. Sixtus laughed through his tears. Annie smiled brightly at her little boy. "Now Sixtus, go to Grandmother's, keep a prayer in your heart for Mama, and have a happy day!"

Joel looked at Annie. Her red hair was splayed around her face in every direction like the sun. Her freckled cheeks were rosy. "God be with you," Joel said in a rush of emotion as he bent down and kissed her.

"Joel," Annie said after the kiss, "hurry now and don't worry. This is the strongest I've ever felt before a birth."

Joel nodded and stood up. "Farewell, my beloved." He turned to Julianne. "Thank you, Juli. I'll have mother and the girls here as soon as I can."

"*Sooner* would be better." Julianne gave Joel and Sixtus a quick hug before they left.

A half hour passed. There was a knock at the door. Julianne opened it with Sariah fussing in her arms. "Oh, Almon, I hoped you were my mother!" Juli exclaimed in dismay.

"Why on earth would you want me to be your mother? I thought you would be glad I am me!" Almon laughed as he reached around the baby and kissed Julianne.

"Annie's about to have the baby!"

Almon's green eyes widened. "I'll come back later," he said as he started to leave.

"Stay, I need you." Julianne grabbed him with her free hand and pulled him into the house. "Tend Sariah. Give her a piece of hard bread dipped in molasses." Julianne handed him the baby as Annie cried out from the bedroom.

"Thank you," Julianne called back as she ran to the aid of her sister-in-law.

Fifteen minutes later, Annie gave birth to an infant son. The baby came into the world with a wet mass of matted black hair. Julianne deftly pinched off the cord and wrapped the squealing child in a blanket. She laid the baby against Annie's breast. Portions of Annie's hair, now plastered with sweat, stuck to her forehead.

"Thank you, my friend," Annie whispered to Julianne. Annie stared in awe at her baby. She cupped his shoulders in one hand and ran a fingertip along his arms and legs. She counted his tiny fingers and toes.

Julianne took a deep breath as she watched Annie. What an unutterable joy it would be to have a child of her own! A mixture of joy, relief, and longing filled her. She had been with Annie during the births of three out of her four children. She remembered

Annie's first delivery, the beautiful child that had been named after Julianne, the little girl who had died. Juli impulsively put her arms around the mother and baby and hugged them. "Oh, Annie, you did it! How I hope you are with me when I deliver my first! How I hope I am as brave and strong as you!"

* * *

In the nearby room, Almon, who had heard the baby's first cry, continued to bounce little Sariah vigorously on his knee. "This is the way the gentlemen ride, the gentlemen ride, the gentlemen ride," he chanted, as the baby girl flew up and down. Sariah squealed with glee. Almon stopped suddenly, and the tiny girl with brown, curly hair stared at him open-mouthed, her hazel eyes bright. She whined, wanting him to play more.

"Poor baby Sari." Almon smiled slyly as he started bouncing her again. His green eyes gleamed. "Your life has changed forever. You have been usurped by a brother who squeals like a baby pig."

* * *

Within an hour, Joel returned to his home with Julia, Almera, and Susan. They found Almon in the kitchen, trying to eat bread and cheese with Sariah on his lap, the little girl sticky with molasses as she gnawed on a hard crust of bread.

"You have a new son in the other room," Almon said to Joel as he chewed a bite of cheese. Joel grinned boyishly. Sariah whined and reached out to her father.

"I'll see if they are ready for you, Joel," Julia said. She stepped quickly into the adjoining bedroom.

"Joel," Julia called out from the bedroom door. "Your wife is asking for you."

When Joel started to leave the room, Sariah whined, twisted, and reached out to him. She began to cry, getting molasses all over Almon's shirt.

Almon groaned and held Sariah at arm's length. Almera deftly took Sariah from Almon. Then Susan dipped a cloth in water and began cleaning the little girl up.

Almon swallowed his cheese and stood up, noticing that Joel had left the bedroom door completely ajar. Almon walked over. He looked in and saw that all was in order. Only a pile of soiled bedclothes indicated the drama that had taken place just an hour ago. Annie and the infant were now cleaned up and resting comfortably under a fresh quilt.

Almon watched as Annie looked up at Joel and smiled. "Our son, Nephi. All went well, Joel. Julianne helped me! It was the easiest birth so far."

Joel kissed his wife and tenderly picked up his son. After admiring the miracle of the child, he handed him to his mother. Julia began to cry.

"Are you all right, Mother Johnson?" Annie questioned softly.

Julia nodded and swallowed. "Dear Annie, our Father in Heaven has taken my David, but has given you this beautiful child in almost the same breath. I am grateful to Him for the baby's well-being and for your safety."

Joel put his arm around his mother's shoulder, and Annie's eyes filled with tears. She looked at her mother-in-law. "How I wish your David were with us rejoicing today."

Almon felt Julianne take his hand. She led him out of the room. In the kitchen, Julianne wrapped her cloak around her shoulders and handed Almon his coat. "Let's go outside for a moment of privacy," she suggested.

As they walked, the sky was cloudy and the ground hard and cold. Julianne tucked their entwined hands into the pocket of her cloak. Almon spoke. "If that were our son, I would name him David."

Juli stopped and kissed Almon's cheek. "Annie and Joel decided a long time ago to name their son Nephi. I'm glad that our son will be David's namesake."

Almon felt a sudden panic rise inside of him. Yet instead of bolting, he wrapped Julianne in his arms and held her close. Why did he have the urge to run? Why was he suddenly afraid of the very thing he wanted most in the world? Was it because he found it taxing taking care of little Sariah for just an hour? Was it because he feared losing his freedom?

"How long before we can marry?" Julianne whispered. Almon heard the urgency in her voice. He hesitated. Julianne rushed forward, "Things can change so fast, Almon. I don't want to wait long."

Almon continued to hold her close. "I can't support a wife yet. I need to be able to provide for you and a family."

"I'm not afraid to be poor, Almon," Juli said softly. "Most of the Saints in Kirtland are poor."

"This spring," Almon said, his heart pounding against hers. "I'll rent some land and get crops in."

Julianne's face lighted with joy. She kissed him and continued their walk, almost skipping now as she exclaimed, "Almon, as I watched Annie with her sweet baby, how I yearned for our little ones!"

Almon suddenly laughed at his own fear. "It will be heaven, Juli!" He grabbed her and kissed her long and tenderly.

* * *

December 16, 1833

A few days later, Seth and Lyman walked together to a priesthood meeting at the Whitney store. Snowflakes flurried around them. Once in the store, they immediately went to the upstairs class-room. The room was nearly full, and they quickly found a place to sit on a back bench. A few moments later, Brigham Young arrived, dusting the snow off his hat and shoulders. Just before the meeting started, he shook Lyman's hand and squeezed onto the bench next to him. After an opening prayer and hymn, the Prophet stood before the group and began speaking.

Seth and Lyman watched in awe as the Prophet's countenance changed. They had never seen him receive a revelation before. Tears came to both men's eyes as a peculiar transparency enveloped Joseph—that calmness reminiscent of a clear, summer morning. His fair features took on a look that was heavenly, pale like the snow, but warm like a hearth fire in winter. Each sentence was spoken slowly and clearly with a pause when it ended. Brother Frederick wrote it down. The revelation continued. There was no back-tracking, no sound in the room other than the Prophet's voice, the scratch of the quill, and the awe-filled breathing of the brethren.

> *"They that have been scattered shall be gathered.*
> *"And all they who have mourned shall be comforted.*
> *"And all they who have given their lives for my name shall be crowned.*
> *"Therefore, let your hearts be comforted concerning Zion; for all flesh is in mine hands; be still and know that I am God.*
> *"Zion shall not be moved out of her place, notwithstanding her children are scattered."*

There was not a dry eye in the room as the men thought of the suffering families in Missouri. The revelation continued:

> *"And the lord of the vineyard said unto one of his servants: Go and gather together the residue of my servants, and take all the strength of mine house, which are my warriors, my young men, and they that are of middle age also among all my servants, who are the strength of mine house, save those only whom I have appointed to tarry;*
> *"And go ye straightway unto the land of my vineyard, and redeem my vineyard; for it is mine; and I have bought it with money . . .*
> *"And his servant went straightway, and did all things whatsoever his lord commanded him; and after many days all things were fulfilled."*

* * *

Four days later, Philastus Hurlbut arrived in the Kirtland area in a coach attached to a horse-driven sleigh. Though it wasn't snowing, the day was cold and windy. Hurlbut went directly to the tavern to get a warm drink and spend the night. His personal belongings were still in his room in the Johnson home. Upon entering the tavern, he saw Ezekiel Johnson sitting at a back table. Hurlbut approached.

"Hello Father Johnson."

Ezekiel looked up, his eyes bloodshot. "Evening Philastus."

"I suppose we will only see each other in here from now on. Even Seth's Christian nature would be tried by my continuing presence in your home. No, I shall leave your family until I have safely disposed of Smith's visage as a prophet. That won't be difficult with the evidence I've gathered. Once your family is over the shock, perhaps they will applaud rather than hate me! Until then, would you be my spy in Kirtland and tell me what mischief Joe Smith is up to?"

Ezekiel eyed Hurlbut darkly. "Joseph Smith's people have been driven from Jackson County, Missouri. Women and children are dying from exposure. I suppose that's the mischief on his mind right now."

Hurlbut nodded and sat down at Ezekiel's table. He pulled off his gloves. He leaned toward Ezekiel and spoke confidentially. "Don't misunderstand me, Zeke. I know about Jackson County. I too sorrow over such a needless calamity. But Joe Smith is to blame for those people's suffering, not the Jackson County boys. They were protecting their own. Smith must be stopped."

Ezekiel snorted and took another drink. Hurlbut ordered a drink, then continued with an amiable smile, "How is my cousin?"

"Lyman's fair."

"And do you have a new grandchild?"

Ezekiel nodded. "Aye. A boy."

Hurlbut continued nonchalantly. "How about the rest of your family? How are David and Seth?"

Ezekiel studied him for a moment, then shook his head. "You don't know, do you?"

Hurlbut's eyes narrowed quizzically. "Know what?"

Ezekiel's voice was bitter and his look haggard. "David's dead. Quick consumption. Worked himself to death in that temple brickyard."

For a moment, Philastus was silent. Then intense anger surged through him. Joseph Smith had stolen Hurlbut's hopes for marriage and David Johnson's life! Philastus stood up and struck the table with the full force of his powerful fist. He shouted over the din of conversation. "There will be no more sacrifices to Joe Smith's God!" Every eye in the tavern turned to him. "Mormonism will fall, or I will see Joseph Smith to his grave! I will wash my hands in his blood! Who will stand by me?" A shout went up. A cacophony of voices joined the fray.

"Let's tear down them temple walls!"

"Grandison Newell can get us a cannon."

"Shoot Joe Smith! He's the kingpin."

Hurlbut raised his hand to quiet the crowd and held up his satchel. "I have affidavits—testimonies from the leading citizens of Palmyra, New York, Smith's old neighbors. They describe the villainy of Joe Smith and his family. Even his father-in-law testifies against him. He would rather have his poor daughter dead than married to Smith. I also have a manuscript written by a deceased gentleman, from which Joe Smith and Sidney Rigdon copied the historical parts of the Book of Mormon. You will no longer have to worry about your daughters being stolen by Mormonites. We will kill the cat, and the mice will run free!"

* * *

As Philastus worked the crowd, Ezekiel stood up and left the tavern. Riding his mule against the wind, he crossed the bridge over the Chagrin River into Kirtland. The wind was cold on his face, and his gloveless hands were red and callused. He didn't stop until he was at the Whitney Store. Without speaking to anyone, he walked straight upstairs and knocked on the door to Joseph Smith's apartment. Emma answered with her baby in her arms. Ezekiel took off his hat. He felt suddenly embarrassed by the smell of whisky on him.

"Mr. Johnson," Emma said carefully. "Can I help you?"

"Ma'am, I need to speak to your husband."

"He recently returned from the new printing office. He and Carlos are downstairs in the kitchen eating a late supper. You may join them."

Ezekiel walked downstairs. When he entered the small kitchen, the two men at the table looked up. Ezekiel nodded to Don Carlos, then abruptly addressed Joseph. "Hurlbut's back. He's working the crowd at the tavern—turning them into vigilantes. He plays dirty—has affidavits from your old neighbors and your wife's father. If he can't break down Mormonism, he'll kill you. Says he'll wash his hands in your blood. They're threatening your temple. Talking about a cannon. I'd advise you to get a bodyguard. Make sure your temple workers carry firearms."

Joseph stood up, his blue eyes somber. "Thank you, Father Johnson, for warning us."

"I'm tired of burying Mormon men. If you can't protect your own, maybe you ought to get out of this prophet business."

Joseph looked straight into Ezekiel's eyes. "I cannot, sir, until God releases me."

Ezekiel did not look away. "Then watch your back." He nodded curtly, having finished his business with the Smiths. "Joseph. Carlos. I'll see you boys around." He turned and walked out of the room.

After Ezekiel left, Don Carlos looked at his brother and took a deep breath. "Joseph, I believe we have a friend amongst our enemies."

Joseph nodded. "And enemies, Carlos, amongst our friends."

* * *

The next afternoon was clear and cold. Seth rode to the Shermans' home and found Lyman outside building a split-rail fence.

"Lyman," Seth said as he helped Lyman lift one of the logs, "When Pa came home last night, he mentioned that Philastus is back. He'll soon be moving out of our house."

Lyman nodded, but did not speak. Seth could feel the tension moving through his friend. Yet he went on, knowing that Lyman would hear the news eventually. "He's rallying the anti-Mormons in Mentor, increasing his rhetoric, swearing he'll destroy Mormonism or kill Joseph himself. He says he brought back proof that Joseph is a fraud. Last night he had the men in the tavern riled to the point of violence. They were threatening to shoot the Prophet and tear down the walls of the temple. Before Pa came home, he went to Joseph and warned him to be careful. Today Joseph filed a complaint against Philastus with the justice of the peace. They will serve a warrant for Philastus's arrest."

Lyman and Seth set the log into place. When Lyman turned to Seth his expressive eyes were spheres of pain and anger. He spoke through clenched teeth. "D. P. wants to kill the Prophet of God!" He was silent for a moment, then exclaimed, "Seth, I can't comprehend it. Once I promised Philastus that I would always be his friend, his brother. That Philastus is dead. Worse than dead!"

Seth put a hand on Lyman's shoulder. The world had seemed empty and fragile since David's death. Yet, he knew that Lyman suffered the greater loss. "My friend," Seth said. "We both have lost brothers this year."

* * *

On the evening of January seventh, Lyman held the reins steady as he maneuvered the horse-driven sleigh toward the Painesville jail. He was taking blankets and supplies to Philastus. Three days ago, Hurlbut had been forced to appear before the justice of the peace in Painesville Township. He had been arrested for threatening the life and property of Joseph Smith Jr. After requesting a continuance, Hurlbut had been informed that he would have to remain in jail for ten days—until the case could be heard.

The full moon rose and lighted the road of packed snow before Lyman. As he neared the jail, Lyman's jaw was rigid. He flicked the reins and drove the horse onward. Lyman looked older than he had looked just months ago. The softness of his features had vanished, replaced by lines of pain and fortitude, an almost fierce nobility.

This task had not been Lyman's idea. He came out of respect for the wishes of his mother and mother-in-law. The sleigh contained blankets and personal items that Philastus had left at the Johnson home. His mother had even sent a pot of warm stew. Lyman knew that she held onto the hope that her nephew could be redeemed. Lyman shook his head as he reined in the horse near the jail. He took a deep breath, certain that this trip was futile.

After knocking on the door of the adjoining house, Lyman briefly explained his errand to the justice of the peace, William Holbrook. A few moments later, Holbrook helped Lyman carry the blankets and food into the jail. A single candle stood on a stool. Philastus sat on a bed, wearing a heavy coat, shuffling through papers. Thick quilts covered his legs. Upon seeing Lyman, Philastus's eyes widened in surprise. He put the papers on the floor. Despite his warm clothing, Lyman noticed that Philastus was pale, and his lips were slightly blue from the cold. The years of their kinship felt like a weight in Lyman's heart.

"Have you come to gloat, Lyman?" Philastus asked cynically.

"I've brought a pot of stew from Mother and the things you left at the Johnsons'." When Philastus didn't answer, Lyman turned and stepped toward the door.

Hurlbut cleared his throat and held up a gloved hand. "Wait." Lyman stopped as if summoned. He turned slowly around. Hurlbut addressed the justice of the peace. "Mr. Holbrook, could I have a few moments alone with my cousin?"

Holbrook nodded. "Sure thing, Mr. Hurlbut. Mr. Sherman, I'll need your firearm."

Lyman handed his gun to Holbrook. The justice of the peace left the room. Philastus pointed at the stack of papers, "Lyman, I have affidavits from people in Palmyra, from Isaac Hale. They prove that the whole Smith tribe are base, lying rogues!"

Lyman stared at Philastus. "I know firsthand what the Smiths are like and so do you. Even if you honestly believe that Joseph is not a prophet, how can you be so cruel to Sister Emma, to Mother and Father Smith as to print those lies?"

Hurlbut coughed. "I seek the truth! You should be seeking vengeance for this injustice against your cousin, not heralding a false prophet." He coughed again.

Lyman's shoulders sagged. It was no use arguing with him. "Eat the stew Mother sent before it gets cold."

Philastus's voice was bitter. "So Aunt Asenath pities me. There's a good Christian woman. *Agree with your enemies quickly while you are in the way with them. If ye do it unto the least of these, my brethren, ye have done it unto me.* And here I sit, suffering in prison for the truth, like a disciple of Christ. "

Lyman tensed. Hurlbut continued. "What satisfaction it would give me to kill your deranged prophet! To do all the world a favor!" Philastus saw Lyman's fists clench. He goaded him. "Come on, Lyman, hit me! Give me the chance to knock some sense into your thick skull! Why would Joe Smith be afraid of me when he has the Almighty to protect him?"

Suddenly Lyman saw his cousin for what he was—a proud and angry man fighting against the very power that could heal him. D. P. was kicking against the pricks like Alma the Younger and Saul of old. But an angel would not come to Philastus. He had had his chance to know the truth. Lyman felt the wave of rage pass through him, and as it receded, tremendous sadness filled him like rising water. "Forgive me, Philastus," he said softly.

Hurlbut was taken off guard. "Forgive you for what, Lyman? I don't blame you. You are only a pawn on Joseph Smith's board."

"You would have been better off had I never baptized you into the Church of Christ."

Hurlbut recoiled. "Smith's church is not Christ's Church!"

Lyman's eyes, brimming with tears, bored into his cousin. "Philastus, you have no idea what you're fighting against."

Philastus looked steadily back at his cousin. "Go home, Lyman. Keep Delcena and the children inside tonight."

Lyman went to the door. He looked back at his cousin one last time. "May God have mercy on your soul."

* * *

Late that night, while Delcena slept, Lyman lay awake. He rose from the bed and kneeled on the cold floor. He prayed that he would do enough good to outweigh his cousin's evil works, and that Philastus's heart would be softened enough to prevent him from committing murder, that his soul might not be lost forever. Then Lyman beseeched the Lord to protect Delcena and the children, the Prophet Joseph, and the restored Church of Christ.

After closing his prayer, Lyman climbed back into bed. He was almost asleep when the sound of cannons shook their house. Delcena awakened and clung to him. Thirteen rounds were fired before the night was silent again. "Philastus knew of this," Lyman whispered. "He warned me to stay inside tonight."

When all was quiet, Lyman dressed and went outside. He made his way to the temple site. Father Smith and Hyrum were already there. The temple walls stood. There had been no casualties. A few minutes later the Prophet and Don Carlos arrived, followed by Bishop Whitney and Seth. The men spoke in low voices. Lyman bowed his head, thanking his Heavenly Father that there was no blood on his cousin's hands that night.

* * *

When Seth returned home, his parents and Nancy were sitting in the kitchen close to the fire. Julia's rocking chair stilled, and she looked up at him anxiously.

"No one is hurt," Seth assured her. "The walls of the temple stand."

"Did you check on Delcena?" Ezekiel questioned.

Seth nodded. "Of course. They're fine."

"What was Lyman thinking—moving his family so close to that temple site?" Ezekiel growled. No one responded.

A moment later, Nancy addressed her brother. "Seth," Nancy said quietly, "when you go upstairs, tell the rest that all is well. We sent them back to bed, but I'd wager they're awake."

Seth nodded and smiled at Nancy. "You'd best turn in too. Dawn is around the corner."

After Nancy and Seth left the room, Ezekiel stood up and stared into the fire. He spoke to his wife, but did not look at her. His voice was bitter. "David is dead! Cannons have been fired in the direction of Delcena's home! Will you continue down this futile course until more of our children are destroyed, until all love between us is cold?"

When Julia did not answer, Ezekiel spun toward her, his eyes ablaze. "How long will you live this way? How long?"

Julia looked into his eyes. "Until the Savior comes again."

Ezekiel turned and stalked out of the room. Julia heard the door to Philastus's old room slam shut. Julia went into her bedroom and curled up under her quilt. She did not cry. There were no tears left.

15

Oh Zion, how I love
Thy great and holy cause
Could I thy wicked foes remove
And safe enforce thy laws.

How would I leap for joy
And labor day and night
Their evil works all to destroy
And put their hosts in flight.

Joel Hills Johnson
(*Diary,* 64)

February 1834

The wind howled outside as Julia called her children together for
evening prayers. Just as they were about to kneel around the
hearth, there was a knock at the front door. William ran to open it.
Almera followed him. She immediately recognized Samuel
Prescott, the man who shared a carpenter shop with her father. She
recalled how he had come with the coffin following David's death.

Prescott grinned past William, his eyes meeting Almera's. The
storm raged outside. William pushed the door closed. "Hello Miss.
You seem destined to greet me every time I call. Do you answer the
door for every guest?"

Almera colored slightly. "It is a habit of mine, Mr. Prescott. Do come in."

"You are expecting something then—a surprise each time the door opens. Is there a name attached to such a beautiful face?" he asked boldly.

Almera retained her composure. "Almera, sir."

"A name to fit your loveliness."

Seth joined the group at the door. "Hello, Mr. Prescott. What brings you here during this storm?"

"Tidings from your father. He's spending the night in Mentor. At the tavern."

"It's kind of you to show such concern for our family."

"I like your father. I'm a much younger man than he is and can weather a storm."

"You're welcome to join us in Bible reading and prayers."

Prescott shook his head. "No thank you." He shook Seth's hand. Then he focused on Almera. He took her hand in his. "Miss Almera, may I call on you this week?"

Almera felt his fingers, warm on a freezing day, callused from carpentry much like her father's. Her heart beat a little faster. But he wasn't a member of the Church. Seth's face was a mask of protective concern. Almera tried to hide the emotion in her voice when she spoke. "Mr. Prescott, I must decline. I haven't been feeling well this winter and wouldn't be good company."

Samuel Prescott's fair features darkened. "I'll return in the spring when you're feeling better." He dropped her hand, opened the door, and left without closing the door behind him.

Wind and snow swept in. Nine-year-old William pushed the door closed once again. Then he turned to Almera, his cheeks chapped and his brown eyes dancing. Will put his hand over his heart and sighed dramatically. "A lovely name to fit such loveliness!" he mimicked.

Almera grabbed for her little brother, but he ducked away and raced into the sitting room. William ran over to Mary and kneeled at her feet. He took her hand and kissed it, pretending Mary was Almera and he, Mr. Prescott. Making his voice sound deep, he sighed dramatically. "Almera, I shall return in the spring when you are well again!" With a slurp, he kissed Mary's hand once more. Mary jerked away, disgusted.

George doubled over laughing, and Esther giggled. Amos jumped up and down, laughing loudly, his blond curls bouncing. William glanced over at Almera and Seth in the doorway as if he were gauging their reaction. Almera rolled her eyes at him, but Seth wasn't smiling.

"William," Seth reprimanded above the clatter in the room, "it isn't right to make sport of other people."

In response, William stood up and pantomimed loading a shotgun. "I'm Mr. Seth Johnson," the boy said, pushing his chest out. "And this shell has your name on it if you dare come to court one of my sisters!" At that, Julianne, Almera, Joe, and Benjamin burst out laughing. Even Susan smiled.

* * *

A week later, on a dismal snowy day, Julianne and Susan washed the woolens in the kitchen. Each time a load was finished, Julia and Almera hung them out to dry on lines stretching across the sitting room. The room was chill as the wet clothing sucked the warmth from the fire. Nancy sat close to the hearth, twisting cotton yarn for stockings.

Benjamin burst in the front door and barreled into the sitting room. His face was flushed, and snow dusted his shoulders. "Brother Joseph has received another revelation!" he eagerly announced. Julia and Almera stopped hanging the clothing. Julianne and Susan hurried in from the kitchen. Nancy's hands stilled as she looked at Benjamin.

With an audience now, Ben continued. "The Lord has directed the strength of His house, the young and middle-aged men, to travel to Missouri to take supplies to the Saints and help them return to Zion. He says that angels will go before them. The Prophet will lead them like Moses led the children of Israel!"

Julia's hands fluttered unconsciously. "Benjamin, was Seth there?"

Ben nodded. "He's talking with Almon and Lyman now. Almon was ordained an elder this morning."

"Almon was ordained an elder?" Julianne repeated, her eyes wide.

"Yes," Benjamin went on. "Brother Joseph said it was time. He said that Almon will go with Zion's Camp and do great things."

"Are they going to fight the Missouri mobs?" Susan asked.

"That's why they're going," Ben said, sounding a bit irked. "To lead the people back to the land of Zion. I don't think the mobs will just let them walk back into Jackson County."

"Did the Prophet say how many men will go?" Julia asked. A knot of fear had formed in her stomach.

Ben responded. "All but a few who will be called to tarry. Brother Joseph and other missionaries are going east in a few days to gather more men. Mother, George Albert Smith is going to Missouri, and he isn't much older than I am. Maybe Joe E. and I can go. We'll march with Seth, Lyman, and Almon."

Julia shook her head. "No. Neither of you have been baptized. Besides, with Seth going, I need you and Joe here." For the first time, she felt an awkward surge of gratitude for Ezekiel's opposition. The thought of her Seth being in danger shook her very core. With David gone, how could she bear another loss?

Ben's eyebrows knit together, and his mood darkened. "But Mother, the revelation said that those not willing to lay down their lives for Christ's sake aren't worthy to be called his disciples. Angels will protect Zion's Camp."

Julia was silent. She didn't know how to answer her son. Nancy spoke. "Ben, did the Prophet say when the men would leave for Missouri?"

Ben nodded and answered shortly. "In the spring. After the crops are planted." Then he turned back to his mother. "Mother, I need to obey the Prophet."

Julia understood the earnest passion in Benjamin's eyes. She would postpone this battle, but she would not lose it. "Son, we'll talk about this later, when Seth is home."

Julia's mind was troubled as she worked the remainder of the morning, praying constantly in her heart that the Prophet would receive another revelation calling Seth and Joel to tarry in Kirtland. Distracted, she did not respond when William, George, Esther, and Amos played tag in the sitting room, dodging about the clean clothes and accidentally knocking the woolens off the lines. Nor did she chastise Almera for shouting angrily at them.

* * *

Back in the kitchen, wringing out the laundry, Julianne's tears fell onto the wet clothing.

"Don't cry," Susan said quietly. "The Lord will protect them."

"I don't want Almon to become crippled like Nancy. Or to die like David. And how could we survive without Seth?" Juli cried.

Susan left the washboard and put her arm around her sister. "I don't know," she whispered.

"Susie, will you help me put some trim on my Sunday dress?" Juli sobbed. "I want to marry Almon now. So that we have a little time together."

"Of course," Susan said with tears in her eyes.

Julianne hugged Susan as she cried. She wanted desperately to have a little bit of time as Almon's wife before he left on this dangerous mission that could snatch him away from her for the rest of her life. Oh, why did David have to die and destroy every illusion of security?

* * *

That evening when the family sat around the table for supper, Ezekiel was in a dark mood. Word traveled fast to the tavern. He had heard that afternoon that Joseph Smith was planning a military operation to redeem so-called Zion.

He looked over at Seth. "Do you plan on going to Missouri with that foolhardy group Joseph Smith is putting together?"

Seth put his fork down and looked steadily at his father. "Yes, Pa. You have always taught me to honor my commitments, never to break my word. I have to go and help our people who've been driven from their homes. They bought and paid for their land. Even the governor admits that the law is on their side. But he doesn't have a militia willing to enforce it. Some things are worth fighting for."

Ezekiel chewed his lower lip. "I suppose Joel's going too."

Seth shook his head. "No. Brother Joseph has asked him to stay here and work the sawmill."

Ezekiel sniffed. "Why does he need to cut logs when there won't be men here to build anything?"

"Joel's working on shingles for the temple roof."

"What about Lyman?" Ezekiel snapped.

"He's going."

Ezekiel glanced at Julianne, then back at Seth. "And young Almon Babbitt?"

Seth nodded. "Nearly all the young men are going."

Ezekiel shook his head as if this was unbelievable. He glared at Seth. "Not only are you leaving your families defenseless, but the Missouri mobs will be waiting for you Mormon boys. I didn't raise you to die on some cursed Missouri prairie. Your fate would be worse than David's. At least he died at home, surrounded by the people who love him."

"I only have one life to live, Pa. I have to live it the best I can." Seth's eyes were both gentle and unyielding as he spoke. Ezekiel looked away from his son. The look in Seth's eyes reminded him too much of Julia.

* * *

During this interchange, Joe E. watched Ben. His brother sat on the edge of his seat. Joe knew how much Ben wanted to go on Zion's Camp with Seth. Joe was glad that Ben was wise enough to keep quiet for the moment and not start a bigger row, but Joe also knew that Ben hadn't given up hope. Joe sighed. He thought about how he prayed each day for the suffering people in Missouri. Perhaps Zion's Camp was an answer to those prayers. Yet he didn't feel it like Ben. He didn't want to go. Maybe he was a coward and lacked faith. But he also clearly perceived how much his mother wanted him to stay home, how much she needed him. With Seth going, Joe knew that it would be his job to take care of her, to comfort her, and to organize and direct his younger brothers.

Joe looked around the table. The only sounds were the clicking of silverware and the chewing of food. No one dared talk with that grim look on Pa's face. Joe took a deep breath. He thought of how he sometimes still cried at night when he thought of David. He shuddered at the thought of Seth in danger, and he hoped that his father would stop Ben from going.

A few days ago he had gotten a letter from Morris telling him that Rachel and Blanchard were planning to get married someday. Joe shook his head as he remembered laughing and picking wild-flowers in the lonely gulf with Rachel. There were a few pretty girls in Kirtland, but none who compared to her. Just a few years ago Joe had found fun around each corner. He was sixteen now, and worry lined his brow.

* * *

That night, in an upstairs bedroom, Esther's young body jerked to a sitting position as screams wracked her six-year-old frame. Mary, who shared a bed with Esther, shook her younger sister gently, trying to wake her up. "It's a nightmare, Esther, wake up."

"Dragons! Dragons!" Esther shrieked, her eyes wide open in terror. "Seth! Don't! David! David!" The little girl moaned as she sobbed.

"Esther, wake up! Please wake up," Mary shouted.

Awakened by their sisters' cries, Susan and Julianne ran into the room. Julianne gathered Esther into her arms and rocked her back and forth on the bed. Susan sat down by Mary. When little

Esther realized where she was, she buried her head deeper into Julianne's shoulder, continuing to sob.

"It was just a nightmare," Julianne assured. "Tell us what it was about and you'll feel better."

"There were dragons outside our house," Esther whimpered. "Spitting fire. They killed David. Seth went outside to fight them, but they were too big and strong." Esther's breathing was labored, and she shuddered. Julianne continued to hug her baby sister, her own eyes filling with tears. Feeling helpless, she could not promise little Esther that such a nightmare wouldn't come to pass.

Suddenly, Susan's soft voice filled the room as she continued the dream-story. "Sir Almon the Magnificent rode up with Lyman the Faithful at his side. With swords of lightning they slew the dragons and rescued Seth the Benevolent. Inside the house, Ezekiel the Kind and his brave wife, Julia, doused every fire the dragons had started."

Susan stopped talking. Nancy stood at the doorway. She had slowly climbed the stairs with her crutches when she heard Esther scream. Nancy continued the story, her eyes shining with tears. "Sir David the Valiant was buried on the hill where the maple trees grew. And every day, his loved one's watered his grave with their tears. A maple tree took root close to where Sir David lay. All those who rested in its shade became strong, loving, and wise. And though the family continued to mourn for David, they felt his love every day when the sun rose in the morning."

Esther whimpered. "Juli, I don't like sad stories."

"But sad stories can be beautiful too," Julianne whispered, holding Esther tightly. "If we become like Nancy and Susie and make them so."

* * *

Four days later, Seth and Lyman lifted a granite stone with the help of Almon, Don Carlos, and Burr Riggs. They were working to repair a portion of the temple. The night before, vigilantes from

Mentor had broken down one of the emerging walls and had tried to set the structure on fire. Luckily the vandals had been chased away by a handful of young men who had set their dogs on them.

After the final stone was set back in place, Lyman shaded his eyes in the cloudless winter sunlight. He looked over at the nearby Methodist church where Philastus held many of his anti-Mormon meetings. Lyman thought about how his cousin was now out of jail after posting bond for good behavior. The justice of the peace had ruled that Joseph Smith Jr. had reason to believe that Doctor Philastus Hurlbut would kill him, maim him, or destroy his property. Another trial would be held in Chardon on March thirty-first, where a final judgment would be rendered.

Lyman turned to Seth and nodded in the direction of the Methodist church. "Philastus could be over there right now planning his next attack against Joseph and the temple. I wish there was a way to stop him."

Seth looked at his friend. "I know. But the Prophet teaches that we must build up the kingdom of God. We can't allow ourselves to be distracted from that work by those who lay in wait to destroy."

Lyman nodded. The two stood in silence for a moment. Then, their attention was diverted when they overheard the ensuing conversation between their three young companions, Almon, Don Carlos, and Burr Riggs.

"Brother Burr," Almon said as he merrily trilled the r's on his tongue. "When do you and Lovina plan to get married?"

The spirited, taciturn Burr tossed his head. "I'd marry Lovina today if her father would let me. But he won't give permission until after we get back from Missouri. I'll have to prove myself in battle before I win my bride."

"I wish I were going to Zion," Don Carlos said, his handsome face serious. "But Joseph insists that I stay here and help print *The Star.*"

Almon chuckled. "Don't murmur, Carlos. Enjoy tarrying in Kirtland and courting the lovely Miss Agnes." At the mention of Agnes's name, Don Carlos's color rose.

Burr eyed Almon. "And what of you, Brother Babbitt? Do you plan to marry Sister Julianne before or aft our jaunt to avenge Zion?"

Almon grinned. "Before! I'm a lucky man. We're thinking about the first of April."

"Excuse me, brethren," Seth said as he interrupted Almon and stepped in front of Don Carlos and Burr. "A word with you in private, Brother Babbitt."

Lyman chuckled as he watched Almon walk meekly away with Seth. "There's one thing worse than having a girl with a protective father," he said to his young friends. "And that would be adding an elder brother into the mix."

* * *

"Why do you speak of marrying my sister when you haven't yet asked my father for her hand? Now that I know your intentions, you will hear my feelings on the subject," Seth said briskly. His eyes, usually so deep and kind, had fire in them.

Almon had never seen Seth angry before. He tried to sound nonchalant. "Seth, I assumed Julianne had told you our plans. Julianne has already spoken with your father and assures me he will grant permission. I plan to officially ask him this week. I want your blessing too. I want the whole family's blessing."

"But you will not have my blessing if you marry her before we go to Missouri. Think of the danger it puts her in—binding herself to someone whose life is at stake. Some of us might not come back. *You* might not come back. If you left her with child, she would become a young widow with a baby, alone and penniless. Her chances of marrying someone else would diminish. I beg you not to marry her now for your own selfish reasons."

Almon sputtered. "My own selfish reasons! Seth, I'm guilty of a lot of things, but not this. I love your sister. I'm not the one insisting on getting married now. It's Juli! I'd rather wait until I have something more to offer her. She's too good for me as it is."

For a moment Seth chewed on this information, eyeing the young man next to him, trying to decide whether or not he was completely honest.

Almon went on, his eyes flashing. "But don't get your hopes up, Seth; I don't plan to let Julianne slip away just because she's too good for me. I'm too selfish for that. But I'm not trying to get her to marry me before we leave. Why don't you talk to Julianne about it? Convince her to hold off. I'd rather wait until we get back and I'm settled. But I'll tell you another thing. If she'll only have me now, I won't lose her. I don't know about you, but I plan on coming back from Missouri!" Almon took a breath.

Seth's shoulders relaxed. Almon's reaction impressed him a good deal. "Almon, you must talk with her about waiting. Insist on it. She won't forgive me for meddling."

"And you think she'll forgive me for changing her wedding date? And agree to wait for me?" Almon asked, looking slightly panicked.

Seth smiled, amused. "Yes. And I think in the course of your lifetime together, she'll forgive you for a great deal more serious things. She's promised herself to you, Almon. I know Juli. She'll wait for you to come back. If we both come back whole, your union will have my blessing."

"I'm coming back, Seth," Almon repeated. "And you're coming with me. I'm holding you to your word."

* * *

The next morning, Almon walked over to the Johnsons' shortly after breakfast. It had been freezing cold the previous night, but the morning was sunny and chill. It was the season when the maple sap ran. Almon found Julianne outside replacing the buckets on the tapped maple trees. Almon snuck up behind her and put his hands over her eyes. "Who, who, whooo?" he hooted like an owl.

Julianne put her hands over his. "You, you, youuu!" she returned, laughing. He moved his hands around her waist, turned her around and kissed her.

"Why are you here so early this morning?" Juli asked after the kiss. Her nose was pink from the cold, and her brown eyes sparkled in the sunlight.

Not answering directly, Almon inspected the maple sap dripping from the hollowed elderberry branches inserted into the holes in the trees. "Looks like you're getting a fair amount of sap this year."

"We hope to make five hundred pounds of sugar," Juli said.

Almon helped Julianne attach the buckets to the trees. When they were finished, he put his arms around her again. "Julianne Johnson, will you marry me—"

Julianne laughed and interrupted him. "Yes, a hundred times, yes. Ask me again each day until the wedding."

Almon gently put his forefinger on her lips to stop her from going on. "Juli," he said, his green eyes serious. "I hadn't finished the sentence. Will you marry me when I return from Missouri? Not now, but then."

"Almon." The sparkle fled from Julianne's eyes. "Are you unsure about marrying me?"

"No, my darling, a hundred times, no."

"Then why should we wait? Why have you changed your mind?" Julianne's voice sounded bewildered.

"Seth talked to me yesterday."

"Seth? What does Seth have to do with our decision? Father will allow us to wed."

"But Seth is reasonable, Juli."

Julianne closed her eyes. "I don't want reasonable anymore."

Almon continued. "Seth is right as well. I won't tie you to me before I leave, not when your whole future is at stake. No matter how much I want to. Don't blame Seth. He has your welfare at heart. But when I get back, dearest, nothing will stop me from taking you as my bride."

Julianne could not contain her tears. "Don't you understand, Almon? Don't you know why I want to get married now? If you were staying here we could get married anytime. The spring. The fall. It wouldn't matter. But you might not come back! Seth might not come back!"

Almon held her tight and stroked her hair with his gloved hand. Tears burned in his bright green eyes. Two years ago, he had not realized a love like this was possible. But it was painful too. When he spoke, his voice was defiant. "I will come back, Julianne Johnson. Let all the powers of earth and hell combine against me, but I will still come back to you. And I will bring Seth home with me."

* * *

On Saturday, March twenty-ninth, Joseph Smith, Sidney Rigdon, and Frederick G. Williams walked out of the council room together. Their planning and prayers that day had revolved around three things: the court case against D. P. Hurlbut, which was to begin on the following Monday; the Church's growing debt due to the arrival of poor Saints in Kirtland, coupled with the cost of building the temple; and the organization and preparation for the trek to Missouri. Two days previous, Joseph had come back to Kirtland following his Eastern mission for the purpose of gathering funds and men for Zion's Camp. Despite mounting pressures, he planned to spend the rest of the day with Emma and his little ones.

As the men walked outside into the bright sunlight, Sidney Rigdon was the first to see Benjamin Johnson loitering expectantly near the front door of the building. "Young man, what can I do for you?" Brother Rigdon asked.

"I—I'd like a word with Brother Joseph," Benjamin stuttered.

Sidney Rigdon looked over at Joseph. "The Prophet has a lot on his mind, son, and his family is waiting for him."

"It's all right, Sidney. I have a few minutes to walk and talk with Brother Bennie. If you brethren would excuse us," Joseph said as he smiled warmly at Benjamin.

The day was bright and windy. As they walked together, the Prophet asked Benjamin what was on his mind. Benjamin took a deep breath and began. "I want to go with Seth, Lyman, and Almon—with all of you—with Zion's Camp." Benjamin continued, speaking quickly. He had rehearsed this speech in his mind over and over again. "I'm not needed at home. My brother Joe and my three younger brothers can do the necessary work. I—I want to do the will of God, and to have the blessings of all those willing to lay down their lives for the gospel of Christ."

Joseph stopped and looked deeply into the eyes of the earnest fifteen-year-old. He put a hand on the Ben's shoulder. "Benjamin Johnson," he said compassionately and clearly. "I deem it best for you to remain in Kirtland because of the opposition of your father. I promise you that no loss will come to you from waiting. For although you are not fully a member of the Church, you have partaken of every hope, desire, and spiritual influence of those around you. The Lord knows the intent of your heart and will bless you abundantly." Then the Prophet's face lighted into a smile. "Bennie, be at peace!"

Tears gathered in Benjamin's eyes as he felt the power of God through His servant, Joseph Smith Jr. Benjamin nodded. He was filled with an unspeakable joy at the deep realization that he was living in a day when God had placed a prophet again on the earth. Joseph embraced young Benjamin. Then the two parted, both individuals intent on giving their lives to the Lord.

* * *

Lyman sat between his sister Cornelia and his mother on a bench in the Chardon Courtroom. His youngest sister, Electa, had stayed home. The place was packed with curious spectators, most of whom were not members of the Church, but who had come to hear the "Mormon Trial." They were there to see Joe Smith for themselves, as well as Doctor P. Hurlbut, the exposer of the Mormon mystery.

The trial progressed through a long list of witnesses. Lyman and his mother and sisters had not been subpoenaed. Lyman inwardly thanked the Prophet for this kindness toward his family. They would not have to testify against their kinsman.

Later in the afternoon, Mr. Birchard, the presiding judge, sat stone-faced as he listened to each testimony. A witness sat down, and Sister Copley took the stand. She described how Hurlbut had once come to her home and voiced threats against the Prophet, Joseph Smith. On cross-examination, Hurlbut's lawyer asked Sister Copley why she had not reported any of Hurlbut's threats to Smith.

The middle-aged lady colored slightly and answered. "I didn't think that any human being had the power to hurt a prophet."

Philastus's lawyer sniffed. "It seems, Madam, that Joe himself appears to have placed little reliance upon his divine invulnerability; for he testified today that he is afraid of bodily injury from the defendant."

The judge interrupted. "That comment, sir, has nothing to do with this case. Next witness, please."

After the final witness, the judge called for a short break in which he could review the testimonies. The whispering voices in the room reminded Lyman of swarming bees. He felt his mother take his hand.

Five minutes later, the judge called the court back into session. After looking through the papers at his desk, he asked the accused to stand. "Doctor Philastus Hurlbut, I find you guilty of the charges brought against you. You are required to post a good-behavior bond of two hundred dollars and to pay the court costs totaling one hundred twelve dollars and fifty cents. You must also have two respectable individuals provide additional sureties guaranteeing your good behavior in general, and especially toward Joseph Smith Jr. for the period of six months." The judge pounded the podium with his gavel. "Case dismissed."

Lyman stared at the profile of his cousin. He knew Philastus well. He read the embarrassment and anger in his features. Asenath Hurlbut Sherman touched her son's elbow. Her voice sounded very tired. "Lyman, Cornelia, let's go. It's over now."

Cornelia stood up and straightened her shoulders. She looked at her brother. His glasses were steamy in the warm room. "There is no joy in this victory," she commented with a matter-of-fact sigh.

"No," Lyman said as he glanced once more at Philastus, who was now talking with his attorney. "Only sorrow." Philastus Hurlbut did not watch as his closest relatives turned away from him and left the courtroom.

16

Show mercy unto Zion Lord
That faith and truth with love divine
And righteousness may be restored
That all her children may be thine.

That all thy saints with one accord
May unto thee their homage bring
And thou forever be adored
As Zion's Savior, Lord, and King.

Joel Hills Johnson
(*Diary,* 69)

The early May afternoon was warm and muggy. Nancy and Susan sat in the shade of the porch, sewing clothing for the destitute Missouri Saints. In the distance, they saw John Murdock approach.

"He's one of the kindest men in all the Church," Nancy commented

"And he's a widower," Susan added.

Nancy looked over at her sister. Susan was now concentrating on her sewing. Nancy spoke. "Maybe we should talk to Almera about getting to know him."

Susan didn't look up, but added. "I was thinking of you, Nance."

Nancy's eyes widened. Her heart warmed toward her sister, realizing that Susie was probably the only person on earth who actually thought she had something to offer a man. Yet Nancy knew the truth. The last thing John Murdock or any man needed was a crippled wife.

"He's too short for me," Nancy commented with a smile. Susan giggled and shook her head. No further conversation was possible, because John Murdock walked up to them and doffed his hat. "Morning ladies, is Seth home?"

Susan shook her head. "No, but we expect him soon. Sit down for a moment while I get you some refreshment."

"Thank you, miss," John commented. Susan put her sewing aside and went into the house. Mr. Murdock sat on a chair opposite Nancy.

Nancy felt her face color slightly when she thought of how Susan purposely left her alone with Brother Murdock. They weren't expecting Seth back for at least an hour.

Nancy forced her thoughts from herself. "How are you Brother Murdock?" she asked.

"As right as rain," John answered. "And you, Sister Nancy?'

"Very well, thank you. Are you ready for the journey?"

John Murdock nodded. "I was ready the moment Brother Joseph announced the march to Missouri. My little ones are there. I haven't seen them since last August when the Lord called me on a mission. My boys are with Bishop Partridge, and my little girl, Phebe, is living with the Gilberts. I pray that I will be able to stay in Missouri and build a home for them and help rebuild Zion."

To have a home. To rebuild Zion. Nancy wondered what it would be like to be able to dream such dreams. Yet, she knew that Brother Murdock's life had been anything but easy. Nancy had heard how he wept when the Saints were driven from Zion. It had been terrible for him, knowing that his children were suffering and in danger, while he was far away on a mission, unable to help them. When the march to Zion was announced, he had been the first to volunteer. "I hope your prayers are answered," Nancy said softly. "I'm glad that you will be with your little ones soon."

The door opened and closed. Esther came outside and sidled up to Nancy. "Susie is bringing out cider and cake. Like tea time in England. She says I can have some too."

John grinned at Esther and held out his hand. "Sounds like it's going to be a fine snack. What's your name, sweetheart?"

"Esther Johnson," Esther replied primly as she shook John's hand.

"You're just a little bigger than my girl, Phebe. Are you about seven years old?"

"Six."

John clapped his hands together. "Perfect! That's my Phebe's age."

"Could Phebe come over and meet me?" Esther asked. "I'm tired of playing with boys."

"I'm sorry, Miss Esther," John said. "Phebe is in Missouri. But I'll see her soon and tell her about you."

"Are you going there with my brother Seth?" Esther questioned. John nodded. "That I am."

"Maybe you could bring Phebe back to Kirtland with you."

"I'm hoping to stay in Missouri with her, Miss Esther," John said. "But perhaps all the Saints will gather to Zion soon. Then you will move to Missouri. You and Phebe could have an English tea time together."

Susan came out the front door carrying a tray of cider and cake. Ezekiel followed her. "Hello, John," Ezekiel said. There was tobacco in his mouth. The lines of his face had become harder and more pronounced since David's death.

Murdock stood up and shook his hand. As Susan offered the refreshments to their guest, Ezekiel sat down heavily.

Esther left Nancy's side and climbed on her father's lap. Ezekiel kissed the top of her head.

After the group drank their cider and ate their cake, John Murdock thanked them and explained that he needed to leave and continue his errand. He spoke to Ezekiel, "Father Johnson, could you tell Seth that there's a meeting at the new schoolhouse tomorrow at four o'clock? President Smith wants all of the men marching with Zion's Camp to attend."

Ezekiel's blue eyes darkened. "John, you are the only man in Kirtland who has any business going to Missouri right now. You have children there. But blood will flow when a Mormon army comes riding into Jackson County."

John's voice was both friendly and firm. "You don't understand, Father Johnson. Joseph and the other brethren feel as much obligation as I do. Our bonds of faith make the Saints in Missouri family to all of us."

Ezekiel's voice hardened. "Speaking of family, I talked to your father-in-law yesterday."

"Is he in good health?" John asked cautiously. His late wife's father was Orris Clapp, one of the most influential members of Kirtland's Anti-Mormon Committee.

"Yes. He's hoping you come to your senses, that you bring your younguns back here to Kirtland."

John's look became as grim as his host's. "Why? So he can turn my own flesh and blood against me and the Church of Christ?"

Ezekiel eyed John Murdock. "I suppose that might be one of his reasons. His daughter died, and his grandchildren are far away. A man doesn't take kindly to losing his family."

John Murdock continued, his voice bitter. "Father Johnson, it was my father-in-law's Campbellite brethren who tarred and feathered the Prophet, which led to the death of little Joseph Murdock Smith. Did Orris Clapp fire that cannon toward the temple? Did he lead those who tore down the wall?"

Ezekiel shook his head as he spit tobacco juice into an empty cup. "No, John. That wasn't Orris Clapp. That was Grandison Newell."

* * *

Sunday, May 4, 1834

Seth, Lyman, Almon, and Julianne squinted in the bright afternoon sunlight as they listened to the Prophet. Joseph stood on a trunk in the shade of a newly constructed schoolhouse.

Surrounding the Prophet were many of the men who would travel with him to Missouri. Early the next morning, over one hundred men, calling themselves the Camp of Israel, would leave Kirtland.

Almon held Julianne's hand during the sermon. Their entwined fingers were red and callused from hard work. Almon had labored unceasingly during the past two months helping the Johnsons clear land and plant crops so that he and Julianne would have a portion of the harvest. In turn, Julianne had processed gallons of maple syrup and had worked with the other women in Kirtland to make clothing and gather supplies for the destitute Missouri Saints. In her few free moments, Juli had sewn Almon a new cotton shirt and a pair of trousers—a fresh change of clothing to tuck away in his knapsack. Knowing the stakes of this journey, Julianne trembled. She clung to Almon's hand and hung on every word of the Prophet. The Lord's promises were her hope and Almon's lifeline.

Joseph Smith's blue eyes filled with emotion, and his voice rose in strength as he spoke. "My beloved brethren, I must impress upon you the necessity of being humble on this journey. Exercise faith, patience, and live in obedience to the commands of the Almighty. Do not murmur at the dispensations of providence.

"I bear testimony before God and before all of you of the truth of this work, which God has revealed through me. If each one of us lives as he should before the Lord, keeping His commandments, and not, like the children of Israel, murmuring and disobeying God, we shall all safely return. If we are united and exercise faith, God will deliver us out of the hands of our enemies. But if we, like the children of Israel, forget God and His promises, if we treat lightly His commandments, we will bow beneath the buffetings of Satan and the chastisement of our God."

Julianne's eyes burned. Her Almon was strong willed and energetic. Men were proud by nature. Would the camp be humble enough to return home safely?

After the meeting, Julianne and Almon went in search of a secluded place. They walked along the creek, finding a log near the bank. They sat down and talked for hours of the life they would lead when Almon came back, of how they would name their first son David and their first daughter Ann. As the sun set, its reflection on the water was sucked into darkness, the waterbugs disappearing with the light. Julianne shivered.

Almon kissed the top of her head. "Juli, the Prophet has promised that we'll return."

"He promised you would return if all of you keep the commandments and don't murmur." Julianne's face looked stricken as the darkness fell. "Oh, Almon, a day doesn't go by in our household when someone doesn't murmur. And look at the brethren who already left the Church when Joseph said you were to take munitions and firelocks. Men are proud, Almon, so proud."

Almon, determined to make her laugh one more time, stood up and marched around her, mimicking blowing a bugle. "But we are the priesthood bearers of Israel and will not fail," he shouted, puffing his chest out. "And I, Almon Whiting Babbitt, promise you, Julianne Johnson, that no murmuring word will escape my tongue come high waters and fiery serpents! Smile! You, my dear, own the strongest, bravest, mightiest man of Zion's Camp—body and soul!"

As Almon pulled her to her feet, Julianne laughed through her tears. Almon saw her dimples in the moonlight. "Almon, my boy, my man, my love," she whispered. "You are everything in the world I want, now and always. Please be humble and come back to me."

"I promise," Almon said as he wrapped his arms tightly around her.

* * *

After the meeting, Seth accompanied Lyman to the Sherman home. They walked together, discussing the details of the journey ahead. The first day they would travel toward New Portage, where they would rendezvous with another group of brethren. At that point they would begin traveling in divisions of twelve men. Lyman would travel with Heber Kimball and his company. Seth and Almon would be in the Prophet's mess, which included Zebedee Coltrin, Brigham Young, Frederick G. Williams, and the Prophet's young cousin, George Albert Smith.

Delcena watched as Lyman and Seth approach the house. Her hair hung down in ringlets the way Lyman liked it best. She was knitting. The children played in the yard, Albey toddling, Mary and Alvira laughing and skipping around him. The little girls picked their baby brother up after his frequent tumbles.

A lump formed in Delcena's throat. She knew that Lyman would leave her many times—such was his zeal as an elder and missionary. But this time he and Seth would be traveling a thousand miles, in a large, visible group, passing through country where enemies would like nothing better than to destroy them. Delcena stood up.

Seth shook hands with Lyman in parting, "I'll see you in the morning." Then he embraced his sister. "Good-bye Delcena." She could not stop her tears.

"Delce, have faith," Seth said gently. "Lyman will tell you of the Lord's promises. If the camp is faithful, we will return."

Delcena nodded and wiped her eyes. After Seth left, Lyman and Delcena sat down on the quilt. With his arms around her waist, he told her of Joseph's sermon and the Lord's promises to the men of Zion's Camp. They were interrupted when Albey fell face first in the dirt and screamed. Alvira tried to pick him up, but accidentally dropped him again. Lyman stood up and jogged over to them. He lifted Albey in his arms and wiped the dirt from his face with a handkerchief. When Albey quieted, he picked Mary up in the other arm. Alvira mounted him piggy-back with her arms wrapped tightly around his neck. His children shrieked with laughter as Lyman galloped around the yard with all three in tow.

After fifteen minutes of this, he skidded to a stop by Delcena and dumped the children on the blanket. As the little ones laughed, Delcena looked at Lyman. There were tears in his eyes as well. She knew the thought in both their hearts. Could this be their last night together on this earth?

* * *

At dawn the next morning, while Julia added a few things to Seth's knapsack in the kitchen, Seth bid farewell to his brothers and sisters who had gathered in the sitting room. First, he picked up Amos and hugged him.

"Will you bring me back something?" the little boy questioned.

"How about some smooth rocks from the Missouri River?"

"Round ones for marbles!" Amos exclaimed.

"I want some too!" Esther piped up. "And tell Phebe Murdock to be my friend someday!" Seth put Amos down and hugged his little sister, promising that he wouldn't forget.

Then he shook hands with George and Will. George requested a rattlesnake skin, and Will told him to shoot the Missourians before they shot him.

"We are going to escort the Saints back to their land, not to shoot the Missourians," Seth corrected.

"But they might shoot you, so be ready," George advised.

At the thought of Seth being shot at, Mary crumbled into tears. Seth turned to her. She quickly opened her fist and handed Seth a handkerchief. It was folded up until it was very small. Seth unfolded it and saw that Mary had embroidered his initials in fancy, sweeping script. "Thank you, darling Mary," he said as he put his arm around the sobbing adolescent. "I'll keep it in my pocket and think of you every day. God will be with us both." Mary nodded, gave Seth a fierce hug, and then ran from the room.

Almera blinked back her tears. "I'll never forgive you if you don't come back," she exclaimed as she hugged him.

Seth focused on her for a moment. This sister had grown into such a beautiful, passionate woman. "Remember, Almera," he said gently, "that this short life is only a sliver of eternity, and that we are all in God's hands." Almera nodded, blinded by tears.

"Good-bye, dear Seth," Susan said softly.

Seth embraced her. She was his quiet sister with inner sight. A quote describing Sue came into his mind. *There is something in a face, an air, and a peculiar grace, which boldest painter cannot trace.* Seth smiled at her, "How I'll miss you, Susie!"

"And I you," Susan said, her eyes dry and her voice quiet.

A moment later, Joe embraced Seth tightly and wished him good luck.

"Take care of Mother while I'm gone," Seth said during the embrace.

"You can depend on it," Joe said.

"Keep up your studies," Seth advised. "And try your hand at poetry. If something happens to me, comfort the others with your cheer."

Joseph swallowed hard. "I wouldn't have any cheer left. May God bless and keep you."

Seth looked into his brother's eyes. Joe would have a burden to carry while he was gone. "Good-bye, dear Joe."

A moment later, Benjamin embraced Seth, unable to talk for the tears streaming down his cheeks. He was afraid he wouldn't see his brother again.

"Dearest Bennie," Seth exclaimed, scarcely able to hold back his own tears. "May heaven watch over you as you grow to manhood! How proud I am of you!"

Julianne put her arms around both of her brothers. "Benja," she said, her brown eyes moist, "Almon has promised to bring Seth back to us." She gulped. "And Seth, you must promise to keep an eye on Almon. Exhort him to humility."

Seth smiled and nodded, "With all diligence."

Nancy was the final sibling to whom Seth bid good-bye. She sat on the couch, for she had been coughing lately and was very tired. Seth worried about her most of all. They were close in age and shared so many memories. Thoughts of their childhood together passed through his mind like streams of colors. He remembered her love for animals, the way she rode horses for pleasure, the books they had read together, the hours they had spent tutoring their younger brothers and sisters. He visualized the horror of her accident and thought of how she had nurtured him when his mind was ill.

"Good-bye, Nancy, my dear, dear sister," Seth said as he sat down by her. "Do all in your power to get well and to be here when I return."

"Oh, Seth, I will!" Nancy cried. She coughed once more and saw the shadow of worry in Seth's eyes. It was like Seth to think of another even at a time like this. Nancy held back her tears and smiled. "Seth, do you remember years ago when Uncle Joel sent us the *The Letters of Junius* to study?"

Seth nodded.

Nancy went on, "I looked over them the other day and one seems to fit this parting. *We owe it to our ancestors to preserve entire those rights, which they have delivered to our care: we owe it to our posterity, not to suffer their dearest inheritance to be destroyed.* Seth, that's what you're doing, preserving the Saints' rights in this blessed nation, ensuring all of our inheritances. I'm so proud of you. How blessed I am to have a brother of such strength and goodness!"

Seth held his sister close, too emotional to speak.

Ezekiel stood at the door. He looked like he had just rolled out of bed. His gray hair was awry, his eyes red, and his jaw tense as he watched Nancy and Seth. Ezekiel took his gun, *Betsy,* from the mantle. Seth stood up. "Take this," Ezekiel said gruffly. "It's a far better piece than your musket."

"Thank you, Pa," Seth responded as he handled the weapon and fingered the silver trim. He had never killed a man. The thought of doing so sickened him. He spoke quietly. "I'll only use this to defend the lives of the innocent."

Ezekiel nodded as his gray eyes looked into his son's brown ones. "Your word is your bond, son. Do your best to come back to us."

"I will." With *Betsy* in one hand, Seth embraced his father.

Julia came into the room with Seth's knapsack. "I've packed you some pork, honey, and cornbread. And another pair of stockings."

After Seth thanked her, Julia held him close as if she didn't want to ever let him go, as if she wanted to remember the look and feel of him forever. "Thank you, dearest Seth, for your goodness and faithfulness," Julia said. "Our prayers and love follow you every moment of each day. Angels will go with Zion's Camp."

"And I pray that guardian angels will watch over all of you whom I love so dearly," Seth said. His eyes burned with tears. He shouldered his knapsack and walked out the door.

* * *

Tuesday, May 13—eight days later

Sweat dripped from Lyman, Seth, and Almon as they and two other men heaved the ropes attached to Parley P. Pratt's wagon. Their backs bent into their work. Their feet were blistered and sore from walking twenty-seven miles that day in the humid weather. Elder Pratt, who had broken his harness three miles away from the encampment, sat in the wagon seat whistling and singing as the men pulled him to camp. Initially, Lyman and Seth were so intent on the work that they ignored Parley's song. Brother Pratt seemed to be the only one having a good time. But after Almon began singing, they joined in, an electricity in the air pushing them forward, giving them the strength and will to continue.

> *"Hark and listen to the trumpeters,*
> *They sound for volunteers;*
> *On Zion's bright and flowery mound*
> *Behold their officers.*
> *Their garment white, their armors bright,*
> *With courage bold they stand,*
> *Enlisting Soldiers for their king*
> *To march to Zion's land.*
> *It sets my heart all on a flame*
> *A soldier to be.*
> *I will enlist, gird up my arms,*
> *And fight for liberty.*
> *We want no cowards in our band,*
> *Who will their colours fly;*
> *We call for valiant-hearted men*
> *Who are not afraid to die."*

When their task was complete, Seth and Almon bade Lyman good night. Lyman left to rejoin his company. The trumpet sounded, signaling time for evening prayer. Almon and Seth listened as the Prophet beseeched their Father in Heaven to protect and guide them on this journey.

After the prayer, Zebedee Coltrin, the company cook, fed Seth and Almon a scanty meal of fried pork and bread. "Better save some of your dinner for breakfast," Coltrin moodily warned them. "The two men sent ahead for flour came back empty-handed."

Following the meal, Seth watered and fed their company's horses, while Almon gathered up a bunch of fallen leaves to soften the ground that he and Seth would be sleeping on. Almon spread out both men's bedrolls. When Seth came back, he dropped onto his blanket next to Almon.

"How are your feet?" Seth asked as they stretched out under their blankets. It was warm at the moment, but the night would turn cold.

"Dandy," Almon answered. "Long as I don't take my boots off and let 'em swell up." Almon wrapped his blanket around himself and immediately fell asleep.

Despite his exhaustion, Seth again prayed, asking the Lord for strength on this journey and to protect his family in Kirtland. Then he lay awake listening to the hoot of an owl and the water rippling in the creek. After staring at the stars for a time, he rolled over. The ground was hard beneath the leaves. In the moonlight, he looked at Almon, who slept peacefully. Seth sighed, thinking of how well Almon endured the hardships of camp life. He remembered the previous morning, when their only food had been raw pork and sour bread. Almon had eaten it with relish. Seth had found it difficult to swallow, despite his hunger. With his stomach growling, Seth closed his eyes, and exhaustion pressed him into a dreamless sleep.

Seth awakened long before dawn. The trumpet had not yet sounded. He was stiff and cold, and his blankets were icy. As Seth stood up, pain lanced through his feet. He limped over to the water bucket to get a drink. He had to break through three-quarters of an inch of ice that had formed during the night. Seth took a long sip from the ladle as most of the camp continued to slumber.

Wide-awake, Seth walked around the camp in the dark as his feet limbered and his limping decreased. A hundred yards away, Seth saw that the Prophet was up, carrying a lantern. Joseph walked over to Seth and suggested they walk together to the edge of camp where Moses Martin was on sentry duty. They found Brother Martin, propped in a sitting position against a tree, with his sword in his arms, snoring vigorously.

Joseph raised an eyebrow at Seth. "It's good we weren't attacked last night." With a smile, Joseph deftly slipped Brother Martin's sword out of its scabbard. "Evidence," Joseph said quietly, "when we explain that we must call a court-martial. But for now, we'll let Brother Moses sleep."

Seth looked at the slumbering man. Martin's head was bent at an odd angle, and his mouth was wide open. "The poor fellow's exhausted," Seth commented. "I'm sure he didn't mean to fall asleep while on duty."

Joseph nodded compassionately. "And I will heartily recommend that he be acquitted. I think every man on the jury will agree." Joseph suddenly chuckled and added, "as long as we don't select Brother Sylvester as a jurist."

Seth smiled at the Prophet's humor. Sylvester Smith had been complaining regularly.

Joseph sighed as he looked back again at the snoring guard. "But it is dangerous for a sentry to fall asleep on duty. Spies have been following the camp, and we don't know when we might be attacked. How are you holding up, Brother Seth? Did your wet, bloody stockings freeze on your feet last night like mine?"

Seth smiled. The Prophet's companionship warmed him. "Yes, sir. But I'm doing tolerably well despite my abused stockings." Then the trumpet sounded, and the two men joined their brethren on bended knees, imploring the Lord's blessings for that day.

* * *

A week later, on Tuesday, May twentieth, the men of Zion's Camp endured a particularly grueling day. As they pitched their tents that evening, their boots and trousers were caked with mud. The roads has been very bad, requiring the men to attach ropes to the tongues of the wagons and pull beside their horses in mud deeper than the tops of their boots.

In the evening, they set up camp near a creek. Lyman walked down to the water to clean the mud speckles off his glasses. While Lyman squatted down, three well-dressed men rode up on horses. The animals were bay colored, finely muscled, and well groomed.

"Hello, sir." A dark-haired, blue-eyed, middle-aged gentleman tipped his hat. "You're with a large company. Where's your camp from, and where are you going?"

Lyman stood up, put his dripping spectacles back on, and looked at the men. Lyman's answer was friendly and rehearsed. "We're from the east and we're heading west looking for places to settle."

"Is that right?" another man asked coldly. He wore a seal-skin cap that drooped down over one of his eyes. He pointed his gun at Lyman.

Lyman met the man's eyes with a steady nod. "That's right."

The man snorted. "If you are Mormons on your way to Jackson County, Missouri, let this be a warning. If you make it through Indianapolis, which is doubtful, you'll never live to cross the Mississippi."

Lyman turned his head toward the man who originally addressed him. "You'd be wise to tell your friend to put away his firearm and be friendly. Like you said, we're a large company."

The first man told his companion to put away the gun.

"Let's get a look at the whole company," the third man suggested to his companions as if Lyman wasn't there.

Lyman spoke up. "Come with me. You're welcome to share our dinner."

The men dismounted and followed Lyman, leading their horses. After they had entered the camp, the seal-skin-capped man elbowed his companion and pointed to Frederick G. Williams, who was older than most of the men and of a more stately demeanor. They left Lyman and walked up to where Dr. Williams ate with Joseph and the rest of their mess. "Where are you folks from?" the first man questioned.

"I'm from Vermont," Brigham Young answered amicably.

"New York," Joseph said nonchalantly.

"Me too. Chautauqua County," Seth offered.

"Massachusetts," George Albert chimed in.

"Ohio," Almon added, his green eyes flashing with life.

The seal-skin-capped man eyed Almon. "And where are you headed, boy?"

"We're all from the east, and as soon as we've had our dinner, we're headed to the west." Almon grinned buoyantly. The man was clearly not amused.

The first man addressed Dr. Williams once more. "Sir, are you the leader of these men?"

"No, sir."

"Then could you point us to the man who is?"

Dr. Williams shrugged. "No one in particular leads us."

The stranger pressed. "Is there not a general to take charge of such a large company?"

Frederick responded, "We're a hodgepodge group of wanderers traveling together for safety—just scouting out the country for places to settle. Sometimes one takes charge and sometimes another, so as not to throw the burden on anyone in particular."

The second man spoke with sarcasm. "Then I warn you fellows to take care. The citizens of Indianapolis have heard rumors that an army of Mormons will pass through their city. These religious fanatics are on their way west to slaughter the good people of Jackson County, Missouri. They won't be allowed to pass through Indianapolis alive."

Almon could not hold his tongue. "Sir, your warning is appreciated. If we run into those fanatical fiends, we'll high-tail it out of here. They won't get wind of the Indianapolis ambush from us. Good luck to you fellows."

Clearly frustrated, the three horsemen spun around and left the camp. Frederick G. Williams grinned at Almon. "Young man, just who are you calling a fanatical fiend?"

Almon laughed. "The whole bunch of us fine fellows!"

Joseph swallowed his last bit of sour milk. He chuckled as he looked over at Almon and Dr. Williams. "The two of you make a dandy pair of liars! It's good to know you are honest men!"

"This is no laughing matter," Sylvester Smith said tensely, standing on the periphery of the group. They all turned to look at him. He glared at Joseph. The black dog lying at Joseph's side, which old Father Baker had given him as protection, growled. Joseph stroked the animal, and he immediately quieted and licked Joseph's hand. Sylvester Smith continued. "We have to pass through Indianapolis tomorrow morning. What do you plan to do? Lead a ragtag army to the slaughter?"

Joseph looked steadily at Sylvester Smith. "I promise you, Brother Sylvester, in the name of the Lord, that we will not be disturbed, but we will pass through Indianapolis without the people knowing it."

Sylvester glared at Joseph. "And just how do you plan to do that with a company as large as this?"

Joseph was quiet for a moment, as if waiting. Almon spoke. "I've an idea. When we get near the place, we'll separate; each wagon will enter the town a short distance from the others. Many of us will ride in the wagons and not be seen. Others will walk down different streets."

Joseph smiled and nodded at Almon, "And we'll leave the inhabitants wondering just when that big company will come along."

* * *

The sun beat down mercilessly on Monday, May twenty-sixth, as Zion's Camp journeyed across the first arm of the prairie. The only water lay in stagnant, putrid pools. The men saw a deer a short distance away. John Murdock, who was familiar with the prairie, explained that the deer was actually miles away; its seeming near-ness was an optical illusion due to the flatness of the country. Joseph Hancock and Almon didn't believe him and went in pursuit. But they were vastly disappointed at the distance and returned to the camp at noon without the deer, but burning with thirst. The company had stopped to rest at one of the sloughs.

Almon found Seth sitting in the shade of a wagon, holding a water bucket. To Almon's dismay, the bucket contained miry water from the slough, full of red, worm-like creatures called wigglers.

"Thirsty?" Seth asked.

For the first time on the journey, Almon cursed.

Seth raised his eyebrows. "Young George Albert showed me how to strain the water. You line your top and bottom teeth together and hold them tight. Then you drink. The creatures can't get in, but dribble down your chin."

"You have to be joking."

"Watch." Seth demonstrated. He swallowed a bit without gagging, which he considered quite a success. Almon would have laughed as the watery wrigglers slid down the gentlemanly Seth's chin if he weren't so horribly thirsty. Almon grabbed the bucket from Seth and drank the sickening water, straining the wrigglers with his teeth. The warm, putrid water scarcely dented his thirst.

It was nearly evening when the camp came to the house of a Mr. Wayne, the only settler in the vicinity. On seeing the large company suffering from thirst, the grungy, gray-haired man gave them free access to his well. "I know you fellows are Mormons, so don't deny it," he said as he watched the men drink. "Three men looking for you passed by my place last week. I think it a shame that you people aren't free to enjoy your religion as you please in the United States of America."

After thanking Mr. Wayne and drinking their fill, the refreshed men crossed the Embarrass River and camped a mile away on a western branch. As Joseph and his company set up their tent, they found three prairie rattlesnakes. Zebedee Coltrin told Almon to go and get an ax so they could kill the snakes.

The Prophet put his hand on Almon's arm, detaining him. "Let them alone—don't hurt them. How will the serpent ever lose his venom, while the servants of God possess the same disposition, and continue to make war upon it? Men must become harmless before the brute creation; and when men lose their vicious disposi-tions and cease to destroy the animal race, the lion and the lamb can dwell together, and the sucking child can play with the serpent in safety. We should not kill a serpent, bird, or an animal of any kind during our journey, unless it is necessary to preserve ourselves from hunger."

Following Joseph's counsel, Brigham Young, Seth, and Almon found sticks and carried the snakes across to the other side of the creek. As Almon waded through the water, the snake hissed and struck at his stick. Almon felt like shutting the serpent up by kicking its head off. But he remembered his promise to Julianne and refrained. Still he wasn't sure he agreed with this particular teaching of the Prophet. Seth, on the other hand, seemed in complete agreement and ready to make friends with any snake who came his way. *But he'd sing a different tune if his sisters were around,* Almon thought wryly. *He scarcely lets a man, much less a snake, near one of them.*

* * *

That night, at eleven o'clock, the picket guards awakened Joseph and quickly explained that to the southeast they had seen many campfires, which they knew must be the mob coming to destroy them. While the guards awakened the other captains, Joseph instantly arose and went to look. He immediately realized their mistake. It was the moon rising through the scattering of trees that fringed the prairie, making it look like the reflection of campfires. Joseph had seen such a sight before on another trip to Zion. He knew that the view would become increasingly beautiful as the moon rose over the broad prairie. He raised his gun and discharged it in the air—a call for all the men to come to arms.

Within ten minutes the whole camp was before him in companies, paraded and ready for battle. Almon's eyes flashed. He held a pistol in one hand and a sword in the other. Lyman's face was grim. Seth's knuckles were white as he gripped Ezekiel's gun. With all his men now standing before him, Joseph grinned in delight. The baffled men stared blankly at their commander.

"The picket guards have been fooled. There is no danger near tonight," Joseph called out. "It is only the moon, not the fires of the enemy. All is well. What a sight it will be to watch the moon rise above the broad prairie. It is well worth getting out of bed to see. And I am overjoyed at how quickly you were ready to defend our camp!"

Seth took a deep breath and whispered to his companions. "Even the beauty of the night does not seem enough reason for Brother Joseph to sound a false alarm, to cause such panic and horror to arise in the hearts of other men." But Almon laughed at the joke, and Lyman's eyes widened in awe as the twinkling lights merged into one glowing sphere rising above the horizon.

"Hurrah for Israel!" Lyman cried out. The rest of the camp joined in the shout.

The young, fair-headed Prophet threw his head back and opened his arms wide in the moonlight, full of joy at being with his brethren on such a glorious night.

* * *

On June fourth, the camp arrived at the banks of the Mississippi. The state of Missouri loomed a mile and a half away, on the opposite shore. The men were edgy, for they remembered the warning from the mob's spies—that they would never be allowed to cross the river alive. With only one flatboat to ferry the entire party across the expanse of water, it would take a full two days of going back and forth before the task was accomplished. In the meantime, they would be split up, waiting on opposite shores, their strength divided, vulnerable to the enemy's advances.

To make matters worse, they had slept but little the previous night. They had heard shots to the west of them and answering shots to the east. Joseph had doubled the guards and had been up all night with his men. Fortunately, it had turned out to be a false alarm.

At dawn, after morning prayers and a bowl of corn mush with sugar, Seth and Almon were among the first group to cross the river with Captain Brigham Young, Frederick G. Williams, and three other men. The morning was fresh, and a cool mist rose from the water. They arrived on the opposite shore without incident, the four horses having swum alongside the boat.

The horses scrambled up the shore and shook off the water. After the men had unloaded the barge, Brigham pulled Seth and Almon aside. "I have an assignment for the two of you. Take two of the horses and ride to the branch of the Church in Bowling Green. Gather what men and supplies you can. We'll be heading toward the Allred Settlement where we'll stay for a few days. Be careful and meet us there."

Seth and Almon quickly agreed and wasted no time in tacking up the horses. As they rode away, Seth was relieved to get away from the terse mood in the camp, where men's tempers were short due to the stress of fatigue and fear. He quietly prayed that a spirit of patience and unity be with his brethren while they were gone. Perhaps this mission in gathering more men and supplies would rally the spirit of the camp. Seth thanked the Lord that he was allowed to be an instrument in His hands.

Almon's thoughts were elsewhere. He was proud to be chosen once again for a special assignment and could scarcely wait to write Julianne about it. He remembered how a week ago, he and Dr. Williams had disguised themselves as a traveling physician and his apprentice son. Together they had scouted out the mood of the people in Springfield, Illinois. He and Frederick had eaten well at the tavern, talked to everyone they met, mailed a number of letters, and purchased two kegs of gunpowder for the camp. Almon had enjoyed it a great deal. He hoped to enjoy this assignment with Seth as much. Perhaps the Bowling Green Saints would have an extra feather bed for him to sleep in that night. Such a luxury would be heavenly indeed!

*   *   *

June 7, 1834

Almon was not disappointed in the excursion. When they met back up with the camp three days later, he was in a festive mood. The Bowling Green Saints had treated them with gratitude and kindness. Almon had slept in a bed and consumed food and sweet milk to his heart's content. He and Seth had preformed their task well and brought back five additional men, two wagons filled with supplies, and four more horses.

After checking in with Joseph, Almon noticed Levi Hancock sitting dismally under a maple tree, fingering a handmade fife. Almon squatted down on the ground next to Levi. He was ten years older than Almon, but seemed much younger. Levi was a talkative, witty fellow, who liked to sing and make up rhymes. "Brother Levi, why so melancholy?" Almon questioned. "We're all here in Missouri, safe and sound."

Levi eyed him as he put the flute down, picked up a handful of dried grass, and began twisting the ends. "I keep thinkin' about the row between Sylvester and the Prophet."

Almon grinned. "Which one?" The captain of Levi's company, Sylvester Smith, had balked at Joseph's decisions a number of times throughout the journey.

"The one that beat all the rest," Levi said. "But you weren't here to see it."

Almon's green eyes gleamed. He was interested. "I'd like to hear about it."

As Levi talked, he kept twisting and tying the weeds until they took on the shape of a dog. "Our company was the very last one to cross the river. While I waited, I whittled a fife out of a large joint of sweet alder. Let me tell you, it wasn't much fun waiting there alone with the rest of the camp on the other side. We were left by ourselves and would have been helpless in an attack. Anyway, when we finally crossed, we were so happy to be safely in Missouri. Once on the bank, Sylvester lined us up single file, and we marched smartly to camp accompanied by the notes of my fife. Sylvester led the way.

"As we came up the rise in sight of the camp, Brother Joseph's watchdog runs up to us barking and growling, heading straight for Sylvester."

"Did he bite him?" Almon asked, his eyes widening. He wished he'd been there to see it.

Levi shook his head. "Nope. Joseph called him off. But it made me mad. Here we had to wait until the very last. We're trying to make the best of it, and that dog attacks us! Sylvester cursed at Joseph and threatened to kill his dog."

Almon whistled. "I'd wager that didn't go over well—when you consider that Brother Joseph sticks up for rattlers. That dog's a long sight more important to him than a snake. What did Joseph do?"

"He didn't do anything but take his dog with him into the tent. But the next morning he preached that proverb—*a soft answer turneth away wrath.* He talked about how the Lord won't protect us if we can't overcome the spirit of wrath and wickedness. If we don't repent, a scourge could devastate our camp. He explained that such a vengeful spirit keeps men in misery. Then Joseph gave examples of a vengeful spirit. 'If any man injures me I will injure him, If he insults me I will kill him. If a dog growls at me, I'll show him who's the master. If a dog bites me I'll kill it.'

"Sylvester walks up from feeding his horses just when Joseph says the bit about the dog. Sylvester shouts at Joseph, 'If your dog bites me I *will* kill him!' Joseph responds, 'If you kill my dog, I'll whip you.' Then Joseph continues teaching. 'Brethren, do you see how anger breeds more anger? Brother Sylvester, you must repent of this wicked spirit, or the day will come when you will live to regret it.'"

"Did Sylvester back down?" Almon questioned as he chewed on a piece of grass.

"Nope," Levi commented. "He accused Joseph of prophesying falsehoods in the name of the Lord." Levi handed Almon the dog he had made out of weeds. Then he picked up his fife and stood up. He looked down at Almon. "And I'm afraid that Zion's Camp could be in for some hard times. Looks like we may have a worse enemy to fight than the Missouri mobs."

17

Without, the rain in fitful torrents pour,
And hoarse the wrathful wind doth moan aloud;
The lightnings flash, the crashing thunders roar,
Majestic in their might amid the clouds.

Joseph E. Johnson
(From "Lines Written During a Storm on the Missouri River . . ."
Jottings by the Way, xiv)

June 18, 1834

Seth waded through the waist-high slough, well aware of the enormity of the danger they faced as Zion's Camp marched deeper into Missouri. Parley P. Pratt and Orson Hyde had recently returned from Jefferson City with news that Governor Dunklin had refused to fulfill his promise. *Returning the Mormons to their lands is now impractical,* the governor had told the men who had journeyed a thousand miles under the impression that he would support their efforts. It was no secret that mobs had gathered from Jackson, Ray, and Clay counties, that military action would trigger increased violence. The Missourians planned to slaughter the Mormon Army before they reached Jackson County. To make matters worse, the Prophet lay in Heber Kimball's wagon, ill with chills and fever.

Fighting discouragement and exhaustion, Seth mechanically placed one foot in front of the other. While his body pushed through the mire, his thoughts turned to the Prophet of God. On the journey, Seth had found Brother Joseph to be hardy, deeply compassionate, gregarious, and cheerful. The Prophet had a vibrant will and was seasoned to hardship. Unlike many of the men in the camp, Seth had remained uncomplaining, even when he occasionally did not understand the reasons for some of the camp leaders' decisions.

In addition, Seth had passed much of the march with and around Almon and had come to know him well. A natural leader, Almon was quick to ask questions and give suggestions to the Prophet, but he had never lagged in his support, whether his counsel was accepted or not. Seth's trust and respect for Almon had grown substantially. Yet last night, Seth had dreamed that it was David, not Almon, who marched by his side. David's arm had been around Seth's shoulders, and it was David's words of encouragement that were whispered in Seth's ears.

There was a loud, wet, sucking sound as Seth dragged his foot from the sludge. At the next step, the ground angled, and the footing was firm. In a few steps, he was on dry ground. They marched on. When darkness approached, they found themselves on a small, grassy prairie surrounded by a thicket of hazel brush. General Lyman Wight halted the men and instructed them to set up camp.

Seth looked around and shook his head. There was no cover here. They were completely exposed and highly vulnerable to attack.

"I suppose it's sleep here or in the mire," Almon commented as if he were reading Seth's thoughts.

"We could march on to some place safe," Seth suggested.

Almon shook his head emphatically. "I can't go another step. You'd have to carry me on your back, like General Wight carried Joseph Young through the slough." .

Seth eyed Almon and raised his dark eyebrows. "Do you actually suppose I'd do that?"

Almon chuckled. "I'd lay money on it."

As they were setting up camp, Seth and Almon watched Joseph Smith emerge from Heber's wagon. The Prophet surveyed their campsite. Though his face was flushed from fever, it was clear that he was concerned. He spoke briefly to Frederick G. Williams, then walked toward the thicket alone.

In the dark thicket, weak and ill, with hazel brush pressing on each side of him, Joseph kneeled down privately. He poured his soul out in prayer, fervently beseeching his Heavenly Father to suffer no evil to come upon the company in this vulnerable location. When he came out of the thicket, the moon was high, and most of the men slumbered.

Though exhausted, Seth had not been able to fall asleep. As Joseph walked by his tent, Seth spoke, his low voice breaking through the sound of the wind rustling the prairie grasses. "Brother Joseph, are you feeling better?" he questioned.

"Yes, Brother Seth," Joseph said quietly. "I've sweat out the fever. And I have received an assurance from God that no harm will befall us this night."

Seth lay down and closed his eyes. Now he would sleep soundly. He put aside the other question that dallied in his mind. *What about tomorrow?*

* * *

When the bugle sounded at daybreak, signalling morning prayers, Lyman Sherman came to Seth and Almon's tent. The three men kneeled together, praying in turn for the Lord to guide them through this dangerous time and to watch over their family. Following prayers, the men gathered to hear the Prophet's counsel.

Joseph suggested the camp leave immediately and breakfast later. Their current position was unsafe. The Prophet continued, "Today, if all goes well, we will be with our brethren in Clay County by nightfall. Greater love hath no man than this—that he is willing to lay down his life for his friends. You have shown this great love. Your sacrifice is akin to the sacrifice of Abraham. I pray continually that our blood will not water the ground of Missouri, that there will be a peaceful end to this crisis. That Zion will be redeemed."

During the morning's march, Lyman walked next to Luke Johnson, a charismatic, emotional young man. Luke was not related to Ezekiel's family, but was the son of John and Elsa Johnson. They were faithful members who had owned a large farm in Hiram, Ohio, where the Prophet had lived for a time.

As they journeyed near Richmond, the camp marched past a yard where a black woman labored in a garden near the road, her back bent like a willow branch. The woman straightened up as the men walked by. Her head pivoted as she glanced furtively toward the farmhouse, then back at the men. Her dark eyes met Luke's. "Come here, massa!" she cried out, waving her arms, beckoning.

Luke immediately stepped out of formation and walked up to the fence. Lyman followed a short distance behind, ready to help Luke if a problem arose.

She glanced furtively around, then spoke quickly. "There is a company of men here who are fixing to kill you this morning as you pass through."

"Thank you, ma'am. Do you know where we can stop safely to breakfast?"

She wrung her hands together, clearly agitated. "Yes, massa! Two mile up the road on the south side lives a farmer who's friendly to the Mormons."

"God bless you." Luke tipped his hat.

Twenty-five minutes later, the company stopped at the suggested farm and was not disappointed. They dined on a hearty breakfast of corndodger and bacon. The farmer supplied them with all the milk they could drink. After breakfast, Dr. Williams asked Seth to find out how much money the farmer wanted for the milk.

Seth approached the farmer and made his polite offer. The farmer looked into the Mormon's dark, gentle eyes. The farmer shook Seth's hand but refused payment, saying, "He is a mean man that will sell milk. I could have let you have more if I had known you were coming. You have many enemies around here. You will most likely meet with some trouble. It's an awful shame."

The noon sun shone high in the cloudless sky as the company left, refreshed by the farmer's generosity and the filling meal. They marched quickly, excited about the prospect of greeting the Saints in Clay County before nightfall. As the day progressed, their excitement waned. A number of frustrating setbacks hindered their progress. One wagon broke. The wheels ran off of four others. The entire company had to stop and wait each time a wagon was repaired. They had traveled fifteen miles by dusk, only half of what they had hoped. As the gray shadows of twilight replaced the vibrant colors of the day, they neared an elevated piece of land between the forks of the Little Fishing and Big Fishing Rivers. The men waded across the Little Fishing River, the water only to their ankles. Then they stopped for the night.

After supper, Seth and Almon were pitching their tent when five heavily armed men galloped into the camp. The horsemen shot their guns into the air. The men of Zion's Camp surrounded them on foot, their hands near their weapons. The five horses danced nervously under their riders.

Emboldened by too much drink, the Missourians were not intimidated by the number of Mormons. One of them laughed roughly. "We jist wanted to see what you cursed Mormons looked like before you're all dead. There are sixty men from Ray, forty from Lafayette, seventy from Clay, and two hundred from Jackson close on your heels! Each is well armed and has sworn to kill you. You will see hell before morning!"

"Hope you enjoyed your last supper!" another man shouted. Then he cursed, calling the Mormons every foul name he could think of.

Jenkins Salisbury came up to Joseph and spoke in a low voice. "We could easily kill these dogs and attack the rest unaware."

Joseph stared at the five on horseback. He turned back to Jenkins. "No," Joseph said levelly. "The Lord will give us a bramble to keep the dogs off tonight."

The Missourians spun their horses and galloped away. Captain Brigham Young asked the question that was in all of their minds. "Brother Joseph, what should we do now?"

Joseph looked to the southwest. Part of the sky was clear and crimson as the sun set. But a small black cloud was growing quickly and appeared to be moving toward them. The wind began to blow.

"A squall is coming," Joseph said. "Go to your tents and pray there tonight. Get what sleep you can. God is in this storm."

A few minutes later, after praying within their tent, Seth and Almon were lying on their backs on their bedrolls. Wind whipped the sides of the tent, and thunder rumbled as they numbly fell asleep. An hour later, they awoke to Lyman yelling and their tent blowing down around them. Thunder roared in concert with the torrents of wind, rain, and hail. "Get your firearms!" Lyman shouted. "We'll take cover in that old church!"

Pelted by the storm, Seth and Almon stumbled out of bed with their weapons in hand. They ran with Lyman and the other brethren to an old deserted meetinghouse. Once inside, the men lay down on the wooden benches, dripping wet. Lightning pierced the sky, and the inside of the church was instantaneously bright. In the seconds of light, Lyman and Seth saw the grin on Almon's face as plain as at noonday.

"What's he so happy about?" Lyman asked Seth.

"I figure he's crazy from the storm," Seth said as he pulled his sopping hat down over his eyes to try to sleep, despite the flashing lightning and his drenched clothing.

Almon chuckled. "Joseph got it right again. The Missourians won't be crossing the Big Fishing River tonight. It sure is good being friends with a prophet."

"'Tis a sin to gloat," Lyman commented with a smile as he took his glasses off and tucked them into his pocket. Seth said a prayer in his heart, thanking God for their safety, and asking Him to protect their enemies from the vengeance of the storm. Seth Johnson realized that the Missourians did not understand what they did anymore than the Romans who crucified the Lord. They had no idea that Joseph was a prophet of the living God.

When the men woke up in the morning, they went outside. Clean air and rushing water greeted them. The Big Fishing River raged, forty feet deep; the Little Fishing River was nearly as high. A short distance away, the ground was covered with tree branches that had been cut off by the hail. In spite of the calamity, the camp's horses and supplies were intact. Later they learned that things had not gone so well for the mob. Their enemies had indeed planned to attack and destroy the Mormons that night. But the storm had exploded, and the usually docile rivers had risen thirty feet in barely half an hour, making them impossible to ford. One member of the mob had been killed when struck by lightning. Another Missourian's hand had been torn off by his frantic horse.

* * *

The men moved the camp four miles up the divide between the rivers. Unable to travel farther because of the high water, they pitched their tents near the residence of Brother Cooper. The following morning, three grim-faced men rode into camp. The foremost was in military uniform.

Almon stared at them coolly and whispered to Seth. "Have the Missouri dogs come again?"

Seth's eyes widened as he observed their demeanor. These men did not appear either threatening or friendly. "I don't think so."

The man in uniform announced that he was Colonel Sconce from Ray County and requested a conference with the leaders of the camp. They dismounted. As the Mormon men stared at them silently and suspiciously with weapons in hand, Colonel Sconce continued, his voice trembling. "I am not here to threaten battle, but to find out your intentions. I see that an Almighty Power protects this people. I started from Richmond, Ray County, with a fixed determination to destroy you, but was kept back by the storm, and wasn't able to reach you."

Brigham Young stepped forward. "I'm Captain Young. Please sit down with us, and we will tell you our intentions."

After the Missourians were seated, the Prophet arose and stepped forward, making himself known for the first time on the journey. He spoke at length about the persecution of the Saints, detailing the suffering of his people in Jackson County. His voice rang with emotion, and his clear, blue eyes shone with tears. "We have left our dear wives and little ones alone without protection. We have walked a thousand miles to assist our people, to bring them clothing and other necessities of life. We only want to reinstate them on their own lands, which they lawfully purchased. We have no desire to injure any people, but only to administer to the wants of our afflicted friends."

When Joseph finished speaking, Colonel Sconce spoke, his voice breaking. "I thank the Almighty for stopping us! Murdering you would have been a crime beyond repair." The colonel stood and shook Joseph's hand. His men followed suit. Colonel Sconce took a deep breath and added his heartfelt promise. "We will do all in our power to stop the prejudice spreading against you throughout the countryside."

As Seth watched the three men ride away, he too wept, knowing that his prayers had been answered. The Lord's protective hand during the storm had been two-sided—the lives of Israel's men had been saved, and the souls of some honest, misled Missourians had been shielded from sin.

* * *

The following afternoon, Joseph received a revelation. As the breeze ruffled through his fair, sun-streaked hair, the men of Zion's Camp gathered around. Joseph read to them the words of God:

> *"Therefore, in consequence of the transgressions of my people, it is expedient in me that mine elders should wait for a little season for the redemption of Zion—*

"That they themselves may be prepared, and that my people may be taught more perfectly, and have experience, and know more perfectly concerning their duty, and the things which I require at their hands.

"And this cannot be brought to pass until mine elders are endowed with power from on high.

"For behold, I have prepared a great endowment and blessing to be poured out upon them, inasmuch as they are faithful and continue in humility before me . . .

"For behold, I do not require at their hands to fight the battles of Zion; for as I said in a former commandment, even so will I fulfil—I will fight your battles . . .

"And again I say unto you, sue for peace, not only to the people that have smitten you, but also to all people;

"And lift up an ensign of peace, and make a proclamation of peace unto the ends of the earth . . .

"Therefore be faithful; and behold, and lo, I am with you even unto the end. Even so. Amen."

Almon's heart pounded as he absorbed the impact of the revelation. The battle had ended before it began! He listened as the Prophet told the men that they could soon return to their families. But Almon had not come to fail! He had come to be part of a glorious victory, where all of Missouri saw the power of God as the innocent were led back to their lands, singing the praises of their deliverers. But that was not to be. Of course, he could now return to Julianne, to all of the promises of their life together. But he would not return in triumph. Almon wanted to ask the Prophet why the Lord had led them to failure. But Almon had promised that he would not complain. The taste was bitter in his mouth, but he held his tongue.

Men in the camp muttered. John Murdock's head hung down. Almon gritted his teeth. He knew how much Brother Murdock had wanted to gain an inheritance in Zion for himself and his children. Almon glanced at Seth and saw that he looked pale and numb, his eyes exhausted and expressionless. A chill ran through Almon. Two men from the camp had fallen ill with cholera in the past two days. It was over, but not finished. They were defeated without having the chance to fight! They were a long way from home. He wanted to shout out his frustration.

But it was Lyman's voice, not Almon's, that rose above the muttering of those around them. "All is well, my friends! God is with us. We will be endowed with power from on high! The time will come when Zion will be redeemed. For now, we can go home to our loved ones!"

* * *

The next morning, Seth, Lyman, and Almon journeyed with the faithful men of Zion's Camp around the heads of the Fishing River, across a prairie and woodland, to A. Sidney Gilbert's residence. As they walked, John Murdock fell into pace beside Seth.

"Mornin', Brother Seth," John commented.

"Mornin' John," Seth returned. He felt unusually tired, and his face was drawn.

John continued "Today I see my little Phebe. She's living with Brother and Sister Gilbert. I guess it isn't time to redeem Zion, but I'll soon be reunited with my little girl."

"You'll have your part of heaven today, John," Seth said quietly. "Are your boys there too?"

John shook his head. "No. Orrice and Johnny are in the southwest part of the county with the Colesville Saints, helping them whitewash their new log meetinghouse. I'll go there after I see Phebe."

Seth spoke. "I'm glad for you and your children, John."

A short time later, the men from Zion's Camp arrived at the Gilbert settlement. While Brother Gilbert greeted the Prophet, a six-year-old girl stood outside the door of the house, holding Sister Gilbert's hand. John Murdock broke ranks with his brethren and ran toward them.

The child looked up at the woman with her. "My papa?"

Sister Gilbert smiled, nodded, and nudged Phebe toward the father she hadn't seen for a year, whose vision blurred with tears of joy.

While John Murdock enfolded his daughter in his arms, Brother Gilbert instructed the men to pitch their tents close by, on the banks of the Rushing River in a field owned by Brother Burkett.

Before they set up camp, the Prophet explained that the men no longer were required to travel with their companies. That night Lyman moved into Seth and Almon's tent.

* * *

Near midnight, Almon and Lyman awoke to Seth's cries of agony. "I cannot see! God help me!" Seth groaned, doubled over. The tent reeked of sickness.

"Cholera! Oh, Lord, save my dear brother!" Lyman cried out in prayer.

"Get him on his feet," Almon shouted as he put his arms around Seth and dragged him out of the tent.

Almon and Lyman heard the screams of other men as they moved Seth forward, one supporting each side of him.

"Fight this!" Almon shouted in Seth's ear. Then to Lyman, "Make him run!"

With brutal strength, despite Seth's screams, Lyman and Almon forced Seth to move forward. They made Seth run, while he cramped and purged, until the blood circulated in his veins, until his sight returned. Then the three crawled back into the tent, surrounded by the smell of sickness. Seth's fever raged. Almon and Lyman blessed Seth, but his agony continued.

As the sky turned pink with dawn, Lyman and Almon stepped outside for a moment to talk. Almon wanted to plug his ears as they heard and saw man after man attacked by the devastating enemy, cholera. Brigham Young walked up to them, his voice filled with pain. "Has anyone in your tent been struck?"

"Brother Seth," Lyman answered.

Brigham continued. "Dr. Williams is up at the Gilbert's. He'll come to you as soon as he can. Brother Joseph tried to rebuke the disease but cannot. Because of our murmuring, we are left alone! Joseph said that our prayers might mitigate the disease, but will not end it altogether."

Almon watched as Brigham Young walked toward the next tent. Then he cursed as he grabbed his shotgun. Had they come all this way to rot and die? Rage filled his eyes. He was a warrior and would not be defeated. He had not come to fail! He might not be able to return the Saints to their lands, but he *would* bring Seth home.

Lyman paled at Almon's look. "Almon, will I lose one brother to death and the other to apostasy?"

Almon spoke between clenched teeth. "No. You'll lose neither. I'm going to shoot some squirrels and make a broth for Seth. Take care of him until I'm back."

While Almon stalked toward the woodland, Lyman took a bucket of water into the tent. He washed away the filth and sponged Seth's feverish body. Almon returned with two squirrels and made a broth. Seth sipped a portion, then cramped and purged again and again.

* * *

Almon and Lyman took turns nursing Seth. Three hours before dawn, Lyman dozed. He awoke to Heber Kimball's voice at the door. "Brothers, Eber Wilcox died. We need help burying him."

"Seth is stricken. I'll not leave him," Almon returned.

"I'll go," Lyman said. He reached over and touched Seth's shoulder. Then he ducked out of the tent, weeping.

"Bring your gun," Heber said through his own tears. "Our enemies threaten even now."

With three other men, Lyman rolled Brother Wilcox into his blankets. After this, they laid his body on a sled, each man pulling a rope with one hand and holding a gun in the other. They took the body to a little bluff by the side of a small stream that emptied into Rushing Creek. Lyman and Heber dug the grave while the other three stood with their firearms to defend them. Then they carefully rolled the body in, covered it with soft leaves and bushes, and replaced the earth. When they returned to the camp, Brother Hitchcock was dead. They began their task once more.

By breakfast time, Lyman had aided in the burial of five of his brethren. As he walked back to camp, it felt as if the giant talons of a hawk had gripped him. Lyman fell, writhing in pain. With a tremendous exertion of prayer and will, he stumbled to his feet, then jumped and thrashed his arms. With strength far greater than his own, he ran. He did not stop until the cramping was over, and he thanked God that he was extricated from the grip of death. When he returned to the tent, he lay down, trembling.

"You too?" Almon asked in horror.

"I will live. God has given me strength. The cramping has ceased," Lyman whispered.

Seth, who remained doubled over, gasped, his pain excruciating. "Father in Heaven, have mercy on me! Send David to escort me home!"

"Shut up about David," Almon snapped as he gripped Seth's shoulders. "*I'm* taking you home. I'll carry you to Kirtland on my back, if I must!" Seth vomited with Almon's hands on him, with Almon's will seeping into him, insistent that he live.

An hour later, Dr. Frederick Williams brought a mixture of whisky and raw flour to the tent as a medicine for the disease. Almon threatened physical violence if Seth and Lyman did not immediately drink it. Dr. Williams administered the medication. Then Brother Frederick looked over at Almon and added, "One of the afflicted has plunged himself into the cold water of the river. It helped."

Seth groaned, the medicine causing additional cramping. "We're going to the river," Almon said as he began stripping off both his own and Seth's shirt and trousers.

With Almon's arms around Seth, the two men walked slowly into the cold, fast-moving current until the water was nearly shoulder high. Seth shook like a leaf in a strong wind; his knees buckled as pain knifed through his abdomen. As Almon struggled to hold Seth upright, his feet slipped in the muddy river bottom, and his grip on Seth faltered. The river pulled Seth away from him. Terrified, Almon lunged forward desperately. Swallowing a curse, he cried out, "Lord, help me!"

Miraculously, Almon had Seth in his arms. His muscles hardened around his friend. It felt as if David's former strength rushed through Almon. He was like an island fastened to the river bottom, steady and upright, with the cold water swirling around him. Seth's cramps suddenly subsided and his body slumped, no longer rigid in pain. With Seth weak and nearly unconscious, Almon put him on his back and carried him out of the water. Almon's heart pounded. "Seth, God has not forsaken us," Almon cried out, weeping as he set Seth's feet on the shore. "Live!"

That night, Seth was able to retain a portion of the broth Almon spooned into his cracked, dry lips.

* * *

From the porch, Julia watched Joe E., Ben, and Ezekiel cut the hay with scythes. Her heart ached for Joe in particular. Unused to hard physical labor, Joe swung the scythe awkwardly. Zeke put his scythe down and walked toward the well to get a drink of water.

Julia left the porch and met him there. "Don't push Joe too hard," she said quietly. "I'm worried about him." She dipped the cup into the bucket and handed Ezekiel a drink.

Ezekiel gulped down the water. Then he shook his head shortly. "A man needs to know more than book learning to get on in the world. With David dead and Seth gone, it's prime time for Joe to learn that."

"But he could cut himself, Zeke. Gangrene could set in."

"Joe's careful, and he's not complaining," Ezekiel retorted. "There are ladies in Kirtland who are raking their own hay into cocks with their babies on their backs. It is shameful, but if the

Mormons don't get the hay in, their stock will starve this winter, and children won't have enough milk to grow strong. Delcena's lucky that she has us. I don't understand men leaving their wives and children like this."

"Zeke, the people in Missouri are destitute. They've been unlawfully driven from their land. Don't you understand that?"

"I understand it, and I don't like it. But Seth ought to be here with his family, not on some pointless march where he could get himself killed."

Julia bristled. "Seth needs his father's prayers, not his criticism."

"A wife is what he needs," Ezekiel retorted. "Preferably, one who will listen to him." Julia swallowed, turned, and walked into the house.

Later that afternoon, Nancy looked pale as she sat in the corner of the room writing a letter to Seth. Additional worry crept into Julia. Although Nancy's cough had subsided, she had lost weight during the past two months. Julia trembled at her own lack of faith. Julia's love for God had remained constant, but her confidence that she could bear up in the face of trials had been shaken since David's death. She felt afraid when her children coughed, tripped, or cut themselves during work or play.

Julia donned her bonnet and set off to the Whitney Store. She intended to buy the herbs she needed to brew a strengthening drink for Nancy. She walked over to where Zeke and the boys were mowing and told them her plans.

Ezekiel didn't take his eyes off her face as she spoke. To Julia, it felt as if he were looking inside of her, rather than at her. Was she like a book that he knew how to read after years of experience? Did that happen whenever a couple had been married as long as the two of them? They knew each other so intimately, and could hurt each other so deeply.

Ezekiel turned to his son. "Joe, put your scythe away and go with your mother. She'll need your help."

As they walked to the store, Julia looked over at Joe. He was covered with sweat, and his face was red from the sun. She noticed that his eyes were bloodshot and that he frequently took out his hand-kerchief and blew his nose. If she had noticed David's cough before he became desperately ill, would she have been able to save him?

Julia tucked her hand protectively under her son's elbow. "Are you all right, Joe?" she questioned.

"It's just hay fever, Mother," Joe commented. He sneezed. There was worry in Julia's dark eyes. Joe continued with a smile. "I'm fine. I can say *Blue Beard Bashaw beat a Bumble Bee at Balsora* without coughing." Joe laughed. Then he coughed again.

"Joe, I don't want you to mow anymore," Julia said. "You're not well. I'll speak to your father when we get home."

"Mother," Joe said. "Seth, Almon, and Lyman are putting their lives on the line. The least I can do is learn to mow the hay."

"That is exactly why you must not mow the hay," Julia rejoined with tears in her eyes.

Joe put his arm around her as they walked up the steps into the store. "No, Mother," he said quietly. "This year I work in the fields beside Pa. And I trust in God like you've always taught me."

Inside the store, Julia saw Jared Carter at the counter speaking to Elizabeth Whitney. Julia blinked back her tears, straightened her shoulders, and walked up to him.

"Welcome back, Brother Jared." Julia shook his hand, remembering that Brother Carter had not been counseled to go with Zion's Camp. He had been instructed to continue his mission, then to work on the temple and strengthen the Saints in Kirtland.

"Hello, Mother Johnson." Brother Carter smiled at her.

Julia turned to Elizabeth Whitney. "Has there been any word from Zion's Camp?"

Elizabeth shook her head. "Not this week. But we believe they are in Missouri now. Our fasting and prayers will increase—if that is possible."

Tears stung Julia's eyes. Seth could already be dead.

Jared Carter spoke gently. "Mother Johnson, I saw Don Carlos this morning. The two of us would like to come visit you occasionally, to see how your family fares, and bless you in any way we can. Would Father Johnson oppose?"

"My husband is away most evenings," Julia said. "And you are always welcome. With Seth gone, and Joel so busy, there are rarely any priesthood holders in my home. We feel that void every day."

"Have faith, Mother Johnson," Jared Carter said. "I believe that Brother Seth will come home safely to you. Carlos and I will stop by soon."

On the way home, Joe took Julia's hand. "Mother," he promised, "someday Ben and I will hold the priesthood of God. We will know what to do to bless the family. David and Seth have shown us the way."

* * *

On the evening of June twenty-ninth, Lyman and Almon sat outside, eating a supper of corn mush and honey, while Seth slept in the tent. For two days, Almon had plunged Seth into cold water, day and night, sometimes hourly, whenever the cramping began anew. Now, much of Seth's pain had ceased, although his fever continued. Earlier that day, Dr. Williams had told the men that he believed Seth was out of immediate danger, though he still needed time to convalesce.

In contrast, most of Lyman's strength had returned. After swallowing a mouthful of food, he spoke to Almon. "Brother Heber is preparing to leave in the morning for Kirtland. You should think about going. Help the family finish getting the hay in. I'll stay here until Seth is strong enough to travel."

Almon shook his head. "I'm seeing this thing through. You go. You have a wife and children. Tell Julianne I love her and that Seth and I will be home before fall."

Lyman nodded and embraced Almon with tears in his eyes. "I'll tell Miss Julianne that you are a singular man, the most valiant brother, and the most faithful friend."

18

When foes combine! And thou are friend
My victory is won
Their works of darkness quickly end
Like night before the sun.

My God to thee my soul looks up
Thy grace my thoughts employ
Thou are my glory, life, and hope,
And fount of every joy.

Joel Hills Johnson
(*Diary*, 65)

July 3, 1834

Around noon, Almon came back to the tent carrying a bowl of corn mush and a Missouri-cured ham. "Feeling better?" he asked when he found Seth sitting outside.

Seth nodded slightly. The very effort of sitting upright in the chair taxed him physically. There were dark shadows under his eyes, and his face was gaunt and pale. Although there had not been any new cases of cholera, some of the men still battled between life and death. "How's Brother Gilbert?" Seth questioned.

Almon shook his head and breathed out slowly. "He didn't make it."

Seth closed his eyes for a moment. "And little Phebe Murdock?"

"She's still alive. John has been at her side ever since he came back from the Colesville settlement three days ago," Almon commented.

Details of the child's life passed through Seth's mind. The little girl had lost her mother and endured the horror of the expulsion from Jackson County. She was now battling cholera and fighting for her life. She wasn't any older than his baby sister, Esther.

Seth slowly ate a small portion of corn mush. Afterwards he thanked Almon, then went back into the tent to lie down. He slept for several hours. When he awakened, he felt somewhat stronger. He walked slowly around the camp, working to regain his strength. He saw John Murdock emptying a chamber pot into the creek. Seth spoke, "Hello John."

Murdock looked up and nodded. "Brother Seth. Good to see you on your feet."

"My prayers are with Phebe," Seth said. "How is she?"

John Murdock looked at the ground and shook his head. "I should have taken her with me to see her brothers, but she was afraid of the Missourians. She wanted to stay with Sister Gilbert until I came back for her. When Brother Page brought me word that she was ill and Brother Gilbert dead—I left my boys and came back as quickly as I could."

"I'm sorry, John," Seth said gently as he put his hand on his shoulder.

Murdock swallowed as he looked up and met Seth's eyes. "She holds to life by a single thread. I should pray for her suffering to end, for her to join her mama who is in heaven. It's wrong of me to try to keep her here when she suffers so," John choked. "But she's my only little girl now."

"I know, John," Seth said gently.

John Murdock fought tears. "I'd best get back to her, Brother Seth. Thank you."

"May God be with you and Phebe," Seth added.

John Murdock nodded. "And you, Brother Seth."

Seth went back to the tent. Almon wasn't there. Weakly, he kneeled before the Lord and prayed for little Phebe Murdock, an innocent child dying of cholera. He prayed fervently that her suffering would end, whether in life or in death. He imagined the reunion little Phebe might soon have with her mother. He prayed for Brother John to be comforted if Phebe died. He thought about David and the rest of those who died in the Lord. The thought of the end of earthly suffering and the blessed rest of heaven filled Seth with hope.

Then suddenly, it felt as if an unseen power interrupted the direction of Seth's prayer. The images of his living brothers and sisters entered his mind with an overwhelming force. He saw them on their knees, begging their Father in Heaven for his safe return. He felt the depth of their need. Seth's prayer changed course. He asked his Father in Heaven for the health and strength to return home so that he could finish his mission on earth.

* * *

On Sunday, at daybreak, Phebe Murdock's spirit left her body as her father held her in his arms. She was six years, three months, and twenty-seven days old. A short time later, Henry Rawlins awakened Seth, for John had asked that he join them for the burial. Seth ducked out of the tent as Almon continued to sleep.

Phebe was buried a little after sunrise. Seth watched in reverence as John laid two split shakes in the bottom of the grave, and one on each side. Then he softened the grave with straw, gently lowered his child's body in, laid two shakes across, and covered it over with earth. As John Murdock bowed his head in prayer, the new sun rose in the sky, and Seth, who stood near to strengthen the bereaved father, felt heaven reaching down to earth and lovingly bearing away the sweet soul of a little girl.

Around noon that day, the Prophet came from the home of Lyman Wight to counsel and strengthen those who remained camped near the Gilbert residence. He grieved when he heard of

Phebe's suffering and death. He embraced John Murdock and wept with him. He counseled John to remain in Missouri with his young sons and become a member of the high council in Zion.

Then the Prophet turned to Almon and Seth. "My dear brethren, the Lord has strengthened and preserved your lives. It's now time to return to Kirtland and our families. Tuesday, whoever is ready to travel should meet me at the Marsh's home in Eastern Clay County. We'll start for Kirtland Wednesday morning."

Almon looked at Seth. Seth nodded and turned to the Prophet. "We'll be there."

* * *

The morning grew hot as Almera walked the four miles to the carpenter shop. A gentleman had dropped off an order for a table at the house. She had offered to take it to Ezekiel. It had been cool when she set out, but now her cheeks were pink and her brow moist.

Sam Prescott looked up when she opened the door. He was the only person in the shop. "Hello, Miss Almera," he said with a short nod as he continued shaving the wood from a board.

"Good morning, Mr. Prescott," Almera returned, her color deepening. "Do you know where I might find my father?"

Prescott put his tools down and stood up. "He left an hour ago after he read the paper. I thought he went home. The news hit him hard. I didn't think he would care a whit about Joseph Smith's death, but maybe it's the fact that your brother is there."

All color drained from Almera's face. Prescott's blue eyes did not leave her image. He walked over to her. "Sit down Miss Almera," he said as he guided her to a chair. "Forgive me for this shock. I thought you knew. There was a battle. Joseph Smith is dead. There's an article in today's newspaper."

"Show it to me," Almera whispered. Her voice sounded strange and dry. Samuel Prescott went to a table and picked up a copy of *The Chardon Spectator and Geauga Gazette*. He pulled up a chair close to Almera and pointed to a small article. "Looks like it originated in Richmond. Maybe it's a false report. If not, I pray that your brother survived." He shook his head. "It's too bad. I know you put a lot of stock in your prophet."

Almera read the words of the short article with dry eyes and shaking hands.

A MORMON BATTLE.—A letter received, by a gentleman in this neighbourhood, direct from Missouri, stating that a body of well armed Mormons, lead on by their great prophet, Joe Smith, lately attempted to cross the river into Jackson county. A party of the citizens of Jackson county opposed their crossing, and a battle ensued, in which, Joe Smith was wounded in the leg, and the Mormons obliged to retreat: that Joe Smith's limb was amputated, but he died three days after the operation.

Almera stood up on the verge of panic. "I have to go."
Prescott put his arm around her. "Did you walk?"
Almera nodded numbly.
"Wait here. I'll drive you in my wagon."
"Thank you," Almera whispered. She felt as if she might faint. On the drive home, Prescott looked over at Almera periodically. She stared straight ahead, her eyes blinking and full of tears, her pretty mouth quivering. She had no idea how attractive Samuel Prescott found her at the moment, how he wished he could to take her somewhere alone and forcefully kiss her, bringing forth the passion he felt certain lay dormant inside of her. Instead, the wagon headed steadily toward the Johnson home.

When they arrived, Prescott leapt down, took Almera's hand, and helped her out of the wagon. He kissed her fingertips. "I'm always close by," he said.

After he left, Almera ran into the house. All was quiet. "Is anyone home?" she cried out as she broke down sobbing.

Nancy, who was in the sitting room, called to her. "I'm here, Mera, dearest Mera."

Almera stumbled into the sitting room. "The newspaper says that Joseph is dead. Where is everyone?"

Nancy nodded with tears in her eyes. "We read the report. Most of the family is at the Shermans'. The boys are cutting Lyman's hay. Julianne and the little ones are with Delcena. Mother and Susan are at the Whitney Store awaiting news."

Nancy stroked Almera's hair. "We don't think it's true," she said softly. "So many lies are printed about us. If Brother Joseph were dead, one of the brethren would have sent word. They would have found a way."

Almera sobbed. "What if the Prophet has died? What if Seth is gone?"

"God will not desert us," Nancy assured. "I know that. Even if the Prophet and Seth were to die, they would be near us. It doesn't feel like David's gone, but on the other side of a door, which will one day open for each of us."

"I would that the door stay closed forever!" Almera cried.

"But Mera, there is light behind the door, the light of our Savior."

"But there's such pain here, Nancy." Almera wept. "You know that more than any of us."

Nancy felt tears fill her own eyes. Almera was right; there was pain everywhere, in each step she took every single day. "But there is no pain in heaven," she whispered. "Only joy."

* * *

July 22, 1834

Seth and Almon gathered with the Prophet and sixteen other men near the eastern bank of the Okaw River before daylight. The group had been traveling for nearly two weeks. They had forded the river the night before in log canoes. Despite the danger and deprivation of the journey, Seth had grown stronger. The men had already breakfasted and said morning prayers. At the moment, the men's discussion centered on the green-headed flies that would attack the horses as soon as the sun rose and they attempted to cross the prairie.

"Those flies can kill a horse in thirty minutes on the prairie," Joseph commented as he looked out across the sea of grass.

"What I don't get is why they don't bite the horses in the timber," George Albert observed.

"There's no rhyme or reason." Almon shook his head.

"We'll go ahead in groups of two, interspersing ourselves across the prairie," Joseph suggested. "Frederick will handle the wagon reins. The first two men will run with the team, one on each side, whipping the flies. When they tire out and fall behind, two more brethren will take over. We'll do this until we get the team and wagon across the prairie and into the timber."

After a prayer, the men spread out along the prairie. When Ezra Thayre and George Albert fell behind, Seth and Almon sprinted to the frightened horses, the wagon barreling behind the animals. They whipped at the cloud of green-headed flies swarming toward the horses. As flies buzzed in their eyes and mouths, the men dripped with sweat, their legs churning and their arms wildly waving the whips. When Seth tripped and fell, Almon continued another few paces. Then William Smith and Martin Harris were to the team in an instant, whipping the flies and running.

Seth pulled himself to his feet, jaggedly sucking in air. "I lost my footing," he said.

"It's all right. We got far enough." Almon viciously slapped a fly off his arm. "You are doing mighty well, Seth."

"The Lord strengthens me."

Almon grinned. "I'm thankful I don't have to carry you on my back. Come on, let's get across this prairie and another day closer to home."

* * *

The men arrived in Richmond, Indiana, in the evening. Some of the men went to find food and lodging while others, including Almon and Seth, waited by the wagon with the Prophet. Dr.

Williams bought a newspaper. He sat down on the wagon seat and began reading.

A few minutes later, Frederick Williams leapt down from the wagon and walked quickly to the Prophet, who was sitting on the back of the wagon with his legs dangling, reading the Bible. "Joseph," he said, "there's an article here about us. Says we were in a battle and you were wounded in the leg."

Joseph grinned and moved his leg back and forth as if he were testing to see if it worked. Dr. Williams continued. "Your limb was amputated, and three days later you died of mortification."

Almon laughed from where he was leaning against the wagon, chewing a piece of grass. "You're the best-looking dead man I've ever seen, Brother Joseph."

The Prophet seemed not to have heard Almon's comment. Joseph's grin evaporated. "Let's find that editor and set him straight. Emma and my parents will be so grieved!"

The men walked together to the printing press. Joseph went into the brick building, accompanied by Dr. Williams, Almon, and Seth. When inside, Joseph cleared his throat and asked to speak to the editor of the paper. A man with a thin mustache approached them. He was chewing tobacco. He introduced himself and shook Joseph's hand. "I'm the editor. How can I help you, sir?"

Joseph held out the newspaper article. "I'm Joseph Smith, the man mentioned in this report. You have printed falsehoods. There was no battle in Jackson County, and I am not dead. I ask you to write another article and print the truth."

The man raised his eyebrows and spit out the tobacco. "Let me get this straight. You're Joseph Smith, the great Mormon prophet?"

"I am."

"And these ragtag fellows are part of your army?"

"Yes, sir."

The man laughed. "Young fellow, you look more like a prankster than a prophet."

"He's Joseph Smith," Almon said steadily.

"He is." Seth nodded in agreement.

"And there are fifteen more men in town who will testify to it," Dr. Williams added.

The editor snorted. "I don't know you fellows' game." He pointed to the paper in Joseph's hand. "But I know the sources that story came from. I assure you that they were reliable. Besides, if Joseph Smith were alive, why would he prance in here and announce himself? If I printed an article about him passing through Richmond, his enemies would be on his tail. His life wouldn't be worth the paper in your hand."

Joseph's face reddened. "Sir, I have a wife, children, and an aged mother and father. I'm here because of the suffering and terror they must feel in consequence of the falsehoods printed in your paper! I beg you to print the truth."

"Falsehoods! Pshaa! You are no more the Mormon prophet than I am the president of the United States. You fellows leave now, or I'll have you thrown out."

* * *

July 26, 1834

Lyman walked with Heber C. Kimball and his company toward Kirtland late in the afternoon. The sky was cloudless and the day hot and humid. The men were bearded, dirty, and bedraggled, having walked thirty-five to forty miles a day. Just outside of town they embraced each other and prayed together, thanking the Lord for their health and safety. Joyful anticipation filled them. Within an hour they would be with their families.

With a pounding heart, Lyman walked up to his house. Only silence greeted him. He immediately realized that Delcena and the children were gone. He looked around. Much of his hay had been cut and rolled into bundles.

He went into the house. Alvira's doll was on the floor. An ember still burned in the hearth. Lyman walked into his room. It looked as if the bed had been quickly made that morning, the trundle bed pushed hastily underneath.

Lyman took clean trousers and a fresh shirt out of his bureau. Although disappointed that his family was not there to greet him, he now had the opportunity to meet them properly. He walked to the creek, where he bathed and shaved. Then he went back into the house and looked in the mirror. His face was leaner than three months ago and deeply tanned. Yet, other than that, he looked like he did any other day. He was home, finally home.

Lyman walked out the door and set off down the road. He had only walked a hundred yards when he saw a wagon coming toward him. He grinned with excitement, knowing who it was. He heard Joe E. crack the whip to hurry the mule. He recognized the shape of the woman sitting next to her brother with a little boy in her lap, her face wet as she wept for joy. He heard the welcoming shouts of two little girls as they stood up in the back of the wagon, yelling and pointing at him. "Look! Look! There's Papa! There he is!"

Lyman ran toward them. Joe pulled the mule to a halt. Delcena handed Joe the baby. She was out of the wagon in an instant and headed toward her husband. Then she was in his arms. Lyman held his wife so tightly that her feet lifted off the ground. "Lyman, Lyman. I love you. I love you," she said, while their little girls danced around them.

* * *

An hour later Joe was back at home. He had left Delcena and the children at their house with Lyman. Yesterday the *Painesville Telegraph* had carried an article stating that seventeen persons in Joe Smith's army had died of cholera. Joe remembered how his father, after reading the article, had set off for the shop, his face a mask of sorrow and pain. Ezekiel had not returned home last night. The rest of the family had prayed into the wee hours of the morning, hoping beyond hope that the news of cholera was as false as they believed the report of the Prophet's death to be.

Now Joe could tell his family with certainty that no battle had taken place, that the Prophet lived. But he had to tell them the truth of the second article. People were dead from cholera. They had nearly lost Seth.

Once in the house, Joe sat down and took his mother's hand. "Lyman is back. Seth and Almon are alive but not home yet."

Within seconds, Joe's brothers and sisters anxiously gathered around. Benjamin's foot bounced up and down nervously. Julianne wrung her hands together.

"When will Seth be home?" Mary cried.

Joe explained. "Seth had cholera, but he lived through it. Dr. Williams said he was out of danger when Lyman left." Joe took a breath and went on. "But Seth wasn't strong enough to travel. Lyman offered to stay with him, but Almon wouldn't leave Seth's side. He sent Lyman home to tell us to expect them before fall."

"Did Almon have cholera too?" Julianne asked.

Joe shook his head. "He was hearty the whole time. Lyman was struck, but recovered quickly. Seth was struck hard. He nearly died. Almon, with God's help, kept him alive."

Julia felt tears prick her eyes. Her son was alive, but he suffered so far away. She asked her children to pray with her. The family knelt together. Julia wept as she thanked God for preserving her son's life and for Almon's goodness in taking care of him. She thanked her Father in Heaven for the glorious restoration of the gospel and for preserving the Prophet's life. She prayed for the families of those who had died of cholera and beseeched the Lord to return Seth and Almon to their family circle. Then she prayed for each of her children, and for peace and faith to abide in her heart and home.

During the prayer, Jared Carter and Don Carlos Smith came to the door. They stood silently outside with folded arms as they listened. After hearing "Amen," Jared quietly opened the door. He saw that good family together on their knees combining their faith. Only one sat in a chair, bowing her head near the rest because she could not kneel. He remembered speaking to David Johnson so long ago, on that bright day when he was rebaptized. Now, Brother David was dead, and Sister Nancy remained crippled.

"Come with me, Brother Carlos," Jared whispered. Guided by the Holy Spirit, Jared Carter and Don Carlos Smith walked to Nancy and laid their hands on her head. Julia Johnson and her children looked up from their prayer.

Jared Carter spoke. "Sister Nancy Johnson, by the power of the holy Melchizedek Priesthood and in the name of Jesus Christ I command you to lay aside your crutches and arise and walk."

Trembling, Nancy handed her crutches to Benjamin, who kneeled near her chair. She stood on her feet, her legs shaking. Slowly, she put one foot in front of the other. "There is no pain," she sobbed as she stepped forward more confidently. "Oh, Mother! Mother! There is no pain!"

* * *

Benjamin rode Leo hard to the Mentor tavern. After tying the horse to the post, he went in and looked around for his father.

"Young man, who are you looking for?" the bartender called out.

"My father, Ezekiel Johnson," Benjamin answered.

"Zeke works at the shop late sometimes. Check there."

But instead of going to the shop, Benjamin galloped home. Nancy heard him run into the house. She carefully stood up. "Bennie, did you find Pa?"

Benjamin nodded breathlessly "He's at the shop. You can catch him before he goes to the tavern."

Joe and Ben each took one of Nancy's hands and helped her walk outside. With Benjamin's hand in hers, she stepped gingerly into the wagon seat.

"Nancy, child," Julia asked gently, "don't you want one of us to go with you? You don't know what shape your father will be in."

"Mama," Nancy said with shining eyes. "I'm not alone. The Lord is with me, and I feel David near." Then she took the reins in her hands.

* * *

Ezekiel felt the smooth grain of the cupboard he was working on. He looked up as the door to the shop opened. His eldest daughter stood on the threshold. Her color was high, and her eyes shone with tears.

"Nancy, has something happened?" he asked as he stood up.

"Yes, Papa," she said with tears running down her cheeks. "Something wonderful." She began walking toward her father.

"Darlin,' your crutches," Ezekiel cried out as he lurched toward her, holding his arms out to stop her from falling.

Nancy stopped and stood tall. She was now laughing through her tears, her cheeks apple red like when she was a little girl. "Papa, Papa, I can walk! God has healed me!"

She stepped forward. Ezekiel clutched her to him. "Nancy, dear, what is this?"

"Jared Carter gave me a blessing. The pain is gone, Papa."

Ezekiel's eyes filled with tears as he held his daughter in his arms. "I don't understand." His voice was confused as tears wet his ruddy cheeks.

"What, Papa?" Nancy whispered. "What don't you understand?"

"If there is a God, why would He be so cruel as to take David from us, and then be so kind as to heal you?" Ezekiel wept.

Nancy closed her eyes and held her father close. "I don't know, Papa. But I do know how much David hoped I would walk again. David's prayers for me have been answered."

* * *

The family was seated at the supper table on Monday, August fourth, when there was a knock at the door. Ezekiel stood up. He opened the door and saw two men standing before him. The tallest was rail thin, bearded, and filthy. The other was shorter and even dirtier.

Ezekiel would not have recognized his son in this bedraggled hobo had it not been for Seth's eyes. "Seth!" Ezekiel cried out as he clasped him to his heart. Julia and all of his children except for Nancy left the table and raced to the door.

"Stop!" Ezekiel thundered. "Let Mother have a chance to hug her son before you knock him over!"

Julianne was the only one who did not freeze in her tracks. Her eyes were on Almon as he held out his arms to her. As if she hadn't heard her father's command, Julianne sprinted to her love, her skirts flying recklessly behind her. Almon lifted her high and swung her around and around, the two laughing and crying. And while the family cheered and wept, Julia put her hands on Seth's face and held him close.

Then Ezekiel looked at Nancy sitting at the table with tears of joy running down her face. When Almon set Julianne down, Ezekiel spoke again. His voice cracked. "Let Nancy be the next to come over and hug her brother."

Stunned, Seth realized that there were no crutches next to Nancy's chair. His dear sister stood up and quickly walked over to him. Weeping now, Seth hugged her tightly. "Seth," Nancy whispered as they embraced, "I am healed in body. I am whole."

Then the Johnson children broke loose. They ran to Seth and Nancy, shouting, laughing, weeping, and climbing over one another to hug their brother. Unspeakable joy filled the Johnson home.

ᘗᕈᶜ NOTES ᕉᕈ

CHAPTER 1

There were several articles written in the local newspapers to discredit the new "Mormonite" religion. One specific article in *The Fredonia Censor* reported the failure to heal Nancy Johnson, as quoted in the text of Chapter 1. In sarcasm it also notes the death of Joseph Brackenbury, the missionary who died in the Johnson home:

> Death of a Mormon Preacher. —Died, in Pomfret on Saturday, 7th inst. *Joseph H. Brackenbury,* a 'Mormon Preacher.' He recently came to this town from Ohio, in company with one or two individuals of the same society. —They preached, exhorted, and with great *zeal* and *apparent* humility, attempted to propagate their doctrines. . . . In confirmation of their doctrine and divine mission, they *professed* to have the power to heal the sick, and raise the dead. It is credibly reported that they attempted twice without effect, to heal a Miss Nancy Johnson. . . . The company of Brackenbury attempted also to heal him, and since his [decease], to raise him from the dead. (*The Fredonia Censor,* Vol. XI, No. 44, Wednesday, January 25, 1832)

Seth's coming to accompany Ben home after a short stay in Kirtland, appearing "perfectly sound in mind" (Johnson, B. F., *My Life's Review,* 8) did occur in the fall of 1832, although the specific conversations, blessings, and counsel of the Prophet while in Kirtland were imagined to take place. Joseph Smith was likely aware of the Johnson family and their desire to move to Kirtland as seen in Joel's statement that he was "counseled" by the Prophet to buy property in Kirtland (Johnson, J. H., Diary, 12–13).

CHAPTER 2

Mr. Goldfinger, Joe's Old Indian friend is a fictional character; however, Joe's interest in the culture and his involvement in championing the cause of the Native American was a theme throughout his life. As an adult, he organized a company of Indians and went to Washington, D.C., in defense of their rights. In a summary of his diary it states, "He became imbued with the idea of obtaining justice . . . by drawing attention to their plight in the nation's capital by presenting their wrongs before the Indian Commission and the President of the United States, Millard Fillmore" (*Register of the Papers of Joseph Ellis Johnson* [1817–1882], 11).

Amicus wrote several letters published in the *American Eagle* (Westfield, N.Y.), during 1832–1833, some on the subject of Mormonism. It is not certain that Joseph or any of the Johnsons wrote these articles; however, years later "when Joseph wrote poetry and articles for the press, his favorite nom de plume was Amicus" (Johnson, Rufus, *Trail to Sundown,* 65), and the content seems consistent with his values and beliefs.

Ellicott, the seat of Chautauqua County, and the Jamestown and Busti area, about twenty to thirty miles south of Pomfret, was frequented by the early missionaries and became a gathering place for early Mormon families in New York prior to moving to Kirtland, Ohio. *The Early History of the Town of Ellicott,* written in 1897, not only documents the presence of the Saints and purpose of this area for the Mormons, but the general feeling in the community about them. "This was one of the headquarters, a gathering place preparatory to a removal to Kirkland, Ohio, of that religious parasite, Mormonism. At one time there were nearly 300 of them" (Hazeltine, Gilbert W., 343). Smallpox, or what was thought to be smallpox, did break out in the Mormon settlement and was the cause of animosity between the citizens of Jamestown and the Mormons. Hazeltine refers to this time as the "Jamestown Mormon War" (345). The timing of the outbreak of smallpox among the Mormons has been altered slightly. Smallpox was first reported in January 1833 (*The American Eagle,* Vol. 2, No. 8, Westfield, N.Y., January 22, 1833).

Philastus Hurlbut did have a home in Ellicott. The documentation of Hurlbut's residence is found in a notice in the local newspaper. This notice in *The Jamestown Journal* offers a reward for the return of his lost wallet.

LOST, In the village of Jamestown, or between the village and Causadaga Creek, on Thursday the 13th inst. a small leather wallet, containing about three dollars in cash, and a promissory note given by A. & S. R. Gilson to the bearer for $10.00.

Any person finding said wallet, and returning it to me at Plumb's Mills, shall be handsomely rewarded.

D. P. HURLBUT.
Ellicott, September 20, 1832.

(*Jamestown Journal,* No. 326, Wednesday, September 26, 1832).

It is not certain that the Shermans resided with Hurlbut; however, there are also historical records that place Lyman and Delcena as living in the area at that time: some family records place Albey Sherman's (Lyman and Delcena's son) birthplace as Jamestown, on October 30, 1832; and, the Hiram and Rebecca Burdick Winter's family history record Lyman performing baptisms of their extended family in Jamestown, June 1833 (Olsen, Beth Randall, *Among the Remnant Who Lingered,* 15).

Lyman may have initially verbally guessed that the gift of tongues was of the devil (Esplin, Ronald K. "The Emergence of Brigham Young and the Twelve to Mormon Leadership," 93). However, the incident of Brigham Young visiting the Sherman family is based upon a letter Benjamin F. Johnson wrote to Elder Gibbs in 1905. The letter was requested by Elder Gibbs as recommended by the First Presidency to address Benjamin's knowledge of events in the early days of the Church. In this letter he stated:

Brigham Young started with his brother from their home in the state of New York, to visit the Prophet at Kirtland, and on their way called upon us . . . and remaining overnight with my sister's husband, Lyman R. Sherman. And while at evening in animated conversation upon the gifts as promised to accompany the gospel, the spirit came upon Brother Sherman in mighty power, and he opened his mouth in an unknown tongue, to the great surprise and joy to all, and I think that Brother Brigham also at that time received the gift. (Johnson, B. F., "Gibb's letter," 1905, as printed in E. Dale LeBaron's thesis, "Benjamin Franklin Johnson, Colonizer, Public Servant, and Church Leader," 344)

Brigham Young's history is consistent with Benjamin's account. "We visited many friends on the way, and some branches of the Church. We exhorted them and prayed with them, and I spoke in tongues. Some pronounced it genuine and from the Lord, and others pronounced it of the devil" (*Manuscript History of Brigham Young*).

CHAPTER 3

The meeting that Seth and Joel attend the night before Jared Carter's mission is not known to have specifically taken place. However, it is based upon information given in Jared Carter's journal. He says that while preaching in Amherst and the surrounding areas, "the Lord blessed my soul in advance in meeting with my brethren," and having "felt moved upon by the spirit to go to Michigan" he leaves on a mission Friday, November 30, 1833 (Carter, Jared, Journal, 21).

The scene of Almon writing and then sending a letter to Julianne by way of Ben was written for plot development to portray the growing feelings of Almon for Julianne. Little is known about the specifics of their relationship; however, it is assumed that it grew and began to blossom during this period of time.

Joe's relationship with Rachel Risley is based on a friendship that continued into adulthood. In his personal papers there is some correspondence from a Mrs. Blanchard Darby. The letters are familiar, friendly, and reminiscent of mutual friends and childhood places. No first or maiden name is given, and so the fictional name of Rachel Risley is used to portray this young friend of Joe, who shared some common interests and a friendship in his youth. The surname Risley is common to that area and is taken from the Historical Risley Mansion in Fredonia (Fredonia Chamber of Commerce, 1999–2000). The letters are dated January 15, 1865; October 22, 1865; and November 8, 1868 and are found in "The Papers of Joseph Ellis Johnson (1817–1882)." The "stolen kisses" Joe remembers in the text of the novel are based on a poem he wrote later in his life:

In autumn, when the mellow fruit was red,
To "paring-bees" with lightened step we tread;
. . . We peeled the fruit, told yarns, and joked and laughed,
We kissed the girls . . .
("The Old Schoolhouse" in *Jottings by the Way,* xix)

Joel was incorrectly listed as a missionary in Fredonia, New York, in a derogatory article in the local newspaper (*The Fredonia Censor,* Vol. XII., No. 36, Fredonia, N.Y., Wed., Nov. 28, 1832).

> *The Mormonites.* —It is our humiliating duty to record the fact, that two of the preachers* of this fanatical sect have visited our city, endeavoring to propagate their strange doctrines, and it is said that about fifteen persons here became converts, having been led away by their delusions . . .

> . . . The preachers intended visiting the cities and principal towns in New England—We are informed that they have recently visited Lynn where they have endeavored to make a favorable impression, by the appearance of great sincerity.

> —*N. Y. Paper.*

— — — — — — — — —

> * One of these we believe is Joel H. Johnson of this town.

> —*Censor.*

Joel was in Ohio at this time. According to other historical records, the two missionaries traveling through New England and New York were most likely Orson Hyde and Samuel Smith ("History of Orson Hyde," *The Latter-day Saints' Millennial Star* 26, 1864).

CHAPTER 4

The primary setting of this chapter takes place in Fredonia, which is the sister community and closest town to Pomfret. Fredonia's history does include having "the first natural gas well in the United States (1821)" and a documented "visit by General Lafayette in 1825" (*Fredonia Chamber of Commerce,* 1999–2000). In 1933, it was still one of the only places in the United States that used natural gas. Ben's memory of being taken to see the French General Lafayette is fictional and written to promote the plot of the story; however, the Johnson family was living in the area at that time, and they were likely aware of his visit and may have witnessed it.

The "Amicus" article quoted in this chapter from *The American Eagle,* a local newspaper, was actually written one year earlier (May 8, 1832). The date is changed for plot consideration because the subsequent articles written by and about "Amicus" used in later chapters were written in May 1833.

CHAPTER 5

The information presented in this chapter concerning smallpox in Jamestown is taken from newspaper articles of the time (*The Jamestown Journal,* Vol. VII, No. 343, Wednesday, January 23, 1833; No. 344, Wednesday, January 30, 1833; No. 345, Wednesday, February 6, 1833; No. 346, Wednesday, February 13, 1833; and *The Fredonia Censor,* Vol. XIII, No. 5 Fredonia, N.Y., Wednesday, April 24, 1833). Although it is not recorded in family records that Lyman knew and blessed a woman who died with smallpox, Mrs. Clark was reported to have died of the disease on the evening of February 5, 1833 (*The Jamestown Journal,* Vol. VII, No. 345, Wednesday, February 6, 1833).

There was some difficulty in determining whether the disease was smallpox or a milder illness referred to as varioloid. It caused great concern in the community and escalated the anti-Mormon sentiment. Written in response to public concern about the outbreak, a local doctor, Dr. Proudfit, says that he did not believe the cases to be smallpox (*The Jamestown Journal,* Vol. VII, No. 344, Wednesday, January 30, 1833).

However, Dr. Proudfit's diagnosis is challenged in a subsequent newspaper article:

Dr. Proudfit considers it as too mild a complaint for smallpox and thinks the worst cases that he has seen, have indicated no danger. Now it is possible that another person might have thought it a dangerous complaint, but this could not prove it to be smallpox, neither does Dr. Proudfit's estimate of its mildness prove it to be varioloid. . . . If the disease thus far has proved to be generally mild for smallpox, it may be satisfactorily accounted for from the fact that it occurred at a favorable season of the year, and in a healthy situation. (*The Jamestown Journal,* Vol. VII, No. 346, Wednesday, February 13, 1833)

The "brotherly" relationship of Lyman and D. P. Hurlbut as presented in this novel is not historically documented in journals or other records.

However, the probable familial relationship (detailed in the next paragraph), that both were in the area of Jamestown/Ellicott at the same time, and the fact that D. P. lives with the Johnson family in Kirtland for a period of time create the possibility of this close relationship. There is little information identifying the parents of D. P. Hurlbut. Lyman Sherman and his mother, Asenath Hurlbut, are most likely close relatives because of the proximity of their residence in New York and in Kirtland; in addition, there is a connection with the Benjamin Winchester family. One of Asenath's brothers, Asel Hurlbut, married Sarah Winchester, Benjamin's aunt. Winchester says that D. P. Hurlbut often stayed in his father's home (*The Origin of the Spaulding Story*, Philadelphia, 1840, 4) when traveling. Asenath and Asel are two of twelve children listed on the family group record of their parents, David and Dorcas Hurlbut. It is most likely that Philastus is a child of one of Asenath or Asel's siblings. In Benjamin Winchester's book, *The Origin of the Spaulding Story*, he gives background information about Hurlbut's journey to Kirtland:

> He embraced the faith of the church of the Latter Day Saints, and soon started for Kirtland, Ohio; ostensibly to cultivate an acquaintance with the brethren there. On his way, he passed through the place in which I resided; he was not ordained at this time. (4, 5)

The exact timing and instance when D. P. Hurlbut learns of the Spaulding Story is unknown. However, it is known that the Spaulding claims originated in Erie County, and Hurlbut could have heard of it while traveling or staying with his Hurlbut/Winchester relations.

Hurlbut's initials, D. P., standing for Doctor Philastus, represent an unusual given name. Philastus was very uncommon, even for that period of time. And, as stated in this chapter, he was given the name Doctor, being "the seventh son of his mother," probably because of following folklore:

> A seventh son is always a lucky or especially gifted person, often gifted with occult powers. He makes a good doctor; he usually has instinctive knowledge of magic and medicinal herbs; and the seventh son can stop hemorrhages. Throughout England, Scotland, Ireland, and the United States in general, any seventh child is regarded as having exceptional healing powers. (*Funk & Wagnall's Standard Dictionary of Folklore Mythology and Legend*, Volume two: J–Z, 1950)

Although we don't know the exact circumstances under which Hurlbut met Lovina Williams, W. R. Hine, a nonmember living in the Kirtland area, said, "I became acquainted with D. P. Hurlbut before he left the Mormons. He courted Dr. Williams' beautiful daughter, and told her he had a revelation to marry her; she told him when she received a revelation they would be married" (*Dale W. Adams Research,* Box 1, Folder 1). Although it is imagined that Hurlbut rescued Lovina's friend, the incident itself is based on a real incident:

> Lovina and a few of her girl friends were walking on a plank in the mill pond a quarter of a mile from the school house. Some of the girls were waiting for a turn and in a hurry to be on the plank. . . . One girl became frightened and lost her balance, falling into the water. Their cries for help were heard in time to rescue the girl. (Williams, Rebecca S., *After One Hundred Years,* 70)

The revelation now referred to as *The Word of Wisdom* was revealed February 27, 1833. Joel Hills Johnson was present on that occasion. He says, "I was with Joseph Smith, the Prophet, when the Word of Wisdom was given by revelation. . . . I was then thirty-one years of age, and had used tobacco somewhat extravagantly for fifteen years. . . . I knew that God had spoken" (Johnson, J. H., *Voice From the Mountains,* 12). Zebedee Coltrin said that of the twenty-two men present, all used tobacco except for two. When Joseph read the revelation, "they all laid aside their pipes and use of tobacco" (*Joseph Smith's Kirtland,* 97). It is not known if Hurlbut was actually in attendance.

CHAPTER 6

Although this particular excursion of Almon Babbitt to Cincinnati is fictional, the Joel Hills (Julia's brother) family did live in the Cincinnati area at this time.

Joseph Smith records that Hurlbut came to his home March 13, 1833, and spent a considerable time conversing about the Book of Mormon. Although the details of this conversation were not found in any historical documents, the tone of the meeting was likely positive since Hurlbut is listed as being presented and ordained an elder as recorded by Joseph Smith, March 18, 1833 (Journal History, 13, 18 March, 1833).

John Murdock was Julia Smith's biological father. She was the adopted daughter of Emma and Joseph. Murdock boarded with the Prophet and

Emma during the beginning of the School of the Prophets until he left on his mission to New York, April 3, 1833 (Murdock, John, Autobiograhy and Diary). It is likely he spent time with his little daughter; however, he never did disclose that he was her father. This is stated in a letter dated January 20, 1859 from John in Utah replying to a correspondence from Julia. He explains to her, "Sister Smith requested me not to make my self known to the children as being their Father: It was a hard request and I said but little on the subject" (Murdock, S. Reed, *John Murdock, His Life and His Legacy*, 293). The fictional scene during the School of the Prophets when John is reminiscing as the Prophet Joseph washes his feet is based upon a description to Julia of her mother's death in this same letter.

The manner in which the School of the Prophets was conducted was based upon Zebedee Coltrin's remarks. He says that it began with the salutation as found in the Doctrine and Covenants, followed by the washing of feet by Joseph, and the administration of the sacrament. These remarks are found in the minutes of the Salt Lake City School of the Prophets, October 3, 1883. The scene of the washing of feet in the School of the Prophets is based upon several documented events (Journal History, 23, 24 January, 1833).

John Murdock and Zebedee Coltrin arrived in Jamestown, April twelfth and in Pomfret, April fifteenth. John Murdock stated in his journal, "12th arrived at Jame's Town (Jamestown), found 2 brothers and 2 sisters sick with smallpox. We fasted, prayed, and laid on hands in the name of the Lord, and they were healed. On Sunday we broke bread with the Church and strengthened them. 15th arrived at Pomfret. Found the Church healthful both temporally and spiritually" (Murdock, John, Autobiography and Diary).

Although the specific scene of the Johnsons' breaking of the line is fictional, it is based on significant historical data. Jamestown, referred to as "a gathering place," became the backdrop of the "Jamestown Mormon War." Due to the scare of smallpox, fences were constructed across "third street at Lafayette" as a barrier set to isolate the area of town in which the Mormons lived. "Big Simmons, the watchman" would use a large hickory stick to hit those trying to leave the fenced area. It was stated that those who were hit by the hickory stick while trying to leave complained of a headache, fainted, or lay in the street until cared for by some of their people (Hazeltine, Gilbert W., *The Early History of Ellicott*, 345).

CHAPTER 7

Although the details of the missing letter and reactions of individual family members concerning the move to Kirtland are limited, Julia and the children began their journey in the spring (Johnson, Rufus, *Trail to Sundown*, 42). "Time passed, and no letter of instruction came; and being compelled to give possession of our home, we started for Ohio" (Johnson, B. F., *My Life's Review*, 8). The exact date of their departure is unknown. However, Benjamin says that they arrived in early June, 1833 (8).

The uncle of the Prophet Joseph, John Smith and his family, stopped in Westfield, New York, on their way to Kirtland in order to stay and worship with the congregation there. Members of the Johnson family met the John Smith family as they were traveling (Johnson, Rufus, *Trail to Sundown*, 43). Although there is no historical documentation that Seth, David, or Benjamin specifically met the Smiths in Westfield or were present in the barn, the date, place, and details of the experience did occur and are recorded by George A. Smith:

> On the 17th [May] we arrived at Silver Creek, Chautauqua Co., New York, . . . We attended meetings. . . . We traveled to Westfield, where there was a branch of the church; my father preached in the evening. I was so sleepy I could not keep awake; I went to the wagon, but was so sleepy that I could not get in to bed, although my bed was made there, but fell asleep by the wagon. While here one of bro. Brown's horses died, in consequence of which he began to doubt the work of the Lord; for, said he, "If this was the work of the Lord, he would not suffer our horses to die when we are on the way to Zion." (Journal History, 1 May, 1833)

The letters to and from "Amicus" are found in the local Westfield news-paper, *The American Eagle,* in May 1833 on the dates represented in the text of the chapter. The paper indicates that although the letter from Amicus was published May 28, the letter was written May 22, 1833 (*The American Eagle,* Vol. 2, No. 25 Westfield, N.Y., May 21, 1833; No. 26, May 28). Although, the authorship of the Amicus letters is not absolute, the dates of these letters fit within the time frame of the Johnson's residence in Pomfret and their subsequent move to Kirtland.

CHAPTER 8

The exact date of the Johnsons' arrival in Kirtland is not recorded, and their greeting by the Prophet is fictional. However, Julia and the children did occupy a home on the Kirtland flats in early June (Kirtland land records). This home was close to the Whitney Store, and the property bordered the schoolhouse. At the present time, the schoolhouse has been rebuilt. A small blue house stands nearby. Although changed through the years, the house still contains some of the wooden beams of the original Johnson home (conversation with Keith W. Perkins, author of *Sacred Places in Ohio and Illinois*).

On May 31, Orson Hyde, D. P. Hurlbut's missionary companion, returned to Kirtland and filed charges against him for immoral conduct while on his mission. Although the exact circumstances of Philastus's relationship with Huldah Barnes is not known, it is factual that he knew and was involved with her during his mission. D. P. did not return with Orson, and his whereabouts at the time were unknown. (Broadhurst, Dale, *Crisis at Kirtland*, ch. 2). Philastus was excommunicated on June third, prior to his return to Kirtland, and was "accused of un-Christian conduct with women, while on a mission to the east" (*History of the Church*, 1:352).

For the purpose of plot development, Hurlbut visits Lyman's mother and sisters on his way back to Kirtland. Although this visit is not documented and it is not certain that they were in Thomson, it is important that an association between Philastus and Electa Sherman be introduced. Hurlbut had several documented female relationships at this time, including Electa (Johnson, B.F., *My Life's Review*, 18).

The details of the meeting and the selecting of a plot for the temple are merged from two accounts of this event. Although in *History of the Church*, the events took place over several days (June 3–5), the timing of the events in the novel more closely follow Lucy Mack Smith's account in *A History of Joseph Smith By His Mother*, where a council investigates "the subject of building," including how the brethren envisioned the house to look, concluding with Joseph saying, "I have a plan of the house of the Lord, given by himself, and you will soon see by this, the difference between our calculations and his idea of things" (230). He then gives them the plan, and:

After the close of the meeting, Joseph took the brethren with him, for the purpose of selecting a spot for the building to stand upon. The place which they made choice of was situated in the northeast corner of a field of wheat . . . on the farm upon which we were then living. In a few minutes the fence was removed, and the standing grain was leveled, in order to prepare a place for the building and Hyrum commenced digging a trench for the wall, he having declared that he would strike the first blow upon the house.

On the following Monday, the brethren went to work at the house with great ambition. (230–231)

The *History of the Church* by Joseph states that both Hyrum *and* Reynolds Cahoon, as represented in this chapter, commenced digging the trench. David, Almon, and Don Carlos are not specifically listed as being in attendance at the meeting or afterwards. Reynolds Cahoon, Jared Carter, and Hyrum Smith, were appointed to "take oversight of the building of the house of the Lord," and Joseph, Sidney Rigdon, and Frederick G. Williams, were appointed to obtain "a draft or construction of the inner court of the house," and would have been in attendance at that time (1:352–353).

CHAPTER 9

In this chapter, the events leading up to Hurlbut's actual threat to destroy Joseph Smith are based on many historical accounts. However, the sequencing of events, specifically his marriage proposal to Electa Sherman, was created to provide a reasonable explanation for the timing of Hurlbut's "liberal confession" on June 21 and final excommunication only two days later (*History of the Church*, 1:354–355). He immediately left Kirtland after his reinstatement and was reported to have gone to Thompson, Ohio, on his way to Pennsylvania. There he attempted to seduce another woman (Winchester, *The Origin of the Spaulding Story*, 6), and made boastful statements about deceiving Joseph and the council (*History of the Church*, 1:355; see also *Dale Adams Research*).

There is no evidence to prove that the woman was Electa Sherman; however, the familial connection between the Winchesters and the Shermans make it possible that Electa and her mother could have been staying in Thompson with family, and Winchester would have been aware of Hurlbut's visit and interactions. Benjamin Johnson knew of Hurlbut's interest in Electa, which additionally supports the possibility of the imagined proposal scene of Hurlbut to Electa.

Rejections from both Lovina Williams and Electa Sherman seem to be factors in Hurlbut's quick separation from the Church. A non-Mormon living in Kirtland and speaking of Hurlbut stated, "He courted Mr. Williams' beautiful daughter. . . . Everybody about Kirtland believed he had left the Mormons because she refused him" (Hine, W. R., in *Dale Adams Research*). Benjamin F. Johnson said, "He soon became enamored or greatly in love with Electra . . . and because she despised him for his immorality and rejected his suit, he . . . boastfully declared he would destroy the church" (Johnson, B. F., *My Life's Review*, 18).

The baptismal service in June 1833 in Jamestown, New York, did include those of the Burdick and Winters families, with Lyman Sherman and Sylvester Smith performing the ordinances (Olsen, Beth R., *Among the Remnant Who Lingered,* 15) The song that Lyman sings is from Emma's hymnal. Although this is an imagined scene, it is consistent with what is known about Lyman. It is recorded in the *Journal History* (8 January 1837), that he sang during the sacrament meeting.

CHAPTER 10

Benjamin Winchester described Hurlbut's intentions after his separation from the Mormons. He states,

On discovering he had irretrievably ruined himself with the church, his tactics were changed, and he now determined to demolish, as far as practicable, what he had once endeavored to build up. Now his nefarious purposes were frustrated, he sought to obtain revenge in this manner. Not because he did not conscientiously believe the work of God, as proclaimed by the Latter Day Saints, but because . . . he could no longer hide himself under the cloak of religion, and have a name with the people of God. (*The Origin of the Spaulding Story,* 6)

Hurlbut began to tour the area, giving public lectures against the Mormons in an effort to strike back. He attempted to convince whoever would listen of the dishonest origin of the Book of Mormon. He joined forces with an "anti-Mormon" committee, which included members of the

Kirtland Town Council, the Campbellite ministers from Mentor, and wealthy land owners and businessmen working together to rid their community of the Mormons.

Mentor, the community bordering Kirtland, became an area where those opposing the early Church began to meet and plan their actions to discredit Joseph Smith and the Book of Mormon. Grandison Newell, an established businessman/landowner, and Orris Clapp, a preacher, were two of the leaders of the anti-Mormon committee (*Dale Adams Research*). Orris Clapp was John Murdock's father-in-law (Joseph and Emma Smith's twins' biological grandfather) and a leader of the Campbellites. He had both personal and religious reasons for his involvement in discrediting the Mormon prophet.

It is not known exactly when or where the original meeting occurred that Hurlbut began expounding his theory of the Spaulding manuscript and asked for funding of a research trip to locate Spaulding. However, Benjamin does record that his father spent time in Mentor and did know those who were involved in this well-organized anti-Mormon group.

CHAPTER 11

There is no record that David was at the Smiths' for Don Carlos's ordination. Don Carlos was ordained July 23, 1834, shortly before a ceremony that took place when the cornerstones of the Kirtland Temple were laid. He was ordained for the purpose of participating on this occasion (Backman, M., *The Heavens Resound*, 140). The words of the blessing given by Joseph Smith Sr. to Don Carlos are actually quoted from a blessing given to Carlos shortly before his father died in September, 1840 (Smith, Lucy Mack, *A History of Joseph Smith By His Mother*, 311).

In the ceremony, twenty-four elders were chosen to lay the cornerstones of the temple. Four groups of six elders each laid one of the cornerstones. The group, including the First Presidency of the Church, laid the first cornerstone (Journal History, 23 July 1833). In *My Life's Review*, Benjamin records that his brothers Joel and Seth, and brother-in-law Lyman Sherman, all participated (9). However, Seth and Lyman are not on the list that was reconstructed in 1859 by George A. Smith. In his attempt to remember the twenty-four elders, he reads the list to "Orson Hyde who said that he did not know of any cause for altering it, although he could not remember distinctly what happened on that occasion" (Journal History, 23 July 1833).

The hymn sung in the meeting is from Emma's hymnbook 114–115, hymn 84, verses 4–5.

Although family histories place Ezekiel as a carpenter in Mentor (Cluff & Gibson, *Johnson Gems,* 21), there is no information that he worked with Samuel Prescott. Samuel Prescott did live in the area and is introduced here to provide a link for the Johnson story to move forward. Although there is no concrete documentation or record, a Johnson family tale is that Brigham Young shared a carpenter's bench with Ezekiel for a short period of time.

Oliver Cowdery did travel to Kirtland from Independence to tell the news of the situation of the Saints in Missouri. Joseph Smith originally planned that the temple be made of bricks, a project in which the Johnsons were very involved.

It is a fact that Philastus Hurlbut did live with the Johnson family at this time (Johnson, B. F., *My Life's Review*); however, the reasons behind the decision to let him stay for a period of time and the feelings of different family members about him are extrapolated considering the plot, relationships, and characterizations of the novel.

Hurlbut began lectures in Kirtland when he returned, as represented in this chapter. However, it is likely, but not documented, that some of the Johnson family may have attended those lectures. In the 1830s there was a Methodist meetinghouse in the southeast corner of the cemetery, just north of the Kirtland temple, facing the temple on Maple Street. This church was burned by arsonists in 1838 (Berrett & Parkin, *Sacred Places,* 29).

CHAPTER 12

October fourth is the day before Joseph Smith started on his mission to Canada (*History of the Church*, 1:416). It is also exactly forty days before the fulfillment of the "prophecy" of Joseph Smith. The hunting scene involving Joseph and the Johnsons imaginatively sets up the circumstances of this prophecy, which is based on an article written by Philo Dibble in the *Juvenile Instructor,* January 1892. It says that sometime in the fall of 1833 Joseph said, "Forty days shall not pass and the stars shall fall from heaven." Although it is not known exactly when the prophecy was made, Philo Dibble relates the interesting experience of Joseph Hancock, which happened on the thirty-ninth day, one day before a meteor shower that was witnessed throughout the United States (McConkie, *Remembering Joseph*, 338).

In Joel Hills Johnson's autobiography it states that they were employed in making bricks for the temple until September 25 because the temple was to be made of stone and not bricks.

There are no records to indicate that David was an elder at the time that he died. The details of David's death, which are consistent, include:

Through his ambition in labors upon the [brick] yard, and in procuring wood with which to burn the brick, overtasked his strength, took severe cold, commenced bleeding at the lungs, lingered for a few weeks in quick consumption, and died as he has lived—a true latter-Day Saint. His last testimony was given through the gift of tongues, which was interpreted by Bro. Don Carlos Smith, who as his friend and companion, was present at his death, which occurred Oct. 30, 1833 (Johnson, B. F., *My Life's Review*, 9).

At the time of Joseph's and Sidney Rigdon's mission to Canada, Frederick Williams was left in charge of Kirtland, and Oliver Cowdery was securing the purchase of a printing press (*History of the Church*, 1:418). It was planned that Don Carlos would aid Oliver in running the press. The first edition of this paper included the obituary of David as reflected in the text of this chapter. (*The Evening and Morning Star*, December 1833; Lisonbee, Janet. *Obituaries and Life Sketches*).

It is not known who made the casket for David.

CHAPTER 13

Joseph's arrival in Kirtland and the feelings he expresses in his conversation with Ezekiel concerning David's death are based on a letter addressed to Brother Moses Nickerson. The Prophet Joseph wrote that he arrived in Kirtland on:

The fourth ultimo, after a fatiguing journey . . . [and] . . . found our families and the Church in this place well, generally. Nothing of consequence happened while we were absent, except the death of one of our brethren—David Johnson—a young man of great worth as a private citizen among us, the loss of whom we justly mourn. (Journal History, 19 Nov. 1833)

There are several accounts of "the night of the falling stars," which occurred November 13, 1833. The meteor shower was viewed throughout the United States (*History of the Church*, 1:440). Although the scene of the Johnsons watching the stars together with thoughts of David present in their minds was imagined, Benjamin does record his witness in *My Life's Review*: "For the heavens were full of blazing storm, from zenith to horizon, and a view more sublime and terrible the eyes of man may never have seen. . . . I gazed upon the scene with wondering awe, but with a full realization of its purport as a sign of the last days" (10).

Among many other accounts, there was a story told in the *Juvenile Instructor*, January 1892, that "Joseph Hancock . . . and another brother were out hunting game and got lost." They wandered about until night, and found themselves at the house of a man who claimed knowing of Joseph Smith's prophecy that the stars would fall in forty days, and asked the men what they thought of the Prophet, now that thirty-nine days had passed and the prophecy was not fulfilled. Brother Hancock stayed that night at the house of the unbeliever and "the whole heavens were lit up with the falling meteors" (McConkie, *Remembering Joseph*, 338). There is no record of Almon being the other brother; however, it is likely he knew and worked with Joseph Hancock making bricks. When the Johnsons made brick for the temple, they used the brickyard originally belonging to Joseph and Thomas Hancock (Johnson, B. F., *My Life's Review*, 9).

Parley P. Pratt described the sight he and the exiled Saints witnessed from their shanty, make-shift camps in the Missouri bottoms:

The firmament . . . seemed enveloped in splendid fireworks, as if every star in the broad expanse had been hurled from its course, and sent lawless through the wilds of ether. Thousands of bright meteors were shooting through space in every direction, with long trains of light following in their course. This lasted for several hours, and was only closed by the dawn of the rising sun. Every heart was filled with joy at this majestic display of signs and wonders, showing the near approach of the coming of the Son of God. (*Autobiography of Parley P. Pratt,* 103)

In writing of this powerful experience, which brought great comfort to the Saints, some details were pieced together from the various accounts, including the fact that Oliver and Joseph stood together at the Smith's front gate witnessing the signs from heaven (Ira Ames journal, as found in McConkie, *Remembering Joseph,* 338). Joseph relates this experience, "I arose and to my great joy, beheld the stars fall from heaven like a shower of hailstones; . . . a sure sign that the coming of Christ is close at hand. In the midst of this shower of fire, I was led to exclaim, 'How marvelous are Thy works, O Lord!'" (*History of the Church,* 1:439).

CHAPTER 14

Historians have attempted to reconstruct from letters and individual accounts the exact dates and places that coincide with Hurlbut's travel on his anti-Mormon mission to locate the Spaulding Manuscript. Sometime in the month of November he visited at Mrs. Davison's residence in Monson, Massachusetts. There he obtained permission from her to view and take the original papers of her late husband, Solomon Spaulding. She had left them in the possession of her cousin, Mr. Jerome Clark, of Hartwick, New York. Hurlbut's anticipation of receiving the manuscript and subsequent disappointment at not receiving it was deduced from the fact that the manuscript was never published (Broadhurst, Dale, *Crisis at Kirtland*). This is supported in a letter written by Mr. John Haven of an interview with Mrs. Davison and her daughter, Mrs. McKinstry:

Ques.: Where is the manuscript? Ans. Dr. P. Hurlbert [*sic*] came here and took it, and said he would get it printed, and let me have one half of the profits. Ques. Has Dr. P. H. got the manuscript printed? Ans. I received a letter, stating that it did not read as they expected, and they should not print it. (Kirkham, *A New Witness for Christ in America,* 285, as cited in *Dale W. Adams Research*)

Years later, Joseph E. Johnson wrote:

Hurlbut went east and was absent some two or three months—and on his return publicly declared that he could not obtain it, but instead brought several affidavits from persons who claimed to have heard Solomon Spaulding read his Manuscript Found in 1812, and believed as well as they could remember that the matter and story was the same as printed in the Book of Mormon. . . . According to the sworn statement of M. S. McKinstry, Dr. Hurlbut *did* obtain the Manuscript Found and the only conclusion that can be reasonable is that finding it would spoil his case and ruin his purposes, that manuscript was destroyed or suppressed. ("The Manuscript Found," *Deseret Evening News,* Jan. 3, 1881)

The news of the "melencholly intelegen[ce] of the riot in Zion" (Smith, Joseph, *The Papers of Joseph Smith,* 2:14) is brought to the Prophet Joseph on Monday, November 25, 1833, by Orson Hyde and John Gould, almost three weeks after the Missouri Saints had been forced to leave Independence. The words of Joseph's response in this chapter are consistent with Lucy Mack Smith's record as well as the sentiment and feeling found in a letter Joseph wrote December 10, 1833: "Brethren, when we learn your sufferings, it awakens every sympathy of our hearts; it weighs us down; we cannot refrain from tears, . . . and I myself should have been with you" (Journal History, 10 Dec. 1833).

It is not recorded that Seth and Lyman were included when Joseph received the revelation concerning Zion. However, the revelation was received on December 16 (Journal History, 16 December 1833), and Oliver Cowdery was heard to have "dramatically announced" that they had received news from heaven (Bushman, Richard, *Rough Stone Rolling,* 229).

Hurlbut returned to Kirtland and began to give lectures about what he had found—the story of the manuscript and statements from Palmyra to discredit Joseph and his family. The anti-Mormon feeling was escalating during this time period. Thirteen rounds were shot toward the temple from a cannon about half a mile northwest the morning of January 8, 1834. At this time, Joseph was assigned a bodyguard, and guards were placed around the temple site to protect it from vandals. Joseph Smith charged Hurlbut with threatening his life and property in early January 1834. Joseph Smith also assigned bodyguards for himself and Sidney Rigdon at this time (Broadhurst, Dale, *Crisis at Kirtland*; see also *Dale W. Adams Research*).

There is no documentation that Ezekiel went to Joseph Smith's home with Hurlbut's plans; however, the intent of Ezekiel is consistent with

Benjamin's statement that although his father was regarded as "an opposer, knew all their secrets," he did not keep these secrets from those close to him who were active believers of the Prophet Joseph (Johnson, B. F., *My Life's Review,* 19).

CHAPTER 15

It is documented that the Prophet Joseph counsels Benjamin not to go with Zion's Camp. Ben's desire to go and his feelings are also expressed in the following entry from *My Life's Review:*

Zion's Camp was preparing to start, in which I desired to accompany my brother Seth, and brother-in-law L. R. Sherman, with A. W. Babbitt, who was to marry my sister Julia. But the Prophet deemed it not best for me to go, owing to the opposition of my father, and as I had not yet received my baptism. I was assured by the Prophet Joseph that no loss should come to me for waiting, for although not fully a member I had partaken of every hope, desire, and spiritual influence with which those around me were animated. It was with a joy almost unspeakable that I realized that I was living in a day when God had a prophet upon the earth. (10)

The court case between D. P. Hurlbut and Joseph Smith is found in the court records of Chardon, Geauga, Ohio, beginning March 31, 1834. Joseph records that he went up to Chardon on March 31, and that "the court has not brought forward Hurlbut's trial yet, and we were engaged in issuing subpoenas for witnesses." Joseph Smith continues, "My soul delighteth in the law of the Lord, for He forgiveth my sins, and will confound mine enemies." Joseph then attends court the next two days and returns to Kirtland on April 4 (Journal History, April 1, 1834), awaiting the court's decision, which comes April ninth. "Dr. Philastus Hurlburt be bound over, under two hundred dollar bonds, to keep the peace for six months, and pay the cost, which amounted to nearly three hundred dollars, all of which was in answer to our prayers, for which I thank my Heavenly Father" (Journal History, April 9, 1834).

It is not documented that Lyman, his mother, and sister were present during the court proceedings. The local newspaper *The Chardon Spectator and Geauga Gazette* on April 12, 1834 printed the following article related to the trial.

Mormon Trial. —Great interest was excited in the public mind, in this country, in relation to the complaint of Joseph Smith, jun., the great prophet, and originator of Mormonism, against Doctor P. Hurlburt, the exposer of the Mormon mystery. The complaint was made, before a justice of the peace, to bind Hurlburt to keep the peace toward the Prophet. The justice ordered Hurlburt to enter into bonds to keep the peace, and to appear before the Court of Common Pleas. On Tuesday last, the case was heard before the court. The court-house was filled almost to suffocation, with an eager and curious crowd of spectators, to hear the Mormon trial, as it was called. A great number of witnesses attended, and were examined, chiefly members of the Mormon society, among whom was the renowned Prophet himself. It appeared that Hurlburt had been a disciple of Mormonism, and was ordained an elder by Joe himself, but for misconduct, as the Mormon witnesses alleged, was excommunicated. After this, he discovered that Joe was a false prophet, and the Book of Mormon a cheat: —began lecturing against it, and examining and collecting proof that the story of the Book of Mormon was taken from a manuscript romance, written by one Spalding [*sic*], who formerly lived at Conneaut and who died before publication. Many witnesses testified to threats of revenge from Hurlburt. One witness, who testified to the threats of Hurlburt, on cross-examination being asked the reason why she had not communicated these threats to Smith, answered that she did not believe Hurlburt, or any other human being, had the power to hurt the Prophet;—but Joe himself appears to have placed little reliance upon his divine invulnerability;—for he testified that he became afraid of bodily injury from the defendant. The Court finally ordered Hurlburt to find security in the sum of Two Hundred Dollars, to keep the peace for the period of six months.

In the chapter, the female witness in the newspaper article is given the name of Sister Copley. It is known that a Mary Copley was a witness during the trial, but she may or may not have been this woman.

CHAPTER 16

In August of 1832, John Murdock received a revelation that he would be called on a mission to the east; however, he was told that "it is not expedient that you should go until your children are provided for, and sent up kindly to the bishop in Zion" (D&C, Section 99). He did not leave until April of 1833, after the children were sent to Bishop Partridge in Independence. The children were then placed in separate families in Missouri. Phebe was four, and was placed in the home of Algernon Sidney Gilbert. Gilbert and his wife, Elizabeth Rollins, welcomed Phebe into their home along with their nieces, Elizabeth and Caroline Rollins, the two young girls who were credited with saving many of the papers of the "Book of Commandments" when the printing press was destroyed in Independence.

Although it is historically accurate that Seth, Almon, and Lyman all marched with Zion's Camp, they did not leave any personal written accounts. The incidents and scenes of Zion's Camp were primarily written based of the histories of George Albert Smith, Levi Hancock, John Murdock, and Heber C. Kimball. The *History of the Church* was also used extensively in writing the Zion's Camp experience.

Lyman's thoughts and feelings about leaving his family and joining Zion's Camp mirrored the actual statement of Heber C. Kimball. "We started on the 5th of May, and truly this was a solemn morning to me. I took leave of my wife and children and friends, not expecting ever to see them again" (Journal of Heber C. Kimball).

Some information about the organization of Zion's Camp is recorded in various records and accounts. In *History of the Church,* Joseph Smith writes,

> I . . . divided the whole band and into companies of twelve, leaving each company to elect its own captain, who assigned each man in his respective company his post and duty. . . . We purchased flour and meal, baked our own bread, and cooked our own food, generally, which was good, though sometimes scanty; and sometimes we had johnny-cake, or corn-dodger, instead of flour bread. Every night before retiring to rest, at the sound of the trumpet, we bowed before the Lord . . . and at the sound of the morning trumpet, about four o'clock, every man was again on his knees before the Lord. (2:64–65)

The original history of Zion's Camp, written by Frederick G. Williams, and the list of companies, was lost. Although, Seth, Almon, and Lyman's placement in companies is not certain, it is also not arbitrary. It is noted that

Seth and Almon traveled home to Kirtland in a group with Joseph Smith and his cousin, George A. Smith (Smith, G. A., *History of George Albert Smith*, 32), and that Lyman Sherman traveled back with Heber C. Kimball (*History of Heber C. Kimball*). Brigham Young, George A. Smith and Zebedee Coltrin were in the same company with the Prophet (Smith, George A., *History of George A. Smith*; see also Launius, R. D., *Zion's Camp*, 56).

The song sung by Parley P. Pratt as his wagon is being pulled is a song that was recorded in Reuben McBride's journal. (He was a member of Zion's Camp.) Although, the scene is fictional, it was said that when this song was sung, there was "electricity in the air" (Launius, R. D., *Zion's Camp*, 52).

The Moses Martin incident actually happened a few days later than represented in this chapter.

During this chapter, Almon, Lyman, and Seth were placed in the day-to-day experience of Zion's Camp as presented in various journals and accounts. However, two incidents of their involvement are documented. Almon did go with Frederick G. Williams "in disguise" on May 30, 1833 (*History of the Church*, 2:76) "ahead into Springfield to learn the feelings of the people and procure some ammunition" (Smith, George A., *History of George Albert Smith*, 7); and in the *History of the Church* it states, "Elders Seth Johnson and Almon W. Babbitt, who had been sent to the Bowling Green Branch to gather recruits, returned to the camp on the morning of the 7th with a small company, two wagons and several horses" (2:87).

CHAPTER 17

The trek of Zion's Camp through the "slough half a mile wide" is found in the Prophet's account of that specific day (Journal History, 18 June 1834). He says he was sick and rode in Elder Kimball's wagon. Without any provisions, most of the men waded through mud and water up to their waists. That day, after arriving at the location of their campsite, the Prophet was very concerned about their vulnerability, knowing that sixty of the Jackson county mob had just joined the Ray county mob. He said:

When I . . . viewed our unsafe location, considering the danger of an attack from our enemies, I almost forgot my sickness, went some distance in the brush, bowed down and prayed my Heavenly Father to suffer no evil to come upon us, but keep us safe through the night. I obtained an assurance that we should be safe until morning. . . . All was quiet in the camp through the night.

It is not included in the records that Lyman was with Luke Johnson when he was called over and warned by "a black woman in a gentleman's garden, that there is a company of men lying in wait here, who are calculating to kill you this morning as you pass through" (Journal History, 18 June 1834), or that Seth was the individual who asked for milk; however, these incidents did occur.

Levi Hancock said that "the greatest miracle in our favor was when we had got between the two fishing rivers on a high ridge by a log meeting-house." All of the journals relate this incident; however, there are various details in each account, which have been used in writing this chapter. While on this "elevated piece of land" (Kimball, Heber C., *Excerpts from the Journal of Heber C. Kimball*), five men rode into camp cussing and swearing that the Mormons would be dead before morning because there was an army before and behind them. Levi Hancock writes that Jenkins Salisbury "wanted Joseph to let him fight." Joseph tells him not to, for "the Lord will give us a bramble to keep off the dogs this night" (Hancock, Levi, Journal). Wilford Woodruff then stated that when the five men were in camp there was not a cloud in the sky, but when they left:

> A small cloud like a black spot appeared in the north west, and it began to unroll itself like a scroll, and in a few minutes the whole heavens were covered with a pall as black as ink. This indicated a sudden storm which soon broke upon us with wind, rain, thunder and lightning and hail. Our beds were soon afloat and our tents blown down over our heads. We all fled into a Baptist meetinghouse. As the Prophet Joseph came in shaking the water from his hat and clothing he said, "Boys, there is some meaning to this, God is in this storm." We sang praises to God and lay all night on benches under cover while our enemies were in the pelting storm. (*History of the Church*, 2:104)

Although all histories of Zion's Camp document the spread and devastation of cholera, Heber C. Kimball's journal provides much of the detail used in this chapter. Lyman's involvement in caring for those with cholera is fictional. The scene of caring for the sick and dying is based on Heber's account. Lyman's symptoms in contracting cholera, his response and reaction, and subsequent healing, was also taken from Heber's recorded experience:

I was instantly struck blind, and saw no way that whereby I could free myself from the disease, only to exert myself by jumping and thrashing myself about, until my sight returned to me, and my blood began to circulate in my veins. I started and ran some distance, and by this means, through the help of God, I was enabled to extricate myself from the grasp of death. (*History of the Church*, 2:116)

Seth did nearly die of cholera during Zion's Camp (Johnson, B. F. *My Life's Review*, 11). No detailed account is written of his illness. The discovery that plunging and bathing in cold water would bring relief and healing was found in Heber C. Kimball's journal. During four days, sixty-eight of the members of Zion's Camp were afflicted with the disease; fourteen died (Kimball, Heber C., *Excerpts from the Journal of Heber C. Kimball*).

CHAPTER 18

Phebe Murdock's death was recorded in her father John's journal. He said, "On the 30th, word came to me that my daughter Phebe was sick nigh unto death, of cholera, . . . I immediately went and took care of her till July 6th when the Spirit left the body just at the break of day." She was buried a little after sunrise in the morning. Murdock describes her burial. "She was decently laid out, and they dug a grave and we laid 2 split shakes in the bottom and one each side and laid in some straw, and laid the corpse on it, laid 2 sticks across and covered it over, and that was her coffin." John stayed in Missouri until he baptized his eight-year-old son, John, September 23. He left the next day for Ohio (Murdock, John, Autobiography and Diary, 16–17).

The Saints in Kirtland would have heard various reports from the newspapers that were not accurate. The quoted article in the text of the chapter was published in the *Chardon Spectator and Geauga Gazette* on July 12, 1834. That time period was difficult in Kirtland, as a variety of reports about the outbreak of cholera surfaced (*Painesville Telegraph*, Friday, July 25, 1834).

Almon and Seth's return trip back to Ohio with the Prophet is recorded in a day-by-day account in George Albert Smith's history. A few of the trials and hardships the men encountered on the return home are included in the chapter, including that "the green-headed flies, which were immense in numbers . . . would kill a horse in 30 minutes if he were tied on the prairie" (36). The following Sunday evening, July 27 when they arrived in Richmond, he records:

The Richmond newspaper published that day had announced to the world the astounding news that 'Joe Smith' the Mormon leader had had a battle with the mob in Jackson County, had been wounded in the leg, had the limb amputated, and three days afterwards had died of mortification. Joseph visited the editor, but had difficulty to convince him that he was not really dead, the editor feeling assured he had published the true state of the case. (38)

The exact date and details of Nancy's healing are not recorded; however, Jared Carter and "other elders" healed her that summer. It is not known that Don Carlos was one of the elders, but he did not go on Zion's Camp and was probably in Kirtland that summer also. Benjamin writes:

In the course of the summer elder Jared Carter, a man then of mighty faith, came with other elders to our house, and seeing sister Nancy upon her crutches commanded her in the name of Jesus Christ of Nazareth to leave her crutches and walk, which she at once did, and never again did she use them, altho for years she had borne no weight upon her broken joint. We all knew it to be the power of God, and almost felt to shout Hosanna! to think our beloved sister was again sound in limb and able to walk. (Johnson, B. F., *My Life's Review,* 11)

SELECTED BIBLIOGRAPHY

Backman, Milton V., Jr. *The Heavens Resound.* Salt Lake City: Deseret Book, 2002.

Berrett, Lamar C. and Max H. Parkin, eds. *Sacred Places, Missouri, A Comprehensive Guide to Early LDS Historical Sites.* Salt Lake City: Deseret Book, 2004.

Bushman, Richard Lyman. *Joseph Smith: Rough Stone Rolling.* New York, NY: Knopf, 2005.

Collier, Fred C. and William S. Harwell, eds. *Kirtland Council Minute Book.* Salt Lake City: Collier's Publishing, 1996.

Cannon, Donald Q. and Lyndon W. Cook, eds. *Far West Record: Minutes of the Church of Jesus Christ of Latter-day Saints, 1830–1844.* Salt Lake City: Deseret Book, 1983.

Carter, Jared. Journal of Jared Carter. Provo, UT: L. Tom Perry Special Collections, Harold B. Lee Library, Brigham Young University.

Dale W. Adams Research Collection on Mormons in Ohio. Provo, UT: L. Tom Perry Special Collections, Harold B. Lee Library, Brigham Young University, 2002.

Esplin, Ronald K. "The Emergence of Brigham Young and the Twelve to Mormon Leadership," 1830–1841: a dissertation presented to the Department of History at Brigham Young University.

Hancock, Levi W. *The Levi Hancock Journal, 1803–1836.* United States: s.n., 1983. Provo, UT: L. Tom Perry Special Collections, Harold B. Lee Library, Brigham Young University.

Hazeltine, Gilbert W. *The Early History of the Town of Ellicott.* Jamestown, NY: Journal Print. Co. 1887.

Johnson, Benjamin Franklin. *My Life's Review, Autobiography of Benjamin Franklin Johnson.* Provo, UT: Grandin, 1997, and Benjamin F. Johnson Family Organization, 1999.

Johnson, George Washington. *Diary of George W. Johnson.* Provo, UT: Brigham Young University, 1940.

—. *Jottings by the Way.* St. George, UT: C. E. Johnson, 1882.

Johnson, Joel Hills. *Diary of Joel Hills Johnson.* Provo, UT: Brigham Young University, 1945.

Johnson, Joseph Ellis. *The Papers of Joseph Ellis Johnson.* Salt Lake City, UT: Special Collections Department of University of Utah Libraries.

Johnson, Rufus D. *J.E.J. Trail to Sundown, Casadaga to Casa Grande, 1817–1882, The Story of a Pioneer: Joseph Ellis Johnson.* Salt Lake City: Deseret News Press, 1961.

Journal History of the Church of Jesus Christ of Latter-day Saints.

Kimball, Heber C. *The Journal of Heber C. Kimball.* Originally published: Salt Lake City: Juvenile Instructor Office, 1882.

Le Baron, Dale E., "Benjamin Franklin Johnson, Colonizer, Public Servant, and Church Leader," Thesis.

Le Baron, Dale E. *Benjamin Franklin Johnson, Friend to the Prophets.* Provo, UT: Grandin, 1997.

Lisonbee, Janet. *Obituaries and Life Sketches of the Early Saints Who Died in the Kirtland, Ohio Area.* Kirtland, OH: The Community of Christ, 2003.

Madsen, Susan A. *The Lord Needed a Prophet.* Salt Lake City: Deseret Book, 1900.

McConkie, Mark L. *Remembering Joseph: Personal Recollections of Those Who Knew the Prophet Joseph Smith.* Salt Lake City: Deseret Book, 2003.

Murdock, John. Autobiography and Diary, 1830–ca.1867. Provo, UT: L. Tom Perry Special Collections, Harold B. Lee Library, Brigham Young University.

Murdock, S. Reed. *John Murdock: His Life and His Legacy.* Layton, UT: Summerwood Publishers, 2000.

Olsen, Beth Radmall. *Among The Remnant Who Lingered: The History of Rebecca Burdick and Hiram Winters and Their Families.* Orem, UT: Micro Dynamics Electronic Publishing, 1997.

Pratt, Parley P. *Autobiography of Parley P. Pratt.* Salt Lake City: Deseret Book, 1973.

Smith, George Albert. *History of George Albert Smith.* Provo, UT: L. Tom Perry Special Collections, Harold B. Lee Library, Brigham Young University.

Smith, Lucy Mack. *History of Joseph Smith by His Mother, Lucy Mack Smith.* Salt Lake City: Bookcraft, 1958.

Smith, Joseph, Jr. *History of the Church of Jesus Christ of Latter-Day Saints.* 7 Vols. ed. B. H. Roberts. Salt Lake City: Deseret Book, 1980.

—. *The Papers of Joseph Smith.* 2 Vols.

Winchester, Benjamin. *The Origin of the Spaulding Story, Concerning the Manuscript Found.* Philadelphia: Brown, 1840.

Williams, Rebecca S. *Meet Dr. Frederick Granger Williams and His Wife Rebecca Swain Williams . . . After One Hundred Years!* Independence, MO: Zion's Printing and Publishing, 1951.

Young, Brigham. *Manuscript History of Brigham Young, 1801–1844.* ed. Elden J. Watson. Salt Lake City: Smith Secretarial Service, 1978.

TIMELINE

A Banner Is Unfurled Volume I and
The Church of Jesus Christ of Latter-day Saints Historical Timeline

1787
Fourteen-year-old Ezekiel Johnson runs away from home, leaving his mother and abusive step-father.

1797
Ezekiel Johnson travels to Grafton, Massachusetts, and meets Julia Hills.

1801
January 12
Ezekiel Johnson and Julia Hills marry.

1805
December 23
Joseph Smith born to Joseph Smith Sr. and Lucy Mack Smith, Sharon, Vermont.

1820
Early spring
The Prophet Joseph Smith receives First Vision in a grove of trees in Palmyra and Manchester Townships, New York, near his home.

1823
September 21–22
Joseph Smith visited by Angel Moroni and told of the Book of Mormon record. Joseph views the gold plates buried in a nearby hill (Cumorah).

1827
January 18
Joseph Smith marries Emma Hale.

September 22
Joseph Smith obtains the gold plates from Moroni at the Hill Cumorah.

1829
January 15
Ezekiel and Julia's youngest son, Amos Partridge, is born.

January 16
Delcena Johnson and Lyman Sherman are married.

May 15
John the Baptist confers the Aaronic Priesthood on Joseph Smith and Oliver Cowdery in Harmony, Pennsylvania.

May
Joseph Smith and Oliver Cowdery receive the Melchizedek Priesthood from Peter, James, and John near the Susquehanna River between Harmony, Pennsylvania, and Colesville, New York.

June
Translation of the Book of Mormon completed. The Three Witnesses and the Eight Witnesses are shown the gold plates.

1830
February
The decision is made that Joel and Annie will move to Ohio.

March 26
First printed copies of the Book of Mormon available, Palmyra, New York.

April 6
The Church organized in Fayette Township, New York.

August
Delcena and Lyman have twins, a son and a daughter. (Their baby boy dies that first year.) Nancy is thrown from a horse and is told by the physician that she will never walk again.

September
David goes with Joel to Ohio. Settling in Amherst, Loraine County, Ohio, Joel partners with John Clay in building a sawmill.

September–October
First missionaries called to preach to the Lamanites (Native Americans).

October
David returns to Pomfret for the purpose of moving Annie to join Joel. Ezekiel is drinking more, Nancy is not well, and there is increased stress in the Johnson home.

November
Seth and Ezekiel leave to spend the winter in Cincinnati.

December
David returns to Amherst with Annie and Sixtus.

1831
January
Joseph and Emma move to Kirtland.

March
Annie attends the "Mormonite" meetings and is the first in the family to be fully converted. In time, Joel joins her at the meetings, critically, yet faithfully, comparing the doctrine of the Book of Mormon and the Bible. David meets Don Carlos Smith, reads the Book of Mormon, and also gains a testimony of this new, controversial religion.

April 30
Joseph and Emma's twins are born and live only three hours.

May
Annie is baptized.

May 9
Joseph and Emma adopt the Murdock twins (Julia and Joseph).

June 1
Joel is baptized by Sylvester Smith. David's baptism is performed by Edson Fuller who is distracted and "under the influence of an evil spirit" (Carter, 11) during the ordinance. David feels dissatisfied about the circumstances of his baptism.

July
Almon Babbitt is healed by Jared Carter. (Church meeting in Barney's barn is protected from the downpour.)

July 20
Site for the city of Zion (the New Jerusalem) in Independence, Missouri, revealed to the Prophet Joseph Smith.

August
A letter from Joel, with the Book of Mormon, arrives in Pomfret, informing the family of his, Annie's, and David's conversion. Seth and Julia write back to Joel expressing their concern.

September and October
In Pomfret, Julia and her children are studying the Book of Mormon while Ezekiel is staying in Fredonia to work. Seth struggles inwardly about the truth of the book, while most of the family receives a testimony.

September 20
Joel is ordained an elder.

October 25–26
Joel Hills Johnson meets the Prophet Joseph Smith in Orange, Ohio, at a general conference. Orange is located 15 miles south of Kirtland. About 65 members of the Church live in that area at this time.

Fall/Winter
Joel and David, with Almon Babbitt, arrive in Pomfret to share their testimonies with the family. Missionaries Joseph Brackenbury and Edmund Durfee arrive in the area and stay in the Johnson's home. Lyman Sherman and Julia decide to get baptized. Shortly after their baptisms, Seth's prayers are answered as he receives a witness of the Book of Mormon.

Ezekiel returns from Fredonia and does not allow the younger children who are not of age to be baptized.

1832
January
Seth, Nancy, and Julianne are baptized shortly after Lyman and Julia.

January 7
Elder Brackenbury dies of "bilious colic." After the funeral of Elder Brackenbury, during the middle of the night, the Johnson men check the graveyard and intercept medical students attempting to dig up the body of the beloved missionary.

Spring
There is great persecution in Western New York, some focused specifically on the Johnson family's baptism, and the failure to heal Elder Brackenbury and Nancy.

Benjamin returns with Joel to Amherst.

January 25
Joseph Smith is sustained president of High Priesthood at the Amherst, Ohio, conference.

February 16
Revelation of postmortal state of mankind (D&C 76).

February 18
Annie gives birth to baby Sariah.

March 24
Joseph and Sidney Rigdon tarred and feathered at Hiram, Ohio.

March 29
Joseph M., the adopted son of Joseph and Emma Smith, dies.

April
Joseph Smith travels to Jackson County, Missouri.

June
Joseph Smith arrives in Kirtland after a delay at Greenville, Indiana.

Summer
Seth, Ezekiel, Susan, and others travel to Kirtland. Ezekiel seems to be favorably impressed by the Prophet Joseph Smith. In Amherst, at Joel's home, a "mania" overcomes Seth.

Ezekiel returns with Seth to Pomfret, Benjamin stays in Amherst to help Joel with the coming harvest.

In New York, David is rebaptized by Jared Carter.

October
Joseph Smith travels to Albany, New York, New York City, and Boston, with Newell K. Whitney.

October 30
Lyman and Delcena's son, Albey Lyman Sherman, is born.
Seth is stronger and chooses to go and get Benjamin from Ohio.

Ezekiel tells Seth that he is going to sell the farm in Pomfret and move the family to Chicago.

November 6
Joseph Smith returns to Kirtland; his son Joseph III is born.